THE DECAMERON
OF
GIOVANNI BOCCACCIO

THE DECAMERON

OF

GIOVANNI BOCCACCIO

FAITHFULLY TRANSLATED BY

J. M. RIGG

WITH AN ILLUSTRATED INTRODUCTION AND
SIXTEEN HAND-COLOURED ILLUSTRATIONS FROM ORIGINAL
DRAWINGS BY

LOUIS CHALON

VOLUME THE FIRST

LONDON : PRIVATELY PRINTED FOR THE NAVARRE
SOCIETY LIMITED

Made in Great Britain.   Printed by Neill & Co. Ltd., Edinburgh

CONTENTS.

PAGE
INTRODUCTION xiii

PROEM 1

FIRST DAY 4

NOVEL I.—*Ser Ciappelletto cheats a holy friar by a false confession, and dies ; and, having lived as a very bad man, is, on his death, reputed a saint, and called San Ciappelletto* . . . 22

NOVEL II.—*Abraham, a Jew, at the instance of Jehannot de Chevigny, goes to the court of Rome, and having marked the evil life of the clergy, returns to Paris, and becomes a Christian* . . 34

NOVEL III.—*Melchisedech, a Jew, by a story of three rings averts a danger with which he was menaced by Saladin* . . . 38

NOVEL IV.—*A monk lapses into a sin meriting the most severe punishment, justly censures the same fault in his abbot, and thus evades the penalty* 41

NOVEL V.—*The Marchioness of Monferrato by a banquet of hens seasoned with wit checks the mad passion of the King of France* . 45

NOVEL VI.—*A worthy man by an apt saying puts to shame the wicked hypocrisy of the religious* 48

NOVEL VII.—*Bergamino, with a story of Primasso and the Abbot of Cluny, finely censures a sudden access of avarice in Messer Cane della Scala* 51

NOVEL VIII.—*Guglielmo Borsiere by a neat retort sharply censures avarice in Messer Ermino de' Grimaldi* . . . 56

NOVEL IX.—*The censure of a Gascon lady converts the King of Cyprus from a churlish to an honourable temper* . . 59

PAGE

NOVEL X.—*Master Alberto da Bologna honourably puts to shame a
lady who sought occasion to put him to shame in that he was in
love with her*   61

SECOND DAY   67

NOVEL I.—*Martellino pretends to be a paralytic, and makes it appear
as if he were cured by being placed upon the body of St. Arrigo.
His trick is detected ; he is beaten and arrested, and is in peril of
hanging, but finally escapes*   68

NOVEL II.—*Rinaldo d'Asti is robbed, arrives at Castel Guglielmo,
and is entertained by a widow lady; his property is restored to
him, and he returns home safe and sound*   .   .   .   73

NOVEL III.—*Three young men squander their substance and are
reduced to poverty. Their nephew, returning home a desperate
man, falls in with an abbot, in whom he discovers the daughter of
the King of England. She marries him, and he retrieves the losses
and re-establishes the fortune of his uncles*   .   .   .   79

NOVEL IV.—*Landolfo Ruffolo is reduced to poverty, turns corsair, is
captured by Genoese, is shipwrecked, escapes on a chest full of
jewels, and, being cast ashore at Corfu, is hospitably entertained
by a woman, and returns home wealthy*   .   .   .   87

NOVEL V.—*Andreuccio da Perugia comes to Naples to buy horses,
meets with three serious adventures in one night, comes safe out of
them all, and returns home with a ruby*   .   .   .   92

NOVEL VI.—*Madam Beritola loses two sons, is found with two kids
on an island, goes thence to Lunigiana, where one of her sons takes
service with her master, and lies with his daughter, for which he
is put in prison. Sicily rebels against King Charles, the son is
recognized by the mother, marries the master's daughter, and, his
brother being discovered, is reinstated in great honour*   .   .   104

NOVEL VII.—*The Soldan of Babylon sends one of his daughters overseas, designing to marry her to the King of Algarve. By divers
adventures she comes in the space of four years into the hands of
nine men in divers places. At last she is restored to her father,
whom she quits again in the guise of a virgin, and, as was at
first intended, is married to the King of Algarve*   .   .   117

CONTENTS.

PAGE

NOVEL VIII.—*The Count of Antwerp, labouring under a false accusation, goes into exile. He leaves his two children in different places in England, and takes service in Ireland. Returning to England an unknown man, he finds his sons prosperous. He serves as a groom in the army of the King of France; his innocence is established, and he is restored to his former honours* . 137

NOVEL IX.—*Bernabò of Genoa, deceived by Ambrogiuolo, loses his money and commands his innocent wife to be put to death. She escapes, habits herself as a man, and serves the Soldan. She discovers the deceiver, and brings Bernabò to Alexandria, where the deceiver is punished. She then resumes the garb of a woman, and with her husband returns wealthy to Genoa* . . 152

NOVEL X.—*Paganino da Monaco carries off the wife of Messer Ricciardo di Chinzica, who, having learned where she is, goes to Paganino and in a friendly manner asks him to restore her. He consents, provided she be willing. She refuses to go back with her husband. Messer Ricciardo dies, and she marries Paganino* . 164

THIRD DAY 174

NOVEL I.—*Masetto da Lamporecchio feigns to be dumb, and obtains a gardener's place at a convent of women, who with one accord make haste to lie with him* 177

NOVEL II.—*A groom lies with the wife of King Agilulf, who learns the fact, keeps his own counsel, finds out the groom and shears him. The shorn shears all his fellows, and so comes safe out of the scrape.* 184

NOVEL III.—*Under cloak of confession and a most spotless conscience, a lady, enamoured of a young man, induces a booby friar unwittingly to provide a means to the entire gratification of her passion* . 189

NOVEL IV.—*Dom Felice instructs Fra Puccio how to attain blessedness by doing a penance. Fra Puccio does the penance, and meanwhile Dom Felice has a good time with Fra Puccio's wife* . . 198

NOVEL V.—*Zima gives a palfrey to Messer Francesco Vergellesi, who in return suffers him to speak with his wife. She keeping silence, he answers in her stead, and the sequel is in accordance with his answer* 203

PAGE

NOVEL VI.—*Ricciardo Minutolo loves the wife of Filippello Fighinolfi, and knowing her to be jealous, makes her believe that his own wife is to meet Filippello at a bagnio on the ensuing day; whereby she is induced to go thither, where, thinking to have been with her husband, she discovers that she has tarried with Ricciardo* . 209

NOVEL VII.—*Tedaldo, being in disfavour with his lady, departs from Florence. He returns thither after a while in the guise of a pilgrim, has speech of his lady, and makes her sensible of her fault. Her husband, convicted of slaying him, he delivers from peril of death, reconciles him with his brothers, and thereafter discreetly enjoys his lady* 217

NOVEL VIII.—*Ferondo, having taken a certain powder, is interred for dead; is disinterred by the abbot, who enjoys his wife; is put in prison and taught to believe that he is in purgatory; is then resuscitated, and rears as his own a boy begotten by the abbot upon his wife* 232

NOVEL IX.—*Gillette of Narbonne cures the King of France of a fistula, craves for spouse Bertrand de Roussillon, who marries her against his will, and hies him in despite to Florence, where, as he courts a young woman, Gillette lies with him in her stead, and has two sons by him; for which cause he afterwards takes her into favour and entreats her as his wife* 241

NOVEL X.—*Alibech turns hermit, and is taught by Rustico, a monk, how the Devil is put in hell. She is afterwards conveyed thence, and becomes the wife of Neerbale* 250

FOURTH DAY 258

NOVEL I.—*Tancred, Prince of Salerno, slays his daughter's lover, and sends her his heart in a golden cup: she pours upon it a poisonous distillation, which she drinks and dies* 265

NOVEL II.—*Fra Alberto gives a lady to understand that she is beloved of the Angel Gabriel, in whose shape he lies with her sundry times; afterward, for fear of her kinsmen, he flings himself forth of her house, and finds shelter in the house of a poor man, who on the morrow leads him in the guise of a wild man into the piazza, where, being recognized, he is apprehended by his brethren and imprisoned.* 275

CONTENTS.

PAGE

NOVEL III.—*Three young men love three sisters, and flee with them to Crete. The eldest of the sisters slays her lover for jealousy. The second saves the life of the first by yielding herself to the Duke of Crete. Her lover slays her, and makes off with the first: the third sister and her lover are charged with the murder, are arrested and confess the crime. They escape death by bribing the guards, flee destitute to Rhodes, and there in destitution die* .   . 284

NOVEL IV.—*Gerbino, in breach of the plighted faith of his grandfather, King Guglielmo, attacks a ship of the King of Tunis to rescue thence his daughter. She being slain by those aboard the ship, he slays them, and afterwards he is beheaded* .   .   . 291

NOVEL V.—*Lisabetta's brothers slay her lover: he appears to her in a dream, and shews her where he is buried: she privily disinters the head, and sets it in a pot of basil, whereon she daily weeps a great while. The pot being taken from her by her brothers, she dies not long after* 296

NOVEL VI.—*Andreuola loves Gabriotto: she tells him a dream that she has had; he tells her a dream of his own, and dies suddenly in her arms. While she and her maid are carrying his corpse to his house, they are taken by the Signory. She tells how the matter stands, is threatened with violence by the Podestà, but will not brook it. Her father hears how she is bested; and, her innocence being established, causes her to be set at large; but she, being minded to tarry no longer in the world, becomes a nun* .   . 302

NOVEL VII.—*Simona loves Pasquino; they are together in a garden; Pasquino rubs a leaf of sage against his teeth, and dies; Simona is arrested, and, with intent to shew the judge how Pasquino died, rubs one of the leaves of the same plant against her teeth, and likewise dies* 309

NOVEL VIII.—*Girolamo loves Salvestra: yielding to his mother's prayers he goes to Paris; he returns to find Salvestra married; he enters her house by stealth, lays himself by her side, and dies; he is borne to the church, where Salvestra lays herself by his side, and dies* 313

NOVEL IX.—*Sieur Guillaume de Roussillon slays his wife's paramour, Sieur Guillaume de Cabestaing, and gives her his heart to eat. She, coming to wit thereof, throws herself from a high window to the ground, and dies, and is buried with her lover* .   . 318

PAGE

NOVEL X.—*The wife of a leech, deeming her lover, who has taken an opiate, to be dead, puts him in a chest, which, with him therein, two usurers carry off to their house. He comes to himself, and is taken for a thief; but, the lady's maid giving the Signory to understand that she had put him in the chest which the usurers stole, he escapes the gallows, and the usurers are mulcted in moneys for the theft of the chest* 322

ILLUSTRATIONS TO VOL. I.

To face page

THE SOLDAN OF BABYLON'S DAUGHTER DANCING.—SECOND DAY, SEVENTH STORY . . . . . *Frontispiece*

THE DINNER OF HENS.—FIRST DAY, FIFTH STORY . . 45

RINALDO D'ASTI AND THE WIDOW LADY.—SECOND DAY, SECOND STORY 76

OSBECH AND THE CAPTIVES.—SECOND DAY, SEVENTH STORY . 109

THE LADY AND THE FRIAR.—THIRD DAY, THIRD STORY . 140

GREEN GEESE.—FOURTH DAY, INTRODUCTION . . . 173

THE THREE RINGS.—FIRST DAY, THIRD STORY . . . 204

THE DAUGHTER OF THE KING OF TUNIS.—FOURTH DAY, FOURTH STORY 269

SIMONA SPINNING.—FOURTH DAY, SEVENTH STORY . . 300

INTRODUCTION.

SON of a merchant, Boccaccio di Chellino di Buonaiuto, of Certaldo in Val d'Elsa, a little town about midway between Empoli and Siena, but within the Florentine " contado," Giovanni Boccaccio was born, most probably at Paris, in the year 1313. His mother, at any rate, was a Frenchwoman, whom his father seduced during a sojourn at Paris, and afterwards deserted. So much as this Boccaccio has himself told us, under a transparent veil of allegory, in his *Ameto*. Of his mother we would fain know more, for his wit has in it a quality, especially noticeable in the Tenth Novel of the Sixth Day of the *Decameron*, which marks him out as the forerunner of Rabelais, and prompts us to ask how much more his genius may have owed to his French ancestry. His father was of sufficient standing in Florence to be chosen Prior in 1321 ; but this brief term of office—but two months—was his last as well as his first experience of public life. Of Boccaccio's early years we know nothing more than that his first preceptor was the Florentine grammarian, Giovanni da Strada, father of the poet Zanobi da Strada, and that, when he was about ten years old, he was bound apprentice to a merchant, with whom he spent the next six years at Paris, whence he returned to Florence with an inveterate repugnance to commerce. His father then proposed to make a canonist of him ; but the study of Gratian proved hardly more congenial than the routine of the counting-house to the lad, who had already evinced a taste for letters ; and a sojourn at Naples, where under the *régime* of the enlightened King Robert there were coteries of learned men, and even Greek was not altogether unknown, decided his future career. According to Filippo Villani his choice was finally fixed by a visit to the tomb of Vergil on the Via Puteolana, and, though the modern critical spirit is apt to discount such stories, there can be no doubt that such a pilgrimage would be apt to make a deep, and perhaps enduring, impression upon a nature ardent and sensitive, and already conscious of extraordinary powers. His stay at Naples was also in another respect a turning-point in his life ; for it was there that, as we gather from the *Filocopo*, he first saw the blonde beauty, Maria, natural daughter of King Robert, whom he has immortalized as Fiammetta. The place was the church of San Lorenzo, the day the 26th of March, 1334. Boccaccio's admiring gaze was observed by the lady, who, though married, proved no Laura, and forthwith returned his love in equal measure. Their *liaison* lasted several years, during which Boccaccio recorded the various phases of their passion with exemplary assiduity in verse and prose. Besides paying her due and discreet homage in sonnet and canzone, he associated her in one way or another, not only with the *Filocopo* (his prose romance of *Florio* and *Biancofiore*, which he professes to have written to pleasure her), but with the *Ameto*, the *Amorosa Visione*, the *Teseide*, and the *Filostrato*; and in *L'Amorosa Fiammetta* he wove out of their relations a romance in which her lover, who is there called *Pamfilo*, plays Æneas to her Dido, though with somewhat less tragic consequences. The *Proem* to the *Decameron* shews us the after-glow of his passion ; the lady herself appears as one of the " honourable company," and her portrait, as in the act of receiving the laurel wreath at the close of the Fourth Day, is a masterpiece of tender and delicate delineation.

Boccaccio appears to have been recalled to Florence by his father in 1341 ; and it was probably in that year that he wrote *L'Amorosa Fiammetta* and the allegorical prose pastoral (with songs interspersed) which he entitled *Ameto*, and in which Fiammetta masquerades in green as one of the nymphs. The *Amorosa Visione*, written about the same time, is not only an allegory but an acrostic, the initial letters of its fifteen hundred triplets composing two sonnets and a ballade in honour of Fiammetta, whom he here for once ventures to call by her true name. Later came the *Teseide*, or romance of Palamon and Arcite, the first extant rendering of the story, in twelve books, and the *Filostrato*, nine books of the loves and woes of Troilus and Cressida. Both these poems are in *ottava rima*, a metre which, if Boccaccio did not invent it, he was the first to apply to such a purpose. Both works were dedicated to Fiammetta. A graceful idyll in the same metre, *Ninfale Fiesolano*, was written later, probably at Naples in 1345. King Robert was then dead, but Boccaccio enjoyed the favour of Queen Joan, of somewhat doubtful memory, at whose instance he hints in one of

Frontispiece to the first illustrated edition of the *Decameron*, Venice, 1492. (A. W. Pollard's *Italian Book Illustrations*, Seeley and Co.)

his later letters th.it he wrote the *Decameron*. Without impugning Boccaccio's veracity we can hardly but think that the *Decameron* would have seen the light, though Queen Joan had withheld her encouragement. He had probably been long meditating it, and gathering materials for it, and we may well suppose that the outbreak of the plague in 1348, by furnishing him with a sombre background to heighten the effect of his motley pageant, had far more to do with accelerating the composition than aught that Queen Joan may have said.

That Boccaccio was not at Florence during the pestilence is certain; but we need not therefore doubt the substantial accuracy of his marvellous description of the state of the stricken city, for the course and consequences of the terrible visitation must have been much the same in all parts of Italy, and as to Florence in particular, Boccaccio could have no difficulty in obtaining detailed and abundant information from credible eye-witnesses. The introduction of Fiammetta, who was in all probability at Naples at the time, and in any case was not a Florentine, shews, however, that he is by no means to be taken literally, and renders it extremely probable that the facetious, irrepressible, and privileged Dioneo is no other than himself. At the same time we cannot deem it either impossible, or very unlikely, that in the general relaxation of morale, which the plague brought in its train, refuge from care and fear was sought in the diversions which he describes by some of those who had country-seats to which to withdraw, and whether the " contado " was that of Florence or that of Naples is a matter of no considerable importance.[1] It is probable

---

[1] As to the palaces in which the scene is laid, Manni (*Istoria del Decamerone*, Par. ii. cap. ii.) identifies the first with a villa near Fiesole, which can be no other than the Villa Palmieri, and the second (*ib.* cap. lxxvi.) with the Podere della Fonte, or so-called Villa del Boccaccio, near Camerata. Baldelli's theory, adopted by Mrs. Janet Ann Ross (*Florentine Villas*, 1901), that the Villa di Poggio Gherardi was the first, and the Villa Palmieri the second, retreat is not to be reconciled with Boccaccio's descriptions. The Villa Palmieri is not remote enough for the second and more sequestered retreat, nor is it, as that is said to have been, situate on a low hill amid a plain, but on the lower Fiesolean slope. The most rational supposition would seem to be that Boccaccio, who had seen many a luxurious villa, freely combined his experiences in the description of his palaces and pleasaunces, and never expected to be taken *au pied de la lettre*.

that Boccaccio's father was one of the victims of the pestilence; for he was dead in 1350, when his son returned to Florence to live thenceforth on the modest patrimony which he inherited. It must have been about this time that he formed an intimacy with Petrarch, which, notwithstanding marked diversity of temperament, character and pursuits, was destined to be broken only by death. Despite his complaints of the malevolence of his critics in the *Proem* to the Fourth Day of the *Decameron*, he had no lack of appreciation on the part of his fellow-citizens, and was employed by the Republic on several missions; to Bologna, probably with the view of averting the submission of that city to the Visconti in 1350; to Petrarch at Padua in March 1351, with a letter from the Priors announcing his restitution to citizenship, and inviting him to return to Florence, and assume the rectorship of the newly founded university; to Ludwig of Brandenburg with overtures for an alliance against the Visconti in December of the same year; and in the spring of 1354 to Pope Innocent VI. at Avignon in reference to the approaching visit of the Emperor Charles IV. to Italy. About this time, 1354–5, he threw off, in striking contrast to his earlier works, an invective against women, entitled *Laberinto d' Amore*, otherwise *Corbaccio*, a coarse performance occasioned by resentment at what he deemed capricious treatment by a lady to whom he had made advances. To the same period, though the date cannot be precisely fixed, belongs his Life of Dante, a work of but mediocre merit. Somewhat later, it would seem, he began the study of Greek under one Leontius Pilatus, a Calabrian, who possessed some knowledge of that language, and sought to pass himself off as a Greek by birth.

Leontius was of coarse manners and uncertain temper, but Boccaccio was his host and pupil for some years, and eventually procured him the chair of Greek in the university of Florence. How much Greek Boccaccio learned from him, and how far he may have been beholden to him in the compilation of his elaborate Latin treatise *De Genealogia Deorum*, in which he essayed with very curious results to expound the inner meaning of mythology, it is impossible to say. In 1361 he seems to have had serious thoughts of devoting himself to religion, being prodigiously impressed by the menaces, monitions, and revelations of a dying Carthusian of Siena. One of the revelations concerned a matter which Boccaccio had supposed to be known only to Petrarch and himself. He accordingly confided his anxiety to Petrarch, who persuaded him to amend his life without renouncing the world. In 1362 he revisited Naples, and in the following year spent three months with Petrarch at Venice. In 1365 he was sent by the Republic of Florence on a mission of conciliation to Pope Urban V. at Avignon. He was employed on a like errand on the Pope's return to Rome in 1367. In 1368 he revisited Venice, and in 1371 Naples; but in May 1372 he returned to Florence, where on 25th August 1373 he was appointed lecturer on the Divina Commedia, with a yearly stipend of 100 fiorini d'oro. His lectures, of which the first was delivered in the church of San Stefano near the Ponte Vecchio, were discontinued owing to ill health, doubtless aggravated by the distress which the death of Petrarch (20th July 1374) could not but cause him, when he had got no farther than the seventeenth Canto of the *Inferno*. His commentary is still occasionally quoted. He died, perhaps in the odour of sanctity, for in later life he was a diligent collector of relics, at Certaldo on 21st December 1375, and was buried in the parish church. His tomb was desecrated, and his remains were dispersed, owing, it is said, to a misunderstanding, towards the close of the eighteenth century. His library, which by his direction was placed in the Convent of Santo Spirito at Florence, was destroyed by fire about a century after his death.

Besides the *De Genealogia Deorum* Boccaccio wrote other treatises in Latin, which need not here be specified, and sixteen *Eclogues* in the same language, of which he was by no means a master. As for his minor works in the vernacular, the earlier of them shew that he had not as yet wrought himself free from the conventionalism which the polite literature of Italy inherited from the Sicilians. It is therefore inevitable that the twentieth century should find the *Filocopo*, *Ameto*, and *Amorosa Visione* tedious reading. The *Teseide* determined the form in which Pulci, Boiardo, Bello, Ariosto, Tasso, and, with a slight modification, our own Spenser were to write, but its readers are now few, and are not likely ever again to be numerous. Chaucer drew upon it for the *Knight's Tale*, but it is at any rate arguable that his retrenchment of its perhaps inordinate length was judicious, and that what he gave was better than what he borrowed. Still, that it had such a redactor as Chaucer is no small testimony to its

THE PROCESSION TO THE GARDEN.   THE TELLING OF THE STORIES.

From the first illustrated edition of the *Decameron*. (A. W. Pollard's *Italian Book Illustration*, Seeley and Co.)

merit; nor was it only in the *Knight's Tale* that he was indebted to it : the description of the Temple of Love in the *Parlement of Foules* is taken almost word for word from it. Even more considerable and conspicuous is Chaucer's obligation to Boccaccio in the *Troilus and Criseyde*, about a third of which is borrowed from the *Filostrato*. Nor is it a little remarkable that the same man, that in the *Teseide* and *Filostrato* founded the chivalrous epic, should also, and in the same period of his literary activity, have written the first, and not the least powerful and artistic of psychologic romances, for even such is *L'Amorosa Fiammetta*.

But whatever may be the final verdict of criticism upon these minor works of Boccaccio, it is impossible to imagine an age in which the *Decameron* will fail of general recognition as, in point alike of invention as of style, one of the most notable creations of human genius. Of few books are the sources so recondite, insomuch that it seems to be certain that in the main they must have been merely oral tradition, and few have exercised so wide and mighty an influence. The profound, many-sided and intimate knowledge of human nature which it evinces, its vast variety of incident, its wealth of tears and laughter, its copious and felicitous diction, inevitably apt for every occasion, and, notwithstanding the frequent harshness, and occasional obscurity of its at times tangled, at times laboured periods, its sustained energy and animation of style must ever ensure for this human comedy unchallenged rank among the literary masterpieces that are truly immortal.

The *Decameron* was among the earliest of printed books, Venice leading the way with a folio edition in 1471, Mantua following suit in 1472, and Vicenza in 1478. A folio edition, adorned with most graceful wood-engravings, was published at Venice in 1492. Notwithstanding the freedom with which in divers passages Boccaccio reflected on the morals of the clergy, the Roman Curia spared the book, which the austere Savonarola condemned to the flames. The tradition that the *Decameron* was among the pile of " vanities " burned by Savonarola in the Piazza della Signoria on the last day of the Carnival of 1497, little more than a year before he was himself burned there, is so intrinsically probable—and accords so well with the extreme paucity of early copies of the work—that it would be the very perversity of scepticism to doubt it. It is by no means to the credit of our

country that, except to scholars, it long remained in England an
almost entirely closed book.[1]   Indeed the first nominally complete
English translation, a sadly mutilated and garbled rendering of the
French version by Antoine Le Maçon, did not appear till 1620,
and though successive redactions brought it nearer to the original,
it remained at the best but a sorry *faute de mieux*.   Such as it was,
however, our forefathers were perforce fain to be content with it.

The first Englishman to render the whole *Decameron* direct
from the Italian was Mr. John Payne ; but his work, printed for
the Villon Society in 1886, was only for private circulation, and
those least inclined to disparage its merits may deem its style somewhat too archaic and stilted adequately to render the vigour and
vivacity of the original.   Accordingly in the present version an
attempt has been made to hit the mean between archaism and
modernism, and to secure as much freedom and spirit as is compatible
with substantial accuracy.

[1] Nevertheless Shakespeare derived indirectly the plot of *All's Well that
Ends Well* from the Ninth Novel of the Third Day, and an element in the
plot of *Cymbeline* from the Ninth Novel of the Second Day.

GRISELDA SURPRISED BY THE MARQUIS.
From the first illustrated edition of the *Decameron*.
(A. W Pollard's *Italian Book Illustrations*, Seeley and Co.)

Beginneth here the book called Decameron, otherwise Prince Galeotto, wherein are contained one hundred novels told in ten days by seven ladies and three young men.

PROEM.

'Tis humane to have compassion on the afflicted; and as it shews well in all, so it is especially demanded of those who have had need of comfort and have found it in others: among whom, if any had ever need thereof or found it precious or delectable, I may be numbered; seeing that from my early youth even to the present I was beyond measure aflame with a most aspiring and noble love[1] more perhaps than, were I to enlarge upon it, would seem to accord with my lowly condition. Whereby, among people of discernment to whose knowledge it had come, I had much praise and high esteem, but nevertheless extreme discomfort and suffering, not indeed by reason of cruelty on the part of the beloved lady, but through superabundant ardour engendered in the soul by ill-bridled desire; the which, as it allowed me no reasonable period of quiescence, frequently occasioned me an inordinate distress. In which distress so much relief was afforded me by the delectable discourse of a friend and his commendable consolations, that I entertain a very solid conviction that to them I owe it that I am not dead. But, as it pleased Him, who, being infinite, has assigned by immutable law an end to all things mundane, my love, beyond all other fervent, and neither to be broken nor bent by any force of determination, or counsel of prudence, or fear of manifest shame or ensuing danger,

[1] For Fiammetta, *i. e.* Maria, natural daughter of Robert, King of Naples.

did nevertheless in course of time abate of its own accord, in such wise that it has now left nought of itself in my mind but that pleasure which it is wont to afford to him who does not adventure too far out in navigating its deep seas ; so that, whereas it was used to be grievous, now, all discomfort being done away, I find that which remains to be delightful. But the cessation of the pain has not banished the memory of the kind offices done me by those who shared by sympathy the burden of my griefs ; nor will it ever, I believe, pass from me except by death. And as among the virtues gratitude is in my judgment most especially to be commended, and ingratitude in equal measure to be censured, therefore, that I show myself not ungrateful, I have resolved, now that I may call myself free, to endeavour, in return for what I have received, to afford, so far as in me lies, some solace, if not to those who succoured me, and who, perchance, by reason of their good sense or good fortune, need it not, at least to such as may be apt to receive it.

And though my support or comfort, so to say, may be of little avail to the needy, nevertheless it seems to me meet to offer it most readily where the need is most apparent, because it will there be most serviceable and also most kindly received. Who will deny, that it should be given, for all that it may be worth, to gentle ladies much rather than to men ? Within their soft bosoms, betwixt fear and shame, they harbour secret fires of love, and how much of strength concealment adds to those fires, they know who have proved it. Moreover, restrained by the will, the caprice, the commandment of fathers, mothers, brothers, and husbands, confined most part of their time within the narrow compass of their chambers, they live, so to say, a life of vacant ease, and, yearning and renouncing in the same moment, meditate divers matters which cannot all be cheerful. If thereby a melancholy bred of amorous desire make entrance into their minds, it is like to tarry there to their sore distress, unless it be dispelled by a change of ideas. Besides which they have much less power to support such a weight than men. For, when men are enamoured, their case is very different, as we may readily perceive. They, if they are afflicted by a melancholy and heaviness of mood, have many ways of relief and diversion ; they may go where they will, may hear and see many things, may hawk, hunt, fish, ride, play or traffic. By which means all are able to compose their minds,

either in whole or in part, and repair the ravage wrought by the
dumpish mood, at least for some space of time ; and shortly after, by
one way or another, either solace ensues, or the dumps become less
grievous.   Wherefore, in some measure to compensate the injustice
of Fortune, which to those whose strength is least, as we see it to be
in the delicate frames of ladies, has been most niggard of support, I,
for the succour and diversion of such of them as love (for others
may find sufficient solace in the needle and the spindle and the reel),
do intend to recount one hundred Novels or Fables or Parables or
Stories, as we may please to call them, which were recounted in ten
days by an honourable company of seven ladies and three young men
in the time of the late mortal pestilence, as also some canzonets sung
by the said ladies for their delectation.   In which pleasant novels
will be found some passages of love rudely crossed, with other
courses of events of which the issues are felicitous, in times as well
modern as ancient : from which stories the said ladies, who shall read
them, may derive both pleasure from the entertaining matters set
forth therein, and also good counsel, in that they may learn what to
shun, and likewise what to pursue.   Which cannot, I believe, come
to pass, unless the dumps be banished by diversion of mind.   And if
it so happen (as God grant it may) let them give thanks to Love,
who, liberating me from his fetters, has given me the power to
devote myself to their gratification.

Beginneth here the first day of the Decameron, in which, when the author has set forth, how it came to pass that the persons, who appear hereafter, met together for interchange of discourse, they, under the rule of Pampinea, discourse of such matters as most commend themselves to each in turn.

As often, most gracious ladies, as I bethink me, how compassionate you are by nature one and all, I do not disguise from myself that the present work must seem to you to have but a heavy and distressful prelude, in that it bears upon its very front what must needs revive the sorrowful memory of the late mortal pestilence, the course whereof was grievous not merely to eye-witnesses but to all who in any other wise had cognisance of it. But I would have you know, that you need not therefore be fearful to read further, as if your reading were ever to be accompanied by sighs and tears. This horrid beginning will be to you even such as to wayfarers is a steep and rugged mountain, beyond which stretches a plain most fair and delectable, which the toil of the ascent and descent does but serve to render more agreeable to them ; for, as the last degree of joy brings with it sorrow, so misery has ever its sequel of happiness. To this brief exordium of woe—brief, I say, inasmuch as it can be put within the compass of a few letters—succeed forthwith the sweets and delights which I have promised you, and which, perhaps, had I not done so, were not to have been expected from it. In truth, had it been honestly possible to guide you whither I would bring you by a road less rough than this will be, I would gladly have so done. But, because without this review of the past, it would not be in my power to shew how the matters, of which you will hereafter read, came to pass, I am almost bound of necessity to enter upon it, if I would write of them at all.

I say, then, that the years of the beatific incarnation of the Son of God had reached the tale of one thousand three hundred and forty-eight, when in the illustrious city of Florence, the fairest of all the cities of Italy, there made its appearance that deadly pestilence, which, whether disesminated by the influence of the celestial bodies, or sent upon us mortals by God in His just wrath by way of retribution for our iniquities, had had its origin some years before in the East, whence, after destroying an innumerable multitude of living beings, it had propagated itself without respite from place to place, and so, calamitously, had spread into the West.

In Florence, despite all that human wisdom and forethought could devise to avert it, as the cleansing of the city from many impurities by officials appointed for the purpose, the refusal of entrance to all sick folk, and the adoption of many precautions for the preservation of health ; despite also humble supplications addressed to God, and often repeated both in public procession and otherwise, by the devout; towards the beginning of the spring of the said year the doleful effects of the pestilence began to be horribly apparent by symptoms that shewed as if miraculous.

Not such were they as in the East, where an issue of blood from the nose was a manifest sign of inevitable death ; but in men and women alike it first betrayed itself by the emergence of certain tumours in the groin or the armpits, some of which grew as large as a common apple, others as an egg, some more, some less, which the common folk called gavoccioli.   From the two said parts of the body this deadly gavocciolo soon began to propagate and spread itself in all directions indifferently ; after which the form of the malady began to change, black spots or livid making their appearance in many cases on the arm or the thigh or elsewhere, now few and large, now minute and numerous.   And as the gavocciolo had been and still was an infallible token of approaching death, such also were these spots on whomsoever they shewed themselves. Which maladies seemed to set entirely at naught both the art of the physician and the virtues of physic ; indeed, whether it was that the disorder was of a nature to defy such treatment, or that the physicians were at fault—besides the qualified there was now a multitude both of men and of women who practised without having received the slightest tincture of medical science—and, being in ignorance of its source, failed to apply the proper remedies ; in either case, not merely were those that recovered few, but almost all within three days from the appearance of the said symptoms, sooner or later, died, and in most cases without any fever or other attendant malady.

Moreover, the virulence of the pest was the greater by reason that intercourse was apt to convey it from the sick to the whole, just as fire devours things dry or greasy when they are brought close to it. Nay, the evil went yet further, for not merely by speech or association with the sick was the malady communicated to the healthy with consequent peril of common death ; but any that touched the clothes of the sick or aught else that had been touched or used by them, seemed thereby to contract the disease.

So marvellous sounds that which I have now to relate, that, had not many, and I among them, observed it with their own eyes, I had hardly dared to credit it, much less to set it down in writing, though I had had it from the lips of a credible witness.

I say, then, that such was the energy of the contagion of the said pestilence, that it was not merely propagated from man to man, but, what is much more startling, it was frequently observed, that things which had belonged to one sick or dead of the disease, if touched by some other living creature, not of the human species, were the occasion, not merely of sickening, but of an almost instan-taneous death. Whereof my own eyes (as I said a little before) had cognisance, one day among others, by the following experience. The rags of a poor man who had died of the disease being strewn about the open street, two hogs came thither, and after, as is their wont, no little trifling with their snouts, took the rags between their teeth and tossed them to and fro about their chaps ; whereupon, almost immediately, they gave a few turns, and fell down dead, as if by poison, upon the rags which in an evil hour they had disturbed.

In which circumstances, not to speak of many others of a similar or even graver complexion, divers apprehensions and imaginations were engendered in the minds of such as were left alive, inclining almost all of them to the same harsh resolution, to wit, to shun and abhor all contact with the sick and all that belonged to them,

thinking thereby to make each his own health secure. Among whom
there were those who thought that to live temperately and avoid all
excess would count for much as a preservative against seizures of this
kind. Wherefore they banded together, and, dissociating themselves
from all others, formed communities in houses where there were no
sick, and lived a separate and secluded life, which they regulated with
the utmost care, avoiding every kind of luxury, but eating and
drinking very moderately of the most delicate viands and the finest
wines, holding converse with none but one another, lest tidings of
sickness or death should reach them, and diverting their minds with
music and such other delights as they could devise. Others, the bias
of whose minds was in the opposite direction, maintained, that to
drink freely, frequent places of public resort, and take their pleasure
with song and revel, sparing to satisfy no appetite, and to laugh and
mock at no event, was the sovereign remedy for so great an evil: and
that which they affirmed they also put in practice, so far as they were
able, resorting day and night, now to this tavern, now to that, drinking
with an entire disregard of rule or measure, and by preference making
the houses of others, as it were, their inns, if they but saw in ther
aught that was particularly to their taste or liking ; which they were
readily able to do, because the owners, seeing death imminent, had
become as reckless of their property as of their lives ; so that most of
the houses were open to all comers, and no distinction was observed
between the stranger who presented himself and the rightful lord.
Thus, adhering ever to their inhuman determination to shun the sick,
as far as possible, they ordered their life. In this extremity of our
city's suffering and tribulation the venerable authority of laws,
human and divine, was abased and all but totally dissolved, for lack
of those who should have administered and enforced them, most of
whom, like the rest of the citizens, were either dead or sick, or so
hard bested for servants that they were unable to execute any
office ; whereby every man was free to do what was right in his
own eyes.

Not a few there were who belonged to neither of the two said
parties, but kept a middle course between them, neither laying the
same restraint upon their diet as the former, nor allowing themselves
the same license in drinking and other dissipations as the latter, but
living with a degree of freedom sufficient to satisfy their appetites,

and not as recluses. They therefore walked abroad, carrying in their hands flowers or fragrant herbs or divers sorts of spices, which they frequently raised to their noses, deeming it an excellent thing thus to comfort the brain with such perfumes, because the air seemed to be everywhere laden and reeking with the stench emitted by the dead and the dying, and the odours of drugs.

Some again, the most sound, perhaps, in judgment, as they were also the most harsh in temper, of all, affirmed that there was no medicine for the disease superior or equal in efficacy to flight; following which prescription a multitude of men and women, negligent of all but themselves, deserted their city, their houses, their estates, their kinsfolk, their goods, and went into voluntary exile, or migrated to the country parts, as if God in visiting men with this pestilence in requital of their iniquities would not pursue them with His wrath wherever they might be, but intended the destruction of such alone as remained within the circuit of the walls of the city; or deeming, perchance, that it was now time for all to flee from it, and that its last hour was come.

Of the adherents of these divers opinions not all died, neither did all escape; but rather there were, of each sort and in every place, many that sickened, and by those who retained their health were treated after the example which they themselves, while whole, had set, being everywhere left to languish in almost total neglect. Tedious were it to recount, how citizen avoided citizen, how among neighbours was scarce found any that shewed fellow-feeling for another, how kinsfolk held aloof, and never met, or but rarely; enough that this sore affliction entered so deep into the minds of men and women, that in the horror thereof brother was forsaken by brother, nephew by uncle, brother by sister, and oftentimes husband by wife; nay, what is more, and scarcely to be believed, fathers and mothers were found to abandon their own children, untended, unvisited, to their fate, as if they had been strangers. Wherefore the sick of both sexes, whose number could not be estimated, were left without resource but in the charity of friends (and few such there were), or the interest of servants, who were hardly to be had at high rates and on unseemly terms, and being, moreover, one and all, men and women of gross understanding, and for the most part unused to such offices, concerned themselves no further than to supply the immediate and expressed wants of the sick, and to watch them die; in which service they themselves not seldom perished with their gains. In consequence of which dearth of servants and dereliction of the sick by neighbours, kinsfolk and friends, it came to pass—a thing, perhaps, never before heard of—that no woman, however dainty, fair or well-born she might be, shrank, when stricken with the disease, from the ministrations of a man, no matter whether he were young or no, or scrupled to expose to him every part of her body, with no more shame than if he had been a woman, submitting of necessity to that which her malady required; wherefrom, perchance, there resulted in after time some loss of modesty in such as recovered. Besides which many succumbed, who with proper attendance, would, perhaps, have escaped death; so that, what with the virulence of the plague and the lack of due tendance of the sick, the multitude of the deaths, that daily and nightly took place in the city, was such that those who heard the tale—not to say witnessed the fact—were struck dumb with amazement. Whereby, practices contrary to the former habits of the citizens could hardly fail to grow up among the survivors.

It had been, as to-day it still is, the custom for the women that were neighbours and of kin to the deceased to gather in his house with the women that were most closely connected with him, to wail with them in common, while on the other hand his male kinsfolk and neighbours, with not a few of the other citizens, and a due proportion of the clergy according to his quality, assembled without, in front of the house, to receive the corpse; and so the dead man was borne on the shoulders of his peers, with funeral pomp of taper and dirge, to the church selected by him before his death. Which rites, as the pestilence waxed in fury, were either in whole or in great part disused, and gave way to others of a novel order. For not only did no crowd of women surround the bed of the dying, but many passed from this life unregarded, and few indeed were they to whom were accorded the lamentations and bitter tears of sorrowing relations; nay, for the most part, their place was taken by the laugh, the jest, the festal gathering; observances which the women, domestic piety in large measure set aside, had adopted with very great advantage to their health. Few also there were whose bodies were attended to the church by more than ten or twelve of their neighbours, and those not the honourable and respected citizens; but a sort of corpse-carriers drawn from the baser ranks, who called themselves becchini [1] and performed such offices for hire, would shoulder the bier, and with hurried steps carry it, not to the church of the dead man's choice, but to that which was nearest at hand, with four or six priests in front and a candle or two, or, perhaps, none ; nor did the priests distress themselves with too long and solemn an office, but with the aid of the becchini hastily consigned the corpse to the first tomb which they found untenanted. The condition of the lower, and, perhaps, in great measure of the middle ranks, of the people shewed even worse and more deplorable ; for, deluded by hope or constrained by poverty, they stayed in their quarters, in their houses, where they sickened by thousands a day, and, being without service or help of any kind, were, so to speak, irredeemably devoted to the death which overtook them. Many died daily or nightly in the public streets ; of many others, who died at home, the departure was hardly observed by their neighbours, until the stench of their putrefying bodies carried the tidings ; and what with their corpses and the corpses of others who died on every hand the whole place was a sepulchre.

It was the common practice of most of the neighbours, moved no less by fear of contamination by the putrefying bodies than by charity towards the deceased, to drag the corpses out of the houses with their own hands, aided, perhaps, by a porter, if a porter was to be had, and to lay them in front of the doors, where any one who made the round might have seen, especially in the morning, more of them than he could count ; afterwards they would have biers brought up, or, in default, planks, whereon they laid them. Nor was it once or twice only that one and the same bier carried two or three corpses at once ; but quite a considerable number of such cases occurred, one bier sufficing for husband and wife, two or three brothers, father and son, and so forth. And times without number it happened, that, as two priests, bearing the cross, were on their way to perform the last office for some one, three or four biers were brought up by the porters in rear of them, so that, whereas the priests supposed that they had but one corpse to bury, they discovered that there were six or eight, or sometimes more. Nor, for all their number, were their

---

[1] Probably from the name of the pronged or hooked implement with which they dragged the corpses out of the houses.

obsequies honoured by either tears or lights or crowds of mourners ; rather, it was come to this, that a dead man was then of no more account than a dead goat would be to-day. From all which it is abundantly manifest, that that lesson of patient resignation, which the sages were never able to learn from the slight and infrequent mishaps which occur in the natural course of events, was now brought home even to the minds of the simple by the magnitude of their disasters, so that they became indifferent to them.

As consecrated ground there was not in extent sufficient to provide tombs for the vast multitude of corpses which day and night, and almost every hour, were brought in eager haste to the churches for interment, least of all, if ancient custom were to be observed and a separate resting-place assigned to each, they dug, for each grave-yard, as soon as it was full, a huge trench, in which they laid the corpses as they arrived by hundreds at a time, piling them up as merchandise is stowed in the hold of a ship, tier upon tier, each covered with a little earth, until the trench would hold no more. But I spare to rehearse with minute particularity each of the woes that came upon our city, and say in brief, that, harsh as was the tenor of her fortunes, the surrounding country knew no mitigation ; for there—not to speak of the castles, each, as it were, a little city in itself—in sequestered village, or on the open champaign, by the way-side, on the farm, in the homestead, the poor hapless husbandmen and their families, forlorn of physicians' care or servants' tendance, perished day and night alike, not as men, but rather as beasts. Wherefore, they too, like the citizens, abandoned all rule of life, all habit of industry, all counsel of prudence ; nay, one and all, as if expecting each day to be their last, not merely ceased to aid Nature to yield her fruit in due season of their beasts and their lands and their past labours, but left no means unused, which ingenuity could devise, to waste their accumulated store ; denying shelter to their oxen, asses, sheep, goats, pigs, fowls, nay, even to their dogs, man's most faithful companions, and driving them out into the fields to roam at large amid the unsheaved, nay, unreaped corn. Many of which, as if endowed with reason, took their fill during the day, and returned home at night without any guidance of herdsman. But enough of the country ! What need we add, but (reverting to the city) that such and so grievous was the harshness of heaven, and perhaps in some degree of man, that, what with the fury of the pestilence, the panic of those whom it spared, and their consequent neglect or desertion of not a few of the stricken in their need, it is believed without any manner of doubt, that between March and the ensuing July upwards of a hundred thousand human beings lost their lives within the walls of the city of Florence, which before the deadly visitation would not have been supposed to contain so many people! How many grand palaces, how many stately homes, how many splendid residences, once full of retainers, of lords, of ladies, were now left desolate of all, even to the meanest servant! How many families of historic fame, of vast ancestral domains, and wealth proverbial, found now no scion to continue the succession! How many brave men, how many fair ladies, how many gallant youths, whom any physician, were he Galen, Hippocrates, or Æsculapius himself, would have pronounced in the soundest of health, broke fast with their kinsfolk, comrades and friends in the morning, and when evening came, supped with their forefathers in the other world!

Irksome it is to myself to rehearse in detail so sorrowful a history. Wherefore, being minded to pass over so much thereof as I fairly can, I say, that our city, being thus well-nigh depopulated, it so happened, as I afterwards learned from one worthy of credit, that on a Tuesday morning after Divine Service the venerable church of Santa Maria Novella was almost deserted save for the presence of seven young ladies habited sadly in keeping with the season. All were connected either by blood or at least as friends or neighbours; and fair and of good understanding were they all, as also of noble birth, gentle manners, and a modest sprightliness. In age none exceeded twenty-eight, or fell short of eighteen years. Their names I would set down in due form, had I not good reason to withhold them, being solicitous lest the matters which here ensue, as told and heard by them, should in after time be occasion of reproach to any of them, in view of the ample indulgence which was then, for the reasons heretofore set forth, accorded to the lighter hours of persons of much riper years than they, but which the manners of to-day have somewhat restricted; nor would I furnish material to detractors, ever ready to bestow their bite where praise is due, to cast by invidious speech the least slur upon the honour of these noble ladies. Wherefore, that what each says may be apprehended without confusion, I intend to give them names more or less appropriate to the character of each. The first, then, being the eldest of the seven, we will call Pampinea, the second Fiammetta, the third Filomena, the fourth Emilia, the fifth we will distinguish as Lauretta, the sixth as Neifile, and the last, not without reason, shall be named Elisa.

'Twas not of set purpose but by mere chance that these ladies met in the same part of the church ; but at length grouping themselves into a sort of circle, after heaving a few sighs, they gave up saying paternosters, and began to converse (among other topics) on the times.

So they continued for a while, and then Pampinea, the rest listening in silent attention, thus began :—" Dear ladies mine, often have I heard it said, and you doubtless as well as I, that wrong is done to none by whoso but honestly uses his reason. And to fortify, preserve, and defend his life to the utmost of his power is the dictate of natural reason in every one that is born. Which right is accorded in such measure that in defence thereof men have been held blameless in taking life. And if this be allowed by the laws, albeit on their stringency depends the well-being of every mortal, how much more exempt from censure should we, and all other honest folk, be in taking such means as we may for the preservation of our life? As often as I bethink me how we have been occupied this morning, and not this morning only, and what has been the tenor of our con-versation, I perceive—and you will readily do the like—that each of us is apprehensive on her own account ; nor thereat do I marvel, but at this I do marvel greatly, that, though none of us lacks a woman's wit, yet none of us has recourse to any means to avert that which we all justly fear. Here we tarry, as if, methinks, for no other purpose than to bear witness to the number of the corpses that are brought hither for interment, or to hearken if the brothers there within, whose number is now almost reduced to nought, chant their offices at the canonical hours, or, by our weeds of woe, to obtrude on the attention of every one that enters, the nature and degree of our sufferings.

" And if we quit the church, we see dead or sick folk carried about, or we see those, who for their crimes were of late condemned to exile by the outraged majesty of the public laws, but who now, in contempt of those laws, well knowing that their ministers are a prey

VOL I.

B

to death or disease, have returned, and traverse the city in packs, making it hideous with their riotous antics ; or else we see the refuse of the people, fostered on our blood, becchini, as they call themselves, who for our torment go prancing about here and there and everywhere, making mock of our miseries in scurrilous songs. Nor hear we aught but :—Such and such are dead ; or, Such and such are dying ; and should hear dolorous wailing on every hand, were there but any to wail. Or go we home, what see we there ? I know not if you are in like case with me ; but there, where once were servants in plenty, I find none left but my maid, and shudder with terror, and feel the very hairs of my head to stand on end ; and turn or tarry where I may, I encounter the ghosts of the departed, not with their wonted mien, but with something horrible in their aspect that appals me. For which reasons church and street and home are alike distressful to me, and the more so that none, methinks, having means and place of retirement as we have, abides here save only we ; or if any such there be, they are of those, as my senses too often have borne witness, who make no distinction between things honourable and their opposites, so they but answer the cravings of appetite, and, alone or in company, do daily and nightly what things soever give promise of most gratification. Nor are these secular persons alone ; but such as live recluse in monasteries break their rule, and give themselves up to carnal pleasures, persuading themselves that they are permissible to them, and only forbidden to others, and, thereby thinking to escape, are become unchaste and dissolute. If such be our circumstances—and such most manifestly they are—what do we here ? what wait we for ? what dream we of ? why are we less prompt to provide for our own safety than the rest of the citizens ? Is life less dear to us than to all other women ? or think we that the bond which unites soul and body is stronger in us than in others, so that there is no blow that may light upon it, of which we need be apprehensive ? If so, we err, we are deceived. What insensate folly were it in us so to believe ! We have but to call to mind the number and condition of those, young as we, and of both sexes, who have succumbed to this cruel pestilence, to find therein conclusive evidence to the contrary. And lest from lethargy or indolence we fall into the vain imagination that by some lucky accident we may in some way or another, when we would, escape—I know not if

your opinion accord with mine—I should deem it most wise in us,
our case being what it is, if, as many others have done before us, and
are still doing, we were to quit this place, and, shunning like death
the evil example of others, betake ourselves to the country, and there
live as honourable women on one of the estates, of which none of us
has any lack, with all cheer of festal gathering and other delights, so
long as in no particular we overstep the bounds of reason. There we
shall hear the chant of birds, have sight of verdant hills and plains, of
cornfields undulating like the sea, of trees of a thousand sorts ; there
also we shall have a larger view of the heavens, which, however harsh
to usward, yet deny not their eternal beauty ; things fairer far for
epe to rest on than the desolate walls of our city. Moreover, we
shall there breathe a fresher air, find ampler store of things meet for
such as live in these times, have fewer causes of annoy. For, though
the husbandmen die there, even as here the citizens, they are
dispersed in scattered homesteads, and 'tis thus less painful to witness.
Nor, so far as I can see, is there a soul here whom we shall desert ;
rather we may truly say, that we are ourselves deserted ; for, our
kinsfolk being either dead or fled in fear of death, no more regardful
of us than if we were strangers, we are left alone in our great
affliction. No censure, then, can fall on us if we do as I propose ;
and otherwise grievous suffering, perhaps death, may ensue. Wherefore, if you agree, 'tis my advice, that, attended by our maids with al.
things needful, we sojourn, now on this, now on the other estate,
and in such way of life continue, until we see—if death should not
first overtake us—the end which Heaven reserves for these events.
And I remind you that it will be at least as seemly in us to leave
with honour, as in others, of whom there are not a few, to stay with
dishonour."

The other ladies praised Pampinea's plan, and indeed were so
prompt to follow it, that they had already begun to discuss the
manner in some detail, as if they were forthwith to rise from their
seats and take the road, when Filomena, whose judgment was
excellent, interposed, saying :—" Ladies, though Pampinea has spoken
to most excellent effect, yet it were not well to be so precipitate as
you seem disposed to be. Bethink you that we are all women ; nor
is there any here so young, but she is of years to understand how
women are minded towards one another, when they are alone

together, and how ill they are able to rule themselves without the guidance of some man. We are sensitive, perverse, suspicious, pusillanimous and timid ; wherefore I much misdoubt, that, if we find no other guidance than our own, this company is like to break up sooner, and with less credit to us, than it should. Against which it were well to provide at the outset." Said then Elisa :—" Without doubt man is woman's head, and, without man's governance, it is seldom that aught that we do is brought to a commendable conclusion. But how are we to come by the men ? Every one of us here knows that her kinsmen are for the most part dead, and that the survivors are dispersed, one here, one there, we know not where, bent each on escaping the same fate as ourselves ; nor were it seemly to seek the aid of strangers ; for, as we are in quest of health, we must find some means so to order matters that, wherever we seek diversion or repose, trouble and scandal do not follow us."

While the ladies were thus conversing, there came into the church three young men, young, I say, but not so young that the age of the youngest was less than twenty-five years ; in whom neither the sinister course of events, nor the loss of friends or kinsfolk, nor fear for their own safety, had availed to quench, or even temper, the ardour of their love. The first was called Pamfilo, the second Filostrato, and the third Dioneo. Very debonair and chivalrous were they all ; and in this troublous time they were seeking if haply, to their exceeding great solace, they might have sight of their fair friends, all three of whom chanced to be among the said seven ladies, besides some that were of kin to the young men. At one and the same moment they recognised the ladies and were recognised by them : wherefore, with a gracious smile, Pampinea thus began :— " Lo, fortune is propitious to our enterprise, having vouchsafed us the good offices of these young men, who are as gallant as they are discreet, and will gladly give us their guidance and escort, so we but take them into our service." Whereupon Neifile, crimson from brow to neck with the blush of modesty, being one of those that had a lover among the young men, said :—" For God's sake, Pampinea, have a care what you say. Well assured am I that nought but good can be said of any of them, and I deem them fit for office far more onerous than this which you propose for them, and their good and honourable company worthy of ladies fairer by far and more tenderly

to be cherished than such as we. But 'tis no secret that they love
some of us here ; wherefore I misdoubt that, if we take them with
us, we may thereby give occasion for scandal and censure merited
neither by us nor by them." "That," said Filomena, "is of no consequence ; so I but live honestly, my conscience gives me no
disquietude ; if others asperse me, God and the truth will take arms
in my defence. Now, should they be disposed to attend us, of a truth
we might say with Pampinea, that fortune favours our enterprise."
The silence which followed betokened consent on the part of the other
ladies, who then with one accord resolved to call the young men, and
acquaint them with their purpose, and pray them to be of their company. So without further parley Pampinea, who had a kinsman
among the young men, rose and approached them where they stood
intently regarding them ; and greeting them gaily, she opened to them
their plan, and besought them on the part of herself and her friends
to join their company on terms of honourable and fraternal comradeship. At first the young men thought she did but trifle with them ;
but when they saw that she was in earnest, they answered with
alacrity that they were ready, and promptly, even before they left
the church, set matters in train for their departure. So all things
meet being first sent forward in due order to their intended place
of sojourn, the ladies with some of their maids, and the three young
men, each attended by a man-servant, sallied forth of the city on
the morrow, being Wednesday, about daybreak, and took the road ;
nor had they journeyed more than two short miles when they
arrived at their destination. The estate[1] lay upon a little hill some
distance from the nearest highway, and, embowered in shrubberies
of divers hues, and other greenery, afforded the eye a pleasant
prospect. On the summit of the hill was a palace with galleries,
halls and chambers, disposed around a fair and spacious court, each
very fair in itself, and the goodlier to see for the gladsome pictures
with which it was adorned ; the whole set amidst meads and gardens
laid out with marvellous art, wells of the coolest water, and vaults of
the finest wines, things more suited to dainty drinkers than to sober
and honourable women. On their arrival the company, to their no
small delight, found their beds already made, the rooms well swept

[1] Identified by tradition with the Villa Palmieri (now Crawford) on the
slope of Fiesole.

and garnished with flowers of every sort that the season could afford, and the floors carpeted with rushes. When they were seated, Dioneo, a gallant who had not his match for courtesy and wit, spoke thus :—" My ladies, 'tis not our forethought so much as your own mother-wit that has guided us hither. How you mean to dispose of your cares I know not ; mine I left behind me within the city-gate when I issued thence with you a brief while ago. Wherefore, I pray you, either address yourselves to make merry, to laugh and sing with me (so far, I mean, as may consist with your dignity), or give me leave to hie me back to the stricken city, there to abide with my cares." To whom blithely Pampinea replied, as if she too had cast off all her cares :—" Well sayest thou, Dioneo, excellent well ; gaily we mean to live ; 'twas a refuge from sorrow that here we sought, nor had we other cause to come hither. But, as no anarchy can long endure, I who initiated the deliberations of which this fair company is the fruit, do now, to the end that our joy may be lasting, deem it expedient, that there be one among us in chief authority, honoured and obeyed by us as our superior, whose exclusive care it shall be to devise how we may pass our time blithely. And that each in turn may prove the weight of the care, as well as enjoy the pleasure, of sovereignty, and, no distinction being made of sex, envy be felt by none by reason of exclusion from the office ; I propose, that the weight and honour be borne by each one for a day ; and let the first to bear sway be chosen by us all, those that follow to be appointed towards the vesper hour by him or her who shall have had the signory for that day ; and let each holder of the signory be, for the time, sole arbiter of the place and manner in which we are to pass our time."

Pampinea's speech was received with the utmost applause, and with one accord she was chosen queen for the first day. Whereupon Filomena hied her lightly to a bay-tree, having often heard of the great honour in which its leaves, and such as were deservedly crowned therewith, were worthy to be holden ; and having gathered a few sprays, she made thereof a goodly wreath of honour, and set it on Pampinea's head ; which wreath was thenceforth, while their company endured, the visible sign of the wearer's sway and sovereignty.

No sooner was Queen Pampinea crowned than she bade all be

silent. She then caused summon to her presence their four maids, and the servants of the three young men, and, all keeping silence, said to them :—" That I may shew you all at once, how, well still giving place to better, our company may flourish and endure, as long as it shall pleasure us, with order meet and assured delight and without reproach, I first of all constitute Dioneo's man, Parmeno, my seneschal, and entrust him with the care and control of all our household, and all that belongs to the service of the hall. Pamfilo's man, Sirisco, I appoint treasurer and chancellor of our exchequer ; and be he ever answerable to Parmeno. While Parmeno and Sirisco are too busy about their duties to serve their masters, let Filostrato's man, Tindaro, have charge of the chambers of all three. My maid, Misia, and Filomena's maid, Licisca, will keep in the kitchen, and with all due diligence prepare such dishes as Parmeno shall bid them. Lauretta's maid, Chimera, and Fiammetta's maid, Stratilia we make answerable for the ladies' chambers, and wherever we may take up our quarters, let them see that all is spotless. And now we enjoin you, one and all alike, as you value our favour, that none of you, go where you may, return whence you may, hear or see what you may, bring us any tidings but such as be cheerful." These orders thus succinctly given were received with universal approval. Whereupon Pampinea rose, and said gaily :— " Here are gardens, meads, and other places delightsome enough, where you may wander at will, and take your pleasure ; but on the stroke of tierce,[1] let all be here to breakfast in the shade."

Thus dismissed by their new queen the gay company sauntered gently through a garden, the young men saying sweet things to the fair ladies, who wove fair garlands of divers sorts of leaves and sang love-songs.

Having thus spent the time allowed them by the queen, they returned to the house, where they found that Parmeno had entered on his office with zeal ; for in a hall on the ground-floor they saw tables covered with the whitest of cloths, and beakers that shone like silver, and sprays of broom scattered everywhere. So, at the bidding of the queen, they washed their hands, and all took their places as marshalled by Parmeno. Dishes, daintily prepared, were served,

---

[1] The canonical hour following prime, roughly speaking about 9 a.m.

and the finest wines were at hand ; the three serving-men did their office noiselessly ; in a word all was fair and ordered in a seemly manner ; whereby the spirits of the company rose, and they seasoned their viands with pleasant jests and sprightly sallies. Breakfast done, the tables were removed, and the queen bade fetch instruments of music ; for all, ladies and young men alike, knew how to tread a measure, and some of them played and sang with great skill : so, at her command, Dioneo having taken a lute, and Fiammetta a viol, they struck up a dance in sweet concert ; and, the servants being dismissed to their repast, the queen, attended by the other ladies and the two young men, led off a stately carol ; which ended they fell to singing ditties dainty and gay. Thus they diverted themselves until the queen, deeming it time to retire to rest, dismissed them all for the night. So the three young men and the ladies withdrew to their several quarters, which were in different parts of the palace. There they found the beds well made, and abundance of flowers, as in the hall ; and so they undressed, and went to bed.

Shortly after none [1] the queen rose, and roused the rest of the ladies, as also the young men, averring that it was injurious to the health to sleep long in the daytime. They therefore hied them to a meadow, where the grass grew green and luxuriant, being nowhere scorched by the sun, and a light breeze gently fanned them. So at the queen's command they all ranged themselves in a circle on the grass, and hearkened while she thus spoke :—

" You mark that the sun is high, the heat intense, and the silence unbroken save by the cicalas among the olive-trees. It were therefore the height of folly to quit this spot at present. Here the air is cool and the prospect fair, and here, observe, are dice and chess. Take, then, your pleasure as you may be severally minded ; but, if you take my advice, you will find pastime for the hot hours before us, not in play, in which the loser must needs be vexed, and neither the winner nor the onlooker much the better pleased, but in telling of stories, in which the invention of one may afford solace to all the company of his hearers. You will not each have told a story before the sun will be low, and the heat abated, so that

---

[1] The canonical hour following sext, *i. e.* 3 p.m.

we shall be able to go and severally take our pleasure where it may seem best to each. Wherefore, if my proposal meet with your approval—for in this I am disposed to consult your pleasure—let us adopt it; if not, divert yourselves as best you may, until the vesper hour."

The queen's proposal being approved by all, ladies and men alike, she added :—"So please you, then, I ordain, that, for this first day, we be free to discourse of such matters as most commend themselves to each in turn." She then addressed Pamfilo, who sat on her right hand, bidding him with a gracious air to lead off with one of his stories. And prompt at the word of command, Pamfilo, while all listened intently, thus began :—

NOVEL I.

Ser Ciappelletto cheats a holy friar by a false confession, and dies; and, having lived as a very bad man, is, on his death, reputed a saint, and called San Ciappelletto.

A SEEMLY thing it is, dearest ladies, that whatever we do, it be begun in the holy and awful name of Him who was the maker of all. Wherefore, as it falls to me to lead the way in this your enterprise of story-telling, I intend to begin with one of His wondrous works, that, by hearing thereof, our hopes in Him, in whom is no change, may be established, and His name be by us forever lauded. 'Tis manifest that, as things temporal are all doomed to pass and perish, so within and without they abound with trouble and anguish and travail, and are subject to infinite perils; nor, save for the especial grace of God, should we, whose being is bound up with and forms part of theirs, have either the strength to endure or the wisdom to combat their adverse influences. By which grace we are visited and penetrated (so we must believe) not by reason of any merit of our own, but solely out of the fulness of God's own goodness, and in answer to the prayers of those who, being mortal like ourselves, did faithfully observe His ordinances during their lives, and are now become blessed for ever with Him in heaven. To whom, as to advocates taught by experience all that belongs to our frailty, we, not daring, perchance, to present our petitions in the presence of so great a Judge, make known our requests for such things as we deem expedient for us. And of His mercy richly abounding to usward we have further proof herein, that, no keenness of mortal vision being able in any degree to penetrate the secret counsels of the Divine mind, it sometimes, perchance, happens, that, in error of judgment, we make one our advocate before His Majesty, who is banished from His presence in eternal exile, and yet He to whom nothing is hidden, having regard rather to the sincerity of our prayers than to our ignorance or the banishment of the intercessor, hears us no less than if the intercessor were in truth one of the blest who enjoy the light of His countenance. Which the story that I am about to relate may serve to make apparent; apparent, I mean, according to the standard or the judgment of man, not of God.

The story goes, then, that Musciatto Franzesi, a great and wealthy merchant, being made a knight in France, and being to attend Charles Sansterre, brother of the King of France, when he came into Tuscany at the instance and with the support of Pope Boniface, found his affairs, as often happens to merchants, to be much involved in divers quarters, and neither easily nor suddenly to be adjusted; wherefore he determined to place them in the hands of commissioners, and found no difficulty except as to certain credits given to some Burgundians, for the recovery of which he doubted whether he could come by a competent agent; for well he knew that the Burgundians were violent men and ill-conditioned and faithless; nor could he call to mind any man so bad that he could with confidence oppose his guile to theirs. After long pondering the matter, he recollected one Ser Ciapperello da Prato, who much frequented his house in Paris. Who being short of stature and very affected, the French who knew not the meaning of Cepparello,[1] but supposed that it meant the same as Cappello, i. e. garland, in their vernacular, called him not Cappello, but Ciappelletto by reason of his diminutive size; and as Ciappelletto he was known everywhere, whereas few people knew him as Ciapperello. Now Ciappelletto's manner of life was thus. He was by profession a notary, and his pride was to make false documents; he would have made them as often as he was asked, and more readily without fee than another at a great price; few indeed he made that were not false, and great was his shame when they were discovered. False witness he bore, solicited or unsolicited, with boundless delight; and, as oaths were in

[1] The diminutive of ceppo, stump or log: more commonly written cepperello (cf. p. 22) or ceppatello. The form ciapperello seems to be found only here.

those days had in very great respect in France, he, scrupling not to forswear himself, corruptly carried the day in every case in which he was summoned faithfully to attest the truth. He took inordinate delight, and bestirred himself with great zeal, in fomenting ill-feeling, enmities, dissensions between friends, kinsfolk and all other folk; and the more calamitous were the consequences the better he was pleased. Set him on murder, or any other foul crime, and he never hesitated, but went about it with alacrity; he had been known on more than one occasion to inflict wounds or death by preference with his own hands. He was a profuse blasphemer of God and His saints, and that on the most trifling occasions, being of all men the most irascible. He was never seen at church, held all the sacraments vile things, and derided them in language of horrible ribaldry. On the other hand he resorted readily to the tavern and other places of evil repute, and frequented them. He was as fond of women as a dog is of the stick : in the use against nature he had not his match among the most abandoned. He would have pilfered and stolen as a matter of conscience, as a holy man would make an oblation. Most gluttonous he was and inordinately fond of his cups, whereby he sometimes brought upon himself both shame and suffering. He was also a practised gamester and thrower of false dice. But why enlarge so much upon him ? Enough that he was, perhaps, the worst man that ever was born.

The rank and power of Musciatto Franzesi had long been this reprobate's mainstay, serving in many instances to secure him considerate treatment on the part of the private persons whom he frequently, and the court which he unremittingly, outraged. So Musciatto, having bethought him of this Ser Cepparello, with whose way of life he was very well acquainted, judged him to be the very sort of person to cope with the guile of the Burgundians. He therefore sent for him, and thus addressed him :—"Ser Ciappelletto, I am, as thou knowest, about to leave this place for good ; and among those with whom I have to settle accounts are certain Burgundians, very wily knaves ; nor know I the man whom I could more fitly entrust with the recovery of my money than thyself. Wherefore, as thou hast nothing to do at present, if thou wilt undertake this business, I will procure thee the favour of the court, and give thee a reasonable part of what thou shalt recover." Ser Ciappelletto, being out of employment, and by no means in easy circumstances, and about to lose Musciatto, so long his mainstay and support, without the least demur, for in truth he had hardly any choice, made his mind up and answered that he was ready to go. So the bargain was struck. Armed with the power of attorney and the royal letters commendatory, Ser Ciappelletto took leave of Messer Musciatto and hied him to Burgundy, where he was hardly known to a soul. He set about the business which had brought him thither, the recovery of the money, in a manner amicable and considerate, foreign to his nature, as if he were minded to reserve his severity to the last. While thus occupied, he was frequently at the house of two Florentine usurers, who treated him with great distinction out of regard for Messer Musciatto ; and there it so happened that he fell sick. The two brothers forthwith placed physicians and servants in attendance upon him, and omitted no means meet and apt for the restoration of his health. But all remedies proved unavailing ; for being now old, and having led, as the physicians reported, a disorderly life, he went daily from bad to worse like one stricken with a mortal disease. This greatly disconcerted the two brothers ; and one day, hard by the room in which Ser Ciappelletto lay sick, they began to talk about him ; saying one to the other :—" What shall we do with this man ? We are hard bested indeed on his account. If we turn him out of the house, sick as he is, we shall not only incur grave censure, but shall evince a signal want of sense ; for folk must know the welcome we gave him in the first instance, the solicitude with which we have had him treated and tended since his illness, during which time he could not possibly do aught to displease us, and yet they would see him suddenly turned out of our house sick unto death. On the other hand he has been so bad a man that he is sure not to confess or receive any of the Church's sacraments ; and dying thus unconfessed, he will be denied burial in church, but will be cast out into some ditch like a dog ; nay, 'twill be all one if he do confess, for such and so horrible have been his crimes that no friar or priest either will or can absolve him; and so, dying without absolution, he will still be cast out into the ditch. In which case the folk of these parts, who reprobate our trade as iniquitous and revile it all day long, and would fain rob us, will seize their opportunity, and raise a tumult, and make a raid upon our houses, crying:—' Away with these Lombard dogs, whom the Church excludes from her pale ; ' and will certainly strip us of our goods, and perhaps take our lives also ; so that in any case we stand to lose if this man die."

Ser Ciappelletto, who, as we said, lay close at hand while they thus spoke, and whose hearing was sharpened, as is often the case, by his malady, overheard all that they said about him. So he called them to him, and said to them :—"I would not have you disquiet yourselves in regard of me, or apprehend loss to befall you by my death. I have heard what you have said of me and have no doubt that 'twould be as you say, if matters took the course you anticipate ; but I am minded that it shall be otherwise. I have committed so many offences against God in the course of my life, that one more in the hour of my death will make no difference whatever to the account. So seek out and bring hither the worthiest and most holy friar you can find, and leave me to settle your affairs and mine upon a sound and solid basis, with which you may rest satisfied." The two brothers had not much hope of the result, but yet they went to a friary and asked for a holy and discreet man to hear the confession of a Lombard that was sick in their house, and returned with an aged man of just and holy life, very learned in the Scriptures, and venerable and held in very great and especial reverence by all the citizens. As soon as he had entered the room where Ser Ciappelletto was lying, and had taken his place by his side, he began gently to comfort him : then he asked him how long it was since he was confessed. Whereto Ser Ciappelletto, who had never been confessed, answered :—"Father, it is my constant practice to be confessed at least once a week, and many a week I am confessed more often ; but true it is, that, since I have been sick, now eight days, I have made no confession, so sore has been my affliction." " Son," said the friar, " thou hast well done, and well for thee, if so thou continue to do ; as thou dost confess so often, I see that my labour of hearkening and questioning will be slight." " Nay but, master friar," said Ser Ciappelletto, " say not so ; I have not confessed so often but that I would fain make a general confession of all my sins that I have committed, so far as I can recall them, from the day of my birth to the present time ; and therefore I pray you, my good father, to question me precisely in every particular just as if I had never been confessed. And spare me not by reason of my sickness, for I had far rather do despite to my flesh than, sparing it, risk the perdition of my soul, which my Saviour redeemed with His precious blood."

The holy man was mightily delighted with these words, which seemed to him to betoken a soul in a state of grace. He therefore signified to Ser Ciappelletto his high approval of this practice; and then began by asking him whether he had ever sinned carnally with a woman. Whereto Ser Ciappelletto answered with a sigh :—" My father, I scruple to tell you the truth in this matter, fearing lest I sin in vain-glory." "Nay, but," said the friar, "speak boldly; none ever sinned by telling the truth, either in confession or otherwise." "Then," said Ser Ciappelletto, "as you bid me speak boldly, I will tell you the truth of this matter. I am virgin even as when I issued from my mother's womb." "Now God's blessing on thee," said the friar, "well done; and the greater is thy merit in that, hadst thou so willed, thou mightest have done otherwise far more readily than we who are under constraint of rule." He then proceeded to ask, whether he had offended God by gluttony. Whereto Ser Ciappelletto, heaving a heavy sigh, answered that he had frequently so offended; for, being wont to fast not only in Lent like other devout persons, but at least three days in every week, taking nothing but bread and water, he had quaffed the water with as good a gusto and as much enjoyment, more particularly when fatigued by devotion or pilgrimage, as great drinkers quaff their wine; and oftentimes he had felt a craving for such dainty dishes of herbs as ladies make when they go into the country, and now and again he had relished his food more than seemed to him meet in one who fasted, as he did, for devotion. "Son," said the friar, "these sins are natural and very trifling; and therefore I would not have thee burden thy conscience too much with them. There is no man, however holy he may be, but must sometimes find it pleasant to eat after a long fast and to drink after exertion." "O, my father," said Ser Ciappelletto, "say not this to comfort me. You know well that I know, that the things which are done in the service of God ought to be done in perfect purity of an unsullied spirit; and whoever does otherwise sins." The friar, well content, replied :—" Glad I am that thou dost think so, and I am mightily pleased with thy pure and good conscience which therein appears; but tell me : hast thou sinned by avarice, coveting more than was reasonable, or withholding more than was right ?" "My father," replied Ser Ciappelletto, "I would not have you disquiet yourself, because I am in the house of these usurers : no part have I in their concerns ; nay, I did but come here to admonish and reprehend them, and wean them from this abominable traffic; and so, I believe, I had done, had not God sent me this visitation. But you must know, that my father left me a fortune, of which I dedicated the greater part to God ; and since then for my own support and the relief of Christ's poor I have done a little trading, whereof I have desired to make gain ; and all that I have gotten I have shared with God's poor, reserving one half for my own needs and giving the other half to them ; and so well has my Maker prospered me, that I have ever managed my affairs to better and better account." "Well done," said the friar ; "but how ? hast thou often given way to anger ?" "Often indeed, I assure you," said Ser Ciappelletto. "And who could refrain therefrom, seeing men doing frowardly all day long, breaking the commandments of God and recking nought of His judgments ? Many a time in the course of a single day I had rather be dead than alive, to see the young men going after vanity, swearing and forswearing themselves, haunting taverns, avoiding the churches, and in short walking in the way of the world rather than in God's way." "My son," said the friar, "this is a righteous wrath ; nor could I find occasion therein to lay a penance upon thee. But did anger ever by any chance betray thee into taking human life, or affronting or otherwise wronging any ?" "Alas," replied Ser Ciappelletto, "alas, sir, man of God though you seem to me, how come you to speak after this manner ? If I had had so much as the least thought of doing any of the things of which you speak, should I believe, think you, that I had been thus supported or God ? These are the deeds of robbers and such like evil men, to whom I have ever said, when any I saw :—'Go, God change your heart.'" Said then the friar :—"Now, my son, as thou hopest to be blest of God, tell me, hast thou never borne false witness against any, or spoken evil of another, or taken the goods of another without his leave ?" "Yes, master friar," answered Ser Ciappelletto, "most true it is that I have spoken evil of another ; for I had once a neighbour who without the least excuse in the world was ever beating his wife, and so great was my pity of the poor creature, whom, when he was in his cups, he would thrash as God alone knows how, that once I

spoke evil of him to his wife's kinsfolk." "Well, well," said the
friar, "thou tellest me thou hast been a merchant ; hast thou ever
cheated any, as merchants use to do ? " " I'faith, yes, master friar,"
said Ser Ciappelletto ; " but I know not who he was ; only that he
brought me some money which he owed me for some cloth that
I had sold him, and I put it in a box without counting it, where
a month afterwards I found four farthings more than there should
have been, which I kept for a year to return to him, but not seeing
him again, I bestowed them in alms for the love of God." "This,"
said the friar, "was a small matter ; and thou didst well to bestow
them as thou didst." The holy friar went on to ask him many
other questions, to which he made answer in each case in this sort.
Then, as the friar was about to give him absolution, Ser Ciappelletto
interposed :—"Sir, I have yet a sin to confess." "What ?" asked the
friar. " I remember," he said, "that I once caused my servant to
sweep my house on a Saturday after none ; and that my observance
of Sunday was less devout than it should have been." "O, my son,"
said the friar, "this is a light matter." "No," said Ser Ciappelletto,
" say not a light matter ; for Sunday is the more to be had in honour
because on that day our Lord rose from the dead." Then said the
holy friar :—"Now is there aught else that thou hast done ? "
" Yes, master friar," replied Ser Ciappelletto, "once by inadvertence
I spat in the church of God." At this the friar began to smile, and
said :—" My son, this is not a matter to trouble about ; we, who are
religious, spit there all day long." "And great impiety it is when
you so do," replied Ser Ciappelletto, " for there is nothing that
is so worthy to be kept from all impurity as the holy temple in which
sacrifice is offered to God." More he said in the same strain, which I
pass over ; and then at last he began to sigh, and by and by to weep
bitterly, as he was well able to do when he chose. And the friar
demanding :—" My son, why weepest thou ? " " Alas, master
friar," answered Ser Ciappelletto, "a sin yet remains, which I have
never confessed, such shame were it to me to tell it ; and as often as
I call it to mind, I weep as you now see me weep, being well assured
that God will never forgive me this sin." Then said the holy friar :—
" Come, come, son, what is this that thou sayst ? If all the sins of
all the men, that ever were or ever shall be, as long as the world shall
endure, were concentrated in one man, so great is the goodness of

God that He would freely pardon them all, were he but penitent and contrite as I see thou art, and confessed them : wherefore tell me thy sin with a good courage." Then said Ser Ciappelletto, still weeping bitterly :—"Alas, my father, mine is too great a sin, and scarce can I believe, if your prayers do not co-operate, that God will ever grant me His pardon thereof." "Tell it with a good courage," said the friar ; "I promise thee to pray God for thee." Ser Ciappelletto, however, continued to weep, and would not speak, for all the friar's encouragement. When he had kept him for a good while in suspense, he heaved a mighty sigh, and said :—"My father, as you promise me to pray God for me, I will tell it you. Know, then, that once, when I was a little child, I cursed my mother ; " and having so said he began again to weep bitterly. " O, my son," said the friar, " does this seem to thee so great a sin ? Men curse God all day long, and He pardons them freely, if they repent them of having so done ; and thinkest thou He will not pardon thee this ? Weep not, be comforted, for truly, hadst thou been one of them that set Him on the Cross, with the contrition that I see in thee, thou wouldst not fail of His pardon." " Alas ! my father," rejoined Ser Ciappelletto, " what is this you say ? To curse my sweet mother that carried me in her womb for nine months day and night, and afterwards on her shoulder more than a hundred times ! Heinous indeed was my offence ; 'tis too great a sin ; nor will it be pardoned, unless you pray God for me."

The friar now perceiving that Ser Ciappelletto had nothing more to say, gave him absolution and his blessing, reputing him for a most holy man, fully believing that all that he had said was true. And who would not have so believed, hearing him so speak at the point of death ? Then, when all was done, he said :—"Ser Ciappelletto, if God so will, you will soon be well ; but should it so come to pass that God call your blessed soul to Himself in this state of grace, is it well pleasing to you that your body be buried in our convent ?" " Yea, verily, master friar," replied Ser Ciappelletto ; " there would I be, and nowhere else, since you have promised to pray God for me ; besides which I have ever had a special devotion to your order. Wherefore I pray you, that, on your return to your convent, you cause to be sent me that very Body of Christ, which you consecrate in the morning on the altar ; because (unworthy though I be) I purpose with your leave to take it, and afterwards the holy and extreme unction, that, though I have lived as a sinner, I may die at any rate as a Christian." The holy man said that he was greatly delighted, that it was well said of Ser Ciappelletto, and that he would cause the Host to be forthwith brought to him; and so it was.

The two brothers, who much misdoubted Ser Ciappelletto's power to deceive the friar, had taken their stand on the other side of a wooden partition which divided the room in which Ser Ciappelletto lay from another, and hearkening there they readily heard and understood what Ser Ciappelletto said to the friar; and at times could scarce refrain their laughter as they followed his confession; and now and again they said one to another :—" What manner of man is this, whom neither age nor sickness, nor fear of death, on the threshold of which he now stands, nor yet of God, before whose judgment-seat he must soon appear, has been able to turn from his wicked ways, that he die not even as he has lived?" But seeing that his confession had secured the interment of his body in church, they troubled themselves no further. Ser Ciappelletto soon afterwards communicated, and growing immensely worse, received the extreme unction, and died shortly after vespers on the same day on which he had made his good confession. So the two brothers, having from his own moneys provided the wherewith to procure him honourable sepulture, and sent word to the friars to come at even to observe the usual vigil, and in the morning to fetch the corpse, set all things in order accordingly. The holy friar who had confessed him, hearing that he was dead, had audience of the prior of the friary; a chapter was convened and the assembled brothers heard from the confessor's own mouth how Ser Ciappelletto had been a holy man, as had appeared by his confession, and were exhorted to receive the body with the utmost veneration and pious care, as one by which there was good hope that God would work many miracles. To this the prior and the rest of the credulous confraternity assenting, they went in a body in the evening to the place where the corpse of Ser Ciappelletto lay, and kept a great and solemn vigil over it; and in the morning they made a procession habited in their surplices and copes, with books in their hands and crosses in front; and chanting as they went, they fetched the corpse and brought it back to their

church with the utmost pomp and solemnity, being followed by
almost all the folk of the city, men and women alike. So it was laid
in the church, and then the holy friar who had heard the confession
got up in the pulpit and began to preach marvellous things of Ser
Ciappelletto's life, his fasts, his virginity, his simplicity and guilelessness and holiness; narrating among other matters that of which
Ser Ciappelletto had made tearful confession as his greatest sin, and
how he had hardly been able to make him conceive that God would
pardon him; from which he took occasion to reprove his hearers;
saying :—" And you, accursed of God, on the least pretext, blaspheme
God and His Mother, and all the celestial court." And much
beside he told of his loyalty and purity ; and, in short, so wrought
upon the people by his words, to which they gave entire credence,
that they all conceived a great veneration for Ser Ciappelletto, and
at the close of the office came pressing forward with the utmost
vehemence to kiss the feet and the hands of the corpse, from which
they tore off the cerements, each thinking himself blessed to have
but a scrap thereof in his possession ; and so it was arranged that
it should be kept there all day long, so as to be visible and accessible
to all. At nightfall it was honourably interred in a marble tomb
in one of the chapels, where on the morrow, one by one, folk came
and lit tapers and prayed and paid their vows, setting there the
waxen images which they had dedicated. And the fame of Ciappelletto's holiness and the devotion to him grew in such measure that
scarce any there was that in any adversity would vow aught to any
saint but he, and they called him and still call him San Ciappelletto,
affirming that many miracles have been and daily are wrought by
God through him for such as devoutly crave his intercession.

So lived, so died Ser Cepperello da Prato, and came to be reputed
a saint, as you have heard. Nor would I deny that it is possible that
he is of the number of the blessed in the presence of God, seeing
that, though his life was evil and depraved, yet he might in his last
moments have made so complete an act of contrition that perchance
God had mercy on him and received him into His kingdom. But,
as this is hidden from us, I speak according to that which appears,
and I say that he ought rather to be in the hands of the devil in hell
than in Paradise. Which, if so it be, is a manifest token of the
superabundance of the goodness of God to usward, inasmuch as He

regards not our error but the sincerity of our faith, and hearkens unto us when, mistaking one who is at enmity with Him for a friend, we have recourse to him, as to one holy indeed, as our intercessor for His grace. Wherefore, that we of this gay company may by His grace be preserved safe and sound throughout this time of adversity, commend we ourselves in our need to Him, whose name we began by invoking, with lauds and reverent devotion and good confidence that we shall be heard.

And so he was silent.

NOVEL II.

Abraham, a Jew, at the instance of Jehannot de Chevigny, goes to the court of Rome, and having marked the evil life of the clergy, returns to Paris, and becomes a Christian.

PAMFILO'S story elicited the mirth of some of the ladies and the hearty commendation of all, who listened to it with close attention until the end. Whereupon the queen bade Neifile, who sat next her, to tell a story, that the commencement thus made of their diversions might have its sequel. Neifile, whose graces of mind matched the beauty of her person, consented with a gladsome good-will, and thus began :—

Pamfilo has shewn by his story that the goodness of God spares to regard our errors when they result from unavoidable ignorance; and in mine I mean to shew you how the same goodness, bearing patiently with the shortcomings of those who should be its faithful witness in deed and word, draws from them contrariwise evidence of His infallible truth ; to the end that what we believe we may with more assured conviction follow.

In Paris, gracious ladies, as I have heard tell, there was once a great merchant, a large dealer in drapery, a good man, most loyal and righteous, his name Jehannot de Chevigny, between whom and a Jew, Abraham by name, also a merchant, and a man of great wealth, as also most loyal and righteous, there subsisted a very close friendship. Now Jehannot, observing Abraham's loyalty and recti-tude, began to be sorely vexed in spirit that the soul of one so worthy and wise and good should perish for want of faith. Where-fore he began in a friendly manner to plead with him, that he should leave the errors of the Jewish faith and turn to the Christian verity, which, being sound and holy, he might see daily prospering and gaining ground, whereas, on the contrary, his own religion was dwindling and was almost come to nothing. The Jew replied that he believed that there was no faith sound and holy except the Jewish faith, in which he was born, and in which he meant to live and die ; nor would anything ever turn him therefrom. Nothing daunted, however, Jehannot some days afterwards began again to ply Abraham with similar arguments, explaining to him in such crude fashion as merchants use the reasons why our faith is better than the Jewish. And though the Jew was a great master in the Jewish law, yet, whether it was by reason of his friendship for Jehannot, or that the Holy Spirit dictated the words that the simple merchant used, at any rate the Jew began to be much interested in Jehannot's arguments, though still too staunch in his faith to suffer himself to be converted. But Jehannot was no less assiduous in plying him with argument than he was obstinate in adhering to his law, insomuch that at length the Jew, overcome by such incessant appeals, said :—" Well, well, Jehannot, thou wouldst have me become a Christian, and I am disposed to do so, provided I first go to Rome and there see him whom thou callest God's vicar on earth, and observe what manner of life he leads and his brother cardinals with him ; and if such it be that thereby, in conjunction with thy words, I may understand that thy faith is better than mine, as thou hast sought to shew me, I will do as I have said : otherwise, I will remain as I am a Jew." When Jehannot heard this, he was greatly distressed, saying to himself :—" I thought to have converted him ; but now I see that the pains which I took for so excellent a purpose are all in vain ; for, if he goes to the court of Rome and sees the iniquitous and foul life which the clergy lead there, so far from turning Christian, had he been converted already, he would without doubt relapse into Judaism." Then turning to Abraham he said :—" Nay, but, my friend, why wouldst thou be at all this labour and great expense of travelling from here to Rome ? to say nothing of the risks both by sea and by land which a rich man like thee must needs run. Thinkest thou not to find here one that can give thee baptism ? And as for any doubts that thou mayst have touching the faith to which I point thee, where wilt thou find greater masters and sages therein than here, to resolve thee of any question thou mayst put to them? Wherefore in my opinion this journey of thine is superfluous. Think that the prelates there are such as thou mayst have seen here, nay, as much better as they are nearer to the Chief Pastor. And so, by my advice thou wilt spare thy pains until some time of indulgence, when I, perhaps, may be able to bear thee company." The Jew replied :— "Jehannot, I doubt not that so it is as thou sayst; but once and for all I tell thee that I am minded to go there, and will never otherwise do that which thou wouldst have me and hast so earnestly besought me to do." "Go then," said Jehannot, seeing that his mind was made up, "and good luck go with thee;" and so he gave up the contest because nothing would be lost, though he felt sure that he would never become a Christian after seeing the court of Rome. The Jew took horse, and posted with all possible speed to Rome; where on his arrival he was honourably received by his fellow Jews. He said nothing to any one of the purpose for which he had come; but began circumspectly to acquaint himself with the ways of the Pope and the cardinals and the other prelates and all the courtiers; and from what he saw for himself, being a man of great intelligence, or learned from others, he discovered that without distinction of rank they were all sunk in the most disgraceful lewdness, sinning not only in the way of nature but after the manner of the men of Sodom, without any restraint of remorse or shame, in such sort that, when any great favour was to be procured, the influence of the courtesans and boys was of no small moment. Moreover he found them one and all gluttonous, wine-bibbers, drunkards, and next after lewdness, most addicted to the shameless service of the belly, like brute beasts. And, as he probed the matter still further, he perceived that they were all so greedy and avaricious that human, nay Christian blood, and things sacred of what kind soever, spiritualities no less than temporalities, they bought and sold for money; which traffic was greater and employed more brokers than the drapery trade and all the other trades of Paris put together; open simony and gluttonous excess being glosed under such specious terms as "arrangement" and "moderate use of creature comforts," as if God could not penetrate the thoughts of even the most corrupt hearts, to say nothing of the signification of words, and would suffer Himself to be misled after the manner of men by the names of things. Which matters,

with many others which are not to be mentioned, our modest and
sober-minded Jew found by no means to his liking, so that, his
curiosity being fully satisfied, he was minded to return to Paris ; which
accordingly he did. There, on his arrival, he was met by Jehannot ;
and the two made great cheer together. Jehannot expected Abraham's
conversion least of all things, and allowed him some days of rest before
he asked what he thought of the Holy Father and the cardinals and
the other courtiers. To which the Jew forthwith replied :—" I think
God owes them all an evil recompense : I tell thee, so far as I was
able to carry my investigations, holiness, devotion, good works or
exemplary living in any kind was nowhere to be found in any clerk ;
but only lewdness, avarice, gluttony, and the like, and worse, if worse
may be, appeared to be held in such honour of all, that (to my thinking) the place is a centre of diabolical rather than of divine activities.
To the best of my judgment, your Pastor, and by consequence all
that are about him devote all their zeal and ingenuity and subtlety
to devise how best and most speedily they may bring the Christian
religion to nought and banish it from the world. And because I see
that what they so zealously endeavour does not come to pass, but
that on the contrary your religion continually grows, and shines
more and more clear, therein I seem to discern a very evident token
that it, rather than any other, as being more true and holy than any
other, has the Holy Spirit for its foundation and support. For which
cause, whereas I met your exhortations in a harsh and obdurate
temper, and would not become a Christian, now I frankly tell you
that I would on no account omit to become such. Go we then to
the church, and there according to the traditional rite of your holy
faith let me receive baptism." Jehannot, who had anticipated a
diametrically opposite conclusion, as soon as he heard him so speak,
was the best pleased man that ever was in the world. So taking
Abraham with him to Notre Dame he prayed the clergy there to
baptise him. When they heard that it was his own wish, they forthwith did so, and Jehannot raised him from the sacred font, and named
him Jean ; and afterwards he caused teachers of great eminence
thoroughly to instruct him in our faith, which he readily learned,
and afterwards practised in a good, a virtuous, nay, a holy life.

NOVEL III.

Melchisedech, a Jew, by a story of three rings averts a great danger with which he was menaced by Saladin.

WHEN Neifile had brought her story to a close amid the commendations of all the company, Filomena, at the queen's behest, thus began :—

The story told by Neifile brings to my mind another in which also a Jew appears, but this time as the hero of a perilous adventure ; and as enough has been said of God and of the truth of our faith, it will not now be inopportune if we descend to mundane events and the actions of men. Wherefore I propose to tell you a story, which will perhaps dispose you to be more circumspect than you have been wont to be in answering questions addressed to you. Well ye know, or should know, loving gossips, that, as it often happens that folk by their own folly forfeit a happy estate and are plunged in most grievous misery, so good sense will extricate the wise from extremity of peril, and establish them in complete and assured peace. Of the change from good to evil fortune, which folly may effect, instances abound ; indeed, occurring as they do by the thousand day by day, they are so conspicuous that their recital would be beside our present purpose. But that good sense may be our succour in misfortune, I will now, as I promised, make plain to you within the narrow compass of a little story.

Saladin, who by his great valour had from small beginnings made himself Soldan of Egypt, and gained many victories over kings both Christian and Saracen, having in divers wars and by divers lavish displays of magnificence spent all his treasure, and in order to meet a certain emergency being in need of a large sum of money, and being at a loss to raise it with a celerity adequate to his necessity,

38

bethought him of a wealthy Jew, Melchisedech by name, who lent at usance in Alexandria, and who, were he but willing, was, as he believed, able to accommodate him, but was so miserly that he would never do so of his own accord, nor was Saladin disposed to constrain him thereto. So great, however, was his necessity that, after pondering every method whereby the Jew might be induced to be compliant, at last he determined to devise a colourably reasonable pretext for extorting the money from him. So he sent for him, received him affably, seated him by his side, and presently said to him :—"My good man, I have heard from many people that thou art very wise, and of great discernment in divine things ; wherefore I would gladly know of thee, which of the three laws thou reputest the true law, the law of the Jews, the law of the Saracens, or the law of the Christians?" The Jew, who was indeed a wise man, saw plainly enough that Saladin meant to entangle him in his speech, that he might have occasion to harass him, and bethought him that he could not praise any of the three laws above another without furnishing Saladin with the pretext which he sought. So, concentrating all the force of his mind to shape such an answer as might avoid the snare, he presently lit on what he sought, saying :—" My lord, a pretty question indeed is this which you propound, and fain would I answer it ; to which end it is apposite that I tell you a story, which, if you will hearken, is as follows :—If I mistake not, I remember to have often heard tell of a great and rich man of old time, who among other most precious jewels had in his treasury a ring of extraordinary beauty and value, which by reason of its value and beauty he was minded to leave to his heirs for ever ; for which cause he ordained, that, whichever of his sons was found in possession of the ring as by his bequest, should thereby be designate his heir, and be entitled to receive from the rest the honour and homage due to a superior. The son, to whom he bequeathed the ring, left it in like manner to his descendants, making the like ordinance as his predecessor. In short the ring passed from hand to hand for many generations ; and in the end came to the hands of one who had three sons, goodly and virtuous all, and very obedient to their father, so that he loved them all indifferently. The rule touching the descent of the ring was known to the young men, and each aspiring to hold the place of honour among them did all he could to persuade his father, who was now old, to leave the ring to him at his death.   The worthy man, who loved them all equally, and knew not how to choose from among them a sole legatee, promised the ring to each in turn, and in order to satisfy all three, caused a cunning artificer secretly to make other two rings, so like the first, that the maker himself could hardly tell which was the true ring. So, before he died, he disposed of the rings, giving one privily to each of his sons ; whereby it came to pass, that after his decease each of the sons claimed the inheritance and the place of honour, and, his claim being disputed by his brothers, produced his ring in witness of right.   And the rings being found so like one to another that it was impossible to distinguish the true one, the suit to determine the true heir remained pendent, and still so remains.   And so, my lord, to your question, touching the three laws given to the three peoples by God the Father, I answer :—Each of these peoples deems itself to have the true inheritance, the true law, the true commandments of God ; but which of them is justified in so believing, is a question which, like that of the rings, remains pendent."   The excellent adroitness with which the Jew had contrived to evade the snare which he had laid for his feet was not lost upon Saladin.   He therefore determined to let the Jew know his need, and did so, telling him at the same time what he had intended to do, in the event of his answering less circumspectly than he had done.

Thereupon the Jew gave the Soldan all the accommodation that he required, which the Soldan afterwards repaid him in full.   He also gave him most munificent gifts with his lifelong amity and a great and honourable position near his person.

NOVEL IV.

A monk lapses into a sin meriting the most severe punishment, justly censures the same fault in his abbot, and thus evades the penalty.

THE silence which followed the conclusion of Filomena's tale was broken by Dioneo, who sate next her, and without waiting for the queen's word, for he knew that by the rule laid down at the commencement it was now his turn to speak, began on this wise :— Loving ladies, if I have well understood the intention of you all, we are here to afford entertainment to one another by story-telling ; wherefore, provided only nought is done that is repugnant to this end, I deem it lawful for each (and so said our queen a little while ago) to tell whatever story seems to him most likely to be amusing. Seeing, then, that we have heard how Abraham saved his soul by the good counsel of Jehannot de Chevigny, and Melchisedech by his own good sense safe-guarded his wealth against the stratagems of Saladin, I hope to escape your censure in narrating a brief story of a monk, who by his address delivered his body from imminent peril of most severe chastisement.

In the not very remote district of Lunigiana there flourished formerly a community of monks more numerous and holy than is there to be found to-day, among whom was a young brother, whose vigour and lustihood neither the fasts nor the vigils availed to subdue. One afternoon, while the rest of the confraternity slept, our young monk took a stroll around the church, which lay in a very sequestered spot, and chanced to espy a young and very beautiful girl, a daughter, perhaps, of one of the husbandmen of those parts, going through the fields and gathering herbs as she went. No sooner had

41

he seen her than he was sharply assailed by carnal concupiscence, insomuch that he made up to and accosted her ; and (she hearkening) little by little they came to an understanding, and unobserved by any entered his cell together.   Now it so chanced that, while they fooled it within somewhat recklessly, he being overwrought with passion, the abbot awoke and passing slowly by the young monk's cell, heard the noise which they made within, and the better to distinguish the voices, came softly up to the door of the cell, and listening discovered that beyond all doubt there was a woman within. His first thought was to force the door open ; but, changing his mind, he returned to his chamber and waited until the monk should come out.

Delightsome beyond measure though the monk found his intercourse with the girl, yet was he not altogether without anxiety. He had heard, as he thought, the sound of footsteps in the dormitory, and having applied his eye to a convenient aperture had had a good view of the abbot as he stood by the door listening.   He was thus fully aware that the abbot might have detected the presence of a woman in the cell.   Whereat he was exceedingly distressed, knowing that he had a severe punishment to expect ; but he concealed his vexation from the girl while he busily cast about in his mind for some way of escape from his embarrassment.   He thus hit on a novel stratagem which was exactly suited to his purpose.   With the air of one who had had enough of the girl's company he said to her :—" I shall now leave you in order that I may arrange for your departure hence unobserved.   Stay here quietly until I return."   So out he went, locking the door of the cell, and withdrawing the key, which he carried straight to the abbot's chamber and handed to him, as was the custom when a monk was going out, saying with a composed air :— " Sir, I was not able this morning to bring in all the faggots which I had made ready, so with your leave I will go to the wood and bring them in."   The abbot, desiring to have better cognisance of the monk's offence, and not dreaming that the monk knew that he had been detected, was pleased with the turn matters had taken, and received the key gladly, at the same time giving the monk the desired leave.   So the monk withdrew, and the abbot began to consider what course it were best for him to take, whether to assemble the brotherhood and open the door in their presence, that, being witnesses of

the delinquency, they might have no cause to murmur against him
when he proceeded to punish the delinquent, or whether it were not
better first to learn from the girl's own lips how it had come about.
And reflecting that she might be the wife or daughter of some man
who would take it ill that she should be shamed by being exposed to
the gaze of all the monks, he determined first of all to find out who
she was, and then to make up his mind. So he went softly to the
cell, opened the door, and, having entered, closed it behind him.
The girl, seeing that her visitor was none other than the abbot, quite
lost her presence of mind, and quaking with shame began to weep.
Master abbot surveyed her from head to foot, and seeing that she
was fresh and comely, fell a prey, old though he was, to fleshly
cravings no less poignant and sudden than those which the young
monk had experienced, and began thus to commune with himself:—
"Alas! why take I not my pleasure when I may, seeing that I
never need lack for occasions of trouble and vexation of spirit? Here
is a fair wench, and no one in the world to know. If I can bring her
to pleasure me, I know not why I should not do so. Who will
know? No one will ever know; and sin that is hidden is half
forgiven; this chance may never come again; so, methinks, it were
the part of wisdom to take the boon which God bestows." So
musing, with an altogether different purpose from that with which
he had come, he drew near the girl, and softly bade her to be
comforted, and besought her not to weep; and so little by little he
came at last to show her what he would be at. The girl, being
made neither of iron nor of adamant, was readily induced to gratify
the abbot, who after bestowing upon her many an embrace and
kiss, got upon the monk's bed, where, being sensible, perhaps, of the
disparity between his reverend portliness and her tender youth, and
fearing to injure her by his excessive weight, he refrained from lying
upon her, but laid her upon him, and in that manner disported
himself with her for a long time. The monk, who had only pretended to go to the wood, and had concealed himself in the dormitory,
no sooner saw the abbot enter his cell than he was overjoyed to
think that his plan would succeed; and when he saw that he had
locked the door, he was well assured thereof. So he stole out of his
hiding-place, and set his eye to an aperture through which he saw
and heard all that the abbot did and said. At length the abbot,

having had enough of dalliance with the girl, locked her in the cell and returned to his chamber. Catching sight of the monk soon afterwards, and supposing him to have returned from the wood, he determined to give him a sharp reprimand and have him imprisoned, that he might thus secure the prey for himself alone. He therefore caused him to be summoned, chid him very severely and with a stern countenance, and ordered him to be put in prison. The monk replied trippingly :—"Sir, I have not been so long in the order of St. Benedict as to have every particular of the rule by heart ; nor did you teach me before to-day in what posture it behoves the monk to have intercourse with women, but limited your instruction to such matters as fasts and vigils. As, however, you have now given me my lesson, I promise you, if you also pardon my offence, that I will never repeat it, but will always follow the example which you have set me."

The abbot, who was a shrewd man, saw at once that the monk was not only more knowing than he, but had actually seen what he had done ; nor, conscience-stricken himself, could he for shame mete out to the monk a measure which he himself merited. So pardon given, with an injunction to bury what had been seen in silence, they decently conveyed the young girl out of the monastery, whither, it is to be believed, they now and again caused her to return.

NOVEL V.

The Marchioness of Monferrato by a banquet of hens seasoned with wit checks the mad passion of the King of France.

THE story told by Dioneo evoked at first some qualms of shame in the minds of the ladies, as was apparent by the modest blush that tinged their faces : then exchanging glances, and scarce able to refrain their mirth, they listened to it with half-suppressed smiles. On its conclusion they bestowed upon Dioneo a few words of gentle reprehension with intent to admonish him that such stories were not to be told among ladies. The queen then turned to Fiammetta, who was seated on the grass at her side, and bade her follow suit ; and Fiammetta with a gay and gracious mien thus began :—

The line upon which our story-telling proceeds, to wit, to shew the virtue that resides in apt and ready repartees, pleases me well ; and as in affairs of love men and women are in diverse case, for to aspire to the love of a woman of higher lineage than his own is wisdom in man, whereas a woman's good sense is then most conspicuous when she knows how to preserve herself from becoming enamoured of a man, her superior in rank, I am minded, fair my ladies, to shew you by the story which I am now to tell, how by deed and word a gentlewoman both defended herself against attack, and weaned her suitor from his love.

The Marquis of Monferrato, a paladin of distinguished prowess, was gone overseas as gonfalonier of the Church in a general array of the Christian forces. Whose merits being canvassed at the court of Philippe le Borgne, on the eve of his departure from France on the same service, a knight observed, that there was not under the stars a couple comparable to the Marquis and his lady ; in that, while the Marquis was a paragon of the knightly virtues, his lady for beauty and honour was without a peer among all the other ladies of the world. These words made so deep an impression on the mind of the King of France that, though he had never seen the lady, he fell ardently in love with her, and, being to join the armada, resolved that his port of embarcation should be no other than Genoa, in order that, travelling thither by land, he might find a decent pretext for visiting the Marchioness, with whom in the absence of the Marquis he trusted to have the success which he desired ; nor did he fail to put his design in execution. Having sent his main army on before, he took the road himself with a small company of gentlemen, and, as they approached the territory of the Marquis, he despatched a courier to the Marchioness, a day in advance, to let her know that he expected to breakfast with her the next morning. The lady, who knew her part and played it well, replied graciously, that he would be indeed welcome, and that his presence would be the greatest of all favours. She then began to commune with herself, what this might import, that so great a king should come to visit her in her husband's absence, nor was she so deluded as not to surmise that it was the fame of her beauty that drew him thither. Nevertheless she made ready to do him honour in a manner befitting her high degree, summoning to her presence such of the retainers as remained in the castle, and giving all needful directions with their advice, except that the order of the banquet and the choice of the dishes she reserved entirely to herself. Then, having caused all the hens that could be found in the country-side to be brought with all speed into the castle, she bade her cooks furnish forth the royal table with divers dishes made exclusively of such fare. The King arrived on the appointed day, and was received by the lady with great and ceremonious cheer. Fair and noble and gracious seemed she in the eyes of the King beyond all that he had conceived from the knight's words, so that he was lost in admiration and inly extolled her to the skies, his passion being the more inflamed in proportion as he found the lady surpass the idea which he had formed of her. A suite of rooms furnished with all the appointments befitting the reception of so great a king, was placed at his disposal, and after a little rest, breakfast-time being come, he and the Marchioness took their places at the same table, while his suite were honourably entertained at other boards according to their several qualities.   Many courses were served with no lack of excellent and rare wines, whereby the King was mightily pleased, as also by the extraordinary beauty of the Marchioness, on whom his eye from time to time rested.   However, as course followed course, the King observed with some surprise, that, though the dishes were diverse, yet they were all but variations of one and the same fare, to wit, the pullet.   Besides which he knew that the domain was one which could not but afford plenty of divers sorts of game, and by forewarning the lady of his approach, he had allowed time for hunting ; yet, for all his surprise, he would not broach the question more directly with her than by a reference to her hens ; so, turning to her with a smile, he said :—"Madam, do hens grow in this country without so much as a single cock ?"   The Marchioness, who perfectly apprehended the drift of the question, saw in it an opportunity, sent her by God, of evincing her virtuous resolution ; so casting a haughty glance upon the King she answered thus :—"Sire, no ; but the women, though they may differ somewhat from others in dress and rank, are yet of the same nature here as elsewhere."   The significance of the banquet of pullets was made manifest to the King by these words, as also the virtue which they veiled.   He perceived that on a lady of such a temper words would be wasted, and that force was out of the question.   Wherefore, yielding to the dictates of prudence and honour, he was now as prompt to quench, as he had been inconsiderate in conceiving, his unfortunate passion for the lady ; and fearing her answers, he refrained from further jesting with her, and dismissing his hopes devoted himself to his breakfast, which done, he disarmed suspicion of the dishonourable purpose of his visit by an early departure, and thanking her for the honour she had conferred upon him, and commending her to God, took the road to Genoa.

NOVEL VI.

A worthy man by an apt saying puts to shame the wicked hypocrisy of the religious.

WHEN all had commended the virtue of the Marchioness and the spirited reproof which she administered to the King of France, Emilia, who sate next to Fiammetta, obeyed the queen's behest, and with a good courage thus began :—

My story is also of a reproof, but of one administered by a worthy man, who lived the secular life, to a greedy religious, by a jibe as merry as admirable. Know then, dear ladies, that there was in our city, not long ago, a friar minor, an inquisitor in matters of heresy, who, albeit he strove might and main to pass himself off as a holy man and tenderly solicitous for the integrity of the Christian Faith, as they all do, yet he had as keen a scent for a full purse as for a deficiency of faith. Now it so chanced that his zeal was rewarded by the discovery of a good man far better furnished with money than with sense, who in an unguarded moment, not from defect of faith, but rather, perhaps, from excess of hilarity, being heated with wine, had happened to say to his boon companions, that he had a wine good enough for Christ Himself to drink. Which being reported to the inquisitor, he, knowing the man to be possessed of large estates and a well-lined purse, set to work in hot haste, "cum gladiis et fustibus," to bring all the rigour of the law to bear upon him, designing thereby not to lighten the load of his victim's misbelief, but to increase the weight of his own purse by the florins, which he might, as he did, receive from him. So he cited him to his presence, and asked him whether what was alleged against him were true. The good man answered in the affirmative, and told him how it had happened. "Then," said our

48

most holy and devout inquisitor of St. John Goldenbeard,[1] " then hast
thou made Christ a wine-bibber, and a lover of rare vintages, as if
He were a sot, a toper and a tavern-haunter even as one of you. And
thinkest thou now by a few words of apology to pass this off as a
light matter ? It is no such thing as thou supposest. Thou hast
deserved the fire ; and we should but do our duty, did we inflict it
upon thee." With these and the like words in plenty he upbraided
him, bending on him meanwhile a countenance as stern as if
Epicurus had stood before him denying the immortality of the soul.
In short he so terrified him that the good man was fain to employ
certain intermediaries to anoint his palms with a liberal allowance of
St. John Goldenmouth's grease, an excellent remedy for the disease of
avarice which spreads like a pestilence among the clergy, and notably
among the friars minors, who dare not touch a coin, that he might
deal gently with him. And great being the virtue of this ointment,
albeit no mention is made thereof by Galen in any part of his
Medicines, it had so gracious an effect that the threatened fire gave
place to a cross, which he was to wear as if he were bound for the
emprise over seas ; and to make the ensign more handsome the
inquisitor ordered that it should be yellow upon a black ground.
Besides which, after pocketing the coin, he kept him dangling about
him for some days, bidding him by way of penance hear mass every
morning at Santa Croce, and afterwards wait upon him at the
breakfast-hour, after which he was free to do as he pleased for the
rest of the day. All which he most carefully observed ; and so it
fell out that one of these mornings there were chanted at the mass
at which he assisted the following words of the Gospel :—You shall
receive an hundredfold and shall possess eternal life. With these
words deeply graven in his memory, he presented himself, as he was
bidden, before the inquisitor, where he sate taking his breakfast, and
being asked whether he had heard mass that morning, he promptly
answered :—" Yes, sir." And being further asked :—" Heardest
thou aught therein, as to which thou art in doubt, or hast thou any
question to propound ? " the good man responded :—" Nay indeed,
doubt have I none of aught that I heard ; but rather assured faith in
the verity of all. One thing, however, I heard, which caused me to

[1] The fiorino d'oro bore the effigy of St. John.

commiserate you and the rest of you friars very heartily, in regard of the evil plight in which you must find yourselves in the other world." "And what," said the inquisitor, "was the passage that so moved thee to commiserate us?" "Sir," rejoined the good man, "it was that passage in the Gospel which says :—You shall receive an hundredfold." "You heard aright," said the inquisitor; "but why did the passage so affect you?" "Sir," replied the good man, "I will tell you. Since I have been in attendance here, I have seen a crowd of poor folk receive a daily dole, now of one, now of two, huge tureens of swill, being the refuse from your table, and that of the brothers of this convent; whereof if you are to receive an hundred-fold in the other world, you will have so much that it will go hard but you are all drowned therein." This raised a general laugh among those who sat at the inquisitor's table, whereat the inquisitor, feeling that their gluttony and hypocrisy had received a home-thrust, was very wroth, and, but that what he had already done had not escaped censure, would have instituted fresh proceedings against him in revenge for the pleasantry with which he had rebuked the base-ness of himself and his brother friars; so in impotent wrath he bade him go about his business and shew himself there no more.

NOVEL VII.

Bergamino, with a story of Primasso and the Abbot of Cluny, finely censures a sudden access of avarice in Messer Cane della Scala.

EMILIA'S charming manner and her story drew laughter and commendation from the queen and all the company, who were much tickled by her new type of crusader. When the laughter had subsided, and all were again silent, Filostrato, on whom the narration now fell, began on this wise :—

A fine thing it is, noble ladies, to hit a fixed mark; but if, on the sudden appearance of some strange object, it be forthwith hit by the bowman, 'tis little short of a miracle. The corrupt and filthy life of the clergy offers on many sides a fixed mark of iniquity at which, whoever is so minded, may let fly, with little doubt that they will reach it, the winged words of reproof and reprehension. Wherefore, though the worthy man did well to censure in the person of the inquisitor the pretended charity of the friars who give to the poor what they ought rather to give to the pigs or throw away, higher indeed is the praise which I accord to him, of whom, taking my cue from the last story, I mean to speak; seeing that by a clever apologue he rebuked a sudden and unwonted access of avarice in Messer Cane della Scala, conveying in a figure what he had at heart to say touching Messer Cane and himself; which apologue is to follow.

Far and wide, almost to the ends of the earth, is borne the most illustrious renown of Messer Cane della Scala, in many ways the favoured child of fortune, a lord almost without a peer among the notables and magnificoes of Italy since the time of the Emperor

Frederic II.   Now Messer Cane, being minded to hold high festival at Verona, whereof fame should speak marvellous things, and many folk from divers parts, of whom the greater number were jesters of every order, being already arrived, Messer Cane did suddenly (for some cause or another) abandon his design, and dismissed them with a partial recompense.   One only, Bergamino by name, a speaker ready and polished in a degree credible only to such as heard him, remained, having received no recompense or congé, still cherishing the hope that this omission might yet turn out to his advantage. But Messer Cane was possessed with the idea that whatever he might give Bergamino would be far more completely thrown away than if he had tossed it into the fire ; so never a word of the sort said he or sent he to him.   A few days thus passed, and then Bergamino, seeing that he was in no demand or request for aught that belonged to his office, and being also at heavy charges at his inn for the keep of his horses and servants, fell into a sort of melancholy ; but still he waited a while, not deeming it expedient to leave.   He had brought with him three rich and goodly robes, given him by other lords, that he might make a brave show at the festival, and when his host began to press for payment he gave him one of the robes ; afterwards, there being still much outstanding against him, he must needs, if he would tarry longer at the inn, give the host the second robe ; after which he began to live on the third, being minded to remain there, as long as it would hold out, in expectation of better luck, and then to take his departure.   Now, while he was thus living on the third robe, it chanced that Messer Cane encountered him one day as he sate at breakfast with a very melancholy visage.   Which Messer Cane observing, said, rather to tease him than expecting to elicit from him any pleasant retort :—" What ails thee, Bergamino, that thou art still so melancholy ?   Let me know the reason why." Whereupon Bergamino, without a moment's reflection, told the following story, which could not have fitted his own case more exactly if it had been long premeditated.

     " My lord, you must know that Primasso was a grammarian of great eminence, and excellent and quick beyond all others in versifying ; whereby he waxed so notable and famous that, albeit he was not everywhere known by sight, yet there were scarce any that did not at least by name and report know who Primasso was.   Now it so

happened that, being once at Paris in straitened circumstances, as
it was his lot to be most of his time by reason that virtue is little
appreciated by the powerful, he heard speak of the Abbot of Cluny,
who, except the Pope, is supposed to be the richest prelate, in regard
of his vast revenues, that the Church of God can shew ; and marvellous and magnificent things were told him of the perpetual court
which the abbot kept, and how, wherever he was, he denied not to
any that came there either meat or drink, so only that he preferred his request while the abbot was at table.   Which when
Primasso heard, he determined to go and see for himself what
magnificent state this abbot kept, for he was one that took great
delight in observing the ways of powerful and lordly men ; wherefore he asked how far from Paris was the abbot then sojourning. He
was informed that the abbot was then at one of his places distant
perhaps six miles ; which Primasso concluded he could reach in time
for breakfast, if he started early in the morning.   When he had
learned the way, he found that no one else was travelling by it, and
fearing lest by mischance he should lose it, and so find himself where
it would not be easy for him to get food, he determined to obviate so
disagreeable a contingency by taking with him three loaves of bread
—as for drink, water, though not much to his taste, was, he supposed,
to be found everywhere.   So, having disposed the loaves in the fold of
his tunic, he took the road and made such progress that he reached
the abbot's place of sojourn before the breakfast-hour.   Having
entered, he made the circuit of the entire place, observing everything,
the vast array of tables, and the vast kitchen well-appointed with all
things needful for the preparation and service of the breakfast, and
saying to himself :—' In very truth this man is even such a magnifico as he is reported to be.'   While his attention was thus occupied,
the abbot's seneschal, it being now breakfast-time, gave order to serve
water for the hands, which being washen, they sat them all down to
breakfast.   Now it so happened that Primasso was placed immediately
in front of the door by which the abbot must pass from his chamber
into the hall ; in which, according to rule of his court, neither wine,
nor bread, nor aught else drinkable or eatable was ever set on the
tables before he made his appearance and was seated.   The seneschal,
therefore, having set the tables, sent word to the abbot, that all
was now ready, and they waited only his pleasure.   So the abbot

gave the word, the door of his chamber was thrown open, and he took a step or two forward towards the hall, gazing straight in front of him as he went.   Thus it fell out that the first man on whom he set eyes was Primasso, who was in very sorry trim.   The abbot, who knew him not by sight, no sooner saw him, than, surprised by a churlish mood to which he had hitherto been an entire stranger, he said to himself :—' So it is to such as this man that I give my hospitality ; ' and going back into the chamber he bade lock the door, and asked of his attendants whether the vile fellow that sate at table directly opposite the door was known to any of them, who, one and all, answered in the negative.   Primasso waited a little, but he was not used to fast, and his journey had whetted his appetite.   So, as the abbot did not return, he drew out one of the loaves which he had brought with him, and began to eat.   The abbot, after a while, bade one of his servants go see whether Primasso were gone.   The servant returned with the answer :—' No, sir, and (what is more) he is eating a loaf of bread, which he seems to have brought with him.' ' Be it so then,' said the abbot, who was vexed that he was not gone of his own accord, but was not disposed to turn him out ; ' let him eat his own bread, if he have any, for he shall have none of ours to-day.'   By and by Primasso, having finished his first loaf, began, as the abbot did not make his appearance, to eat the second ; which was likewise reported to the abbot, who had again sent to see if he were gone.   Finally, as the abbot still delayed his coming, Primasso, having finished the second loaf, began upon the third ; whereof, once more, word was carried to the abbot, who now began to commune with himself and say :—' Alas ! my soul, what unwonted mood harbourest thou to-day ?   What avarice ? what scorn ? and of whom ? I have given my hospitality, now for many a year, to whoso craved it, without looking to see whether he were gentle or churl, poor or rich, merchant or cheat, and mine eyes have seen it squandered on vile fellows without number ; and nought of that which I feel towards this man ever entered my mind.   Assuredly it cannot be that he is a man of no consequence, who is the occasion of this access of avarice in me.   Though he seem to me a vile fellow, he must be some great man, that my mind is thus obstinately averse to do him honour.' Of which musings the upshot was that he sent to inquire who the vile fellow was, and learning that he was Primasso, come to see if what he had heard of his magnificent state were true, he was stricken with shame, having heard of old Primasso's fame, and knowing him to be a great man. Wherefore, being zealous to make him the amend, he studied to do him honour in many ways; and after breakfast, that his garb might accord with his native dignity, he caused him to be nobly arrayed, and setting him upon a palfrey and filling his purse, left it to his own choice, whether to go or to stay. So Primasso, with a full heart, thanked him for his courtesy in terms the amplest that he could command, and, having left Paris afoot, returned thither on horseback."

Messer Cane was shrewd enough to apprehend Bergamino's meaning perfectly well without a gloss, and said with a smile:— " Bergamino, thy parable is apt, and declares to me very plainly thy losses, my avarice, and what thou desirest of me. And in good sooth this access of avarice, of which thou art the occasion, is the first that I have experienced. But I will expel the intruder with the *bâton* which thou thyself hast furnished." So he paid Bergamino's reckoning, habited him nobly in one of his own robes, gave him money and a palfrey, and left it for the time at his discretion, whether to go or to stay.

NOVEL VIII.

Guglielmo Borsiere by a neat retort sharply censures avarice in Messer Ermino de' Grimaldi.

NEXT Filostrato was seated Lauretta, who, when the praises bestowed on Bergamino's address had ceased, knowing that it was now her turn to speak, waited not for the word of command, but with a charming graciousness thus began :—

The last novel, dear gossips, prompts me to relate how a worthy man, likewise a jester, reprehended not without success the greed of a very wealthy merchant; and though the burden of my story is not unlike the last, yet, perchance, it may not on that account be the less appreciated by you, because it has a happy termination.

Know then that in Genoa there dwelt long ago a gentleman, who was known as Messer Ermino de' Grimaldi, and whose wealth, both in lands and money, was generally supposed to be far in excess of that of any other burgher then in Italy; and as in wealth he was without a rival in Italy, so in meanness and avarice there was not any in the entire world, however richly endowed with those qualities, whom he did not immeasurably surpass, insomuch that, not only did he keep a tight grip upon his purse when honour was to be done to another, but in his personal expenditure, even upon things meet and proper, contrary to the general custom of the Genoese, whose wont is to array themselves nobly, he was extremely penurious, as also in his outlay upon his table. Wherefore, not without just cause, folk had dropped his surname de' Grimaldi, and called him instead Messer Ermino Avarizia. While thus by thrift his wealth waxed greater and greater, it so chanced that there came to Genoa a jester of good parts, a man debonair and ready of speech, his name Guglielmo Borsiere, whose like is not to be found to-day, when jesters (to the great reproach be it spoken of those that claim the name and reputation of gentlemen) are rather to be called asses, being without courtly breeding, and formed after the coarse pattern of the basest of churls. And whereas in the days of which I speak they made it their business, they spared no pains, to compose quarrels, to allay heart-burnings, between gentlemen, or arrange marriages, or leagues of amity, ministering meanwhile relief to jaded minds and solace to courts by the sprightly sallies of their wit, and with keen sarcasm, like fathers, censuring churlish manners, being also satisfied with very trifling guerdons ; nowadays all their care is to spend their time in scandal-mongering, in sowing discord, in saying, and (what is worse) in doing in the presence of company things churlish and flagitious, in bringing accusations, true or false, of wicked, shameful or flagitious conduct against one another ; and in drawing gentlemen into base and nefarious practices by sinister and insidious arts. And by these wretched and depraved lords he is held most dear and best rewarded whose words and deeds are the most atrocious, to the great reproach and scandal of the world of to-day ; whereby it is abundantly manifest that virtue has departed from the earth, leaving a degenerate generation to wallow in the lowest depths of vice.

But reverting to the point at which I started, wherefrom under stress of just indignation I have deviated somewhat further than I intended, I say that the said Guglielmo was had in honour, and was well received by all the gentlemen of Genoa ; and tarrying some days in the city, heard much of the meanness and avarice of Messer Ermino, and was curious to see him. Now Messer Ermino had heard that this Guglielmo Borsiere was a man of good parts, and, notwithstanding his avarice, having in him some sparks of good breeding, received him with words of hearty greeting and a gladsome mien, and conversed freely with him and of divers matters, and so conversing, took him with other Genoese that were of his company to a new and very beautiful house which he had built, and after shewing him over the whole of it, said to him :—" Now, Messer Guglielmo, you have seen and heard many things ; could you suggest to me something, the like of which has not hitherto been seen, which I might have painted here in the saloon of this house ? " To which ill-judged question Guglielmo replied:—" Sir, it would not, I think, be in my power to suggest anything the like of which has never been seen, unless it were a sneeze or something similar; but if it so please you, I have something to suggest, which, I think, you have never seen." "Prithee, what may that be?" said Messer Ermino, not expecting to get the answer which he got. For Guglielmo replied forthwith:—"Paint Courtesy here;" which Messer Ermino had no sooner heard, than he was so stricken with shame that his disposition underwent a complete change, and he said:— "Messer Guglielmo, I will see to it that Courtesy is here painted in such wise that neither you nor any one else shall ever again have reason to tell me that I have not seen or known that virtue." And henceforward (so enduring was the change wrought by Guglielmo's words) there was not in Genoa, while he lived, any gentleman so liberal and so gracious and so lavish of honour both to strangers and to his fellow-citizens as Messer Ermino de' Grimaldi

NOVEL IX.

The censure of a Gascon lady converts the King of Cyprus from a churlish to an honourable temper.

EXCEPT Elisa none now remained to answer the call of the queen, and she without waiting for it, with gladsome alacrity thus began :—

Bethink you, damsels, how often it has happened that men who have been obdurate to censures and chastisements have been reclaimed by some unpremeditated casual word. This is plainly manifest by the story told by Lauretta ; and by mine, which will be of the briefest, I mean further to illustrate it ; seeing that, good stories, being always pleasurable, are worth listening to with attention, no matter by whom they may be told.

'Twas, then, in the time of the first king of Cyprus, after the conquest made of the Holy Land by Godfrey de Bouillon, that a lady of Gascony made a pilgrimage to the Holy Sepulchre, and on her way home, having landed at Cyprus, met with brutal outrage at the hands of certain ruffians. Broken-hearted and disconsolate she determined to make her complaint to the king ; but she was told that it would be all in vain, because so spiritless and *fainéant* was he that he not only neglected to avenge affronts put upon others, but endured with a reprehensible tameness those which were offered to himself, insomuch that whoso had any ill-humour to vent, took occasion to vex or mortify him. The lady, hearing this report, despaired of redress, and by way of alleviation of her grief determined to make the king sensible of his baseness. So in tears she presented herself before him and said :—" Sire, it is not to seek redress of the wrong done me that I come here before you: but only that, so please you, I may learn of you how it is that you suffer patiently the wrongs which, as I understand, are done you; that thus schooled by you in patience I may endure my own, which, God knows, I would gladly, were it possible, transfer to you, seeing that you are so well fitted to bear them." These words aroused the hitherto sluggish and apathetic king as it were from sleep. He redressed the lady's wrong, and having thus made a beginning, thenceforth meted out the most rigorous justice to all that in any wise offended against the majesty of his crown.

NOVEL X.

Master Alberto da Bologna honourably puts to shame a lady who sought occasion to put him to shame in that he was in love with her.

AFTER Elisa had done, it only remained for the queen to conclude the day's story-telling, and thus with manner debonair did she begin:—

As stars in the serene expanse of heaven, as in spring-time flowers in the green pastures, so, honourable damsels, in the hour of rare and excellent converse is wit with its bright sallies. Which, being brief, are much more proper for ladies than for men, seeing that prolixity of speech, when brevity is possible, is much less allowable to them; albeit (shame be to us all and all our generation) few ladies or none are left to-day who understand aught that is wittily said, or understanding are able to answer it. For the place of those graces of the spirit which distinguished the ladies of the past has now been usurped by adornments of the person; and she whose dress is most richly and variously and curiously dight, accounts herself more worthy to be had in honour, forgetting, that, were one but so to array him, an ass would carry a far greater load of finery than any of them, and for all that be not a whit the more deserving of honour. I blush to say this, for in censuring others I condemn myself. Tricked out, bedecked, bedizened thus, we are either silent and impassive as statues, or, if we answer aught that is said to us, much better were it we had held our peace. And we make believe, forsooth, that our failure to acquit ourselves in converse with our equals of either sex does but proceed from guilelessness; dignifying stupidity by the name of modesty, as if no lady could be modest and converse with other folk than her maid or laundress or bake-house

woman ; which if Nature had intended, as we feign she did, she would
have set other limits to our garrulousness.   True it is that in this, as
in other matters, time and place and person are to be regarded ;
because it sometimes happens that a lady or gentleman thinking by
some sally of wit to put another to shame, has rather been put to
shame by that other, having failed duly to estimate their relative
powers.   Wherefore, that you may be on your guard against such
error, and, further, that in you be not exemplified the common
proverb, to wit, that women do ever and on all occasions choose the
worst, I trust that this last of to-day's stories, which falls to me to
tell, may serve you as a lesson ; that, as you are distinguished from
others by nobility of nature, so you may also shew yourselves
separate from them by excellence of manners.

There lived not many years ago, perhaps yet lives, in Bologna, a
very great physician, so great that the fame of his skill was noised
abroad throughout almost the entire world.

Now Master Alberto (such was his name) was of so noble a
temper that, being now nigh upon seventy years of age, and all but
devoid of natural heat of body, he was yet receptive of the flames of
love ; and having at an assembly seen a very beautiful widow lady,
Madonna Malgherida de' Ghisolieri, as some say, and being charmed
with her beyond measure, was, notwithstanding his age, no less
ardently enamoured than a young man, insomuch that he was not
well able to sleep at night, unless during the day he had seen the fair
lady's lovely and delicate features.   Wherefore he began to frequent
the vicinity of her house, passing to and fro in front of it, now on
foot now on horseback, as occasion best served.   Which she and many
other ladies perceiving, made merry together more than once, to see
a man of his years and discretion in love, as if they deemed that this
most delightful passion of love were only fit for empty-headed youths,
and could not in men be either harboured or engendered.   Master
Alberto thus continuing to haunt the front of the house, it so
happened that one feast-day the lady with other ladies was seated
before her door, and Master Alberto's approach being thus observed
by them for some time before he arrived, they complotted to receive
him and shew him honour, and then to rally him on his love ; and
so they did, rising with one accord to receive him, bidding him
welcome, and ushering him into a cool courtyard, where they regaled

him with the finest wines and comfits; which done, in a tone of
refined and sprightly banter they asked him how it came about that
he was enamoured of this fair lady, seeing that she was beloved of
many a fine gentleman of youth and spirit.   Master Alberto, being
thus courteously assailed, put a blithe face on it, and answered :—
" Madam, my love for you need surprise none that is conversant
with such matters, and least of all you that are worthy of it.   And
though old men, of course, have lost the strength which love demands for its full fruition, yet are they not therefore without the
good intent and just appreciation of what beseems the accepted lover,
but indeed understand it far better than young men, by reason that
they have more experience.   My hope in thus old aspiring to love
you, who are loved by so many young men, is founded on what I
have frequently observed of ladies' ways at lunch, when they trifle
with the lupin and the leek.   In the leek no part is good, but the
head is at any rate not so bad as the rest, and indeed not unpalatable ;
you, however, for the most part, following a depraved taste, hold it in
your hand and munch the leaves, which are not only of no account
but actually distasteful.   How am I to know, madam, that in your
selection of lovers, you are not equally eccentric ?   In which case I
should be the man of your choice, and the rest would be cast aside."
Whereto the gentle lady, somewhat shame-stricken, as were also her
fair friends, thus made answer :—" Master Alberto, our presumption
has received from you a most just and no less courteous reproof ; but
your love is dear to me, as should ever be that of a wise and worthy
man.   And therefore, saving my honour, I am yours, entirely and
devotedly at your pleasure and command."   This speech brought
Master Alberto to his feet, and the others also rising, he thanked the
lady for her courtesy, bade her a gay and smiling adieu, and so
left the house.   Thus the lady, not considering on whom she exercised her wit, thinking to conquer was conquered herself : against
which mishap you, if you are discreet, will ever be most strictly on
your guard.

As the young ladies and the three young men finished their story-
telling the sun was westering and the heat of the day in great
measure abated.   Which their queen observing, debonairly thus she
spoke :—" Now, dear gossips, my day of sovereignty draws to a close,
and nought remains for me to do but to give you a new queen, by

whom on the morrow our common life may be ordered as she may
deem best in a course of seemly pleasure ; and though there seems to
be still some interval between day and night, yet, as whoso does not
in some degree anticipate the course of time, cannot well provide for
the future ; and in order that what the new queen shall decide to be
meet for the morrow may be made ready beforehand, I decree that
from this time forth the days begin at this hour.   And so in reverent
submission to Him, in whom is the life of all beings, for our comfort
and solace we commit the governance of our realm for the morrow
into the hands of Queen Filomena, most discreet of damsels." So
saying she arose, took the laurel wreath from her brow, and with a
gesture of reverence set it on the brow of Filomena, whom she then,
and after her all the other ladies and the young men, saluted as
queen, doing her due and graceful homage.

Queen Filomena modestly blushed a little to find herself thus
invested with the sovereignty ; but, being put on her mettle by
Pampinea's recent admonitions, she was minded not to seem awkward,
and soon recovered her composure.   She then began by confirming
all the appointments made by Pampinea, and making all needful
arrangements for the following morning and evening, which they
were to pass where they then were.   Whereupon she thus spoke :—
" Dearest gossips, though, thanks rather to Pampinea's courtesy than
to merit of mine, I am made queen of you all ; yet I am not on
that account minded to have respect merely to my own judgment in
the governance of our life, but to unite your wisdom with mine ; and
that you may understand what I think of doing, and by consequence
may be able to amplify or curtail it at your pleasure, I will in few
words make known to you my purpose.   The course observed by
Pampinea to-day, if I have judged aright, seems to be alike commendable and delectable ; wherefore, until by lapse of time, or for some
other cause, it grow tedious, I purpose not to alter it.   So when we
have arranged for what we have already taken in hand, we will go
hence and enjoy a short walk ; at sundown we will sup in the cool ;
and we will then sing a few songs and otherwise divert ourselves,
until it is time to go to sleep.   To-morrow we will rise in the cool
of the morning, and after enjoying another walk, each at his or her
sweet will, we will return, as to-day, and in due time break our fast,
dance, sleep, and having risen, will here resume our story-telling,

wherein, methinks, pleasure and profit unite in superabundant measure. True it is that Pampinea, by reason of her late election to the sovereignty, neglected one matter, which I mean to introduce, to wit, the circumscription of the topic of our story-telling, and its preassignment, that each may be able to premeditate some apt story bearing upon the theme ; and seeing that from the beginning of the world Fortune has made men the sport of divers accidents, and so it will continue until the end, the theme, so please you, shall in each case be the same ; to wit, the fortune of such as after divers adventures have at last attained a goal of unexpected felicity.

The ladies and the young men alike commended the rule thus laid down, and agreed to follow it. Dioneo, however, when the rest had done speaking, said :—" Madam, as all the rest have said, so say I, briefly, that the rule prescribed by you is commendable and delectable ; but of your especial grace I crave a favour, which, I trust, may be granted and continued to me, so long as our company shall endure ; which favour is this : that I be not bound by the assigned theme if I am not so minded, but that I have leave to choose such topic as best shall please me. And lest any suppose that I crave this grace as one that has not stories ready to hand, I am henceforth content that mine be always the last." The queen, knowing him to be a merry and facetious fellow, and feeling sure that he only craved this favour in order that, if the company were jaded, he might have an opportunity to recreate them by some amusing story, gladly, with the consent of the rest, granted his petition. She then rose, and attended by the rest sauntered towards a stream, which, issuing clear as crystal from a neighbouring hill, precipitated itself into a valley shaded by trees close set amid living rock and fresh green herbage. Bare of foot and arm they entered the stream, and roving hither and thither amused themselves in divers ways till in due time they returned to the palace, and gaily supped. Supper ended, the queen sent for instruments of music, and bade Lauretta lead a dance, while Emilia was to sing a song accompanied by Dioneo on the lute.

Accordingly Lauretta led a dance, while Emilia with passion sang the following song :—

> So fain I am of my own loveliness,
> I hope, nor think not e'er
> The weight to feel of other amorousness.

When in the mirror I my face behold,
  That see I there which doth my mind content,
Nor any present hap or memory old
May me deprive of such sweet ravishment.
Where else, then, should I find such blandishment
    Of sight and sense that e'er
My heart should know another amorousness?

Nor need I fear lest the fair thing retreat,
  When fain I am my solace to renew;
Rather, I know, 'twill me advance to meet,
To pleasure me, and shew so sweet a view
That speech or thought of none its semblance true
    Paint or conceive may e'er,
Unless he burn with ev'n such amorousness.

Thereon as more intent I gaze, the fire
  Waxeth within me hourly more and more,
Myself I yield thereto, myself entire,
And foretaste have of what it hath in store,
And hope of greater joyance than before,
    Nay, such as ne'er
None knew; for ne'er was felt such amorousness.

This ballade, to which all heartily responded, albeit its words
furnished much matter of thought to some, was followed by some
other dances, and part of the brief night being thus spent, the queen
proclaimed the first day ended, and bade light the torches, that all
might go to rest until the following morning; and so, seeking their
several chambers, to rest they went.

Endeth here the first day of the Decameron; beginneth the second, in which, under the rule of Filomena, they discourse of the fortunes of such as after divers misadventures have at last attained a goal of unexpected felicity.

THE sun was already trailing the new day in his wake of light, and the birds, blithely chanting their lays among the green boughs, carried the tidings to the ear, when with one accord all the ladies and the three young men arose, and entered the gardens, where for no little time they found their delight in sauntering about the dewy meads, straying hither and thither, culling flowers, and weaving them into fair garlands. The day passed like its predecessor; they breakfasted in the shade, and danced and slept until noon, when they rose, and, at their queen's behest, assembled in the cool meadow, and sat them down in a circle about her. Fair and very debonair she shewed, crowned with her laurel wreath, as for a brief space she scanned the company, and then bade Neifile shew others the way with a story. Neifile made no excuse, and gaily thus began.

NOVEL I.

Martellino pretends to be a paralytic, and makes it appear as if he were cured by being placed upon the body of St. Arrigo. His trick is detected; he is beaten and arrested, and is in peril of hanging, but finally escapes.

OFTEN has it happened, dearest ladies, that one who has studied to raise a laugh at others' expense, especially in regard of things worthy to be had in reverence, has found the laugh turn against himself, and sometimes to his loss: as, in obedience to the queen's command, and by way of introducing our theme, I am about to shew you, by the narrative of an adventure which befell one of our own citizens, and after a course of evil fortune had an entirely unexpected and very felicitous issue.

Not long ago there was at Treviso a German, named Arrigo, a poor man who got his living as a common hired porter, but, though of so humble a condition, was respected by all, being accounted not only an honest but a most holy man; insomuch that, whether truly or falsely I know not, the Trevisans affirm, that on his decease all the bells of the cathedral of Treviso began to toll of their own accord. Which being accounted a miracle, this Arrigo was generally reputed a saint; and all the people of the city gathered before the house where his body lay, and bore it, with a saint's honours, into the cathedral, and brought thither the halt and paralytic and blind, and others afflicted with disease or bodily defects, as hoping that by contact with this holy body they would all be healed. The people thus tumultuously thronging the church, it so chanced that there arrived in Treviso three of our own citizens, of whom one was named Stecchi, another Martellino, and the third Marchese; all three being men whose habit it was to frequent the courts of the nobles and afford spectators amusement by assuming disguises and personating other men. Being entire strangers to the place, and seeing everybody running to and fro, they were much astonished, and having learned the why and wherefore, were curious to go see what was to be seen. So at the inn, where they put up, Marchese began :—"We would fain go see this saint; but for my part I know not how we are to reach the spot, for I hear the piazza is full of Germans and other armed men, posted there by the Lord who rules here to prevent an uproar, and moreover the church, so far as one may learn, is so full of folk that scarce another soul may enter it." Whereupon Martellino, who was bent on seeing what was to be seen, said :—"Let not this deter us; I will assuredly find a way of getting to the saint's body." "How?" rejoined Marchese. "I will tell you," replied Martellino; "I will counterfeit a paralytic, and thou wilt support me on one side and Stecchi on the other, as if I were not able to go alone, and so you will enter the church, making it appear as if you were leading me up to the body of the saint that he may heal me, and all that see will make way and give us free passage." Marchese and Stecchi approved the plan; so all three forthwith left the inn and repaired to a lonely place, where Martellino distorted his hands, his fingers, his arms, his legs, and also his mouth and eyes and his entire face in a manner horrible to contemplate; so that no stranger that saw him could have doubted that he was impotent and paralysed in every part of his body. In this guise Marchese and Stecchi laid hold of him, and led him towards the church, assuming a most piteous air, and humbly beseeching everybody for God's sake to make way for them. Their request was readily granted; and, in short, observed by all, and crying out at almost every step, "make way, make way," they reached the place where St. Arrigo's body was laid. Whereupon some gentlemen who stood by hoisted Martellino on to the saint's body, that thereby he might receive the boon of health. There he lay still for a while, the eyes of all in the church being riveted upon him in expectation of the result; then, being a very practised performer, he stretched, first, one of his fingers, next a hand, afterwards an arm, and so forth, making as if he gradually recovered the use of all his natural powers. Which the people observing raised such a clamour in honour of St. Arrigo that even thunder would have been inaudible. Now it chanced that hard by stood a Florentine, who knew Martellino well, though he had failed to recognise him, when, in such strange guise, he was led into the church; but now, seeing him resume his natural shape, the Florentine recognised him, and at once said with a laugh:—" God's curse upon him. Who that saw him come but would have believed that he was really paralysed?" These words were overheard by some of the Trevisans, who began forthwith to question the Florentine. " How?" said they; " was he then not paralysed?" " No, by God!" returned the Florentine; " he has always been as straight as any of us; he has merely shewn you that he knows better than any man alive how to play this trick of putting on any counterfeit semblance that he chooses." Thereupon the Trevisans, without further parley, made a rush, clearing the way and crying out as they went:—" Seize this traitor who mocks at God and His saints; who, being no paralytic, has come hither in the guise of a paralytic to deride our patron saint and us." So saying, they laid hands on him, dragged him down from where he stood, seized him by the hair, tore the clothes from his back, and fell to beating and kicking him, so that it seemed to him as if all the world were upon him. He cried out:—" Pity, for God's sake," and defended himself as best he could: all in vain, however; the press became thicker and thicker moment by moment. Which Stecchi and Marchese observing began to say one to the other that 'twas a bad business; yet, being apprehensive on their own account, they did not venture to come to his assistance, but cried out with the rest that he ought to die, at the same time, however, casting about how they might find the means to rescue him from the hands of the people, who would certainly have killed him, but for a diversion which Marchese hastily effected. The entire posse of the signory being just outside, he ran off at full speed to the Podestà's lieutenant, and said to him:—" Help, for God's sake; there is a villain here that has cut my purse with full a hundred florins of gold in it; prithee have him arrested that I may have my own again." Whereupon, twelve sergeants or more ran forthwith to the place where hapless Martellino was being carded without a comb, and, forcing their way with the utmost difficulty through the throng, rescued him all bruised and battered from their hands, and led him to the palace; whither he was followed by many who, resenting what he had done, and hearing that

he was arrested as a cutpurse, and lacking better pretext for harassing
him, began one and all to charge him with having cut their purses.
All which the deputy of the Podestà had no sooner heard, than, being
a harsh man, he straightway took Martellino aside and began to
examine him. Martellino answered his questions in a bantering tone,
making light of the arrest ; whereat the deputy, losing patience, had
him bound to the strappado, and caused him to receive a few hints of
the cord with intent to extort from him a confession of his guilt, by
way of preliminary to hanging him. Taken down from the strappado, and questioned by the deputy if what his accusers said were
true, Martellino, as nothing was to be gained by denial, answered :—
" My lord, I am ready to confess the truth ; let but my accusers say,
each of them, when and where I cut his purse, and I will tell you
what I have and what I have not done." " So be it," said the deputy,
and caused a few of them to be summoned. Whereupon Martellino,
being charged with having cut this, that or the other man's purse
eight, six or four days ago, while others averred that he had cut their
purses that very day, answered thus :—" My lord, these men lie in
the throat, and for token that I speak true, I tell you that, so far from
having been here as long as they make out, it is but very lately that
I came into these parts, where I never was before ; and no sooner was
I come, than, as my ill-luck would have it, I went to see the body of
this saint, and so have been carded as you see ; and that what I say
is true, his Lordship's intendant of arrivals, and his book, and also my
host may certify. Wherefore, if you find that even so it is as I say,
hearken not to these wicked men, and spare me the torture and death
which they would have you inflict." In this posture of affairs
Marchese and Stecchi, learning that the Podestà's deputy was dealing
rigorously with Martellino, and had already put him to the strappado,
grew mightily alarmed. " We have made a mess of it," they said to
themselves ; " we have only taken him out of the frying-pan to toss
him into the fire." So, hurrying hither and thither with the utmost
zeal, they made diligent search until they found their host, and told
him how matters stood. The host had his laugh over the affair, and
then brought them to one Sandro Agolanti, who dwelt in Treviso
and had great interest with the Lord of the place. The host laid the
whole matter before Sandro, and, backed by Marchese and Stecchi,
besought him to undertake Martellino's cause. Sandro, after many

a hearty laugh, hied him to the Lord, who at his instance sent for Martellino. The messengers found Martellino still in his shirt before the deputy, at his wits' end, and all but beside himself with fear, because the deputy would hear nothing that he said in his defence. Indeed, the deputy, having a spite against Florentines, had quite made up his mind to have him hanged ; he was therefore in the last degree reluctant to surrender him to the Lord, and only did so upon compulsion. Brought at length before the Lord, Martellino detailed to him the whole affair, and prayed him as the greatest of favours to let him depart in peace. The Lord had a hearty laugh over the adventure, and bestowed a tunic on each of the three. So, congratulating themselves on their unexpected deliverance from so great a peril, they returned home safe and sound.

NOVEL II.

Rinaldo d'Asti is robbed, arrives at Castel Guglielmo, and is entertained by a widow lady; his property is restored to him, and he returns home safe and sound.

THE ladies and the young men, especially Filostrato, laughed inordinately at Neifile's narrative of Martellino's misadventures. Then Filostrato, who sate next Neifile, received the queen's command to follow her, and promptly thus began :—

Fair ladies, 'tis on my mind to tell you a story in which are mingled things sacred and passages of adverse fortune and love, which to hear will perchance be not unprofitable, more especially to travellers in love's treacherous lands; of whom if any fail to say St. Julian's paternoster, it often happens that, though he may have a good bed, he is ill lodged.

Know, then, that in the time of the Marquis Azzo da Ferrara, a merchant, Rinaldo d'Asti by name, having disposed of certain affairs which had brought him to Bologna, set his face homeward, and having left Ferrara behind him was on his way to Verona, when he fell in with some men that looked like merchants, but were in truth robbers and men of evil life and condition, whose company he imprudently joined, riding and conversing with them. They, perceiving that he was a merchant, and judging that he must have money about him, complotted to rob him on the first opportunity; and to obviate suspicion they played the part of worthy and reputable men, their discourse of nought but what was seemly and honourable and leal, their demeanour at once as respectful and as cordial as they could make it; so that he deemed himself very lucky to have met with them, being otherwise alone save for a single mounted servant.

Journeying thus, they conversed, after the desultory manner of travellers, of divers matters, until at last they fell a talking of the prayers which men address to God, and one of the robbers—there were three of them—said to Rinaldo :—" And you, gentle sir, what is your wonted orison when you are on your travels ? " Rinaldo answered :—" Why, to tell the truth, I am a man unskilled, unlearned in such matters, and few prayers have I at my command, being one that lives in the good old way and lets two soldi count for twenty-four deniers ; nevertheless it has always been my custom in journeying to say of a morning, as I leave the inn, a paternoster and an avemaria for the souls of the father and mother of St. Julian, after which I pray God and St. Julian to provide me with a good inn for the night. And many a time in the course of my life have I met with great perils by the way, and evading them all have found comfortable quarters for the night : whereby my faith is assured, that St. Julian, in whose honour I say my paternoster, has gotten me this favour of God ; nor should I look for a prosperous journey and a safe arrival at night, if I had not said it in the morning." Then said his interrogator :—" And did you say it this morning ? " Whereto Rinaldo answered, " Troth, did I," which caused the other, who by this time knew what course matters would take, to say to himself :—" 'Twill prove to have been said in the nick of time ; for if we do not miscarry, I take it thou wilt have but a sorry lodging." Then turning to Rinaldo he said :—" I also have travelled much, and never a prayer have I said, though I have heard them much commended by many ; nor has it ever been my lot to find other than good quarters for the night ; it may be that this very evening you will be able to determine which of us has the better lodging, you that have said the paternoster, or I that have not said it. True, however, it is that in its stead I am accustomed to say the 'Dirupisti,' or the 'Intemerata,' or the 'De profundis,' which, if what my grandmother used to say is to be believed, are of the greatest efficacy." So, talking of divers matters, and ever on the look-out for time and place suited to their evil purpose, they continued their journey, until towards evening, some distance from Castel Guglielmo, as they were about to ford a stream, these three ruffians, profiting by the lateness of the hour, and the loneliness and straitness of the place, set upon Rinaldo and robbed him, and leaving him afoot and in his shirt, said by way of adieu :—

"Go now, and see if thy St. Julian will provide thee with good lodging to-night; our saint, we doubt not, will do as much by us;" and so crossing the stream, they went their way. Rinaldo's servant, coward that he was, did nothing to help his master when he saw him attacked, but turned his horse's head, and was off at a smart pace; nor did he draw rein until he was come to Castel Guglielmo; where, it being now evening, he put up at an inn and gave himself no further trouble. Rinaldo, left barefoot, and stripped to his shirt, while the night closed in very cold and snowy, was at his wits' end, and shivering so that his teeth chattered in his head, began to peer about, if haply he might find some shelter for the night, that so he might not perish with the cold; but, seeing none (for during a recent war the whole country had been wasted by fire), he set off for Castel Guglielmo, quickening his pace by reason of the cold. Whether his servant had taken refuge in Castel Guglielmo or elsewhere, he knew not, but he thought that, could he but enter the town, God would surely send him some succour. However, dark night overtook him while he was still about a mile from the castle; so that on his arrival he found the gates already locked and the bridges raised, and he could not pass in. Sick at heart, disconsolate and bewailing his evil fortune, he looked about for some place where he might ensconce himself, and at any rate find shelter from the snow. And by good luck he espied a house, built with a balcony a little above the castle-wall, under which balcony he purposed to shelter himself until daybreak. Arrived at the spot, he found beneath the balcony a postern, which, however, was locked; and having gathered some bits of straw that lay about, he placed them in front of the postern, and there in sad and sorrowful plight took up his quarters, with many a piteous appeal to St. Julian, whom he reproached for not better rewarding the faith which he reposed in him. St. Julian, however, had not abandoned him, and in due time provided him with a good lodging.

There was in the castle a widow lady of extraordinary beauty (none fairer) whom Marquis Azzo loved as his own life, and kept there for his pleasure. She lived in the very same house beneath the balcony of which Rinaldo had posted himself. Now it chanced that that very day the Marquis had come to Castel Guglielmo to pass the night with her, and had privily caused a bath to be made

ready, and a supper suited to his rank, in the lady's own house.
The arrangements were complete ; and only the Marquis was stayed
for, when a servant happened to present himself at the castle-gate,
bringing tidings for the Marquis which obliged him suddenly to take
horse.   He therefore sent word to the lady that she must not wait
for him, and forthwith took his departure.   The lady, somewhat
disconsolate, found nothing better to do than to get into the bath
which had been intended for the Marquis, sup and go to bed : so
into the bath she went.   The bath was close to the postern on the
other side of which hapless Rinaldo had ensconced himself, and thus
the mournful and quavering music which Rinaldo made as he
shuddered in the cold, and which seemed rather to proceed from a
stork's beak than from the mouth of a human being, was audible to
the lady in the bath.   She therefore called her maid, and said to
her :—" Go up and look out over the wall and down at the postern,
and mark who is there, and what he is, and what he does there."
The maid obeyed, and, the night being fine, had no difficulty in
making out Rinaldo as he sate there, barefoot, as I have said, and in
his shirt, and trembling in every limb.   So she called out to him,
to know who he was.   Rinaldo, who could scarcely articulate for
shivering, told as briefly as he could, who he was, and how and why
he came to be there ; which done, he began piteously to beseech
her not, if she could avoid it, to leave him there all night to perish of
cold.   The maid went back to her mistress full of pity for Rinaldo,
and told her all she had seen and heard.   The lady felt no less pity
for Rinaldo ; and bethinking her that she had the key of the postern
by which the Marquis sometimes entered when he paid her a secret
visit, she said to the maid :—" Go, and let him in softly ; here is
this supper, and there will be none to eat it ; and we can very well
put him up for the night."   Cordially commending her mistress's
humanity, the maid went and let Rinaldo in, and brought him to the
lady, who, seeing that he was all but dead with cold, said to him :—
" Quick, good man, get into that bath, which is still warm."
Gladly he did so, awaiting no second invitation, and was so much
comforted by its warmth that he seemed to have passed from death
to life.   The lady provided him with a suit of clothes, which
had been worn by her husband shortly before his death, and which,
when he had them on, looked as if they had been made for him.   So

he recovered heart, and, while he awaited the lady's commands, gave thanks to God and St. Julian for delivering him from a woful night and conducting him, as it seemed, to comfortable quarters.

The lady meanwhile took a little rest, after which she had a roaring fire put in one of her large rooms, whither presently she came, and asked her maid how the good man did. The maid replied :—" Madam, he has put on the clothes, in which he shews to advantage, having a handsome person, and seeming to be a worthy man, and well-bred." " Go, call him then," said the lady, " tell him to come hither to the fire, and we will sup ; for I know that he has not supped." Rinaldo, on entering the room and seeing the lady, took her to be of no small consequence. He therefore made her a low bow, and did his utmost to thank her worthily for the service she had rendered him. His words pleased her no less than his person, which accorded with what the maid had said : so she made him heartily welcome, installed him at his ease by her side before the fire, and questioned him of the adventure which had brought him thither. Rinaldo detailed all the circumstances, of which the lady had heard somewhat when Rinaldo's servant made his appearance at the castle. She therefore gave entire credence to what he said, and told him what she knew about his servant, and how he might easily find him on the morrow. She then bade set the table, which done, Rinaldo and she washed their hands and sate down together to sup. Tall he was and comely of form and feature, debonair and gracious of mien and manner, and in his lusty prime. The lady had eyed him again and again to her no small satisfaction, and, her wantonness being already kindled for the Marquis, who was to have come to lie with her, she had let Rinaldo take the vacant place in her mind. So when supper was done, and they were risen from the table, she conferred with her maid, whether, after the cruel trick played upon her by the Marquis, it were not well to take the good gift which Fortune had sent her. The maid knowing the bent of her mistress's desire, left no word unsaid that might encourage her to follow it. Wherefore the lady, turning towards Rinaldo, who was standing where she had left him by the fire, began thus :—" So ! Rinaldo, why still so pensive ? Will nothing console you for the loss of a horse and a few clothes ? Take heart, put a blithe face on it, you are at home ; nay more, let me tell you that, seeing you in those clothes which my late husband used to wear, and taking you for him, I have felt, not once or twice, but perhaps a hundred times this evening, a longing to throw my arms round you and kiss you ; and, in faith, I had so done, but that I feared it might displease you." Rinaldo, hearing these words, and marking the flame which shot from the lady's eyes, and being no laggard, came forward with open arms, and confronted her and said :—" Madam, I am not unmindful that I must ever acknowledge that to you I owe my life, in regard of the peril whence you rescued me. If then there be any way in which I may pleasure you, churlish indeed were I not to devise it. So you may even embrace and kiss me to your heart's content, and I will embrace and kiss you with the best of good wills." There needed no further parley. The lady, all aflame with amorous desire, forthwith threw herself into his arms, and straining him to her bosom with a thousand passionate embraces, gave and received a thousand kisses before they sought her chamber. There with all speed they went to bed, nor did day surprise them until again and again and in full measure they had satisfied their desire. With the first streaks of dawn they rose, for the lady was minded that none should surmise aught of the affair. So, having meanly habited Rinaldo, and replenished his purse, she enjoined him to keep the secret, shewed him the way to the castle, where he was to find his servant, and let him out by the same postern by which he had entered. When it was broad day the gates were opened, and Rinaldo, passing himself off as a traveller from distant parts, entered the castle, and found his servant. Having put on the spare suit which was in his valise, he was about to mount the servant's horse, when, as if by miracle, there were brought into the castle the three gentlemen of the road who had robbed him the evening before, having been taken a little while after for another offence. Upon their confession Rinaldo's horse was restored to him, as were also his clothes and money ; so that he lost nothing except a pair of garters, of which the robbers knew not where they had bestowed them. Wherefore Rinaldo, giving thanks to God and St. Julian, mounted his horse, and returned home safe and sound, and on the morrow the three robbers kicked heels in the wind.

NOVEL III.

Three young men squander their substance and are reduced to poverty. Their nephew, returning home a desperate man, falls in with an abbot, in whom he discovers the daughter of the King of England. She marries him, and he retrieves the losses and re-establishes the fortune of his uncles.

THE ladies marvelled to hear the adventures of Rinaldo d'Asti, praised his devotion, and gave thanks to God and St. Julian for the succour lent him in his extreme need. Nor, though the verdict was hardly outspoken, was the lady deemed unwise to take the boon which God had sent her. So they tittered and talked of her night of delight, while Pampinea, being seated by Filostrato, and surmising that her turn would, as it did, come next, was lost in meditation on what she was to say. Roused from her reverie by the word of the queen, she put on a cheerful courage, and thus began :—

Noble ladies, discourse as we may of Fortune's handiwork, much still remains to be said if we but scan events aright, nor need we marvel thereat, if we but duly consider that all matters, which we foolishly call our own, are in her hands, and therefore subject, at her inscrutable will, to every variety of chance and change without any order therein by us discernible. Which is indeed signally manifest everywhere and all day long ; yet, as 'tis our queen's will that we speak thereof, perhaps 'twill not be unprofitable to you, if, notwithstanding it has been the theme of some of the foregoing stories, I add to them another, which, I believe, should give you pleasure.

There was formerly in our city a knight, by name Messer Tedaldo, of the Lamberti, according to some, or, as others say, of the

Agolanti family, perhaps for no better reason than that the occupation of his sons was similar to that which always was and is the
occupation of the Agolanti. However, without professing to
determine which of the two houses he belonged to, I say, that he
was in his day a very wealthy knight, and had three sons, the eldest
being by name Lamberto, the second Tedaldo, and the third
Agolante. Fine, spirited young men were they all, though the
eldest was not yet eighteen years old when their father, Messer
Tedaldo, died very rich, leaving to them as his lawful heirs the
whole of his property both movable and immovable. Finding
themselves thus possessed of great wealth, both in money and in
lands and chattels, they fell to spending without stint or restraint,
indulging their every desire, maintaining a great establishment, and
a large and well-filled stable, besides dogs and hawks, keeping ever
open house, scattering largesses, jousting, and, not content with these
and the like pastimes proper to their condition, indulging every
appetite natural to their youth. They had not long followed this
course of life before the cash left them by their father was exhausted;
and, their rents not sufficing to defray their expenditure, they began
to sell and pledge their property, and disposing of it by degrees, one
item to-day and another to-morrow, they hardly perceived that they
were approaching the verge of ruin, until poverty opened the eyes
which wealth had fast sealed. So one day Lamberto called his
brothers to him, reminded them of the position of wealth and
dignity which had been theirs and their father's before them, and
shewed them the poverty to which their extravagance had reduced
them, and adjured them most earnestly that, before their destitution
was yet further manifest, they should all three sell what little
remained to them and depart thence; which accordingly they did.
Without leave-taking, or any ceremony, they quitted Florence; nor
did they rest until they had arrived in England and established
themselves in a small house in London, where, by living with extreme
parsimony and lending at exorbitant usances, they prospered so well
that in the course of a few years they amassed a fortune; and so,
one by one, they returned to Florence, purchased not a few of their
former estates besides many others, and married. The management
of their affairs in England where they continued their business of
usurers, they left to a young nephew, Alessandro by name, while,

heedless alike of the teaching of experience and of marital and parental duty, they all three launched out at Florence into more extravagant expenditure than before, and contracted debts on all hands and to large amounts. This expenditure they were enabled for some years to support by the remittances made by Alessandro, who, to his great profit, had lent money to the barons on the security of their castles and rents.

While the three brothers thus continued to spend freely, and, when short of money, to borrow it, never doubting of help from England, it so happened that, to the surprise of everybody, there broke out in England a war between the King and his son, by which the whole island was divided into two camps; whereby Alessandro lost all his mortgages of the baronial castles and every other source of income whatsoever. However, in the daily expectation that peace would be concluded between the King and his son, Alessandro, hoping that in that event all would be restored to him, principal and interest, tarried in the island ; and the three brothers at Florence in no degree retrenched their extravagant expenditure, but went on borrowing from day to day. Several years thus passed ; and, their hopes being frustrated, the three brothers not only lost credit, but, being pressed for payment by their creditors, were suddenly arrested, and, their property proving deficient, were kept in prison for the balance, while their wives and little children went into the country parts, or elsewhere, wretchedly equipped, and with no other prospect than to pass the rest of their days in destitution. Alessandro, meanwhile, seeing that the peace, which he had for several years awaited in England, did not come, and deeming that he would hazard his life to no purpose by tarrying longer in the country, made up his mind to return to Italy. He travelled at first altogether alone ; but it so chanced that he left Bruges at the same time with an abbot, habited in white, attended by a numerous retinue, and preceded by a goodly baggage-train. Behind the abbot rode two greybeard knights, kinsmen of the King, in whom Alessandro recognised acquaintances, and, making himself known to them, was readily received into their company. As thus they journeyed together, Alessandro softly asked them who the monks were that rode in front with so great a train, and whither they were bound. "The foremost rider," replied one of the knights, "is a young kinsman of ours, the newly-elected abbot of one of the greatest abbeys of England ; and as he is not of legal age for such a dignity, we are going with him to Rome to obtain the Holy Father's dispensation and his confirmation in the office ; but this is not a matter for common talk." Now the new abbot, as lords are wont to do when they travel, was sometimes in front, sometimes in rear of his train ; and thus it happened that, as he passed, he set eyes on Alessandro, who was still quite young, and very shapely and well-favoured, and as courteous, gracious and debonair as e'er another. The abbot was marvellously taken with him at first sight, having never seen aught that pleased him so much, called him to his side, addressed him graciously, and asked him who he was, whence he came, and whither he was bound. Alessandro frankly told all about himself, and having thus answered the abbot's questions, placed himself at his service as far as his small ability might extend. The abbot was struck by his easy flow of apt speech, and observing his bearing more closely, he made up his mind that, albeit his occupation was base, he was nevertheless of gentle blood, which added no little to his interest in him ; and being moved to compassion by his misfortunes, he gave him friendly consolation, bidding him be of good hope, that if he lived a worthy life, God would yet set him in a place no less or even more exalted than that whence Fortune had cast him down, and prayed him to be of his company as far as Tuscany, as both were going the same way. Alessandro thanked him for his words of comfort, and professed himself ready to obey his every command.

So fared on the abbot, his mind full of new ideas begotten by the sight of Alessandro, until some days later they came to a town which was none too well provided with inns ; and, as the abbot must needs put up there, Alessandro, who was well acquainted with one of the innkeepers, arranged that the abbot should alight at his house, and procured him the least discomfortable quarters which it could afford. He thus became for the nonce the abbot's seneschal, and being very expert for such office, managed excellently, quartering the retinue in divers parts of the town. So the abbot supped, and, the night being far spent, all went to bed except Alessandro, who then asked the host where he might find quarters for the night. "In good sooth, I know not," replied the host ; "thou seest that every place is occupied, and that I and my household must lie on the benches. How-

ever, in the abbot's chamber there are some corn-sacks. I can shew
thee the way thither, and lay a bit of a bed upon them, and there, an
it like thee, thou mayst pass the night very well." "How sayst
thou?" said Alessandro; "in the abbot's chamber, which thou
knowest is small, so that there was not room for any of the monks
to sleep there? Had I understood this when the curtains were
drawn, I would have quartered his monks on the corn-sacks, and
slept myself where the monks sleep." "'Tis even so, however,"
replied the host, "and thou canst, if thou wilt, find excellent quarters
there: the abbot sleeps, the curtains are close drawn; I will go
in softly and lay a small bed there, on which thou canst sleep."
Alessandro, satisfied that it might be managed without disturbing the
abbot, accepted the offer, and made his arrangements for passing the
night as quietly as he could.

The abbot was not asleep; his mind being far too overwrought
by certain newly-awakened desires. He had heard what had passed
between Alessandro and the host, he had marked the place where
Alessandro had lain down, and in the great gladness of his heart had
begun thus to commune with himself:—"God has sent me the
opportunity of gratifying my desire; if I let it pass, perchance it
will be long before another such opportunity occurs." So, being
minded by no means to let it slip, when all was quiet in the inn, he
softly called Alessandro, and bade him lie down by his side. Alessandro made many excuses, but ended by undressing and obeying;
whereupon the abbot laid a hand on Alessandro's breast, and began to
caress him just as amorous girls do their lovers; whereat Alessandro
marvelled greatly, doubting the abbot was prompted to such caresses
by a shameful love. Which the abbot speedily divined, or else surmised from some movement on Alessandro's part, and, laughing,
threw off a chemise which she had upon her, and taking Alessandro's
hand, laid it on her bosom, saying:—"Alessandro, dismiss thy foolish
thought, feel here, and learn what I conceal." Alessandro obeyed,
laying a hand upon the abbot's bosom, where he encountered two
little teats, round, firm and delicate, as they had been of ivory;
whereby he at once knew that 'twas a woman, and without awaiting
further encouragement forthwith embraced her, and would have
kissed her, when she said:—"Before thou art more familiar with me
hearken to what I have to say to thee. As thou mayst perceive, I

am no man, but a woman.   Virgin I left my home, and was going
to the Pope to obtain his sanction for my marriage, when, as Fortune
willed, whether for thy gain or my loss, no sooner had I seen thee
the other day, than I burned for thee with such a flame of love as
never yet had lady for any man.   Wherefore I am minded to have
thee for my husband rather than any other ; so, if thou wilt not
have me to wife, depart at once, and return to thine own place."
Albeit he knew not who she was, Alessandro by the retinue which
attended her conjectured that she must be noble and wealthy, and he
saw that she was very fair ; so it was not long before he answered
that, if such were her pleasure, it was very much to his liking.
Whereupon she sate up, set a ring on his finger, and espoused him
before a tiny picture of our Lord ; after which they embraced, and
to their no small mutual satisfaction solaced themselves for the rest
of the night.   At daybreak Alessandro rose, and by preconcert with
the lady, left the chamber as he had entered it, so that none knew
where he had passed the night : then, blithe at heart beyond measure,
he rejoined the abbot and his train, and so, resuming their journey,
they after many days arrived at Rome.   They had not been there
more than a few days, when the abbot, attended by the two knights
and Alessandro, waited on the Pope, whom, after making the due
obeisance, he thus addressed :—" Holy Father, as you must know
better than any other, whoso intends to lead a true and honourable
life ought, as far as may be, to shun all occasion of error ; for which
cause I, having a mind to live honourably, did, the better to accomplish my purpose, assume the habit in which you see me, and depart
by stealth from the court of my father, the King of England, who
was minded to marry me, young as you see me to be, to the aged
King of Scotland ; and, carrying with me not a little of his treasure,
set my face hitherward that your Holiness might bestow me in
marriage.   Nor was it the age of the King of Scotland that moved
me to flee so much as fear lest the frailty of my youth should, were I
married to him, betray me to commit some breach of divine law, and
sully the honour of my father's royal blood.   And as in this frame of
mind I journeyed, God, who knows best what is meet for every
one, did, as I believe, of His mercy shew me him whom He is pleased
to appoint me for my husband, even this young man " (pointing to
Alessandro) " whom you see by my side, who for nobility of nature

and bearing is a match for any great lady, though the strain of his blood, perhaps, be not of royal purity. Him, therefore, have I chosen, him will I have, and no other, no matter what my father or any one else may think. And albeit the main purpose with which I started is fulfilled, yet I have thought good to continue my journey, that I may visit the holy and venerable places which abound in this city, and your Holiness, and that so in your presence, and by consequence in the presence of others, I may renew my marriage-vow with Alessandro, whereof God alone was witness. Wherefore I humbly pray you that God's will and mine may be also yours, and that you pronounce your benison thereon, that therewith, having the more firm assurance of the favour of Him, whose vicar you are, we may both live together, and, when the time comes, die to God's glory and yours."

Alessandro was filled with wonder and secret delight, when he heard that his wife was the daughter of the King of England; but greater still was the wonder of the two knights, and such their wrath that, had they been anywhere else than in the Pope's presence, they would not have spared to affront Alessandro, and perhaps the lady too. The Pope, on his part, found matter enough for wonder as well in the lady's habit as in her choice; but, knowing that he could not refuse, he consented to grant her request.

He therefore began by smoothing the ruffled tempers of the knights, and having reconciled them with the lady and Alessandro, proceeded to put matters in train for the marriage. When the day appointed was come, he gave a great reception, at which were assembled all the cardinals and many other great lords; to whom he presented the lady royally robed, and looking so fair and so gracious that she won, as she deserved, the praise of all, and likewise Alessandro, splendidly arrayed, and bearing himself not a whit like the young usurer but rather as one of royal blood, for which cause he received due honour from the knights. There, before the Pope himself, the marriage-vows were solemnly renewed; and afterwards the marriage, which was accompanied by every circumstance that could add grace and splendour to the ceremony, received the sanction of his benediction. Alessandro and the lady on leaving Rome saw fit to visit Florence, whither fame had already wafted the news, so that they were received by the citizens with every token of honour. The lady set the three brothers at liberty, paying all their creditors, and reinstated them and their wives in their several properties. So, leaving gracious memories behind them, Alessandro and his lady, accompanied by Agolante, quitted Florence, and arriving at Paris were honourably received by the King. The two knights went before them to England, and by their influence induced the King to restore the lady to his favour, and receive her and his son-in-law with every circumstance of joy and honour. Alessandro he soon afterwards knighted with unwonted ceremony, and bestowed on him the earldom of Cornwall. And such was the Earl's consequence and influence at court that he restored peace between father and son, thereby conferring a great boon on the island and gaining the love and esteem of all the people. Agolante, whom he knighted, recovered all the outstanding debts in full, and returned to Florence immensely rich. The Earl passed the rest of his days with his lady in great renown. Indeed there are those who say, that with the help of his father-in-law he effected by his policy and valour the conquest of Scotland, and was crowned king of that country.

NOVEL IV.

Landolfo Ruffolo is reduced to poverty, turns corsair, is captured by Genoese, is shipwrecked, escapes on a chest full of jewels, and, being cast ashore at Corfu, is hospitably entertained by a woman, and returns home wealthy.

WHEN Pampinea had brought her story to this glorious conclusion, Lauretta, who sate next her, delayed not, but thus began :—

Most gracious ladies, the potency of Fortune is never, methinks, more conspicuous than when she raises one, as in Pampinea's story we have seen her raise Alessandro, from abject misery to regal state. And such being the limits which our theme henceforth imposes on our invention, I shall feel no shame to tell a story wherein reverses yet greater are compensated by a sequel somewhat less dazzling. Well I know that my story, being compared with its predecessor, will therefore be followed with the less interest ; but, failing of necessity, I shall be excused.

Scarce any part of Italy is reputed so delectable as the sea-coast between Reggio and Gaeta ; and in particular the slope which overlooks the sea by Salerno, and which the dwellers there call the Slope of Amalfi, is studded with little towns, gardens and fountains, and peopled by men as wealthy and enterprising in mercantile affairs as are anywhere to be found ; in one of which towns, to wit, Ravello, rich as its inhabitants are to-day, there was formerly a merchant, who surpassed them all in wealth, Landolfo Ruffolo by name, who yet, not content with his wealth, but desiring to double it, came nigh to lose it all and his own life to boot. Know, then, that this man, having made his calculations, as merchants are wont, bought a great ship, which, entirely at his own expense, he loaded with divers sorts of merchandise, and sailed to Cyprus. There he found several other ships, each laden with just such a cargo as his own, and was therefore fain to dispose of his goods at a very cheap rate, insomuch that he might almost as well have thrown them away, and was brought to the verge of ruin. Mortified beyond measure to find himself thus reduced in a short space of time from opulence to something like poverty, he was at his wits' end, and rather than go home poor, having left home rich, he was minded to retrieve his losses by piracy or die in the attempt. So he sold his great ship, and with the price and the proceeds of the sale of his merchandise bought a light bark such as corsairs use, and having excellently well equipped her with the armament and all things else meet for such service, took to scouring the seas as a rover, preying upon all folk alike, but more particularly upon the Turk.

In this enterprise he was more favoured by Fortune than in his trading adventures. A year had scarce gone by before he had taken so many ships from the Turk that not only had he recovered the fortune which he had lost in trade, but was well on the way to doubling it. The bitter memory of his late losses taught him sobriety ; he estimated his gains and found them ample ; and lest he should have a second fall, he schooled himself to rest content with them, and made up his mind to return home without attempting to add to them. Shy of adventuring once more in trade, he refrained from investing them in any way, but shaped his course for home, carrying them with him in the very same bark in which he had gotten them. He had already entered the Archipelago when one evening a contrary wind sprang up from the south-east, bringing with it a very heavy sea, in which his bark could not well have lived. He therefore steered her into a bay under the lee of one of the islets, and there determined to await better weather. As he lay there two great carracks of Genoa, homeward-bound from Constantinople, found, not without difficulty, shelter from the tempest in the same bay. The masters of the carracks espied the bark, and found out to whom she belonged : the fame of Landolfo and his vast wealth had already reached them, and had excited their natural cupidity and rapacity. They therefore determined to capture the bark, which lay without means of escape. Part of their men, well armed with cross-bows and other weapons, they accordingly sent ashore, so posting them that no one could leave the bark without being exposed to the bolts; the rest took to their boats, and rowed up to the side of Landolfo's little craft, which in a little time, with little trouble and no loss or risk, they captured with all aboard her. They then cleared the bark of all she contained, allowing Landolfo, whom they set aboard one of the carracks, only a pitiful doublet, and sunk her. Next day the wind shifted, and the carracks set sail on a westerly course, which they kept prosperously enough throughout the day; but towards evening a tempest arose, and the sea became very boisterous, so that the two ships were parted one from the other. And such was the fury of the gale that the ship, aboard which was poor, hapless Landolfo, was driven with prodigious force upon a shoal off the island of Cephalonia, and broke up and went to pieces like so much glass dashed against a wall. Wherefore the unfortunate wretches that were aboard her, launched amid the floating merchandise and chests and planks with which the sea was strewn, did as men commonly do in such a case; and though the night was of the murkiest and the sea rose and fell in mountainous surges, such as could swim sought to catch hold of whatever chance brought in their way. Among whom hapless Landolfo, who only the day before had again and again prayed for death, rather than he should return home in such poverty, now, seeing death imminent, was afraid; and, like the rest, laid hold of the first plank that came to hand, in the hope that, if he could but avoid immediate drowning, God would in some way aid his escape. Gripping the beam with his legs as best he might, while wind and wave tossed him hither and thither, he contrived to keep himself afloat until broad day: when, looking around him, he discerned nothing but clouds and sea and a chest, which, borne by the wave, from time to time drew nigh him to his extreme terror, for he apprehended it might strike against the plank, and do him a mischief; and ever, as it came near him, he pushed it off with all the little force he had in his hand. But, as it happened, a sudden gust of wind swept down upon the sea, and struck the chest with such force that it was driven against the plank on which Landolfo was, and upset it, and Landolfo went under the waves. Swimming with an energy begotten rather of fear than of strength, he rose to the surface only to see the plank so far from him that, doubting he could not reach it, he made for the chest, which was close at hand ; and resting his breast upon the lid, he did what he could to keep it straight with his arms.   In this manner, tossed to and fro by the sea, without tasting food, for not a morsel had he with him, and drinking more than he cared for, knowing not where he was, and seeing nothing but the sea, he remained all that day, and the following night.   The next day, as the will of God, or the force of the wind so ordered, more like a sponge than aught else, but still with both hands holding fast by the edges of the chest, as we see those do that clutch aught to save themselves from drowning, he was at length borne to the coast of the island of Corfu, where by chance a poor woman was just then scrubbing her kitchen-ware with sand and salt-water to make it shine.   The woman caught sight of him as he drifted shorewards, but making out only a shapeless mass, was at first startled, and shrieked and drew back.   Landolfo was scarce able to see, and uttered no sound, for his power of speech was gone.   However, when the sea brought him close to the shore, she distinguished the shape of the chest, and gazing more intently, she first made out the arms strained over the chest, and then discerned the face and divined the truth.   So, prompted by pity, she went out a little way into the sea, which was then calm, took him by the hair of the head, and drew him to land, chest and all.   Then, not without difficulty she disengaged his hands from the chest, which she set on the head of a little girl, her daughter, that was with her, carried him home like a little child, and set him in a bath, where she chafed and laved him with warm water, until, the vital heat and some part of the strength which he had lost being restored, she saw fit to take him out and regale him with some good wine and comfits.   Thus for some days she tended him as best she could, until he recovered his strength, and knew where he was.   Then, in due time, the good woman, who had kept his chest safe, gave it back to him, and bade him try his fortune.

Landolfo could not recall the chest, but took it when she brought it to him, thinking that, however slight its value, it must suffice for a few days' charges.   He found it very light, and quite lost hope ; but when the good woman was out of doors, he opened it to see what was inside, and found there a great number of precious stones, some set, others unset. Having some knowledge of such matters, he saw at a glance that the stones were of great value; wherefore, feeling that he was still not forsaken by God, he praised His name, and quite recovered heart. But, having in a brief space of time been twice shrewdly hit by the bolts of Fortune, he was apprehensive of a third blow, and deemed it meet to use much circumspection in conveying his treasure home; so he wrapped it up in rags as best he could, telling the good woman that he had no more use for the chest, but she might keep it if she wished, and give him a sack in exchange. This the good woman readily did; and he, thanking her as heartily as he could for the service she had rendered him, threw his sack over his shoulders, and, taking ship, crossed to Brindisi. Thence he made his way by the coast as far as Trani, where he found some of his townsfolk that were drapers, to whom he narrated all his adventures except that of the chest. They in charity gave him a suit of clothes, and lent him a horse and their escort as far as Ravello, whither, he said, he was minded to return. There, thanking God for bringing him safe home, he opened his sack, and examining its contents with more care than before, found the number and fashion of the stones to be such that the sale of them at a moderate price, or even less, would leave him twice as rich as when he left Ravello. So, having disposed of his stones, he sent a large sum of money to Corfu in recompense of the service done him by the good woman who had rescued him from the sea, and also to his friends at Trani who had furnished him with the clothes; the residue he retained, and, making no more ventures in trade, lived and died in honourable estate.

NOVEL V.

*Andreuccio da Perugia comes to Naples to buy horses,
meets with three serious adventures in one night,
comes safe out of them all, and returns home with
a ruby.*

LANDOLFO's find of stones, began Fiammetta, on whom the
narration now fell, has brought to my mind a story in which there are
scarce fewer perilous scapes than in Lauretta's story, but with this
difference, that, instead of a course of perhaps several years, a single
night, as you shall hear, sufficed for their occurrence.

In Perugia, by what I once gathered, there lived a young man,
Andreuccio di Pietro by name, a horse-dealer, who, having learnt
that horses were to be had cheap at Naples, put five hundred florins
of gold in his purse, and in company with some other merchants
went thither, never having been away from home before. On his
arrival at Naples, which was on a Sunday evening, about vespers,
he learnt from his host that the fair would be held on the following
morning. Thither accordingly he then repaired, and looked at
many horses which pleased him much, and cheapening them more
and more, and failing to strike a bargain with any one, he from
time to time, being raw and unwary, drew out his purse of florins
in view of all that came and went, to shew that he meant business.

While he was thus chaffering, and after he had shewn his purse,
there chanced to come by a Sicilian girl, fair as fair could be, but
ready to pleasure any man for a small consideration. He did not see
her, but she saw him and his purse, and forthwith said to herself:—
"Who would be in better luck than I if all those florins were
mine ?" and so she passed on. With the girl was an old woman

also a Sicilian, who, when she saw Andreuccio, dropped behind the
girl, and ran towards him, making as if she would tenderly embrace
him.　The girl observing this said nothing, but stopped and waited
a little way off for the old woman to rejoin her.　Andreuccio turned
as the old woman came up, recognised her, and greeted her very
cordially; but time and place not permitting much converse, she
left him, promising to visit him at his inn; and he resumed his
chaffering, but bought nothing that morning.

Her old woman's intimate acquaintance with Andreuccio had no
more escaped the girl's notice than the contents of Andreuccio's
purse; and with the view of devising, if possible, some way to make
the money, either in whole or in part, her own, she began cautiously
to ask the old woman, who and whence he was, what he did there,
and how she came to know him.　The old woman gave her almost
as much and as circumstantial information touching Andreuccio and his
affairs as he might have done himself, for she had lived a great while with
his father, first in Sicily, and afterwards at Perugia.　She likewise told
the girl the name of his inn, and the purpose with which he had
come to Naples.　Thus fully armed with the names and all else that
it was needful for her to know touching Andreuccio's kith and kin,
the girl founded thereon her hopes of gratifying her cupidity, and
forthwith devised a cunning stratagem to effect her purpose.　Home
she went, and gave the old woman work enough to occupy her all
day, that she might not be able to visit Andreuccio; then, summoning to her aid a little girl whom she had well trained for such services,
she sent her about vespers to the inn where Andreuccio lodged.
Arrived there, the little girl asked for Andreuccio of Andreuccio
himself, who chanced to be just outside the gate.　On his answering
that he was the man, she took him aside, and said :—"Sir, a lady of
this country, so please you, would fain speak with you."　Whereto
he listened with all his ears, and having a great conceit of his person,
made up his mind that the lady was in love with him, as if there
were ne'er another handsome fellow in Naples but himself; so forthwith he replied, that he would wait on the lady, and asked where
and when it would be her pleasure to speak with him.　"Sir," replied
the little girl, "she expects you in her own house, if you be pleased
to come."　"Lead on then, I follow thee," said Andreuccio promptly,
vouchsafing never a word to any in the inn.　So the little girl guided

him to her mistress's house, which was situated in a quarter the character of which may be inferred from its name, Evil Hole. Of this, however, he neither knew nor suspected aught, but, supposing that the quarter was perfectly reputable and that he was going to see a sweet lady, strode carelessly behind the little girl into the house of her mistress, whom she summoned by calling out, " Andreuccio is here ; " and Andreuccio then saw her advance to the head of the stairs to await his ascent. She was tall, still in the freshness of her youth, very fair of face, and very richly and nobly clad. As Andreuccio approached, she descended three steps to meet him with open arms, and clasped him round the neck, but for a while stood silent as if from excess of tenderness ; then, bursting into a flood of tears, she kissed his brow, and in slightly broken accents said :—" O Andreuccio, welcome, welcome, my Andreuccio." Quite lost in wonder to be the recipient of such caresses, Andreuccio could only answer :— " Madam, well met." Whereupon she took him by the hand, led him up into her saloon, and thence without another word into her chamber, which exhaled throughout the blended fragrance of roses, orange-blossoms and other perfumes. He observed a handsome curtained bed, dresses in plenty hanging, as is customary in that country, on pegs, and other appointments very fair and sumptuous ; which sights, being strange to him, confirmed his belief that he was in the house of no other than a great lady. They sate down side by side on a chest at the foot of the bed, and thus she began to speak :— " Andreuccio, I cannot doubt that thou dost marvel both at the caresses which I bestow upon thee, and at my tears, seeing that thou knowest me not, and, maybe, hast never so much as heard my name ; wait but a moment and thou shalt learn what perhaps will cause thee to marvel still more, to wit, that I am thy sister ; and I tell thee, that, since of God's especial grace it is granted me to see one, albeit I would fain see all, of my brothers before I die, I shall not meet death, when the hour comes, without consolation ; but thou, perchance, hast never heard aught of this ; wherefore listen to what I shall say to thee. Pietro, my father and thine, as I suppose thou mayst have heard, dwelt a long while at Palermo, where his good heart and gracious bearing caused him to be (as he still is) much beloved by all that knew him ; but by none was he loved so much as by a gentlewoman, afterwards my mother, then a widow, who, casting aside all respect for her father and brothers, ay, and her honour, grew so intimate with him that a child was born, which child am I, thy sister, whom thou seest before thee. Shortly after my birth it so befell that Pietro must needs leave Palermo and return to Perugia, and I, his little daughter, was left behind with my mother at Palermo ; nor, so far as I have been able to learn, did he ever again bestow a thought upon either of us. Wherefore—to say nothing of the love which he should have borne me, his daughter by no servant or woman of low degree—I should, were he not my father, gravely censure the ingratitude which he shewed towards my mother, who, prompted by a most loyal love, committed her fortune and herself to his keeping, without so much as knowing who he was. But to what end ? The wrongs of long-ago are much more easily censured than redressed ; enough that so it was. He left me a little girl at Palermo, where, when I was grown to be almost as thou seest me, my mother, who was a rich lady, gave me in marriage to an honest gentleman of the Girgenti family, who for love of my mother and myself settled in Palermo, and there, being a staunch Guelf, entered into correspondence with our King Charles ;[1] which being discovered by King Frederic[2] before the time was ripe for action, we had perforce to flee from Sicily just when I was expecting to become the greatest lady that ever was in the island. So, taking with us such few things as we could, few, I say, in comparison of the abundance which we possessed, we bade adieu to our estates and palaces, and found a refuge in this country, and such favour with King Charles that, in partial compensation for the losses which we had sustained on his account, he has granted us estates and houses and an ample pension, which he regularly pays to my husband and thy brother-in-law, as thou mayst yet see. In this manner I live here ; but that I am blest with the sight of thee, I ascribe entirely to the mercy of God ; and no thanks to thee, my sweet brother." So saying she embraced him again, and melting anew into tears kissed his brow.

This story, so congruous, so consistent in every detail, came trippingly and without the least hesitancy from her tongue. Andreuccio remembered that his father had indeed lived at Palermo ; he knew by his own experience the ways of young folk, how prone they are to

[1] Charles II. of Naples, son of Charles of Anjou.
[2] Frederic II. of Sicily, younger son of Peter III. of Arragon.

love ; he saw her melt into tears, he felt her embraces and sisterly
kisses ; and he took all she said for gospel.   So, when she had done,
he answered :—" Madam, it should not surprise you that I marvel,
seeing that, in sooth, my father, for whatever cause, said never a word
of you and your mother, or, if he did so, it came not to my knowledge, so that I knew no more of you than if you had not been ;
wherefore, the lonelier I am here, and the less hope I had of such
good luck, the better pleased I am to have found here my sister.
And indeed, I know not any man, however exalted his station, who
ought not to be well pleased to have such a sister ; much more, then,
I, who am but a petty merchant ; but, I pray you, resolve me of one
thing : how came you to know that I was here ? "   Then answered
she :—" 'Twas told me this morning by a poor woman who is much
about the house, because, as she tells me, she was long in the service
of our father both at Palermo and at Perugia ; and, but that it seemed
more fitting that thou shouldst come to see me at home than that I
should visit thee at an inn, I had long ago sought thee out."   She
then began to inquire particularly after all his kinsfolk by name, and
Andreuccio, becoming ever more firmly persuaded of that which it
was least for his good to believe, answered all her questions.   Their
conversation being thus prolonged and the heat great, she had Greek
wine and sweetmeats brought in, and gave Andreuccio to drink ;
and when towards supper-time he made as if he would leave, she
would in no wise suffer it ; but, feigning to be very much vexed, she
embraced him, saying :—" Alas ! now 'tis plain how little thou carest
for me : to think that thou art with thy sister, whom thou seest for
the first time, and in her own house, where thou shouldst have
alighted on thine arrival, and thou wouldst fain depart hence to go
sup at an inn !   Nay but, for certain, thou shalt sup with me ; and
albeit, to my great regret, my husband is not here, thou shalt see that
I can do a lady's part in shewing thee honour."   Andreuccio, not
knowing what else to say, replied :—" Sister, I care for you with all
a brother's affection ; but if I go not, supper will await me all the
evening at the inn, and I shall justly be taxed with discourtesy."
Then said she :—" Blessed be God, there is even now in the house
one by whom I can send word that they are not to expect thee at the
inn, albeit thou wouldst far better discharge the debt of courtesy by
sending word to thy friends, that they come here to sup ; and then,

if go thou must, you might all go in a body." Andreuccio replied, that he would have none of his friends that evening, but since she would have him stay, he would even do her the pleasure. She then made a shew of sending word to the inn that they should not expect him at dinner. Much more talk followed; and then they sate down to a supper of many courses splendidly served, which she cunningly protracted until nightfall; nor, when they were risen from table, and Andreuccio was about to take his departure, would she by any means suffer it, saying, that Naples was no place to walk about in after dark, least of all for a stranger, and that, as she had sent word to the inn that they were not to expect him at supper, so she had done the like in regard of his bed. Believing what she said, and being (in his false confidence) overjoyed to be with her, he stayed. After supper there was matter enough for talk both various and prolonged; and, when the night was in a measure spent, she gave up her own chamber to Andreuccio, leaving him with a small boy to shew him aught that he might have need of, while she retired with her women to another chamber.

It was a very hot night; so, no sooner was Andreuccio alone than he stripped himself to his doublet, and drew off his stockings and laid them on the bed's head; and nature demanding a discharge of the surplus weight which he carried within him, he asked the lad where this might be done, and was shewn a door in a corner of the room, and told to go in there. Andreuccio, nothing doubting, did so, but, by ill luck, set his foot on a plank which was detached from the joist at the further end, whereby down it went, and he with it. By God's grace he took no hurt by the fall, though it was from some height, beyond sousing himself from head to foot in the ordure which filled the whole place, which, that you may the better understand what has been said, and that which is to follow, I will describe to you. A narrow and blind alley, such as we commonly see between two houses, was spanned by planks supported by joists on either side, and on the planks was the stool; of which planks that which fell with Andreuccio was one. Now Andreuccio, finding himself down there in the alley, fell to calling on the lad, who, as soon as he heard him fall, had run off, and promptly let the lady know what had happened. She hied forthwith to her chamber, and after a hasty search found Andreuccio's clothes and the money in them, for he foolishly thought to secure himself against risk by carrying it always on his person, and thus being possessed of the prize for which she had played her ruse, passing herself off as the sister of a man of Perugia, whereas she was really of Palermo, she concerned herself no further with Andreuccio except to close with all speed the door by which he had gone out when he fell. As the lad did not answer, Andreuccio began to shout more loudly; but all to no purpose. Whereby his suspicions were aroused, and he began at last to perceive the trick that had been played upon him; so he climbed over a low wall that divided the alley from the street, and hied him to the door of the house, which he knew very well. There for a long while he stood shouting and battering the door till it shook on its hinges; but all again to no purpose. No doubt of his misadventure now lurking in his mind, he fell to bewailing himself, saying:—" Alas! in how brief a time have I lost five hundred florins and a sister!" with much more of the like sort. Then he recommenced battering the door and shouting, to such a tune that not a few of the neighbours were roused, and finding the nuisance intolerable, got up; and one of the lady's servant-girls presented herself at the window with a very sleepy air, and said angrily:—" Who knocks below there?" "Oh!" said Andreuccio, "dost not know me? I am Andreuccio, Madam Fiordaliso's brother." "Good man," she rejoined, "if thou hast had too much to drink, go, sleep it off, and come back to-morrow. I know not Andreuccio, nor aught of the fantastic stuff thou pratest; prithee begone and be so good as to let us sleep in peace." "How?" said Andreuccio, "dost not understand what I say? For sure thou dost understand; but if Sicilian kinships are of such a sort that folk forget them so soon, at least return me my clothes, which I left within, and right glad shall I be to be off." Half laughing she rejoined:—" Good man, methinks thou dost dream:" and so saying, she withdrew and closed the window. Andreuccio by this time needed no further evidence of his wrongs; his wrath knew no bounds, and mortification well-nigh converted it into frenzy; he was minded to exact by force what he had failed to obtain by entreaties; and so, arming himself with a large stone, he renewed his attack upon the door with fury, dealing much heavier blows than at first. Wherefore, not a few of the neighbours, whom he had already roused from their beds, set him

down as an ill-conditioned rogue, and his story as a mere fiction
intended to annoy the good woman,[1] and resenting the din which
he now made, came to their windows, just as, when a stranger dog
makes his appearance, all the dogs of the quarter will run to bark at
him, and called out in chorus :—" 'Tis a gross affront to come at this
time of night to the house of the good woman with this silly story.
Prithee, good man, let us sleep in peace ; begone in God's name ; and
if thou hast a score to settle with her, come to-morrow, but a truce
to thy pestering to-night."

Emboldened, perhaps, by these words, a man who lurked within
the house, the good woman's bully, whom Andreuccio had as yet
neither seen nor heard, shewed himself at the window, and said in a
gruff voice and savage, menacing tone :—" Who is below there ? "
Andreuccio looked up in the direction of the voice, and saw standing
at the window, yawning and rubbing his eyes as if he had just been
roused from his bed, or at any rate from deep sleep, a fellow with a
black and matted beard, who, as far as Andreuccio's means of judging
went, bade fair to prove a most redoubtable champion. It was not
without fear, therefore, that he replied :—" I am a brother of the
lady who is within." The bully did not wait for him to finish his
sentence, but, addressing him in a much sterner tone than before,
called out :—" I know not why I come not down and give thee play
with my cudgel, whilst thou givest me sign of life, ass, tedious drivel-
ler that thou must needs be, and drunken sot, thus to disturb our
night's rest." Which said, he withdrew, and closed the window.
Some of the neighbours who best knew the bully's quality gave
Andreuccio fair words. " For God's sake," said they, " good man,
take thyself off, stay not here to be murdered. 'Twere best for thee
to go." These counsels, which seemed to be dictated by charity,
reinforced the fear which the voice and aspect of the bully had
inspired in Andreuccio, who, thus despairing of recovering his money
and in the deepest of dumps, set his face towards the quarter whence
in the daytime he had blindly followed the little girl, and began to
make his way back to the inn. But so noisome was the stench
which he emitted that he resolved to turn aside and take a bath in the
sea. So he bore leftward up a street called Ruga Catalana, and was

---

[1] *I.e.* the bawd.

on his way towards the steep of the city, when by chance he saw two men coming towards him, bearing a lantern, and fearing that they might be patrols or other men who might do him a mischief, he stole away and hid himself in a dismantled house to avoid them. The house, however, was presently entered by the two men, just as if they had been guided thither ; and one of them having disburdened himself of some iron tools which he carried on his shoulder, they both began to examine them, passing meanwhile divers comments upon them. While they were thus occupied, " What," said one, " means this ? Such a stench as never before did I smell the like ! " So saying, he raised the lantern a little ; whereby they had a view of hapless Andreuccio, and asked in amazement :—" Who is there ? " Whereupon Andreuccio was at first silent, but when they flashed the light close upon him, and asked him what he did there in such a filthy state, he told them all that had befallen him. Casting about to fix the place where it occurred, they said one to another :— " Of a surety 'twas in the house of Scarabone Buttafuoco." Then said one, turning to Andreuccio :—" Good man, albeit thou hast lost thy money, thou hast cause enough to praise God that thou hadst the luck to fall ; for hadst thou not fallen, be sure that, no sooner wert thou asleep, than thou hadst been knocked on the head, and lost not only thy money but thy life. But what boots it now to bewail thee ? Thou mightest as soon pluck a star from the firmament as recover a single denier ; nay, 'tis as much as thy life is worth if he do but hear that thou breathest a word of the affair."

The two men then held a short consultation, at the close of which they said :—" Lo now ; we are sorry for thee, and so we make thee a fair offer. If thou wilt join with us in a little matter which we have in hand, we doubt not but thy share of the gain will greatly exceed what thou hast lost." Andreuccio, being now desperate, answered that he was ready to join them. Now Messer Filippo Minutolo, Archbishop of Naples, had that day been buried with a ruby on his finger, worth over five hundred florins of gold, besides other ornaments of extreme value. The two men were minded to despoil the Archbishop of his fine trappings, and imparted their design to Andreuccio, who, cupidity getting the better of caution, approved it ; and so they all three set forth. But as they were on their way to the cathedral, Andreuccio gave out so rank an

odour that one said to the other :—"Can we not contrive that he
somehow wash himself a little, that he stink not so shrewdly?"
"Why yes," said the other, "we are now close to a well, which
is never without the pulley and a large bucket; 'tis but a step
thither, and we will wash him out of hand." Arrived at the well,
they found that the rope was still there, but the bucket had been
removed; so they determined to attach him to the rope, and
lower him into the well, there to wash himself, which done, he
was to jerk the rope, and they would draw him up. Lowered
accordingly he was; but just as, now washen, he jerked the rope, it
so happened that a company of patrols, being thirsty because 'twas a
hot night and some rogue had led them a pretty dance, came to the
well to drink. The two men fled, unobserved, as soon as they caught
sight of the newcomers, who, parched with thirst, laid aside their
bucklers, arms and surcoats, and fell to hauling on the rope, supposing
that it bore the bucket, full of water. When, therefore, they saw
Andreuccio, as he neared the brink of the well, loose the rope and
clutch the brink with his hands, they were stricken with a sudden
terror, and without uttering a word let go the rope, and took to flight
with all the speed they could make. Whereat Andreuccio marvelled
mightily, and had he not kept a tight grip on the brink of the well,
he would certainly have gone back to the bottom and hardly have
escaped grievous hurt, or death. Still greater was his astonishment,
when, fairly landed on *terra firma*, he found the patrols' arms lying
there, which he knew had not been carried by his comrades. He
felt a vague dread, he knew not why; he bewailed once more his
evil fortune; and without venturing to touch the arms, he left the
well and wandered he knew not whither. As he went, however, he
fell in with his two comrades, now returning to draw him out of the
well; who no sooner saw him than in utter amazement they
demanded who had hauled him up. Andreuccio answered that he
knew not, and then told them in detail how it had come about, and
what he had found beside the well. They laughed as they apprehended the circumstances, and told him why they had fled, and who
they were that had hauled him up. Then without further parley,
for it was now midnight, they hied them to the cathedral. They had
no difficulty in entering and finding the tomb, which was a magnificent structure of marble, and with their iron implements they raised

the lid, albeit it was very heavy, to a height sufficient to allow a man to enter, and propped it up. This done, a dialogue ensued. "Who shall go in?" said one. "Not I," said the other. "Nor I," rejoined his companion; "let Andreuccio go in." "That will not I," said Andreuccio. Whereupon both turned upon him and said:— "How? thou wilt not go in? By God, if thou goest not in, we will give thee that over the pate with one of these iron crowbars that thou shalt drop down dead." Terror-stricken, into the tomb Andreuccio went, saying to himself as he did so:—"These men will have me go in, that they may play a trick upon me: when I have handed everything up to them, and am sweating myself to get out of the tomb, they will be off about their business, and I shall be left with nothing for my pains." So he determined to make sure of his own part first; and bethinking him of the precious ring of which he had heard them speak, as soon as he had completed the descent, he drew the ring off the Archbishop's finger, and put it on his own: he then handed up one by one the crosier, mitre and gloves, and other of the Archbishop's trappings, stripping him to his shirt; which done, he told his comrades that there was nothing more. They insisted that the ring must be there, and bade him search everywhere. This he feigned to do, ejaculating from time to time that he found it not; and thus he kept them a little while in suspense. But they, who were in their way as cunning as he, kept on exhorting him to make a careful search, and, seizing their opportunity, withdrew the prop that supported the lid of the tomb, and took to their heels, leaving him there a close prisoner. You will readily conceive how Andreuccio behaved when he understood his situation. More than once he applied his head and shoulders to the lid and sought with might and main to heave it up; but all his efforts were fruitless; so that at last, overwhelmed with anguish he fell in a swoon on the corpse of the Archbishop, and whether of the twain were the more lifeless, Andreuccio or the Archbishop, 'twould have puzzled an observer to determine.

When he came to himself he burst into a torrent of tears, seeing now nothing in store for him but either to perish there of hunger and fetid odours beside the corpse and among the worms, or, should the tomb be earlier opened, to be taken and hanged as a thief. These most lugubrious meditations were interrupted by a sound of persons walking and talking in the church.   They were evidently a numerous company, and their purpose, as Andreuccio surmised, was the very same with which he and his comrades had come thither : whereby his terror was mightily increased.   Presently the folk opened the tomb, and propped up the lid, and then fell to disputing as to who should go in.   None was willing, and the contention was protracted ; but at length one—'twas a priest—said :—" Of what are ye afeared ? Think ye to be eaten by him ?   Nay, the dead eat not the living.   I will go in myself."   So saying he propped his breast upon the edge of the lid, threw his head back, and thrust his legs within, that he might go down feet foremost.   On sight whereof Andreuccio started to his feet, and seizing hold of one of the priest's legs, made as if he would drag him down ; which caused the priest to utter a prodigious yell, and bundle himself out of the tomb with no small celerity. The rest took to flight in a panic, as if a hundred thousand devils were at their heels.   The tomb being thus left open, Andreuccio, the ring still on his finger, sprang out.   The way by which he had entered the church served him for egress, and roaming at random, he arrived towards daybreak at the coast.   Diverging thence he came by chance upon his inn, where he found that his host and his comrades had been anxious about him all night.   When he told them all that had befallen him, they joined with the host in advising him to leave Naples at once.   He accordingly did so, and returned to Perugia, having invested in a ring the money with which he had intended to buy horses.

NOVEL VI.

Madam Beritola loses two sons, is found with two kids on an island, goes thence to Lunigiana, where one of her sons takes service with her master, and lies with his daughter, for which he is put in prison. Sicily rebels against King Charles, the son is recognised by the mother, marries the master's daughter, and, his brother being discovered, is reinstated in great honour.

THE ladies and the young men alike had many a hearty laugh over Fiammetta's narrative of Andreuccio's adventures, which ended, Emilia, at the queen's command, thus began :—

Grave and grievous are the vicissitudes with which Fortune makes us acquainted, and as discourse of such matter serves to awaken our minds, which are so readily lulled to sleep by her flatteries, I deem it worthy of attentive hearing by all, whether they enjoy her favour or endure her frown, in that it ministers counsel to the one sort and consolation to the other. Wherefore, albeit great matters have preceded it, I mean to tell you a story, not less true than touching, of adventures whereof the issue was indeed felicitous, but the antecedent bitterness so long drawn out that scarce can I believe that it was ever sweetened by ensuing happiness.

Dearest ladies, you must know that after the death of the Emperor Frederic II. the crown of Sicily passed to Manfred ; whose favour was enjoyed in the highest degree by a gentleman of Naples, Arrighetto Capece by name, who had to wife Madonna Beritola Caracciola, a fair and gracious lady, likewise a Neapolitan. Now

when Manfred was conquered and slain by King Charles I. at
Benevento, and the whole realm transferred its allegiance to the
conqueror, Arrighetto, who was then governor of Sicily, no sooner
received the tidings than he prepared for instant flight, knowing that
little reliance was to be placed on the fleeting faith of the Sicilians,
and not being minded to become a subject of his master's enemy.
But the Sicilians having intelligence of his plans, he and many other
friends and servants of King Manfred were surprised, taken prisoners
and delivered over to King Charles, to whom the whole island was
soon afterwards surrendered.   In this signal reversal of the wonted
course of things Madam Beritola, knowing not what was become
of Arrighetto, and from the past ever auguring future evil, lest she
should suffer foul dishonour, abandoned all that she possessed, and with
a son of, perhaps, eight years, Giusfredi by name, being also pregnant,
fled in a boat to Lipari, where she gave birth to another male child,
whom she named Outcast.   Then with her sons and a hired nurse
she took ship for Naples, intending there to rejoin her family.
Events, however, fell out otherwise than she expected ; for by stress
of weather the ship was carried out of her course to the desert
island of Ponza,[1] where they put in to a little bay until such time
as they might safely continue their voyage.   Madam Beritola
landed with the rest on the island, and, leaving them all, sought out
a lonely and secluded spot, and there abandoned herself to melancholy
brooding on the loss of her dear Arrighetto.   While thus she spent
her days in solitary preoccupation with her grief it chanced that a
galley of corsairs swooped down upon the island, and, before either
the mariners or any other folk were aware of their peril, made
an easy capture of them all and sailed away ; so that, when Madam
Beritola, her wailing for that day ended, returned, as was her wont,
to the shore to solace herself with the sight of her sons, she found
none there.   At first she was lost in wonder, then with a sudden
suspicion of the truth she bent her eyes seaward, and there saw the
galley still at no great distance, towing the ship in her wake.   Thus
apprehending beyond all manner of doubt that she had lost her sons
as well as her husband, and that, alone, desolate and destitute, she
might not hope that any of her lost ones would ever be restored to

---

[1] The largest, now inhabited, of a group of islets in the Gulf of Gaeta.

her, she fell down on the shore in a swoon with the names of her husband and sons upon her lips.   None was there to administer cold water or aught else that might recall her truant powers ; her animal spirits might even wander whithersoever they would at their sweet will : strength, however, did at last return to her poor exhausted frame, and therewith tears and lamentations, as, plaintively repeating her sons' names, she roamed in quest of them from cavern to cavern. Long time she sought them thus ; but when she saw that her labour was in vain, and that night was closing in, hope, she knew not why, began to return, and with it some degree of anxiety on her own account.   Wherefore she left the shore and returned to the cavern where she had been wont to indulge her plaintive mood.   She passed the night in no small fear and indescribable anguish ; the new day came, and, as she had not supped, she was fain after tierce to appease her hunger, as best she could, by a breakfast of herbs : this done, she wept and began to ruminate on her future way of life. While thus engaged, she observed a she-goat come by and go into an adjacent cavern, and after a while come forth again and go into the wood : thus roused from her reverie she got up, went into the cavern from which the she-goat had issued, and there saw two kids, which might have been born that very day, and seemed to her the sweetest and the most delicious things in the world : and, having, by reason of her recent delivery, milk still within her, she took them up tenderly, and set them to her breast.   They, nothing loath, sucked at her teats as if she had been their own dam ; and thence-forth made no distinction between her and the dam.   Which caused the lady to feel that she had found company in the desert ; and so, living on herbs and water, weeping as often as she bethought her of her husband and sons and her past life, she disposed herself to live and die there, and became no less familiar with the she-goat than with her young.

The gentle lady thus leading the life of a wild creature, it chanced that after some months stress of weather brought a Pisan ship to the very same bay in which she had landed.   The ship lay there for several days, having on board a gentleman, Currado de' Malespini by name (of the same family as the Marquis), who with his noble and most devout lady was returning home from a pilgrim-age, having visited all the holy places in the realm of Apulia.   To

beguile the tedium of the sojourn Currado with his lady, some
servants and his dogs, set forth one day upon a tour through the
island.   As they neared the place where Madam Beritola dwelt,
Currado's dogs on view of the two kids, which, now of a fair size,
were grazing, gave chase.   The kids, pursued by the dogs, made
straight for Madam Beritola's cavern.   She, seeing what was toward,
started to her feet, caught up a stick, and drove the dogs back.
Currado and his lady coming up after the dogs, gazed on Madam
Beritola, now tanned and lean and hairy, with wonder, which she
more than reciprocated.   At her request Currado called off the
dogs; and then he and his lady besought her again and again to
say who she was and what she did there.   So she told them all
about herself, her rank, her misfortunes, and the savage life which
she was minded to le 1.   Currado, who had known Arrighetto
Capece very well, was moved to tears by compassion, and exhausted
all his eloquence to induce her to change her mind, offering to escort
her home, or to take her to live with him in honourable estate as his
sister until God should vouchsafe her kindlier fortune.   The lady
declining all his offers, Currado left her with his wife, whom he bade
see that food was brought thither, and let Madam Beritola, who was
all in rags, have one of her own dresses to wear, and do all that she
could to persuade her to go with them.   So the gentle lady stayed
with Madam Beritola, and after condoling with her at large on her
misfortunes had food and clothing brought to her, and with the
greatest difficulty in the world prevailed upon her to eat and dress
herself.   At last, after much beseeching, she induced her to depart
from her oft-declared intention never to go where she might meet
any that knew her, and accompany them to Lunigiana, taking with
her the two kids and the dam, which latter had in the meantime
returned, and to the gentle lady's great surprise had greeted
Madam Beritola with the utmost affection.   So with the return
of fair weather Madam Beritola, taking with her the dam and the
two kids, embarked with Currado and his lady on their ship, being
called by them—for her true name was not to be known of all—
Cavriuola;[1] and the wind holding fair, they speedily reached the
mouth of the Magra,[2] and landing hied them to Currado's castle;

[1] *I. e.* she-goat.   [2] Between Liguria and Tuscany.

where Madam Beritola abode with Currado's lady in the quality of her maid, serving her well and faithfully, wearing widow's weeds, and feeding and tending her kids with assiduous and loving care.

The corsairs, who, not espying Madam Beritola, had left her at Ponza when they took the ship on which she had come thither, had made a course to Genoa, taking with them all the other folk. On their arrival the owners of the galley shared the booty, and so it happened that as part thereof Madam Beritola's nurse and her two boys fell to the lot of one Messer Guasparrino d'Oria, who sent all three to his house, being minded to keep them there as domestic slaves. The nurse, beside herself with grief at the loss of her mistress and the woful plight in which she found herself and her two charges, shed many a bitter tear. But, seeing that they were unavailing, and that she and the boys were slaves together, she, having, for all her low estate, her share of wit and good sense, made it her first care to comfort them; then, regardful of the condition to which they were reduced, she bethought her, that, if the lads were recognised, 'twould very likely be injurious to them. So, still hoping that some time or another Fortune would change her mood, and they be able, if living, to regain their lost estate, she resolved to let none know who they were, until she saw a fitting occasion; and accordingly, whenever she was questioned thereof by any, she gave them out as her own children. The name of the elder she changed from Giusfredi to Giannotto di Procida; the name of the younger she did not think it worth while to change. She spared no pains to make Giusfredi understand the reason why she had changed his name, and the risk which he might run if he were recognised. This she impressed upon him not once only but many times; and the boy, who was apt to learn, followed the instructions of the wise nurse with perfect exactitude.

So the two boys, ill clad and worse shod, continued with the nurse in Messer Guasparrino's house for two years, patiently performing all kinds of menial offices. But Giannotto, being now sixteen years old, and of a spirit that consorted ill with servitude, brooked not the baseness of his lot, and dismissed himself from Messer Guasparrino's service by getting aboard a galley bound for Alexandria, and travelled far and wide, and fared never the better In the course of his wanderings he learned that his father,

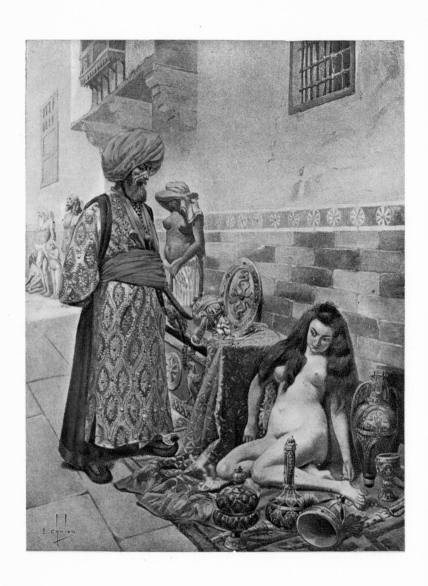

whom he had supposed to be dead, was still living, but kept in prison under watch and ward by King Charles. He was grown a tall handsome young man, when, perhaps three or four years after he had given Messer Guasparrino the slip, weary of roaming and all but despairing of his fortune, he came to Lunigiana, and by chance took service with Currado Malespini, who found him handy, and was well-pleased with him. His mother, who was in attendance on Currado's lady, he seldom saw, and never recognised her, nor she him; so much had time changed both from their former aspect since they last met. While Giannotto was thus in the service of Currado, it fell out by the death of Niccolò da Grignano that his widow, Spina, Currado's daughter, returned to her father's house. Very fair she was and loveable, her age not more than sixteen years, and so it was that she saw Giannotto with favour, and he her, and both fell ardently in love with one another. Their passion was early gratified; but several months elapsed before any detected its existence. Wherefore, growing overbold, they began to dispense with the precautions which such an affair demanded. So one day, as they walked with others through a wood, where the trees grew fair and close, the girl and Giannotto left the rest of the company some distance behind, and, thinking that they were well in advance, found a fair pleasaunce girt in with trees and carpeted with abundance of grass and flowers, and fell to solacing themselves after the manner of lovers. Long time they thus dallied, though such was their delight that all too brief it seemed to them, and so it befell that they were surprised first by the girl's mother and then by Currado. Pained beyond measure by what he had seen, Currado, without assigning any cause, had them both arrested by three of his servants and taken in chains to one of his castles; where in a frenzy of passionate wrath he left them, resolved to put them to an ignominious death. The girl's mother was also very angry, and deemed her daughter's fall deserving of the most rigorous chastisement, but, when by one of Currado's chance words she divined the doom which he destined for the guilty pair, she could not reconcile herself to it, and hasted to intercede with her angry husband, beseeching him to refrain the impetuous wrath which would hurry him in his old age to murder his daughter and imbrue his hands in the blood of his servant, and vent it in some other way, as by close confinement and duress, whereby the culprits should be brought to repent them of their fault in tears. Thus, and with much more to the like effect, the devout lady urged her suit, and at length prevailed upon her husband to abandon his murderous design. Wherefore, he commanded that the pair should be confined in separate prisons, and closely guarded, and kept short of food and in sore discomfort, until further order ; which was accordingly done ; and the life which the captives led, their endless tears, their fasts of inordinate duration, may be readily imagined.

Giannotto and Spina had languished in this sorry plight for full a year, entirely ignored by Currado, when in concert with Messer Gian di Procida, King Peter of Arragon raised a rebellion[1] in the island of Sicily, and wrested it from King Charles, whereat Currado, being a Ghibelline, was overjoyed. Hearing the tidings from one of his warders, Giannotto heaved a great sigh, and said :—" Alas, fourteen years have I been a wanderer upon the face of the earth, looking for no other than this very event ; and now, that my hopes of happiness may be for ever frustrate, it has come to pass only to find me in prison, whence I may never think to issue alive." " How ? " said the warder ; " what signify to thee these doings of these mighty monarchs ? What part hadst thou in Sicily ? " Giannotto answered :—" 'Tis as if my heart were breaking when I bethink me of my father and what part he had in Sicily. I was but a little lad when I fled the island, but yet I remember him as its governor in the time of King Manfred." " And who then was thy father ? " demanded the warder. " His name," rejoined Giannotto, " I need no longer scruple to disclose, seeing that I find myself in the very strait which I hoped to avoid by concealing it. He was and still is, if he live, Arrighetto Capece ; and my name is not Giannotto but Giusfredi ; and I doubt not but, were I once free, and back in Sicily, I might yet hold a very honourable position in the island."

The worthy man asked no more questions, but, as soon as he found opportunity, told what he had learned to Currado ; who, albeit he made light of it in the warder's presence, repaired to Madam Beritola, and asked her in a pleasant manner, whether she had had by Arrighetto a son named Giusfredi. The lady answered, in tears, that, if

---

[1] The Sicilian Vespers, Easter, 1282.

the elder of her two sons were living, such would be his name, and his age twenty-two years. This inclined Currado to think that Giannotto and Giusfredi were indeed one and the same ; and it occurred to him, that, if so it were, he might at once shew himself most merciful and blot out his daughter's shame and his own by giving her to him in marriage ; wherefore he sent for Giannotto privily, and questioned him in detail touching his past life. And finding by indubitable evidence that he was indeed Giusfredi, son of Arrighetto Capece, he said to him :—" Giannotto, thou knowest the wrong which thou hast done me in the person of my daughter, what and how great it is, seeing that I used thee well and kindly, and thou shouldst therefore, like a good servant, have shewn thyself jealous of my honour, and zealous in my interest ; and many there are who, hadst thou treated them as thou hast treated me, would have caused thee to die an ignominious death ; which my clemency would not brook. But now, as it is even so as thou sayst, and thou art of gentle blood by both thy parents, I am minded to put an end to thy sufferings as soon as thou wilt, releasing thee from the captivity in which thou languishest, and setting thee in a happy place, and rein-stating at once thy honour and my own. Thy intimacy with Spina —albeit shameful to both—was yet prompted by love. Spina, as thou knowest, is a widow, and her dower is ample and secure. What her breeding is, and her father's and her mother's, thou knowest : of thy present condition I say nought. Wherefore, when thou wilt, I am consenting, that, having been with dishonour thy friend, she become with honour thy wife, and that, so long as it seem good to thee, thou tarry here with her and me as my son."

Captivity had wasted Giannotto's flesh, but had in no degree impaired the generosity of spirit which he derived from his ancestry, or the whole-hearted love which he bore his lady. So, albeit he ardently desired that which Currado offered, and knew that he was in Currado's power, yet, even as his magnanimity prompted, so, unswervingly, he made answer :—" Currado, neither ambition nor cupidity nor aught else did ever beguile me to any treacherous machination against either thy person or thy property. Thy daughter I loved, and love and shall ever love, because I deem her worthy of my love ; and, if I dealt with her after a fashion which to the mechanic mind seems hardly honourable, I did but commit that fault which is ever congenial to youth, which can never be eradicated so long as youth continues, and which, if the aged would but remember that they were once young and would measure the delinquencies of others by their own and their own by those of others, would not be deemed so grave as thou and many others depict it; and what I did, I did as a friend, not as an enemy. That which thou offerest I have ever desired, and should long ago have sought, had I supposed that thou wouldst grant it, and 'twill be the more grateful to me in proportion to the depth of my despair. But if thy intent be not such as thy words import, feed me not with vain hopes, but send me back to prison there to suffer whatever thou mayst be pleased to inflict; nor doubt that even as I love Spina, so for love of her shall I ever love thee, though thou do thy worst, and still hold thee in reverent regard."

Currado marvelled to hear him thus speak, and being assured of his magnanimity and the fervour of his love, held him the more dear; wherefore he rose, embraced and kissed him, and without further delay bade privily bring thither Spina, who left her prison wasted and wan and weak, and so changed that she seemed almost another woman than of yore, even as Giannotto was scarce his former self. Then and there in Currado's presence they plighted their troth according to our custom of espousals; and some days afterwards Currado, having in the meantime provided all things meet for their convenience and solace, yet so as that none should surmise what had happened, deemed it now time to gladden their mothers with the news. So he sent for his lady and Cavriuola, and thus, addressing first Cavriuola, he spoke:—"What would you say, madam, were I to restore you your elder son as the husband of one of my daughters?" Cavriuola answered:—"I should say, that, were it possible for you to strengthen the bond which attaches me to you, then assuredly you had so done, in that you restored to me that which I cherish more tenderly than myself, and in such a guise as in some measure to renew within me the hope which I had lost: more I could not say." And so, weeping, she was silent. Then, turning to his lady, Currado said:— "And thou, madam, what wouldst thou think if I were to present thee with such a son-in-law?" "A son-in-law," she answered, "that was not of gentle blood, but a mere churl, so he pleased you, would well content me." "So!" returned Currado; "I hope within a few days to gladden the hearts of both of you."

He waited only until the two young folk had recovered their wonted mien, and were clad in a manner befitting their rank. Then, addressing Giusfredi, he said :—"Would it not add to thy joy to see thy mother here?" "I dare not hope," returned Giusfredi, "that she has survived calamities and sufferings such as hers; but were it so, great indeed would be my joy, and none the less that by her counsel I might be aided to the recovery (in great measure) of my lost heritage in Sicily." Whereupon Currado caused both the ladies to come thither, and presented to them the bride. The gladness with which they both greeted her was a wonder to behold, and no less great was their wonder at the benign inspiration that had prompted Currado to unite her in wedlock with Giannotto, whom Currado's words caused Madam Beritola to survey with some attention. A hidden spring of memory was thus touched; she recognised in the man the lineaments of her boy, and awaiting no further evidence she ran with open arms and threw herself upon his neck. No word did she utter, for very excess of maternal tenderness and joy; but, every avenue of sense closed, she fell as if bereft of life within her son's embrace. Giannotto, who had often seen her in the castle and never recognised her, marvelled not a little, but nevertheless it at once flashed upon him that 'twas his mother, and blaming himself for his past inadvertence he took her in his arms and wept and tenderly kissed her. With gentle solicitude Currado's lady and Spina came to her aid, and restored her suspended animation with cold water and other remedies. She then with many tender and endearing words kissed him a thousand times or more, which tokens of her love he received with a look of reverential acknowledgment. Thrice, nay a fourth time were these glad and gracious greetings exchanged, and joyful indeed were they that witnessed them, and hearkened while mother and son compared their past adventures. Then Currado, who had already announced his new alliance to his friends, and received their felicitations, proceeded to give order for the celebration of the event with all becoming gaiety and splendour. As he did so, Giusfredi said to him :—"Currado, you have long given my mother honourable entertainment, and on me you have conferred many boons; wherefore, that you may fill up the measure of your kindness, 'tis now my prayer that you be pleased to gladden my mother and my marriage feast and me with the presence of my brother, now in servitude in the house of Messer Guasparrino d'Oria, who, as I have already told you, made prize of both him and me ; and that then you send some one to Sicily, who shall make himself thoroughly acquainted with the circumstances and condition of the country, and find out how it has fared with my father Arrighetto, whether he be alive or dead, and if alive, in what circumstances, and being thus fully informed, return to us with the tidings." Currado assented, and forthwith sent most trusty agents both to Genoa and to Sicily. So in due time an envoy arrived at Genoa, and made instant suit to Guasparrino on Currado's part for the surrender of Outcast and the nurse, setting forth in detail all that had passed between Currado and Giusfredi and his mother. Whereat Messer Guasparrino was mightily astonished, and said :—"Of a surety there is nought that, being able, I would not do to pleasure Currado ; and true it is that I have had in my house for these fourteen years the boy whom thou dost now demand of me, and his mother, and gladly will I surrender them ; but tell Currado from me to beware of excessive credulity, and to put no faith in the idle tales of Giannotto, or Giusfredi, as thou sayst he calls himself, who is by no means so guileless as he supposes."

Then, having provided for the honourable entertainment of the worthy envoy, he sent privily for the nurse, and cautiously sounded her as to the affair. The nurse had heard of the revolt of Sicily, and had learned that Arrighetto was still alive. She therefore banished fear, and told Messer Guasparrino the whole story, and explained to him the reasons why she had acted as she had done. Finding that what she said accorded very well with what he had learned from Currado's envoy, he inclined to credit the story, and most astutely probing the matter in divers ways, and always finding fresh grounds for confidence, he reproached himself for the sorry manner in which he had treated the boy, and by way of amends gave him one of his own daughters, a beautiful girl of eleven years, to wife with a dowry suited to Arrighetto's rank, and celebrated their nuptials with great festivity. He then brought the boy and girl, Currado's envoy, and the nurse in a well-armed galliot to Lerici, being there met by Currado, who had a castle not far off, where great preparations had been made for their entertainment : and thither accordingly he went with his whole company. What cheer the mother had of her son, the brothers of one another, and all the three of the faithful nurse ; what cheer Messer Guasparrino and his daughter had of all, and all of them, and what cheer all had of Currado and his lady and their sons and their friends, words may not describe; wherefore, my ladies, I leave it to your imagination. And that their joy might be full, God, who, when He gives, gives most abundantly, added the glad tidings that Arrighetto Capece was alive and prosperous. For, when in the best of spirits the ladies and gentlemen had sat them down to feast, and they were yet at the first course, the envoy from Sicily arrived, and among other matters reported, that, no sooner had the insurrection broken out in the island than the people hied them in hot haste to the prison where Arrighetto was kept in confinement by King Charles, and despatching the guards, brought him forth, and knowing him to be a capital enemy to King Charles made him their captain, and under his command fell upon and massacred the French. Whereby he had won the highest place in the favour of King Peter, who had granted him restitution of all his estates and honours, so that he was now both prosperous and mighty. The envoy added that Arrighetto had received him with every token of honour, had manifested the utmost delight on hearing of his lady and son, of whom no tidings had reached him since his arrest, and had sent, to bring them home, a brigantine with some gentlemen aboard, whose arrival might hourly be expected.

The envoy, and the good news which he brought, were heartily welcome; and presently Currado, with some of his friends, encountered the gentlemen who came for Madam Beritola and Giusfredi, and saluting them cordially invited them to his feast, which was not yet half done. Joy unheard-of was depicted on the faces of the lady, of Giusfredi, and of all the rest as they greeted them; nor did they on their part take their places at the table before, as best they might, they had conveyed to Currado and his lady Arrighetto's greetings and grateful acknowledgments of the honour which they had conferred upon his lady and his son, and had placed Arrighetto, to the uttermost of his power, entirely at their service. Then, turning to Messer Guasparrino, of whose kindness Arrighetto surmised nothing, they said that they were very sure that, when he learned the boon which Outcast had received at his hands, he would pay him the like and an even greater tribute of gratitude. This speech ended, they feasted most joyously with the brides and bridegrooms. So passed the day, the first of many which Currado devoted to honouring his son-in-law and his other intimates, both kinsfolk and friends. The time of

festivity ended, Madam Beritola and Giusfredi and the rest felt that
they must leave : so, taking Spina with them, they parted, not
without many tears, from Currado and his lady and Guasparrino, and
went aboard the brigantine, which, wafted by a prosperous wind,
soon brought them to Sicily. At Palermo they were met by
Arrighetto, who received them all, ladies and sons alike, with such
cheer as it were vain to attempt to describe. There it is believed
that they all lived long and happily and in amity with God, being
not unmindful of the blessings which He had conferred upon them.

NOVEL VII.

*The Soldan of Babylon sends one of his daughters over-
seas, designing to marry her to the King of Algarve.
By divers adventures she comes in the space of four
years into the hands of nine men in divers places.
At last she is restored to her father, whom she quits
again in the guise of a virgin, and, as was at first
intended, is married to the King of Algarve.*

HAD Emilia's story but lasted a little longer, the young ladies
would perhaps have been moved to tears, so great was the sympathy
which they felt for Madam Beritola in her various fortunes. But
now that it was ended, the Queen bade Pamfilo follow suit; and he,
than whom none was more obedient, thus began :—

Hardly, gracious ladies, is it given to us to know that which makes
for our good; insomuch that, as has been observable in a multitude
of instances, many, deeming that the acquisition of great riches would
ensure them an easy and tranquil existence, have not only besought
them of God in prayer, but have sought them with such ardour that
they have spared no pains and shrunk from no danger in the quest,
and have attained their end only to lose, at the hands of some one
covetous of their vast inheritance, a life with which before the days
of their prosperity they were well content. Others, whose course,
perilous with a thousand battles, stained with the blood of their
brothers and their friends, has raised them from base to regal estate,
have found in place of the felicity they expected an infinity of cares
and fears, and have proved by experience that a chalice may be
poisoned, though it be of gold, and set on the table of a king. Many

have most ardently desired beauty and strength and other advantages
of person, and have only been taught their error by the death or
dolorous life which these very advantages entailed upon them.
And so, not to instance each particular human desire, I say, in sum,
that there is none of them that men may indulge in full confidence
as exempt from the chances and changes of fortune; wherefore, if we
would act rightly, we ought to school ourselves to take and be
content with that which He gives us, who alone knows and can
afford us that of which we have need.   But, divers as are the
aberrations of desire to which men are prone, so, gracious ladies,
there is one to which you are especially liable, in that you are unduly
solicitous of beauty, insomuch, that, not content with the charms
which nature has allotted you, you endeavour to enhance them with
wondrous ingenuity of art; wherefore I am minded to make you
acquainted with the coil of misadventures in which her beauty
involved a fair Saracen, who in the course of, perhaps, four years was
wedded nine several times.

There was of yore a Soldan of Babylon,[1] by name of Beminedab,
who in his day had cause enough to be well content with his luck.
Many children male and female had he, and among them a daughter,
Alatiel by name, who by common consent of all that saw her was
the most beautiful woman then to be found in the world.   Now the
Soldan, having been signally aided by the King of Algarve[2] in
inflicting a great defeat upon a host of Arabs that had attacked him,
had at his instance and by way of special favour given Alatiel to the
King to wife; wherefore, with an honourable escort of gentlemen
and ladies most nobly and richly equipped, he placed her aboard a
well-armed, well-furnished ship, and, commending her to God, sped
her on her journey.   The mariners, as soon as the weather was
favourable, hoisted sail, and for some days after their departure from
Alexandria had a prosperous voyage; but when they had passed
Sardinia, and were beginning to think that they were nearing their
journey's end, they were caught one day between divers cross winds,
each blowing with extreme fury, whereby the ship laboured so sorely
that not only the lady but the seamen from time to time gave them-

---

[1] *I. e.* according to medieval usage, Egypt.
[2] *I. e.* Garbo, the coast of Africa opposite Andalusia and Granada.

selves up for lost. But still, most manfully and skilfully they struggled might and main with the tempest, which, ever waxing rather than waning, buffeted them for two days with immense unintermittent surges ; and being not far from the island of Majorca, as the third night began to close in, wrapt in clouds and mist and thick darkness, so that they saw neither the sky nor aught else, nor by any nautical skill might conjecture where they were, they felt the ship's timbers part. Wherefore, seeing no way to save the ship, each thought only how best to save himself, and, a boat being thrown out, the masters first, and then the men, one by one, though the first-comers sought with knives in their hands to bar the passage of the rest, all, rather than remain in the leaky ship, crowded into it, and there found the death which they hoped to escape. For the boat, being in such stress of weather and with such a burden quite unmanageable, went under, and all aboard her perished ; whereas the ship, leaky though she was, and all but full of water, yet, driven by the fury of the tempest, was hurled with prodigious velocity upon the shore of the island of Majorca, and struck it with such force as to embed herself in the sand, perhaps a stone's throw from *terra firma*, where she remained all night beaten and washed by the sea, but no more to be moved by the utmost violence of the gale. None had remained aboard her but the lady and her women, whom the malice of the elements and their fears had brought to the verge of death. When it was broad day and the storm was somewhat abated, the lady, half dead, raised her head, and in faltering accents began to call first one and then another of her servants. She called in vain, however ; for those whom she called were too far off to hear. Great indeed was her wonder and fear to find herself thus without sight of human face or sound of other voice than her own ; but, struggling to her feet as best she might, she looked about her, and saw the ladies that were of her escort, and the other women, all prostrate on the deck ; so, after calling them one by one, she began at length to touch them, and finding few that shewed sign of life, for indeed, between grievous sea-sickness and fear, they had little life left, she grew more terrified than before. However, being in sore need of counsel, all alone as she was, and without knowledge or means of learning where she was, she at last induced such as had life in them to get upon their feet, with whom, as none knew where the men were gone, and the ship was now full of water and visibly breaking up, she abandoned herself to piteous lamentations.

It was already none before they descried any one on the shore or elsewhere to whom they could make appeal for help; but shortly after none it so chanced that a gentleman, Pericone da Visalgo by name, being on his return from one of his estates, passed that way with some mounted servants. Catching sight of the ship, he apprehended the circumstances at a glance, and bade one of his servants try to get aboard her, and let him know the result. The servant with some difficulty succeeded in boarding the vessel, and found the gentle lady with her few companions ensconced under shelter of the prow, and shrinking timidly from observation. At the first sight of him they wept, and again and again implored him to have pity on them; but finding that he did not understand them, nor they him, they sought by gestures to make him apprehend their forlorn condition.

With these tidings the servant, after making such survey of the ship as he could, returned to Pericone, who forthwith caused the ladies, and all articles of value which were in the ship and could be removed, to be brought off her, and took them with him to one of his castles. The ladies' powers were soon in a measure restored by food and rest, and by the honour which was paid to Alatiel, and Alatiel alone by all the rest, as well as by the richness of her dress, Pericone perceived that she must be some great lady. Nor, though she was still pale, and her person bore evident marks of the sea's rough usage, did he fail to note that it was cast in a mould of extraordinary beauty. Wherefore his mind was soon made up that, if she lacked a husband, he would take her to wife, and that, if he could not have her to wife, then he would make her his mistress. So this ardent lover, who was a man of powerful frame and haughty mien, devoted himself for several days to the service of the lady with excellent effect, for the lady completely recovered her strength and spirits, so that her beauty far exceeded Pericone's most sanguine conjectures. Great therefore beyond measure was his sorrow that he understood not her speech, nor she his, so that neither could know who the other was; but being inordinately enamoured of her beauty, he sought by such mute blandishments as he could devise to declare his love, and bring her of her own accord to gratify his desire. All in vain, however; she repulsed his advances point blank ; whereby his passion only grew the stronger. So some days passed ; and the lady perceiving Pericone's constancy, and bethinking her that sooner or later she must yield either to force or to love, and gratify his passion, and judging by what she observed of the customs of the people that she was amongst Christians, and in a part where, were she able to speak their language, she would gain little by making herself known, determined with a lofty courage to stand firm and immovable in this extremity of her misfortunes. Wherefore she bade the three women, who were all that were left to her, on no account to let any know who they were, unless they were so circumstanced that they might safely count on assistance in effecting their escape : she also exhorted them most earnestly to preserve their chastity, averring that she was firmly resolved that none but her husband should enjoy her. The women heartily assented, and promised that her injunctions should be obeyed to the utmost of their power.

Day by day Pericone's passion waxed more ardent, being fomented by the proximity and contrariety of its object. Wherefore seeing that blandishment availed nothing, he was minded to have recourse to wiles and stratagems, and in the last resort to force. The lady, debarred by her law from the use of wine, found it, perhaps, on that account all the more palatable ; which Pericone observing determined to enlist Bacchus in the service of Venus. So, ignoring her coyness, he provided one evening a supper, which was ordered with all possible pomp and beauty, and graced by the presence of the lady. No lack was there of incentives to hilarity ; and Pericone directed the servant who waited on Alatiel to ply her with divers sorts of blended wines ; which command the man faithfully executed. She, suspecting nothing, and seduced by the delicious flavour of the liquor, drank somewhat more freely than was seemly, and forgetting her past woes, became frolicsome, and incited by some women who trod some measures in the Majorcan style, she shewed the company how they footed it in Alexandria. This novel demeanour was by no means lost on Pericone, who saw in it a good omen of his speedy success ; so, with profuse relays of food and wine he prolonged the supper far into the night.

When the guests were at length gone, he attended the lady alone to her chamber, where, the heat of the wine overpowering the cold counsels of modesty, she made no more account of Pericone's presence than if he had been one of her women, and forthwith undressed and went to bed. Pericone was not slow to follow her, and as soon as the light was out lay down by her side, and taking her in his arms, without the least demur on her part, began to solace himself with her after the manner of lovers ; which experience—she knew not till then with what horn men butt—caused her to repent that she had not yielded to his blandishments ; nor did she thereafter wait to be invited to such nights of delight, but many a time declared her readiness, not by words, for she had none to convey her meaning, but by gestures.

But this great felicity which she now shared with Pericone was not to last : for not content with making her, instead of the consort of a king, the mistress of a castellan, Fortune had now in store for her a harsher experience, though of an amorous character. Pericone had a brother, twenty-five years of age, fair and fresh as a rose, his name Marato. On sight of Alatiel Marato had been mightily taken with her ; he inferred from her bearing that he stood high in her good graces ; he believed that nothing stood between him and the gratification of his passion but the jealous vigilance with which Pericone guarded her. So musing, he hit upon a ruthless expedient, which had effect in action as hasty as heinous.

It so chanced that there then lay in the port of the city a ship, commanded by two Genoese, bound with a cargo of merchandise for Klarenza in the Morea : her sails were already hoist ; and she tarried only for a favourable breeze. Marato approached the masters and arranged with them to take himself and the lady aboard on the following night. This done he concerted further action with some of his most trusty friends, who readily lent him their aid to carry his design into execution. So on the following evening towards night-fall, the conspirators stole unobserved into Pericone's house, which was entirely unguarded, and there hid themselves, as pre-arranged. Then, as the night wore on, Marato shewed them where Pericone and the lady slept, and they entered the room, and slew Pericone. The lady thus rudely roused wept ; but silencing her by menaces of death they carried her off with the best part of Pericone's treasure, and hied them unobserved to the coast, where Marato parted from his companions, and forthwith took the lady aboard the ship. The wind

was now fair and fresh, the mariners spread the canvas, and the vessel
sped on her course.

This new misadventure, following so hard upon the former, caused
the lady no small chagrin ; but Marato, with the aid of the good St.
Crescent-in-hand that God has given us, found means to afford her
such consolation that she was already grown so familiar with him as
entirely to forget Pericone, when Fortune, not content with her
former caprices, added a new dispensation of woe ; for what with
the beauty of her person, which, as we have often said, was extraordinary, and the exquisite charm of her manners, the two young
men, who commanded the ship, fell so desperately in love with her
that they thought of nothing but how they might best serve and
please her, so only that Marato should not discover the reason of their
assiduous attentions.   And neither being ignorant of the other's love,
they held secret counsel together, and resolved to make conquest of
the lady on joint account : as if love admitted of being held in partnership like merchandise or money.   Which design being thwarted
by the jealousy with which Alatiel was guarded by Marato, they
chose a day and hour, when the ship was speeding amain under canvas,
and Marato was on the poop looking out over the sea and quite off
his guard ; and going stealthily up behind him, they suddenly laid
hands on him, and threw him into the sea, and were already more
than a mile on their course before any perceived that Marato was
overboard.   Which when the lady learned, and knew that he was
irretrievably lost, she relapsed into her former plaintive mood.   But
the twain were forthwith by her side with soft speeches and profuse
promises, which, however ill she understood them, were not altogether
inapt to allay a grief which had in it more of concern for her own
hapless self than of sorrow for her lost lover.   So, in course of time,
the lady beginning visibly to recover heart, they began privily to
debate which of them should first take her to bed with him ; and
neither being willing to give way to the other, and no compromise
being discoverable, high words passed between them, and the dispute
grew so hot, that they both waxed very wroth, drew their knives, and
rushed madly at one another, and before they could be parted by their
men, several stabs had been given and received on either side, whereby
the one fell dead on the spot, and the other was severely wounded in
divers parts of the body.   The lady was much disconcerted to find

herself thus alone with none to afford her either succour or counsel, and was mightily afraid lest the wrath of the kinsfolk and friends of the twain should vent itself upon her. From this mortal peril she was, however, delivered by the intercessions of the wounded man and their speedy arrival at Klarenza.

As there she tarried at the same inn with her wounded lover, the fame of her great beauty was speedily bruited abroad, and reached the ears of the Prince of the Morea, who was then staying there. The Prince was curious to see her, and having so done, pronounced her even more beautiful than rumour had reported her ; nay, he fell in love with her in such a degree that he could think of nought else ; and having heard in what guise she had come thither, he deemed that he might have her. While he was casting about how to compass his end, the kinsfolk of the wounded man, being apprised of the fact, forthwith sent her to him to the boundless delight, as well of the lady, who saw therein her deliverance from a great peril, as of the Prince. The royal bearing, which enhanced the lady's charms, did not escape the Prince, who, being unable to discover her true rank, set her down as at any rate of noble lineage; wherefore he loved her as much again as before, and shewed her no small honour, treating her not as his mistress but as his wife. So the lady, contrasting her present happy estate with her past woes, was comforted ; and, as her gaiety revived, her beauty waxed in such a degree that all the Morea talked of it and of little else : insomuch that the Prince's friend and kinsman, the young, handsome and gallant Duke of Athens, was smitten with a desire to see her, and taking occasion to pay the Prince a visit, as he was now and again wont to do, came to Klarenza with a goodly company of honourable gentlemen. The Prince received him with all distinction and made him heartily welcome, but did not at first shew him the lady. By and by, however, their conversation began to turn upon her and her charms, and the Duke asked if she were really so marvellous a creature as folk said. The Prince replied :— "Nay, but even more so ; and thereof thou shalt have better assurance than my words, to wit, the witness of thine own eyes." So, without delay, for the Duke was now all impatience, they waited on the lady, who was prepared for their visit, and received them very courteously and graciously. They seated her between them, and being debarred from the pleasure of conversing with her, for of their speech she understood little or nothing, they both, and especially the Duke, who was scarce able to believe that she was of mortal mould, gazed upon her in mute admiration ; whereby the Duke, cheating himself with the idea that he was but gratifying his curiosity, drank with his eyes, unawares, deep draughts of the poisoned chalice of love, and, to his own lamentable hurt, fell a prey to a most ardent passion. His first thought, when they had left her, and he had time for reflection, was that the Prince was the luckiest man in the world to have a creature so fair to solace him ; and swayed by his passion, his mind soon inclined to divers other and less honourable meditations, whereof the issue was that, come what might, he would despoil the Prince of his felicity, and, if possible, make it his own. This resolution was no sooner taken than, being of a hasty temperament, he cast to the winds all considerations of honour and justice, and studied only how to compass his end by craft. So, one day, as the first step towards the accomplishment of his evil purpose, he arranged with the Prince's most trusted chamberlain, one Ciuriaci, that his horses and all other his personal effects should, with the utmost secrecy, be got ready against a possible sudden departure: and then at nightfall, attended by a single comrade (both carrying arms), he was privily admitted by Ciuriaci into the Prince's chamber. It was a hot night, and the Prince had risen without disturbing the lady, and was standing bare to the skin at an open window fronting the sea, to enjoy a light breeze that blew thence. So, by preconcert with his comrade, the Duke stole up to the window, and in a trice ran the Prince through the body, and caught him up, and threw him out of the window. The palace was close by the sea, but at a considerable altitude above it, and the window, through which the Prince's body was thrown, looked over some houses, which, being sapped by the sea, had become ruinous, and were rarely or never visited by a soul ; whereby, as the Duke had foreseen, the fall of the Prince's body passed, as indeed it could not but pass, unobserved. Thereupon the Duke's accomplice whipped out a halter, which he had brought with him for the purpose, and, making as if he were but in play, threw it round Ciuriaci's neck, drew it so tight that he could not utter a sound, and then, with the Duke's aid, strangled him, and sent him after his master. All this was accomplished, as the Duke knew full well, without awakening any in the palace, not even the lady, whom he now approached with a light, and holding it over the bed gently uncovered her person, as she lay fast asleep, and surveyed her from head to foot to his no small satisfaction ; for fair as she had seemed to him dressed, he found her unadorned charms incomparably greater. As he gazed, his passion waxed beyond measure, and, reckless of his recent crime, and of the blood which still stained his hands, he got forthwith into the bed ; and she, being too sound asleep to distinguish between him and the Prince, suffered him to lie with her.

But, boundless as was his delight, it brooked no long continuance ; so, rising, he called to him some of his comrades, by whom he had the lady secured in such manner that she could utter no sound, and borne out of the palace by the same secret door by which he had gained entrance ; he then set her on horseback and in dead silence put his troop in motion, taking the road to Athens. He did not, however, venture to take the lady to Athens, where she would have encountered his Duchess—for he was married—but lodged her in a very beautiful villa which he had hard by the city overlooking the sea, where, most forlorn of ladies, she lived secluded, but with no lack of meet and respectful service.

On the following morning the Prince's courtiers awaited his rising until none, but perceiving no sign of it, opened the doors, which had not been secured, and entered his bedroom. Finding it vacant, they supposed that the Prince was gone off privily somewhere to have a few days of unbroken delight with his fair lady ; and so they gave themselves no further trouble. But the next day it so chanced that an idiot, roaming about the ruins where lay the corpses of the Prince and Ciuriaci, drew the latter out by the halter and went off dragging it after him. The corpse was soon recognised by not a few, who, at first struck dumb with amazement, soon recovered sense enough to cajole the idiot into retracing his steps and shewing them the spot where he had found it ; and having thus, to the immeasurable grief of all the citizens, discovered the Prince's body, they buried it with all honour. Needless to say that no pains were spared to trace the perpetrators of so heinous a crime, and that the absence and evidently furtive departure of the Duke of Athens caused him to be suspected both of the murder and of the abduction of the lady. So the citizens were instant with one accord that the Prince's brother, whom they chose as his successor, should exact the debt of vengeance; and he, having satisfied himself by further investigation that their suspicion was well founded, summoned to his aid his kinsfolk, friends and divers vassals, and speedily gathered a large, powerful and well-equipped army, with intent to make war upon the Duke of Athens. The Duke, being informed of his movements, made ready likewise to defend himself with all his power; nor had he any lack of allies, among whom the Emperor of Constantinople sent his son, Constantine, and his nephew, Manuel, with a great and goodly force. The two young men were honourably received by the Duke, and still more so by the Duchess, who was Constantine's sister.

Day by day war grew more imminent; and at last the Duchess took occasion to call Constantine and Manuel into her private chamber, and with many tears told them the whole story at large, explaining the *casus belli*, dilating on the indignity which she suffered at the hands of the Duke, if, as was believed, he really kept a mistress in secret, and beseeching them in most piteous accents to do the best they could to devise some expedient whereby the Duke's honour might be cleared, and her own peace of mind assured. The young men knew exactly how matters stood; and so, without wearying the Duchess with many questions, they did their best to console her, and succeeded in raising her hopes. Before taking their leave they learned from her where the lady was, whose marvellous beauty they had heard lauded so often; and being eager to see her, they besought the Duke to afford them an opportunity. Forgetful of what a like complaisance had cost the Prince, he consented, and next morning brought them to the villa where the lady lived, and with her and a few of his boon companions regaled them with a lordly breakfast, which was served in a most lovely garden. Constantine had no sooner seated himself and surveyed the lady, than he was lost in admiration, inly affirming that he had never seen so beautiful a creature, and that for such a prize the Duke, or any other man, might well be pardoned treachery or any other crime: he scanned her again and again, and ever with more and more admiration; whereby it fared with him even as it had fared with the Duke. He went away hotly in love with her, and dismissing all thought of the war, cast about for some method by which, without betraying his passion to any, he might devise some means of wresting the lady from the Duke.

As he thus burned and brooded, the Prince drew dangerously near the Duke's dominions; wherefore order was given for an advance, and the Duke, with Constantine and the rest, marshalled his forces and led them forth from Athens to bar the Prince's passage of the frontier at certain points. Some days thus passed, during which Constantine, whose mind and soul were entirely absorbed by his passion for the lady, bethought him, that, as the Duke was no longer in her neighbourhood, he might readily compass his end. He therefore feigned to be seriously unwell, and, having by this pretext obtained the Duke's leave, he ceded his command to Manuel, and returned to his sister at Athens. He had not been there many days before the Duchess recurred to the dishonour which the Duke did her by keeping the lady; whereupon he said that of that, if she approved, he would certainly relieve her by seeing that the lady was removed from the villa to some distant place. The Duchess, supposing that Constantine was prompted not by jealousy of the Duke but by jealousy for her honour, gave her hearty consent to his plan, provided he so contrived that the Duke should never know that she had been privy to it; on which point Constantine gave her ample assurance. So, being authorised by the Duchess to act as he might deem best, he secretly equipped a light bark and manned her with some of his men, to whom he confided his plan, bidding them lie to off the garden of the lady's villa; and so, having sent the bark forward, he hied him with other of his men to the villa. He gained ready admission of the servants, and was made heartily welcome by the lady, who, at his desire, attended by some of her servants, walked with him and some of his comrades in the garden. By and by, feigning that he had a message for her from the Duke, he drew her aside towards a gate that led down to the sea, and which one of his confederates had already opened. A concerted signal brought the bark alongside, and to seize the lady and set her aboard the bark was but the work of an instant. Her retinue hung back as they heard Constantine menace with death whoso but stirred or spoke, and suffered him, protesting that what he did was done not to wrong the Duke but solely to vindicate his sister's honour, to embark with his men. The lady wept, of course, but Constantine was at her side, the rowers gave way, and the bark, speeding like a thing of life over the waves, made Egina shortly after dawn. There Constantine and the lady landed, she still lamenting her fatal beauty, and took a little rest and pleasure. Then, re-embarking, they continued their voyage, and in the course of a few days reached Chios, which Constantine, fearing paternal censure, and that he might be deprived of his fair booty, deemed a safe place of sojourn. So, after some days of repose the lady ceased to bewail her harsh destiny, and suffering Constantine to console her as his predecessors had done, began once more to enjoy the good gifts which Fortune sent her.

Now while they thus dallied, Osbech, King of the Turks, who was perennially at war with the Emperor, came by chance to Smyrna; and there learning that Constantine was wantoning in careless ease at Chios with a lady of whom he had made prize, he made a descent by night upon the island with an armed flotilla. Landing his men in dead silence, he made captives of not a few of the Chians whom he surprised in their beds; others, who took the alarm and rushed to arms, he slew; and having wasted the whole island with fire, he shipped the booty and the prisoners, and sailed back to Smyrna. As there he overhauled the booty, he lit upon the fair lady, and knew her for the same that had been taken in bed and fast asleep with Constantine: whereat, being a young man, he was delighted beyond measure, and made her his wife out of hand with all due form and ceremony. And so for several months he enjoyed her.

Now there had been for some time and still was a treaty pending between the Emperor and Basano, King of Cappadocia, whereby Basano with his forces was to fall on Osbech on one side while the Emperor attacked him on the other. Some demands made by Basano, which the Emperor deemed unreasonable, had so far retarded the conclusion of the treaty; but no sooner had the Emperor learned the fate of his son than, distraught with grief, he forthwith conceded the King of Cappadocia's demands, and was instant with him to fall at once upon Osbech while he made ready to attack him on the other side. Getting wind of the Emperor's design, Osbech collected his forces, and, lest he should be caught and crushed between the convergent armies of two most mighty potentates, advanced against the King of Cappadocia. The fair lady he left at Smyrna in the care of a faithful dependant and friend, and after a while joined battle with the King of Cappadocia, in which battle he was slain, and his army defeated and dispersed.   Wherefore Basano with his victorious host advanced, carrying everything before him, upon Smyrna, and receiving everywhere the submission due to a conqueror.

Meanwhile Osbech's dependant, by name Antioco, who had charge of the fair lady, was so smitten with her charms that, albeit he was somewhat advanced in years, he broke faith with his friend and lord, and allowed himself to become enamoured of her.   He had the advantage of knowing her language, which counted for much with one who for some years had been, as it were, compelled to live the life of a deaf mute, finding none whom she could understand or by whom she might be understood ; and goaded by passion, he in the course of a few days established such a degree of intimacy with her that in no long time it passed from friendship into love, so that their lord, far away amid the clash of arms and the tumult of the battle, was forgotten, and marvellous pleasure had they of one another between the sheets.

However, news came at last of Osbech's defeat and death, and the victorious and unchecked advance of Basano, whose advent they were by no means minded to await.   Wherefore, taking with them the best part of the treasure that Osbech had left there, they hied them with all possible secrecy to Rhodes.   There they had not along abode before Antioco fell ill of a mortal disease.   He had then with him a Cypriote merchant, an intimate and very dear friend, to whom, as he felt his end approach, he resolved to leave all that he possessed, including his dear lady.   So, when he felt death imminent, he called them to him and said :—" 'Tis now quite evident to me that my life is fast ebbing away; and sorely do I regret it, for never had I so much pleasure of life as now.   Well content indeed I am in one respect, in that, as die I must, I at least die in the arms of the two persons whom I love more than any other in the world, to wit, in thine arms, dearest friend, and those of this lady, whom, since I have known her, I have loved more than myself.   But yet 'tis grievous to me to know that I must leave her here in a strange land with none to afford her either protection or counsel ; and but that I leave her with thee, who, I doubt not, wilt have for my sake no less care of her than thou wouldst have had of me, 'twould grieve me still more ; wherefore with all my heart and soul I pray thee, that, if I die, thou take her with all else that belongs to me into thy charge, and so acquit thyself of thy trust as thou mayst deem conducive to the peace of my soul. And of thee, dearest lady, I entreat one favour, that I be not forgotten of thee, after my death, so that there whither I go it may still be my boast to be beloved here of the most beautiful lady that nature ever formed. Let me but die with these two hopes assured, and without doubt I shall depart in peace."

Both the merchant and the lady wept to hear him thus speak, and, when he had done, comforted him, and promised faithfully, in the event of his death, to do even as he besought them. He died almost immediately afterwards, and was honourably buried by them. A few days sufficed the merchant to wind up all his affairs in Rhodes ; and being minded to return to Cyprus aboard a Catalan boat that was there, he asked the fair lady what she purposed to do if he went back to Cyprus. The lady answered, that, if it were agreeable to him, she would gladly accompany him, hoping that for love of Antioco he would treat and regard her as his sister. The merchant replied that it would afford him all the pleasure in the world ; and, to protect her from insult until their arrival in Cyprus, he gave her out as his wife, and, suiting action to word, slept with her on the boat in an alcove in a little cabin in the poop. Whereby that happened which on neither side was intended when they left Rhodes, to wit, that the darkness and the comfort and the warmth of the bed, forces of no mean efficacy, did so prevail with them that dead Antioco was forgotten alike as lover and as friend, and by a common impulse they began to wanton together, insomuch that before they were arrived at Baffa, where the Cypriote resided, they were indeed man and wife. At Baffa the lady tarried with the merchant a good while, during which it so befell that a gentleman, Antigono by name, a man of ripe age and riper wisdom but no great wealth, being one that had had vast and various experience of affairs in the service of the King of Cyprus but had found fortune adverse to him, came to Baffa on business ; and passing one day by the house where the fair lady was then living by herself, for the Cypriote merchant was gone to Armenia with some of his wares, he chanced to catch sight of the lady at one of the windows, and, being struck by her extraordinary beauty, regarded her attentively, and began to have some vague recollection of having seen her before, but could by no means remember where.

The fair lady, however, so long the sport of Fortune, but now nearing the term of her woes, no sooner saw Antigono than she remembered to have seen him in her father's service, and in no mean
capacity, at Alexandria. Wherefore she forthwith sent for him,
hoping that by his counsel she might elude her merchant and be
reinstated in her true character and dignity of princess. When he
presented himself, she asked him with some embarrassment whether
he were, as she took him to be, Antigono of Famagosta. He answered
in the affirmative, adding :—" And of you, madam, I have a sort of
recollection, though I cannot say where I have seen you ; wherefore,
so it irk you not, bring, I pray you, yourself to my remembrance."
Satisfied that it was Antigono himself, the lady in a flood of tears threw
herself upon him to his no small amazement, and embraced his neck :
then, after a little while, she asked him whether he had never seen
her in Alexandria. The question awakened Antigono's memory ; he
at once recognised Alatiel, the Soldan's daughter, whom he had thought
to have been drowned at sea, and would have paid her due homage ;
but she would not suffer it, and bade him be seated with her for a
while. Being seated, he respectfully asked her, how, and when and
whence she had come thither, seeing that all Egypt believed for
certain that she had been drowned at sea some years before. " And
would that so it had been," said the lady, " rather than I should
have led the life that I have led ; and so doubtless will my father
say, if he shall ever come to know of it." And so saying, she
burst into such a flood of tears that 'twas a wonder to see. Wherefore Antigono said to her :—" Nay but, madam, be not distressed
before the occasion arises. I pray you, tell me the story of your
adventures, and what has been the tenor of your life ; perchance
'twill prove to be no such matter but, God helping us, we may set it
all straight." " Antigono," said the fair lady, " when I saw thee,
'twas as if I saw my father, and 'twas the tender love by which I
am holden to him that prompted me to make myself known to thee,
though I might have kept my secret ; and few indeed there are,
whom to have met would have afforded me such pleasure as this
which I have in meeting and recognising thee before all others ;
wherefore I will now make known to thee as to a father that which
in my evil fortune I have ever kept close. If, when thou hast heard
my story, thou seest any means whereby I may be reinstated in my

former honour, I pray thee use it. If not, disclose to none that thou hast seen me or heard aught of me."

Then, weeping between every word, she told him her whole story from the day of the shipwreck at Majorca to that hour. Antigono wept in sympathy, and then said :—"Madam, as throughout this train of misfortunes you have happily escaped recognition, I undertake to restore you to your father in such sort that you shall be dearer to him than ever before, and be afterwards married to the King of Algarve. "How ?" she asked. Whereupon he explained to her in detail how he meant to proceed; and, lest delay should give occasion to another to interfere, he went back at once to Famagosta, and having obtained audience of the King, thus he spoke :—"Sire, so please you, you have it in your power at little cost to yourself to do a thing, which will at once redound most signally to your honour and confer a great boon on me, who have grown poor in your service." "How ?" asked the King. Then said Antigono :—"At Baffa is of late arrived a fair damsel, daughter of the Soldan, long thought to be drowned, who to preserve her chastity has suffered long and severe hardship. She is now reduced to poverty, and is desirous of returning to her father. If you should be pleased to send her back to him under my escort, your honour and my interest would be served in high and equal measure ; nor do I think that such a service would ever be forgotten by the Soldan."

With true royal generosity the King forthwith signified his approval, and had Alatiel brought under honourable escort to Famagosta, where, attended by his Queen, he received her with every circumstance of festal pomp and courtly magnificence. Schooled by Antigono, she gave the King and Queen such a version of her adventures as satisfied their inquiries in every particular. So, after a few days, the King sent her back to the Soldan under escort of Antigono, attended by a goodly company of honourable men and women ; and of the cheer which the Soldan made her, and not her only but Antigono and all his company, it boots not to ask. When she was somewhat rested, the Soldan inquired how it was that she was yet alive, and where she had been so long without letting him know how it fared with her. Whereupon the lady, who had got Antigono's lesson by heart, answered thus :—"My father, 'twas perhaps the twentieth night after my departure from you when our ship parted her

timbers in a terrible storm and went ashore nigh a place called
Aguamorta, away there in the West : what was the fate of the men
that were aboard our ship I know not, nor knew I ever; I remember
only, that, when day came, and I returned, as it were, from death to
life, the wreck, having been sighted, was boarded by folk from all the
country-side, intent on plunder ; and I and two of my women were
taken ashore, where the women were forthwith parted from me by
the young men, nor did I ever learn their fate.   Now hear my own.
Struggling might and main, I was seized by two young men, who
dragged me, weeping bitterly, by the hair of the head, towards a
great forest ; but, on sight of four men who were then passing that
way on horseback, they forthwith loosed me and took to flight.
Whereupon the four men, who struck me as persons of great
authority, ran up to me ; and much they questioned me, and much I
said to them ; but neither did they understand me, nor I them.   So,
after long time conferring together, they set me on one of their
horses and brought me to a house, where dwelt a community of
ladies, religious according to their law ; and what the men may have
said I know not, but there I was kindly received and ever honourably
entreated by all ; and with them I did afterwards most reverentially
pay my devotions to St. Crescent-in-Hollow, who is held in great
honour by the women of that country.   When I had been some
time with them, and had learned something of their language, they
asked me who and whence I was : whereto I, knowing that I was in
a convent, and fearing to be cast out as a foe to their law if I told the
truth, answered that I was the daughter of a great gentleman of
Cyprus, who had intended to marry me to a gentleman of Crete ;
but that on the voyage we had been driven out of our course and
wrecked at Aguamorta.   And so I continued, as occasion required,
observing their usages with much assiduity, lest worse should befall
me ; but being one day asked by their superior, whom they call
abbess, whether I was minded to go back to Cyprus, I answered that
there was nought that I desired so much.   However, so solicitous for
my honour was the abbess, that there was none going to Cyprus to
whom she would entrust me, until, two months or so ago, there
arrived some worthy men from France, of whom one was a kinsman
of the abbess, with their wives.   They were on their way to visit the
sepulchre where He whom they hold to be God was buried after He

had suffered death at the hands of the Jews ; and the abbess, learning
their destination, prayed them to take charge of me, and restore me
to my father in Cyprus.   With what cheer, with what honour, these
gentlemen and their wives entertained me, 'twere long to tell.   But,
in brief, we embarked, and in the course of a few days arrived at
Baffa, where it was so ordered by the providence of God, who perchance took pity on me, that in the very hour of our disembarkation
I, not knowing a soul and being at a loss how to answer the gentlemen, who would fain have discharged the trust laid upon them by
the reverend abbess and restored me to my father, fell in, on the
shore, with Antigono, whom I forthwith called, and in our language,
that I might be understood neither of the gentlemen nor of their
wives, bade him acknowledge me as his daughter.   He understood
my case at once, made much of me, and to the utmost of his
slender power honourably requited the gentlemen.   He then brought
me to the King of Cyprus, who accorded me welcome there and
conduct hither so honourable as words of mine can never describe.   If
aught remains to tell, you may best learn it from the lips of Antigono,
who has often heard my story."

Then Antigono, addressing the Soldan, said :—" Sire, what she
has told you accords with what she has often told me, and with
what I have learned from the gentlemen and ladies who accompanied
her.   One thing, however, she has omitted, because, I suppose, it
hardly becomes her to tell it ; to wit, all that the gentlemen and
ladies, who accompanied her, said of the virtuous and gracious and
noble life which she led with the devout ladies, and of the tears and
wailings of both the ladies and the gentlemen, when they parted
with her to me.   But were I to essay to repeat all that they said to
me, the day that now is, and the night that is to follow, were all too
short : suffice it to say so much as this, that, by what I gathered
from their words and have been able to see for myself, you may make
it your boast, that among all the daughters of all your peers that
wear the crown none can be matched with yours for virtue and true
worth."

By all which the Soldan was so overjoyed that 'twas a wonder to
see.   Again and again he made supplication to God, that of His
grace power might be vouchsafed him adequately to recompense all
who had done honour to his daughter, and most especially the King

of Cyprus, for the honourable escort under which he had sent her thither ; for Antigono he provided a magnificent guerdon, and some days later gave him his *congé* to return to Cyprus, at the same time by a special ambassage conveying to the King his grateful acknowledgments of the manner in which he had treated his daughter. Then, being minded that his first intent, to wit, that his daughter should be the bride of the King of Algarve, should not be frustrate, he wrote to the King, telling him all, and adding that, if he were still minded to have her, he might send for her. The King was overjoyed by these tidings, and having sent for her with great pomp, gave her on her arrival a hearty welcome. So she, who had lain with eight men, in all, perhaps, ten thousand times, was bedded with him as a virgin, and made him believe that a virgin she was, and lived long and happily with him as his queen : wherefore 'twas said :—" Mouth, for kisses, was never the worse : like as the moon reneweth her course."

NOVEL VIII.

The Count of Antwerp, labouring under a false accusa-
tion, goes into exile.   He leaves his two children in
different places in England, and takes service in
Ireland.   Returning to England an unknown man, he
finds his sons prosperous.   He serves as a groom in
the army of the King of France ; his innocence is
established, and he is restored to his former honours.

THE ladies heaved many sighs over the various fortunes of the
fair lady : but what prompted those sighs who shall say ?   With
some, perchance, 'twas as much envy as pity of one to whose lot
fell so many nights of delight.   But, however this may be, when
Pamfilo's story was ended, and the laughter which greeted his last
words had subsided, the queen turned to Elisa, and bade her follow
suit with one of her stories.   So Elisa with a cheerful courage thus
began :—

Vast indeed is the field that lies before us, wherein to roam
at large ; 'twould readily afford each of us not one course but ten,
so richly has Fortune diversified it with episodes both strange and
sombre ; wherefore selecting one such from this infinite store, I
say :—That, after the transference of the Roman Empire from the
Franks to the Germans, the greatest enmity prevailed between the
two nations, with warfare perpetual and relentless : wherefore,
deeming that the offensive would be their best defence, the King of
France and his son mustered all the forces they could raise from
their own dominions and those of their kinsmen and allies, and
arrayed a grand army for the subjugation of their enemies.   Before

they took the field, as they could not leave the realm without a
governor, they chose for that office Gautier, Count of Antwerp, a
true knight and sage counsellor, and their very loyal ally and vassal,
choosing him the rather, because, albeit he was a thorough master of
the art of war, yet they deemed him less apt to support its hardships
than for the conduct of affairs of a delicate nature.   Him, therefore,
they set in their place as their vicar-general and regent of the whole
realm of France, and having so done, they took the field.

Count Gautier ordered his administration wisely and in a regular
course, discussing all matters with the queen and her daughter-in-
law ; whom, albeit they were left under his charge and jurisdiction,
he nevertheless treated as his ladies paramount.   The Count was
about forty years of age, and the very mould of manly beauty ; in
bearing as courteous and chivalrous as ever a gentleman might be,
and withal so debonair and dainty, so feat and trim of person that
he had not his peer among the gallants of that day.   His wife was
dead, leaving him two children and no more, to wit, a boy and a
girl, still quite young.   Now the King and his son being thus away
at the war, and the Count frequenting the court of the two said
ladies, and consulting with them upon affairs of state, it so befell
that the Prince's lady regarded him with no small favour, being very
sensible alike of the advantages of his person and the nobility of his
bearing ; whereby she conceived for him a passion which was all the
more ardent because it was secret.   And, as he was without a wife,
and she was still in the freshness of her youth, she saw not why she
should not readily be gratified ; but supposing that nothing stood in
the way but her own shamefastness, she resolved to be rid of that,
and disclose her mind to him without any reserve.   So one day,
when she was alone, she seized her opportunity, and sent for him, as
if she were desirous to converse with him on indifferent topics.   The
Count, his mind entirely aloof from the lady's purpose, presented
himself forthwith, and at her invitation sate down by her side on a
settee.   They were quite alone in the room; but the Count had
twice asked her the reason why she had so honoured him, before,
overcome by passion, she broke silence, and crimson from brow to
neck with shame, half sobbing, trembling in every limb, and faltering
at every word, she thus spoke :—" Dearest friend and sweet my lord,
sagacity such as yours cannot but be apt to perceive how great is the

frailty of men and women, and how, for divers reasons, it varies in different persons in such a degree that no just judge would mete out the same measure to each indifferently, though the fault were apparently the same. Who would not acknowledge that a poor man or woman, fain to earn daily bread by the sweat of the brow, is far more reprehensible in yielding to the solicitations of love, than a rich lady, whose life is lapped in ease and unrestricted luxury? Not a soul, I am persuaded, but would so acknowledge! Wherefore I deem that the possession of these boons of fortune should go far indeed to acquit the possessor, if she, perchance, indulge an errant love; and, for the rest, that, if she have chosen a wise and worthy lover, she should be entirely exonerated. And as I think I may fairly claim the benefit of both these pleas, and of others beside, to wit, my youth and my husband's absence, which naturally incline me to love, 'tis meet that I now urge them in your presence in defence of my passion; and if they have the weight with you which they should have with the wise, I pray you to afford me your help and counsel in the matter wherein I shall demand it. I avow that in the absence of my husband I have been unable to withstand the promptings of the flesh and the power of love, forces of such potency that even the strongest men—not to speak of delicate women—have not seldom been, nay daily are, overcome by them; and so, living thus, as you see me, in ease and luxury, I have allowed the allurements of love to draw me on until at last I find myself a prey to passion. Wherein were I discovered, I were, I confess, dishonoured; but discovery being avoided, I count the dishonour all but nought. Moreover, love has been so gracious to me that not only has he spared to blind me in the choice of my lover, but he has even lent me his most effective aid, pointing me to one well worthy of the love of a lady such as I, even to yourself; whom, if I misread not my mind, I deem the most handsome and courteous and debonair, and therewithal the sagest cavalier that the realm of France may shew. And as you are without a wife, so may I say that I find myself without a husband. Wherefore in return for this great love I bear you, deny me not, I pray you, yours; but have pity on my youth, which wastes away for you like ice before the fire."

These words were followed by such a flood of tears, that, albeit she had intended yet further to press her suit, speech failed her; her eyes drooped, and, almost swooning with emotion, she let her head fall upon the Count's breast. The Count, who was the most loyal of knights, began with all severity to chide her mad passion and to thrust her from him—for she was now making as if she would throw her arms around his neck—and to asseverate with oaths that he would rather be hewn in pieces than either commit, or abet another in committing such an offence against the honour of his lord; when the lady, catching his drift, and forgetting all her love in a sudden frenzy of rage, cried out :—"So! unknightly knight, is it thus you flout my love? Now Heaven forbid, but, as you would be the death of me, I either do you to death or drive you from the world!" So saying, she dishevelled and tore her hair and rent her garments to shreds about her bosom. Which done, she began shrieking at the top of her voice :—"Help! help! The Count of Antwerp threatens to violate me!" Whereupon the Count, who knew that a clear conscience was no protection against the envy of courtiers, and doubted that his innocence would prove scarce a match for the cunning of the lady, started to his feet, and hied him with all speed out of the room, out of the palace, and back to his own house. Counsel of none he sought; but forthwith set his children on horseback, and taking horse himself, departed post haste for Calais. The lady's cries brought not a few to her aid, who, observing her plight, not only gave entire credence to her story, but improved upon it, alleging that the debonair and accomplished Count had long employed all the arts of seduction to compass his end. So they rushed in hot haste to the Count's house, with intent to arrest him, and not finding him, sacked it and razed it to the ground. The news, as glosed and garbled, being carried to the King and Prince in the field, they were mightily incensed, and offered a great reward for the Count, dead or alive, and condemned him and his posterity to perpetual banishment.

Meanwhile the Count, sorely troubled that by his flight his innocence shewed as guilt, pursued his journey, and concealing his identity, and being recognised by none, arrived with his two children at Calais. Thence he forthwith crossed to England, and, meanly clad, fared on for London, taking care as he went to school his children in all that belonged to their new way of life, and especially in two main articles: to wit, that they should bear with resignation the poverty to which, by no fault of theirs, but solely by one of

Fortune's caprices, they and he were reduced, and that they should be most sedulously on their guard to betray to none, as they valued their lives, whence they were, or who their father was. The son, Louis by name, was perhaps nine, and the daughter, Violante, perhaps seven years of age. For years so tender they proved apt pupils, and afterwards shewed by their conduct that they had well learned their father's lesson. He deemed it expedient to change their names, and accordingly called the boy Perrot and the girl Jeannette. So, meanly clad, the Count and his two children arrived at London, and there made shift to get a living by going about soliciting alms in the guise of French mendicants.

Now, as for this purpose they waited one morning outside a church, it so befell that a great lady, the wife of one of the marshals of the King of England, observed them, as she left the church, asking alms, and demanded of the Count whence he was, and whether the children were his. He answered that he was from Picardy, that the children were his, and that he had been fain to leave Picardy by reason of the misconduct of their reprobate elder brother. The lady looked at the girl, who being fair, and of gentle and winning mien and manners, found much favour in her eyes. So the kind-hearted lady said to the Count :—" My good man, if thou art willing to leave thy little daughter with me, I like her looks so well that I will gladly take her ; and if she grow up a good woman, I will see that she is suitably married when the right time comes." The Count was much gratified by the proposal, which he forthwith accepted, and parted with the girl, charging the lady with tears to take every care of her.

Having thus placed the girl with one in whom he felt sure that he might trust, he determined to tarry no longer in London ; wherefore, taking Perrot with him and begging as he went, he made his way to Wales, not without great suffering, being unused to go afoot. Now in Wales another of the King's marshals had his court, maintaining great state and a large number of retainers ; to which court the Count and his son frequently repaired, there to get food ; and there Perrot, finding the marshal's son and other gentlemen's sons vying with one another in boyish exercises, as running and leaping, little by little joined their company, and shewed himself a match or more for them all in all their contests. The marshal's attention being thus drawn to him, he was well pleased with the boy's mien and bearing, and asked who he was. He was told that he was the son of a poor man who sometimes came there to solicit alms. Whereupon he asked the Count to let him have the boy, and the Count, to whom God could have granted no greater boon, readily consented, albeit he was very loath to part with Perrot.

Having thus provided for his son and daughter, the Count resolved to quit the island; and did so, making his way as best he could to Stamford, in Ireland, where he obtained a menial's place in the service of a knight, retainer to one of the earls of that country, and so abode there a long while, doing all the irksome and wearisome drudgery of a lackey or groom.

Meanwhile under the care of the gentle lady at London Violante or Jeannette increased, as in years and stature so also in beauty, and in such favour with the lady and her husband and every other member of the household and all who knew her that 'twas a wonder to see; nor was there any that, observing her bearing and manners, would not have said that estate or dignity there was none so high or honourable but she was worthy of it. So the lady, who, since she had received her from her father, had been unable to learn aught else about him than what he had himself told, was minded to marry her honourably according to what she deemed to be her rank. But God, who justly apportions reward according to merit, having regard to her noble birth, her innocence, and the load of suffering which the sin of another had laid upon her, ordered otherwise; and in His good providence, lest the young gentlewoman should be mated with a churl, permitted, we must believe, events to take the course they did.

The gentle lady with whom Jeannette lived had an only son, whom she and her husband loved most dearly, as well because he was a son as for his rare and noble qualities, for in truth there were few that could compare with him in courtesy and courage and personal beauty. Now the young man marked the extraordinary beauty and grace of Jeannette, who was about six years his junior, and fell so desperately in love with her that he had no eyes for any other maiden; but, deeming her to be of low degree, he not only hesitated to ask her of his parents in marriage, but, fearing to incur reproof for indulging a passion for an inferior, he did his utmost to conceal his love.

Whereby it gave him far more disquietude than if he had avowed it ; insomuch that—so extreme waxed his suffering—he fell ill, and that seriously. Divers physicians were called in, but, for all their scrutiny of his symptoms, they could not determine the nature of his malady, and one and all gave him up for lost. Nothing could exceed the sorrow and dejection of his father and mother, who again and again piteously implored him to discover to them the cause of his malady, and received no other answer than sighs or complaints that he seemed to be wasting away. Now it so happened that one day, Jeannette, who from regard for his mother was sedulous in waiting upon him, for some reason or another came into the room where he lay, while a very young but very skilful physician sate by him and held his pulse. The young man gave her not a word or other sign of recognition ; but his passion waxed, his heart smote him, and the acceleration of his pulse at once betrayed his inward commotion to the physician, who, albeit surprised, remained quietly attentive to see how long it would last, and observing that it ceased when Jeannette left the room, conjectured that he was on the way to explain the young man's malady. So, after a while, still holding the young man's pulse, he sent for Jeannette, as if he had something to ask of her. She returned forthwith ; the young man's pulse mounted as soon as she entered the room, and fell again as soon as she left it. Wherefore the physician no longer hesitated, but rose, and taking the young man's father and mother aside, said to them :— "The restoration of your son's health rests not with medical skill, but solely with Jeannette, whom, as by unmistakable signs I have discovered, he ardently loves, though, so far I can see, she is not aware of it. So you know what you have to do, if you value his life." The prospect thus afforded of their son's deliverance from death reassured the gentleman and his lady, albeit they were troubled, misdoubting it must be by his marriage with Jeannette. So, when the physician was gone, they went to the sick lad, and the lady thus spoke :—"My son, never would I have believed that thou wouldst have concealed from me any desire of thine, least of all if such it were that privation should cause thee to languish ; for well assured thou shouldst have been and shouldst be, that I hold thee dear as my very self, and that whatever may be for thy contentment, even though it were scarce seemly, I would do it for thee; but, for all thou hast so done, God has shewn Himself more merciful to theeward than thyself, and, lest thou die of this malady, has given me to know its cause, which is nothing else than the excessive love which thou bearest to a young woman, be she who she may. Which love in good sooth thou needest not have been ashamed to declare; for it is but natural at thy age; and hadst thou not loved, I should have deemed thee of very little worth. So, my son, be not shy of me, but frankly discover to me thy whole heart; and away with this gloom and melancholy whereof thy sickness is engendered, and be comforted, and assure thyself that there is nought that thou mayst require of me which I will not do to give thee ease, so far as my powers may reach, seeing that thou art dearer to me than my own life. Away with thy shamefastness and fears, and tell me if there is aught wherein I may be helpful to thee in the matter of thy love; and if I bestir not myself and bring it to pass, account me the most harsh mother that ever bore son."

The young man was at first somewhat shamefast to hear his mother thus speak, but, reflecting that none could do more for his happiness than she, he took courage, and thus spoke :—" Madam, my sole reason for concealing my love from you was that I have observed that old people for the most part forget that they once were young; but, as I see that no such unreasonableness is to be apprehended in you, I not only acknowledge the truth of what you say that you have discerned, but I will also disclose to you the object of my passion, on the understanding that your promise shall to the best of your power be performed, as it must be, if I am to be restored to you in sound health." Whereupon the lady, making too sure of that which was destined to fall out otherwise than she expected, gave him every encouragement to discover all his heart, and promised to lose no time and spare no pains in endeavouring to compass his gratification. " Madam," said then the young man, " the rare beauty and exquisite manners of our Jeannette, my powerlessness to make her understand—I do not say commiserate—my love, and my reluctance to disclose it to any, have brought me to the condition in which you see me; and if your promise be not in one way or another performed, be sure that my life will be brief." The lady, deeming that the occasion called rather for comfort than for admonition, replied with a smile :—" Ah ! my son, was this then of all things the secret of thy suffering ? Be of good cheer, and leave me to arrange the affair, when you are recovered." So, animated by a cheerful hope, the young man speedily gave sign of a most marked improvement, which the lady observed with great satisfaction, and then began to cast about how she might keep her promise. So one day she sent for Jeannette, and in a tone of gentle raillery asked her if she had a lover. Jeannette turned very red as she answered :—" Madam, 'twould scarce, nay, 'twould ill become a damsel such as I, poor, outcast from home, and in the service of another, to occupy herself with thoughts of love." Whereto the lady answered :—" So you have none, we will give you one, who will brighten all your life and give you more joy of your beauty ; for it is not right that so fair a damsel as you remain without a lover." " Madam," rejoined Jeannette, " you found me living in poverty with my father, you adopted me, you have brought me up as your daughter; wherefore I should, if possible, comply with your every wish; but in this matter I will render you no compliance, nor do I doubt that I do well. So you will give me a husband, I will love him, but no other will I love ; for, as patrimony I now have none save my honour, that I am minded to guard and preserve while my life shall last." Serious though the obstacle was which these words opposed to the plan by which the lady had intended to keep her promise to her son, her sound judgment could not but secretly acknowledge that the spirit which they evinced was much to be commended in the damsel. Wherefore she said : —" Nay but, Jeannette ; suppose that our Lord the King, who is a young knight as thou art a most fair damsel, craved some indulgence of thy love, wouldst thou deny him ? " " The King," returned Jeannette without the least hesitation, " might constrain me, but with my consent he should never have aught of me that was not honourable." Whereto the lady made no answer, for she now understood the girl's temper ; but, being minded to put her to the proof, she told her son that, as soon as he was recovered, she would arrange that he should be closeted with her in the same room, and be thus able to use all his arts to bring her to his will, saying that it ill became her to play the part of procuress and urge her son's suit upon her own maid. But as the young man, by no means approving this idea, suddenly grew worse, the lady at length opened her mind to Jeannette, whom she found in the same frame as before, and indeed even more resolute. Wherefore she told her husband all that she had done ; and as both preferred that their son should marry beneath him, and live, than that he should remain single and die, they resolved, albeit much discon- certed, to give Jeannette to him to wife ; and so after long debate they did.   Whereat Jeannette was overjoyed, and with devout heart gave thanks to God that He had not forgotten her; nevertheless she still gave no other account of herself than that she was the daughter of a Picard.   So the young man recovered, and blithe at heart as ne'er another, was married, and began to speed the time gaily with his bride.

Meanwhile Perrot, left in Wales with the marshal of the King of England, had likewise with increase of years increase of favour with his master, and grew up most shapely and well-favoured, and of such prowess that in all the island at tourney or joust or any other passage of arms he had not his peer; being everywhere known and renowned as Perrot the Picard.   And as God had not forgotten Jeannette, so likewise He made manifest by what follows that He had not forgotten Perrot.   Well-nigh half the population of those parts being swept off by a sudden visitation of deadly pestilence, most of the survivors fled therefrom in a panic, so that the country was, to all appearance, entirely deserted.   Among those that died of the pest were the marshal, his lady, and his son, besides brothers and nephews and kinsfolk in great number; whereby of his entire household there were left only one of his daughters, now marriageable, and a few servants, among them Perrot.   Now Perrot being a man of such notable prowess, the damsel, soon after the pestilence had spent itself, took him, with the approval and by the advice of the few folk that survived, to be her husband, and made him lord of all that fell to her by inheritance.   Nor was it long before the King of England, learning that the marshal was dead, made Perrot the Picard, to whose merit he was no stranger, marshal in the dead man's room.   Such, in brief, was the history of the two innocent children, with whom the Count of Antwerp had parted, never expecting to see them again.

'Twas now the eighteenth year since the Count of Antwerp had taken flight from Paris, when, being still in Ireland, where he had led a very sorry and suffering sort of life, and feeling that age was now come upon him, he felt a longing to learn, if possible, what was become of his children. The fashion of his outward man was now completely changed; for long hardship had (as he well knew) given to his age a vigour which his youth, lapped in ease, had lacked. So he hesitated not to take his leave of the knight with whom he had so long resided, and poor and in sorry trim he crossed to England, and made his way to the place where he had left Perrot—to find him a great lord and marshal of the King, and in good health, and withal a hardy man and very handsome. All which was very grateful to the old man; but yet he would not make himself known to his son, until he had learned the fate of Jeannette. So forth he fared again, nor did he halt until he was come to London, where, cautiously questing about for news of the lady with whom he had left his daughter, and how it fared with her, he learned that Jeannette was married to the lady's son. Whereat, in the great gladness of his heart, he counted all his past adversity but a light matter, since he had found his children alive and prosperous. But sore he yearned to see Jeannette. Wherefore he took to loitering, as poor folk are wont, in the neighbourhood of the house. And so one day Jacques Lamiens—such was the name of Jeannette's husband—saw him and had pity on him, observing that he was poor and aged, and bade one of his servants take him indoors, and for God's sake give him something to eat; and nothing loath the servant did so. Now Jeannette had borne Jacques several children, the finest and the most winsome children in the world, the eldest no more than eight years old; who gathered about the Count as he ate, and, as if by instinct divining that he was their grandfather, began to make friends with him. He, knowing them for his grandchildren, could not conceal his love, and repaid them with caresses; insomuch that they would not hearken to their governor when he called them, but remained with the Count. Which being reported to Jeannette, she came out of her room, crossed to where the Count was sitting with the children, and bade them do as their master told them, or she would certainly have them whipped. The children began to cry, and to say that they would rather stay with the worthy man, whom they liked much better than their master; whereat both the lady and the Count laughed in sympathy. The Count had risen, with no other intention—for he was not minded to disclose his paternity—

than to pay his daughter the respect due from his poverty to her
rank, and the sight of her had thrilled his soul with a wondrous
delight.   By her he was and remained unrecognised ; utterly
changed as he was from his former self ; aged, grey-haired, bearded,
lean and tanned—in short to all appearance another man than the
Count.

However, seeing that the children were unwilling to leave him,
but wept when she made as if she would constrain them, she bade
the master let them be for a time.   So the children remained with
the worthy man, until by chance Jacques' father came home, and
learned from the master what had happened.   Whereupon, having a
grudge against Jeannette, he said:—" Let them be; and God give
them the ill luck which He owes them : whence they sprang, thither
they must needs return ; they descend from a vagabond on the
mother's side, and so 'tis no wonder that they consort readily with
vagabonds."   The Count caught these words and was sorely pained,
but, shrugging his shoulders, bore the affront silently as he had borne
many another.   Jacques, who had noted his children's fondness for
the worthy man, to wit, the Count, was displeased ; but nevertheless,
such was the love he bore them, that, rather than see them weep, he
gave order that, if the worthy man cared to stay there in his service,
he should be received.   The Count answered that he would gladly
do so, but that he was fit for nothing except to look after horses, to
which he had been used all his life.   So a horse was assigned him,
and when he had groomed him, he occupied himself in playing with
the children.

While Fortune thus shaped the destinies of the Count of Antwerp and his children, it so befell that after a long series of truces
made with the Germans the King of France died, and his crown
passed to his son, whose wife had been the occasion of the Count's
banishment.   The new king, as soon as the last truce with the
Germans was run out, renewed hostilities with extraordinary vigour,
being aided by his brother of England with a large army under the
command of his marshal, Perrot, and his other marshal's son,
Jacques Lamiens.   With them went the worthy man, that is to say,
the Count, who, unrecognised by any, served for a long while in the
army in the capacity of groom, and acquitted himself both in counsel
and in arms with a wisdom and valour unwonted in one of his

supposed rank. The war was still raging when the Queen of France fell seriously ill, and, as she felt her end approach, made a humble and contrite confession of all her sins to the Archbishop of Rouen, who was universally reputed a good and most holy man. Among her other sins she confessed the great wrong that she had done to the Count of Antwerp ; nor was she satisfied to confide it to the Archbishop, but recounted the whole affair, as it had passed, to not a few other worthy men, whom she besought to use their influence with the King to procure the restitution of the Count, if he were still alive, and if not, of his children, to honour and estate. And so, dying shortly afterwards, she was honourably buried. The Queen's confession wrung from the King a sigh or two of compunction for a brave man cruelly wronged ; after which he caused proclamation to be made throughout the army and in many other parts, that whoso should bring him tidings of the Count of Antwerp, or his children, should receive from him such a guerdon for each of them as should justly be matter of marvel ; seeing that he held him acquitted, by confession of the Queen, of the crime for which he had been banished, and was therefore now minded to grant him not only restitution but increase of honour and estate.

Now the Count, being still with the army in his character of groom, heard the proclamation, which he did not doubt was made in good faith. Wherefore he hied him forthwith to Jacques, and begged a private interview with him and Perrot, that he might discover to them that whereof the King was in quest. So the meeting was had ; and Perrot was on the point of declaring himself, when the Count anticipated him :—" Perrot," he said, " Jacques here has thy sister to wife, but never a dowry had he with her. Wherefore that thy sister be not dowerless, 'tis my will that he, and no other, have this great reward which the King offers for thee, son, as he shall certify, of the Count of Antwerp, and for his wife and thy sister, Violante, and for me, Count of Antwerp, thy father." So hearing, Perrot scanned the Count closely, and forthwith recognising him, burst into tears, and throwing himself at his feet embraced him, saying :—" My father, welcome, welcome indeed art thou." Whereupon, between what he had heard from the Count and what he had witnessed on the part of Perrot, Jacques was so overcome with wonder and delight, that at first he was at a loss to know how

to act.   However, giving entire credence to what he had heard, and
recalling insulting language which he had used towards the quondam
groom, the Count, he was sore stricken with shame, and wept, and
fell at the Count's feet, and humbly craved his pardon for all past
offences ; which the Count, raising him to his feet, most graciously
granted him.   So with many a tear and many a hearty laugh the
three men compared their several fortunes ; which done, Perrot and
Jacques would have arrayed the Count in manner befitting his rank,
but he would by no means suffer it, being minded that Jacques, so
soon as he was well assured that the guerdon was forthcoming,
should present him to the King in his garb of groom, that thereby
the King might be the more shamed.   So Jacques, with the Count
and Perrot, went presently to the King and offered to present to him
the Count and his children, provided the guerdon were forthcoming
according to the proclamation.   Jacques wondered not a little as
forthwith at a word from the King a guerdon was produced ample
for all three, and he was bidden take it away with him, so only that
he should in very truth produce, as he had promised, the Count and
his children in the royal presence.   Then, withdrawing a little and
causing his quondam groom, now Count, to come forward with
Perrot, he said :—" Sire, father and son are before you ; the daughter,
my wife, is not here, but, God willing, you shall soon see her."   So
hearing, the King surveyed the Count, whom, notwithstanding his
greatly changed appearance, he at length recognised, and well-nigh
moved to tears, he raised him from his knees to his feet, and kissed
and embraced him.   He also gave a kindly welcome to Perrot, and
bade forthwith furnish the Count with apparel, servants and horses,
suited to his rank; all which was no sooner said than done.   Moreover the King shewed Jacques no little honour, and particularly
questioned him of all his past adventures.

As Jacques was about to take the noble guerdons assigned him for
the discovery of the Count and his children, the Count said to
him :—" Take these tokens of the magnificence of our Lord the
King, and forget not to tell thy father that 'tis from no vagabond
that thy children, his and my grandchildren, descend on the mother's
side."   So Jacques took the guerdons, and sent for his wife and
mother to join him at Paris.   Thither also came Perrot's wife : and
there with all magnificence they were entertained by the Count, to

whom the King had not only restored all his former estates and honours, but added thereto others, whereby he was now become a greater man than he had ever been before. Then with the Count's leave they all returned to their several houses. The Count himself spent the rest of his days at Paris in greater glory than ever.

NOVEL IX.

Bernabò of Genoa, deceived by Ambrogiuolo, loses his money and commands his innocent wife to be put to death. She escapes, habits herself as a man, and serves the Soldan. She discovers the deceiver, and brings Bernabò to Alexandria, where the deceiver is punished. She then resumes the garb of a woman, and with her husband returns wealthy to Genoa.

WHEN Elisa had performed her part, and brought her touching story to a close, Queen Filomena, a damsel no less stately than fair of person, and of a surpassingly sweet and smiling mien, having composed herself to speak, thus began :—

Our engagements with Dioneo shall be faithfully observed ; wherefore, as he and I alone remain to complete the day's narration, I will tell my story first, and he shall have the grace he craved, and be the last to speak. After which prelude she thus began her story :—'Tis a proverb current among the vulgar that the deceived has the better of the deceiver ; a proverb which, were it not exemplified by events, might hardly in any manner be justified. Wherefore, while adhering to our theme, I am minded at the same time, dearest ladies, to shew you that there is truth in this proverb ; the proof whereof should be none the less welcome to you that it may put you on your guard against deceivers.

Know then that certain very great merchants of Italy, being met, as merchants use, for divers reasons proper to each, at a hostelry in Paris, and having one evening jovially supped together, fell a talking of divers matters, and so, passing from one topic to another, they came at last to discuss the ladies whom they had left at home, and one jocosely said :—" I cannot answer for my wife ; but for myself I own, that, whenever a girl that is to my mind comes in my way, I give the go-by to the love that I bear my wife, and take my pleasure of the new-comer to the best of my power." " And so do I," said another, " because I know that, whether I suspect her or no, my wife tries her fortune, and so 'tis do as you are done by ; the ass and the wall are quits." A third added his testimony to the same effect; and in short all seemed to concur in the opinion that the ladies they had left behind them were not likely to neglect their opportunities, when one, a Genoese, Bernabò Lomellin by name, dissociated himself from the rest, affirming that by especial grace of God he was blessed with a wife who was, perhaps, the most perfect paragon to be found in Italy of all the virtues proper to a lady, ay, and in great measure, to a knight or squire ; inasmuch as she was fair, still quite young, handy, hardy, and clever beyond all other women in embroidery work and all other forms of lady's handicraft. Moreover so well-mannered, discreet and sensible was she that she was as fit to wait at a lord's table as any squire or manservant or such like, the best and most adroit that could be found. To which encomium he added that she knew how to manage a horse, fly a hawk, read, write and cast up accounts better than as if she were a merchant; and after much more in the same strain of commendation he came at length to the topic of their conversation, asseverating with an oath that 'twas not possible to find a woman more honest, more chaste than she : nay, he verily believed that, if he remained from home for ten years, or indeed for the rest of his days, she would never think of any of these casual amours with any other man.

Among the merchants who thus gossiped was a young man, Ambrogiuolo da Piacenza by name, who, when Bernabò thus concluded his eulogy of his wife, broke out into a mighty laugh, and asked him with a leer, whether he of all men had this privilege by special patent of the Emperor. Bernabò replied, somewhat angrily, that 'twas a boon conferred upon him by God, who was rather more powerful than the Emperor. To which Ambrogiuolo rejoined :—" I make no doubt, Bernabò, that thou believest that what thou sayst is true ; but, methinks, thou hast been but a careless observer of the nature of things ; otherwise, I do not take thee to be of so gross understanding but that thou must have discerned therein reasons for speaking more judiciously of this matter.   And that thou mayst not think that we, who have spoken with much freedom about our wives, deem them to be of another nature and mould than thine, but mayst know that we have but uttered what common sense dictates, I am minded to go a little further into this matter with thee.   I have always understood, that of all mortal beings created by God man is the most noble, and next after him woman : man, then, being, as is universally believed, and is indeed apparent by his works, more perfect than woman, must without doubt be endowed with more firmness and constancy, women being one and all more mobile, for reasons not a few and founded in nature, which I might adduce, but mean for the present to pass over.   And yet, for all his greater firmness, man cannot withstand—I do not say a woman's supplications, but—the mere lust of the eye which she unwittingly excites, and that in such sort that he will do all that is in his power to induce her to pleasure him, not once, perhaps, in the course of a month, but a thousand times a day.   How, then, shouldst thou expect a woman, mobile by nature, to resist the supplications, the flatteries, the gifts, and all the other modes of attack that an accomplished seducer will employ ?   Thou thinkest that she may hold out !   Nay verily, affirm it as thou mayst, I doubt thou dost not really so think.   Thou dost not deny that thy wife is a woman, a creature of flesh and blood like the rest ; and if so, she must have the same cravings, the same natural propensities as they, and no more force to withstand them ; wherefore 'tis at least possible, that, however honest she be, she will do as others do ; and nought that is possible admits such peremptory denial or affirmation of its contrary as this of thine."

Whereto Bernabò returned :—"I am a merchant and no philosopher, and I will give thee a merchant's answer.   I acknowledge that what thou sayst is true of vain and foolish women who have no modesty, but such as are discreet are so sensitive in regard of their honour that they become better able to preserve it than men, who have no such solicitude ; and my wife is one of this sort." "Doubtless," observed Ambrogiuolo, "few would be found to indulge in these casual amours, if every time they did so a horn grew out on the brow to attest the fact; but not only does no horn make its appearance but not so much as a trace or vestige of a horn, so only they be but prudent; and the shame and dishonour consist only in the discovery : wherefore, if they can do it secretly, they do it, or are fools to refrain. Hold it for certain that she alone is chaste who either had never suit made to her, or, suing herself, was repulsed. And albeit I know that for reasons true and founded in nature this must needs be, yet I should not speak so positively thereof as I do, had I not many a time with many a woman verified it by experience. And I assure thee that, had I but access to this most saintly wife of thine, I should confidently expect very soon to have the same success with her as with others." Then Bernabò angrily :—" 'Twere long and tedious to continue this discussion. I should have my say, and thou thine, and in the end 'twould come to nothing. But, as thou sayst that they are all so compliant, and that thou art so accomplished a seducer, I give thee this pledge of the honour of my wife : I consent to forfeit my head, if thou shouldst succeed in bringing her to pleasure thee in such a sort ; and shouldst thou fail, thou shalt forfeit to me no more than one thousand florins of gold."

Elated by this unexpected offer, Ambrogiuolo replied :—"I know not what I should do with thy blood, Bernabò, if I won the wager; but, if thou wouldst have proof of what I have told thee, lay five thousand florins of gold, which must be worth less to thee than thy head, against a thousand of mine, and, whereas thou makest no stipulation as to time, I will bind myself to go to Genoa, and within three months from my departure hence to have had my pleasure of thy wife, and in witness thereof to bring back with me, of the things which she prizes most dearly, evidence of her compliance so weighty and conclusive that thou thyself shalt admit the fact ; nor do I require ought of thee but that thou pledge thy faith neither to come to Genoa nor to write word to her of this matter during the said three months." Bernabò professed himself well content; and though the rest of the company, seeing that the compact might well have very evil consequences, did all that they could to frustrate it, yet the two men were now so heated that, against the will of the others, they set it down fairly in writing, and signed it each with his own hand. This done, Ambrogiuolo, leaving Bernabò at Paris, posted with all speed for Genoa. Arrived there, he set to work with great caution;

and having found out the quarter in which the lady resided, he learned in the course of a few days enough about her habits of life and her character to know that what Bernabò had told him was rather less than the truth. So, recognising that his enterprise was hopeless, he cast about for some device whereby he might cover his defeat; and having got speech of a poor woman, who was much in the lady's house, as also in her favour, he bribed her (other means failing) to convey him in a chest, which he had had made for the purpose, not only into the house but into the bedroom of the lady, whom the good woman, following Bernabò's instructions, induced to take charge of it for some days, during which, she said, she would be away.

So the lady suffered the chest to remain in the room; and when the night was so far spent that Bernabò thought she must be asleep, he opened it with some tools with which he had provided himself, and stole softly out. There was a light in the room, so that he was able to form an idea of its situation, to take note of the pictures and everything else of consequence that it contained, and to commit the whole to memory. This done, he approached the bed; and observing that the lady, and a little girl that was with her, were fast asleep, he gently uncovered her, and saw that nude she was not a whit less lovely than when dressed: he looked about for some mark that might serve him as evidence that he had seen her in this state, but found nothing except a mole, which she had under the left breast, and which was fringed with a few fair hairs that shone like gold. So beautiful was she that he was tempted at the hazard of his life to take his place by her side in the bed; but, remembering what he had heard of her inflexible obduracy in such affairs, he did not venture; but quietly replaced the bedclothes; and having passed the best part of the night very much at his ease in her room, he took from one of the lady's boxes a purse, a gown, a ring and a girdle, and with these tokens returned to the chest, and locked himself in as before. In this manner he passed two nights, nor did the lady in the least suspect his presence. On the third day the good woman came by preconcert to fetch her chest, and took it back to the place whence she had brought it. So Ambrogiuolo got out, paid her the stipulated sum, and hied him back with all speed to Paris, where he arrived within the appointed time. Then, in presence of the merchants who were witnesses of his altercation with Bernabò, and the wager to which it had given occasion, he told Bernabò that he had won the bet, having done what he had boasted that he would do ; and in proof thereof he first of all described the appearance of the room and the pictures, and then displayed the articles belonging to the lady which he had brought away with him, averring that she had given them to him. Bernabò acknowledged the accuracy of his description of the room, and that the articles did really belong to his wife, but objected that Ambrogiuolo might have learned characteristic features of the room from one of the servants, and have come by the things in a similar way, and therefore, unless he had something more to say, he could not justly claim to have won the bet. " Verily," rejoined Ambrogiuolo, " this should suffice ; but, as thou requirest that I say somewhat further, I will satisfy thee. I say, then, that Madam Zinevra, thy wife, has under her left breast a mole of some size, around which are, perhaps, six hairs of a golden hue." As Bernabò heard this, it was as if a knife pierced his heart, so poignant was his suffering ; and, though no word escaped him, the complete alteration of his mien bore unmistakable witness to the truth of Ambrogiuolo's words. After a while he said :—" Gentlemen, 'tis even as Ambro-giuolo says ; he has won the bet ; he has but to come when he will, and he shall be paid." And so the very next day Ambrogiuolo was paid in full, and Bernabò, intent on wreaking vengeance on his wife, left Paris and set his face towards Genoa. He had no mind, however, to go home, and accordingly halted at an estate which he had some twenty miles from the city, whither he sent forward a servant, in whom he reposed much trust, with two horses and a letter advising the lady of his return, and bidding her come out to meet him. At the same time he gave the servant secret instructions to choose some convenient place, and ruthlessly put the lady to death, and so return to him. On his arrival at Genoa the servant delivered his message and the letter to the lady, who received him with great cheer, and next morning got on horseback and set forth with him for her husband's estate. So they rode on, talking of divers matters, until they came to a deep gorge, very lonely, and shut in by high rocks and trees. The servant, deeming this just the place in which he might without risk of discovery fulfil his lord's behest, whipped out a knife, and seizing

the lady by the arm, said :—" Madam, commend your soul to God,
for here must end at once your journey and your life." Terror-
stricken by what she saw and heard, the lady cried out :—" Mercy
for God's sake ; before thou slay me, tell me at least wherein I have
wronged thee, that thou art thus minded to put me to death."
" Madam," said the servant, "me you have in no wise wronged;
but your husband—how you may have wronged him I know not—
charged me shew you no mercy, but to slay you on this journey,
and threatened to have me hanged by the neck, should I not do so.
You know well how bound I am to him, and that I may not
disobey any of his commands : God knows I pity you, but yet I can
no otherwise." Whereat the lady burst into tears, saying :—" Mercy
for God's sake ; make not thyself the murderer of one that has done
thee no wrong, at the behest of another. The all-seeing God knows
that I never did aught to merit such requital at my husband's hands.
But enough of this for the present : there is a way in which thou
canst serve at once God and thy master and myself, if thou wilt do
as I bid thee : take, then, these clothes of mine and give me in
exchange just thy doublet and a hood; and carry the clothes with
thee to my lord and thine, and tell him that thou hast slain me ;
and I swear to thee by the life which I shall have received at thy
hands, that I will get me gone, and there abide whence news of me
shall never reach either him or thee or these parts." The servant,
being loath to put her to death, soon yielded to pity ; and so he took
her clothes, allowing her to retain a little money that she had, and
gave her one of his worser doublets and a hood ; then, praying her
to depart the country, he left her afoot in the gorge, and returned
to his master, whom he gave to understand that he had not only
carried out his orders but had left the lady's body a prey to wolves.
Bernabò after a while returned to Genoa, where, the supposed
murder being bruited abroad, he was severely censured.

Alone and disconsolate, the lady, as night fell, disguised herself
as best she could, and hied her to a neighbouring village, where,
having procured what was needful from an old woman, she shortened
the doublet and fitted it to her figure, converted her chemise into a
pair of breeches, cut her hair close, and, in short, completely disguised
herself as a sailor. She then made her way to the coast, where by
chance she encountered a Catalan gentleman, by name Segner

Encararch, who had landed from one of his ships, which lay in the offing, to recreate himself at Alba, where there was a fountain. So she made overture to him of her services, was engaged and taken aboard the ship, assuming the name Sicurano da Finale. The gentleman put her in better trim as to clothes, and found her so apt and handy at service that he was exceeding well pleased with her.

Not long afterwards the Catalan sailed one of his carracks to Alexandria. He took with him some peregrine falcons, which he presented to the Soldan, who feasted him once or twice; and noting with approbation the behaviour of Sicurano, who always attended his master, he craved him of the Catalan, which request the Catalan reluctantly granted. Sicurano proved so apt for his new service that he was soon as high in grace and favour with the Soldan as he had been with the Catalan. Wherefore, when the time of year came at which there was wont to be held at Acre, then under the Soldan's sway, a great fair, much frequented by merchants, Christian and Saracen alike, and to which, for the security of the merchants and their goods, the Soldan always sent one of his great officers of state with other officers and a guard to attend upon them, he determined to send Sicurano, who by this time knew the language very well. So Sicurano was sent to Acre as governor and captain of the guard for the protection of the merchants and merchandise. Arrived there, he bestirred himself with great zeal in all matters appertaining to his office; and as he went his rounds of inspection, he espied among the merchants not a few from Italy, Sicilians, Pisans, Genoese, Venetians, and so forth, with whom he consorted the more readily because they reminded him of his native land. And so it befell that, alighting once at a shop belonging to some Venetian merchants, he saw there among other trinkets a purse and a girdle, which he forthwith recognised as having once been his own. Concealing his surprise, he blandly asked whose they were, and if they were for sale. He was answered by Ambrogiuolo da Piacenza, who had come thither with much merchandise aboard a Venetian ship, and hearing that the captain of the guard was asking about the ownership of the purse and girdle, came forward, and said with a smile:—"The things are mine, Sir, and I am not disposed to sell them, but, if they take your fancy, I will gladly give them to you." Observing the smile, Sicurano misdoubted that something had escaped him by which Ambrogiuolo had recognised him; but he answered with a composed air:—"Thou dost smile, perchance, to see me, a soldier, come asking about this woman's gear?" "Not so, Sir," returned Ambrogiuolo; "I smile to think of the manner in which I came by it." "And pray," said Sicurano, "if thou hast no reason to conceal it, tell me, in God's name, how thou didst come by the things." "Why, Sir," said Ambrogiuolo, "they were given me by a Genoese lady, with whom I once spent a night, Madam Zinevra by name, wife of Bernabò Lomellin, who prayed me to keep them as a token of her love. I smiled just now to think of the folly of Bernabò, who was so mad as to stake five thousand florins of gold against my thousand that I could not bring his wife to surrender to me; which I did. I won the bet; and he, who should rather have been punished for his insensate folly, than she for doing what all women do, had her put to death, as I afterwards gathered, on his way back from Paris to Genoa."

Ambrogiuolo had not done speaking before Sicurano had discerned in him the evident cause of her husband's animosity against her, and all her woe, and had made up her mind that he should not escape with impunity. She therefore feigned to be much interested by this story, consorted frequently and very familiarly with Ambrogiuolo, and insidiously captured his confidence, insomuch that at her suggestion, when the fair was done, he, taking with him all his wares, accompanied her to Alexandria, where she provided him with a shop, and put no little of her own money in his hands; so that he, finding it very profitable, was glad enough to stay. Anxious to make her innocence manifest to Bernabò, Sicurano did not rest until, with the help of some great Genoese merchants that were in Alexandria, she had devised an expedient to draw him thither. Her plan succeeded; Bernabò arrived; and, as he was now very poor, she privily arranged that he should be entertained by one of her friends until occasion should serve to carry out her design. She had already induced Ambrogiuolo to tell his story to the Soldan, and the Soldan to interest himself in the matter. So Bernabò being come, and further delay inexpedient, she seized her opportunity, and persuaded the Soldan to cite Ambrogiuolo and Bernabò before him, that in Bernabò's presence Ambrogiuolo might be examined of his boast touching Bernabò's wife, and the truth thereof, if not to be had from him by gentle means, be elicited by torture. So the Soldan, having Ambrogiuolo and Bernabò before him, amid a great concourse of his people questioned Ambrogiuolo of the five thousand florins of gold that he had won from Bernabò, and sternly bade him tell the truth. Still more harsh was the aspect of Sicurano, in whom Ambrogiuolo had placed his chief reliance, but who now threatened him with the direst torments if the truth were not forthcoming. Thus hard bested on this side and on that, and in a manner coerced, Ambrogiuolo, thinking he had but to refund, in presence of Bernabò and many others accurately recounted the affair as it had happened. When he had done, Sicurano, as minister of the Soldan for the time being, turned to Bernabò and said :—" And thy wife, thus falsely accused, what treatment did she meet with at thy hands ?" "Mortified," said Bernabò, " by the loss of my money, and the dishonour which I deemed to have been done me by my wife, I was so overcome by wrath that I had her put to death by one of my servants, who brought me word that her corpse had been instantly devoured by a pack of wolves."

Albeit the Soldan had heard and understood all that had passed, yet he did not as yet apprehend the object for which Sicurano had pursued the investigation. Wherefore Sicurano thus addressed him :—" My lord, what cause this good lady has to boast of her lover and her husband you have now abundant means of judging ; seeing that the lover at one and the same time despoils her of her honour, blasting her fair fame with slanderous accusations, and ruins her husband ; who, more prompt to trust the falsehood of another than the verity of which his own long experience should have assured him, devotes her to death and the devouring wolves ; and, moreover, such is the regard, such the love which both bear her that, though both tarry a long time with her, neither recognises her. However, that you may know full well what chastisements they have severally deserved, I will now cause her to appear in your presence and theirs, provided you, of your especial grace, be pleased to punish the deceiver and pardon the deceived." The Soldan, being minded in this matter to defer entirely to Sicurano, answered that he was well content, and bade produce the lady. Bernabò, who had firmly believed that she was dead, was lost in wonder ; likewise Ambrogiuolo, who now divined his evil plight, and dreading something worse than the

disbursement of money, knew not whether to expect the lady's advent
with fear or with hope.   His suspense was not of long duration ; for,
as soon as the Soldan signified his assent, Sicurano, weeping, threw
herself on her knees at his feet, and discarding the tones, as she
would fain have divested herself of the outward semblance, of a man,
said :—" My lord, that forlorn, hapless Zinevra am I, falsely and
foully slandered by this traitor Ambrogiuolo, and by my cruel
and unjust husband delivered over to his servant to slaughter and
cast out as a prey to the wolves ; for which cause I have now for
six years been a wanderer on the face of the earth in the guise of
a man."   Then rending her robes in front and baring her breast, she
made it manifest to the Soldan and all others who were present,
that she was indeed a woman ; then turning to Ambrogiuolo she
haughtily challenged him to say when she had ever lain with him,
as he had boasted.   Ambrogiuolo said never a word, for he now
recognised her, and it was as if shame had reft from him the power
of speech.   The Soldan, who had never doubted that Sicurano was
a man, was so wonder-struck by what he saw and heard that at
times he thought it must be all a dream.   But, as wonder gave
place to conviction of the truth, he extolled in the amplest terms the
constancy and virtue and seemliness with which Zinevra, erstwhile
Sicurano, had ordered her life.   He then directed that she should
be most nobly arrayed in the garb of her sex and surrounded by a
bevy of ladies.   Mindful of her intercession, he granted to Bernabò
the life which he had forfeited ; and she, when Bernabò threw
himself at her feet and wept and craved her pardon, raised him,
unworthy though he was, to his feet and generously forgave him,
and tenderly embraced him as her husband.   Ambrogiuolo the
Soldan commanded to be bound to a stake, that his bare flesh,
anointed with honey, might be exposed to the sun on one of the
heights of the city, there to remain until it should fall to pieces
of its own accord : and so 'twas done.   He then decreed that the
lady should have the traitor's estate, which was worth not less but
rather more than ten thousand doubloons ; whereto he added, in
jewels and vessels of gold and silver and in money, the equivalent
of upwards of other ten thousand doubloons, having first entertained
her and her husband with most magnificent and ceremonious cheer,
accordant with the lady's worth.   Which done, he placed a ship at

their disposal, and gave them leave to return to Genoa at their pleasure. So to Genoa they returned very rich and happy, and were received with all honour, especially Madam Zinevra, whom all the citizens had believed to be dead, and whom thenceforth, so long as she lived, they held of great consequence and excellency. As for Ambrogiuolo, the very same day that he was bound to the stake, the honey with which his body was anointed attracted such swarms of flies, wasps and gadflies, wherewith that country abounds, that not only was his life sucked from him but his very bones were completely denuded of flesh; in which state, hanging by the sinews, they remained a long time undisturbed, for a sign and a testimony of his baseness to all that passed by. And so the deceived had the better of the deceiver.

NOVEL X.

*Paganino da Monaco carries off the wife of Messer
Ricciardo di Chinzica, who, having learned where
she is, goes to Paganino and in a friendly manner
asks him to restore her.   He consents, provided she
be willing.   She refuses to go back with her husband.
Messer Ricciardo dies, and she marries Paganino.*

THEIR queen's story, by its beauty, elicited hearty commendation
from all the honourable company, and most especially from Dioneo,
with whom it now rested to conclude the day's narration. Again and
again he renewed his eulogy of the queen's story; and then began
on this wise :—

Fair ladies, there is that in the queen's story which has caused
me to change my purpose, and substitute another story for that
which I had meant to tell : I refer to the insensate folly of
Bernabò (well though it was with him in the end) and of all
others, who delude themselves, as he seemed to do, with the vain
imagination that, while they go about the world, taking their
pleasure now of this, now of the other woman, their wives, left
at home, suffer not their hands to stray from their girdles ; as if
we, who are born of them and bred among them, could be ignorant
of the bent of their desires. Wherefore, by my story I purpose
at one and the same time to shew you how great is the folly of
all such, and how much greater is the folly of those who, deeming
themselves mightier than nature, think by sophistical arguments to
bring that to pass which is beyond their power, and strive might
and main to conform others to their own pattern, however little

the nature of the latter may brook such treatment. Know then that there was in Pisa a judge, better endowed with mental than with physical vigour, by name Messer Ricciardo di Chinzica, who, being minded to take a wife, and thinking, perhaps, to satisfy her by the same resources which served him for his studies, was to be suited with none that had not both youth and beauty, qualities which he would rather have eschewed, if he had known how to give himself as good counsel as he gave to others. However, being very rich, he had his desire. Messer Lotto Gualandi gave him in marriage one of his daughters, Bartolomea by name, a maid as fair and fit for amorous dalliance as any in Pisa, though few maids be there that do not shew as spotted lizards. The judge brought her home with all pomp and ceremony, and had a brave and lordly wedding; but in the essay which he made the very first night to serve her so as to consummate the marriage he made a false move, and drew the game much to his own disadvantage; for next morning his lean, withered and scarce animate frame was only to be re-quickened by draughts of vernaccia,[1] artificial restoratives and the like remedies. So, taking a more sober estimate of his powers than he had been wont, the worthy judge began to give his wife lessons from a calendar, which might have served as a horn-book, and perhaps had been put together at Ravenna:[2] inasmuch as, according to his shewing, there was not a day in the year but was sacred, not to one saint only, but to many; in honour of whom for divers reasons it behoved men and women to abstain from carnal intercourse; whereto he added fast-days, Ember-days, vigils of Apostles and other saints, Friday, Saturday, Sunday, the whole of Lent, certain lunar mansions, and many other exceptions, arguing perchance, that the practice of men with women abed should have its times of vacation no less than the administration of the law. In this method, which caused the lady grievous dumps, he long persisted, hardly touching her once a month, and observing her closely, lest another should give her to know working-days, as he had taught her holidays.

[1] A strong white wine.

[2] The saying went, that owing to the multitude of churches at Ravenna every day was there a saint's day.

Now it so befell that, one hot season, Messer Ricciardo thought
he would like to visit a very beautiful estate which he had near
Monte Nero, there to take the air and recreate himself for some
days, and thither accordingly he went with his fair lady. While
there, to amuse her, he arranged for a day's fishing; and so, he in
one boat with the fishermen, and she in another with other ladies,
they put out to watch the sport, which they found so delightsome,
that almost before they knew where they were they were some miles
out to sea. And while they were thus engrossed with the sport, a
galliot of Paganino da Mare, a very famous corsair of those days,
hove in sight and bore down upon the boats, and, for all the speed
they made, came up with that in which were the ladies; and on
sight of the fair lady Paganino, regardless of all else, bore her off to
his galliot before the very eyes of Messer Ricciardo, who was by this
time ashore, and forthwith was gone. The chagrin of the judge,
who was jealous of the very air, may readily be imagined. But
'twas to no purpose that, both at Pisa and elsewhere, he moaned and
groaned over the wickedness of the corsairs, for he knew neither by
whom his wife had been abducted, nor whither she had been taken.
Paganino, meanwhile, deemed himself lucky to have gotten so
beautiful a prize; and being unmarried, he was minded never to
part with her, and addressed himself by soft words to soothe the
sorrow which kept her in a flood of tears. Finding words of little
avail, he at night passed—the more readily that the calendar had
slipped from his girdle, and all feasts and holidays from his mind—
to acts of love, and on this wise administered consolation so effective
that before they were come to Monaco she had completely forgotten
the judge and his canons, and had begun to live with Paganino as
merrily as might be. So he brought her to Monaco, where, besides
the daily and nightly solace which he gave her, he honourably
entreated her as his wife.

Not long afterwards Messer Ricciardo coming to know where
his wife was, and being most ardently desirous to have her back, and
thinking none but he would understand exactly what to do in the
circumstances, determined to go and fetch her himself, being prepared
to spend any sum of money that might be demanded by way of
ransom. So he took ship, and being come to Monaco, he both saw
her and was seen by her; which news she communicated to

Paganino in the evening, and told him how she was minded to behave. Next morning Messer Ricciardo, encountering Paganino, made up to him; and soon assumed a very familiar and friendly air, while Paganino pretended not to know him, being on his guard to see what he would be at. So Messer Ricciardo, as soon as he deemed the time ripe, as best and most delicately he was able, disclosed to Paganino the business on which he had come, praying him to take whatever in the way of ransom he chose and restore him the lady. Paganino replied cheerily :—" Right glad I am to see you here, Sir ; and briefly thus I answer you :—True it is that I have here a young woman ; whether she be your wife or another man's, I know not, for you are none of my acquaintance, nor is she, except for the short time that she has been with me. If, as you say, you are her husband, why, as you seem to me to be a pleasant gentleman, I will even take you to her, and I doubt not she will know you well ; if she says that it is even as you say, and is minded to go with you, you shall give me just what you like by way of ransom, so pleasant have I found you ; otherwise 'twill be churlish in you to think of taking her from me, who am a young man, and as fit to keep a woman as another, and moreover never knew any woman so agreeable." "My wife," said Ricciardo, "she is beyond all manner of doubt, as thou shalt see ; for so soon as thou bringest me to her, she will throw her arms about my neck ; wherefore as thou art minded, even so be it ; I ask no more." "Go we then," said Paganino ; and forthwith they went into the house, and Paganino sent for the lady while they waited in one of the halls. By and by she entered from one of the adjoining rooms all trim and tricked out, and advanced to the place where Paganino and Messer Ricciardo were standing, but never a word did she vouchsafe to her husband, any more than if he had been some stranger whom Paganino had brought into the house. Whereat the judge was mightily amazed, having expected to be greeted by her with the heartiest of cheer, and began to ruminate thus :— Perhaps I am so changed by the melancholy and prolonged heartache, to which I have been a prey since I lost her, that she does not recognise me. Wherefore he said :—" Madam, cause enough have I to rue it that I took thee a fishing, for never yet was known such grief as has been mine since I lost thee ; and now it seems as if thou dost not recognise me, so scant of courtesy is thy greeting. Seest thou not that I am thy Messer Ricciardo, come hither prepared to pay whatever this gentleman, in whose house we are, may demand, that I may have thee back and take thee away with me : and he is so good as to surrender thee on my own terms?" The lady turned to him with a slight smile, and said :—"Is it to me you speak, Sir? Bethink you that you may have mistaken me for another, for I, for my part, do not remember ever to have seen you." "Nay," said Messer Ricciardo, "but bethink thee what thou sayst; scan me closely; and if thou wilt but search thy memory, thou wilt find that I am thy Ricciardo di Chinzica." "Your pardon, Sir," answered the lady, "'tis not, perhaps, as seemly for me, as you imagine, to gaze long upon you; but I have gazed long enough to know that I never saw you before." Messer Ricciardo supposed that she so spoke for fear of Paganino, in whose presence she durst not acknowledge that she knew him : so, after a while, he craved as a favour of Paganino that he might speak with her in a room alone. Which request Paganino granted, so only that he did not kiss her against her will. He then bade the lady go with Messer Ricciardo into a room apart, and hear what he had to say, and give him such answer as she deemed meet. So the lady and Messer Ricciardo went together into a room alone, and sate down, and Messer Ricciardo began on this wise :—"Ah! dear heart of me, sweet soul of me, hope of me, dost not recognise thy Ricciardo that loves thee better than himself? how comes it thus to pass? am I then so changed? Ah! goodly eye of me, do but look on me a little." Whereat the lady burst into a laugh, and interrupting him, said :—"Rest assured that my memory is not so short but that I know you for what you are, my husband, Messer Ricciardo di Chinzica; but far enough you shewed yourself to be, while I was with you, from knowing me for what I was, young, lusty, lively; which, had you been the wise man you would fain be reputed, you would not have ignored, nor by consequence that which, besides food and clothing, it behoves men to give young ladies, albeit for shame they demand it not; which in what sort you gave, you know. You should not have taken a wife if she was to be less to you than the study of the law, albeit 'twas never as a judge that I regarded you, but rather as a bellman of encænia and saints' days, so well you knew them all, and fasts and vigils. And I tell you that, had you imposed the observance of as many saints' days on the labourers that till your lands as on yourself who had but my little plot to till, you would never have harvested a single grain of corn. God in His mercy, having regard unto my youth, has caused me to fall in with this gentleman, with whom I am much closeted in this room, where nought is known of feasts, such feasts, I mean, as you, more devoted to the service of God than to the service of ladies, were wont to observe in such profusion; nor was this threshold ever crossed by Saturday or Friday or vigil or Ember-days or Lent, that is so long; rather here we are at work day and night, threshing the wool, and well I know how featly it went when the matin bell last sounded. Wherefore with him I mean to stay, and to work while I am young, and postpone the observance of feasts and times of indulgence and fasts until I am old: so get you hence, and good luck go with you, but depart with what speed you may, and observe as many feasts as you like, so I be not with you."

The pain with which Messer Ricciardo followed this outburst was more than he could bear, and when she had done, he exclaimed:—"Ah! sweet soul of me, what words are these that thou utterest? Hast thou no care for thy parents' honour and thine own? Wilt thou remain here to be this man's harlot, and to live in mortal sin, rather than live with me at Pisa as my wife? Why, when he is tired of thee, he will cast thee out to thy most grievous dishonour. I will ever cherish thee, and ever, will I nill I, thou wilt be the mistress of my house. Wouldst thou, to gratify this unbridled and unseemly passion, part at once with thy honour and with me, who love thee more dearly than my very life? Ah! cherished hope of me, say not so again: make up thy mind to come with me. As I now know thy bent, I will henceforth constrain myself to pleasure thee: wherefore, sweet my treasure, think better of it, and come with me, who have never known a happy hour since thou wert reft from me." The lady answered:—"I expect not, nor is it possible, that another should be more tender of my honour than I am myself. Were my parents so, when they gave me to you? I trow not; nor mean I to be more tender of their honour now than they were then of mine. And if now I live in mortar sin, I will ever abide there until it be pestle sin:[1] concern yourself no further

---

[1] A poor jeu de mots, mortaio, mortar, being substituted for mortale.

on my account. Moreover, let me tell you, that, whereas at Pisa
'twas as if I were your harlot, seeing that the planets in conjunction
according to lunar mansion and geometric square intervened between
you and me, here with Paganino I deem myself a wife, for he holds
me in his arms all night long and hugs and bites me, and how he
serves me, God be my witness. Ah! but you say you will constrain
yourself to serve me : to what end ? to do it on the third essay,
and raise it by stroke of bâton ? I doubt not you are become a
perfect knight since last I saw you. Begone, and constrain yourself
to live ; for here, methinks, your tenure is but precarious, so hectic
and wasted is your appearance. Nay more ; I tell you this, that,
should Paganino desert me (which he does not seem disposed to do
so long as I am willing to stay with him), never will I return to
your house, where for one while I staid to my most grievous loss
and prejudice, but will seek my commodity elsewhere, than with
one from whose whole body I could not wring a single cupful of sap.
So, again, I tell you that here is neither feast nor vigil ; wherefore
here I mean to abide ; and you, get you gone, in God's name with
what speed you may, lest I raise the cry that you threaten to
violate me."

Messer Ricciardo felt himself hard bested, but he could not but
recognise that, worn out as he was, he had been foolish to take a
young wife ; so sad and woebegone he quitted the room, and, after
expending on Paganino a wealth of words which signified nothing,
he at last gave up his bootless enterprise, and leaving the lady to her
own devices, returned to Pisa ; where for very grief he lapsed into
such utter imbecility that, when he was met by any with greeting or
question in the street, he made no other answer than "the evil hole
brooks no holiday," and soon afterwards died. Which when Paganino
learned, being well assured of the love the lady bore him, he made
her his lawful wife ; and so, keeping neither feast nor vigil nor Lent,
they worked as hard as their legs permitted, and had a good time.
Wherefore, dear my ladies, I am of opinion that Messer Bernabò in
his altercation with Ambrogiuolo rode the goat downhill.[1]

This story provoked so much laughter that the jaws of every one
in the company ached ; and all the ladies by common consent

[1] *I. e.* argued preposterously, the goat being the last animal to carry a
rider comfortably downhill.

acknowledged that Dioneo was right, and pronounced Bernabò a blockhead. But when the story was ended and the laughter had subsided, the queen, observing that the hour was now late, and that with the completion of the day's story-telling the end of her sovereignty was come, followed the example of her predecessor, and took off her wreath and set it on Neifile's brow, saying with gladsome mien, "Now, dear gossip, thine be the sovereignty of this little people ; " and so she resumed her seat. Neifile coloured somewhat to receive such honour, shewing of aspect even as the fresh-blown rose of April or May in the radiance of the dawn, her eyes rather downcast, and glowing with love's fire like the morning-star. But when the respectful murmur, by which the rest of the company gave blithe token of the favour in which they held their queen, was hushed, and her courage revived, she raised herself somewhat more in her seat than she was wont, and thus spoke :—"As so it is that I am your queen, I purpose not to depart from the usage observed by my predecessors, whose rule has commanded not only your obedience but your approbation. I will therefore in few words explain to you the course which, if it commend itself to your wisdom, we will follow. To-morrow, you know, is Friday, and the next day Saturday, days which most folk find somewhat wearisome by reason of the viands which are then customary, to say nothing of the reverence in which Friday is meet to be held, seeing that 'twas on that day that He who died for us bore His passion ; wherefore 'twould be in my judgment both right and very seemly, if, in honour of God, we then bade story-telling give place to prayer. On Saturday ladies are wont to wash the head, and rid their persons of whatever of dust or other soilure they may have gathered by the labours of the past week ; not a few, likewise, are wont to practise abstinence for devotion to the Virgin Mother of the Son of God, and to honour the approaching Sunday by an entire surcease from work. Wherefore, as we cannot then completely carry out our plan of life, we shall, I think, do well to intermit our story-telling on that day also. We shall then have been here four days ; and lest we should be surprised by new-comers, I deem it expedient that we shift our quarters, and I have already taken thought for our next place of sojourn. Where, being arrived on Sunday, we will assemble after our sleep ; and, whereas to-day our discourse has had an ample

172 DECAMERON. [SECOND DAY.

field to range in, I propose, both because you will thereby have more time for thought, and it will be best to set some limits to the license of our story-telling, that of the many diversities of Fortune's handi-work we make one our theme, whereof I have also made choice, to wit, the luck of such as have painfully acquired some much-coveted thing, or having lost, have recovered it. Whereon let each meditate some matter, which to tell may be profitable or at least delectable to the company, saving always Dioneo's privilege."

All applauded the queen's speech and plan, to which, therefore, it was decided to give effect. Thereupon the queen called her seneschal, told him where to place the tables that evening, and then explained to him all that he had to do during the time of her sovereignty. This done, she rose with her train, and gave leave to all to take their pleasure as to each might seem best. So the ladies and the men hied them away to a little garden, where they diverted themselves a while; then supper-time being come, they supped with all gay and festal cheer. When they were risen from the table, Emilia, at the queen's command, led the dance, while Pampinea, the other ladies responding, sang the ensuing song.

> Shall any lady sing, if I not sing,
>   I to whom Love did full contentment bring?
>
> Come hither, Love, thou cause of all my joy,
>   Of all my hope, and all its sequel blest,
>   And with me tune the lay,
>   No more to sighs and bitter past annoy,
>   That now but serve to lend thy bliss more zest;
>   But to that fire's clear ray,
>   Wherewith enwrapt I blithely live and gay,
>   Thee as my God for ever worshipping.
>
> 'Twas thou, O Love, didst set before mine eyes,
>   When first thy fire my soul did penetrate,
>   A youth to be my fere,
>   So fair, so fit for deeds of high emprise,
>   That ne'er another shall be found more great,
>   Nay, nor, I ween, his peer:
>   Such flame he kindled that my heart's full cheer
>   I now pour out in chant with thee, my King.

And that wherein I most delight is this,
That as I love him, so he loveth me:
So thank thee, Love, I must.
For whatsoe'er this world can yield of bliss
Is mine, and in the next at peace to be
I hope through that full trust
I place in him.   And thou, O God, that dost
It see, wilt grant of joy thy plenishing.

Some other songs and dances followed, to the accompaniment of divers sorts of music; after which, the queen deeming it time to go to rest, all, following in the wake of the torches, sought their several chambers. The next two days they devoted to the duties to which the queen had adverted, looking forward to the Sunday with eager expectancy.

Endeth here the second day of the Decameron, beginneth the third, in which, under the rule of Neifile, discourse is had of the fortune of such as have painfully acquired some much-coveted thing, or, having lost, have recovered it.

THE dawn of Sunday was already changing from vermilion to orange, as the sun hasted to the horizon, when the queen rose and roused all the company. The seneschal had early sent forward to their next place of sojourn ample store of things meet with folk to make all things ready, and now seeing the queen on the road, and the decampment, as it were, begun, he hastily completed the equipment of the baggage-train, and set off therewith, attended by the rest of the servants, in rear of the ladies and gentlemen. So, to the chant of, perhaps, a score of nightingales and other birds, the queen, her ladies and the three young men trooping beside or after her, paced leisurely westward by a path little frequented and overgrown with herbage and flowers, which, as they caught the sunlight, began one and all to unfold their petals. So fared she on with her train, while the quirk and the jest and the laugh passed from mouth to mouth ; nor had they completed more than two thousand paces when, well before half tierce,[1] they arrived at a palace most fair and sumptuous, which stood out somewhat from the plain, being situate upon a low eminence. On entering, they first traversed its great halls and dainty chambers furnished throughout with all brave and meet appointments ; and finding all most commendable, they reputed its lord a magnifico. Then descending, they surveyed its spacious and cheerful court, its vaults of excellent wines and copious springs of most cool water, and found it still more commendable. After which, being fain of rest, they sat them down in a gallery

[1] *I. e.* midway between prime and tierce, about 7.30 a.m.

which commanded the court, and was close imbosked with leafage
and such flowers as the season afforded, and thither the discreet
seneschal brought comfits and wines most choice and excellent,
wherewith they were refreshed. Whereupon they hied them to a
walled garden adjoining the palace; which, the gate being opened,
they entered, and wonder-struck by the beauty of the whole passed
on to examine more attentively the several parts. It was bordered
and traversed in many parts by alleys, each very wide and straight as
an arrow and roofed in with trellis of vines, which gave good promise
of bearing clusters that year, and, being all in flower, dispersed such
fragrance throughout the garden as blended with that exhaled by
many another plant that grew therein made the garden seem
redolent of all the spices that ever grew in the East. The sides of
the alleys were all, as it were, walled in with roses white and red
and jasmine; insomuch that there was no part of the garden but one
might walk there not merely in the morning but at high noon in
grateful shade and fragrance, completely screened from the sun. As
for the plants that were in the garden, 'twere long to enumerate
them, to specify their sorts, to describe the order of their arrangement;
enough, in brief, that there was abundance of every rarer species that
our climate allows. In the middle of the garden, a thing not less
but much more to be commended than aught else, was a lawn of
the finest turf, and so green that it seemed almost black, pranked with
flowers of, perhaps, a thousand sorts, and girt about with the richest
living verdure of orange-trees and cedars, which shewed not only
flowers but fruits both new and old, and were no less grateful to the
smell by their fragrance than to the eye by their shade. In the
middle of the lawn was a basin of whitest marble, graven with
marvellous art; in the centre whereof—whether the spring were
natural or artificial I know not—rose a column supporting a figure
which sent forth a jet of water of such volume and to such an
altitude that it fell, not without a delicious plash, into the basin in
quantity amply sufficient to turn a mill-wheel. The overflow was
carried away from the lawn by a hidden conduit, and then, re-
emerging, was distributed through tiny channels, very fair and
cunningly contrived, in such sort as to flow round the entire lawn,
and by similar derivative channels to penetrate almost every part of
the fair garden, until, re-uniting at a certain point, it issued thence,

and, clear as crystal, slid down towards the plain, turning by the way two mill-wheels with extreme velocity to the no small profit of the lord. The aspect of this garden, its fair order, the plants and the fountain and the rivulets that flowed from it, so charmed the ladies and the three young men that with one accord they affirmed that they knew not how it could receive any accession of beauty, or what other form could be given to Paradise, if it were to be planted on earth. So, excellently well pleased, they roved about it, plucking sprays from the trees, and weaving them into the fairest of garlands, while songsters of, perhaps, a score of different sorts warbled as if in mutual emulation, when suddenly a sight as fair and delightsome as novel, which, engrossed by the other beauties of the place, they had hitherto overlooked, met their eyes. For the garden, they now saw, was peopled with a host of living creatures, fair and of, perhaps, a hundred sorts; and they pointed out to one another how here emerged a cony, or there scampered a hare, or couched a goat, or grazed a fawn, or many another harmless, all but domesticated, creature roved carelessly seeking his pleasure at his own sweet will. All which served immensely to reinforce their already abundant delight. At length, however, they had enough of wandering about the garden and observing this thing and that : wherefore they repaired to the beautiful fountain, around which were ranged the tables, and there, after they had sung half-a-dozen songs and trod some measures, they sat them down, at the queen's command, to breakfast, which was served with all celerity and in fair and orderly manner, the viands being both good and delicate; whereby their spirits rose, and up they got, and betook themselves again to music and song and dance, and so sped the hours, until, as the heat increased, the queen deemed it time that whoso was so minded should go to sleep. Some there were that did so; others were too charmed by the beauty of the place to think of leaving it; but tarried there, and, while the rest slept, amused themselves with reading romances or playing at chess or dice. However, after none, there was a general *levée*; and, with faces laved and refreshed with cold water, they gathered by the queen's command upon the lawn, and, having sat them down in their wonted order by the fountain, waited for the story-telling to begin upon the theme assigned by the queen. With this duty the queen first charged Filostrato, who began on this wise.

NOVEL I.

*Masetto da Lamporecchio feigns to be dumb, and obtains
a gardener's place at a convent of women, who with
one accord make haste to lie with him.*

FAIREST ladies, not a few there are both of men and of women,
who are so foolish as blindly to believe that, so soon as a young
woman has been veiled in white and cowled in black, she ceases to
be a woman, and is no more subject to the cravings proper to her
sex, than if, in assuming the garb and profession of a nun, she had
put on the nature of a stone : and if, perchance, they hear of aught
that is counter to this their faith, they are no less vehement in their
censure than if some most heinous and unnatural crime had been
committed ; neither bethinking them of themselves, whom unrestricted liberty avails not to satisfy, nor making due allowance for
the prepotent forces of idleness and solitude. And likewise not a
few there are that blindly believe that, what with the hoe and the
spade and coarse fare and hardship, the carnal propensities are utterly
eradicated from the tillers of the soil, and therewith all nimbleness of
wit and understanding. But how gross is the error of such as so
suppose, I, on whom the queen has laid her commands, am minded,
without deviating from the theme prescribed by her, to make manifest
to you by a little story.

In this very country-side of ours there was and yet is a convent of
women of great repute for sanctity—name it I will not, lest I should
in some measure diminish its repute—the nuns being at the time of
which I speak but nine in number, including the abbess, and all
young women. Their very beautiful garden was in charge of a
foolish fellow, who, not being content with his wage, squared

accounts with their steward, and hied him back to Lamporecchio, whence he came.   Among others who welcomed him home was a young husbandman, Masetto by name, a stout and hardy fellow, and handsome for a contadino, who asked him where he had been so long.   Nuto, as our good friend was called, told him.   Masetto then asked how he had been employed at the convent, and Nuto answered :—"I kept their large and beautiful garden in good trim, and, besides, I sometimes went to the wood to fetch the faggots, I drew water, and did some other trifling services ; but the ladies gave so little wage that it scarce kept me in shoes.   And moreover they are all young, and, I think, they are one and all possessed of the devil, for 'tis impossible to do anything to their mind ; indeed, when I would be at work in the kitchen-garden, 'put this here,' would say one, 'put that here,' would say another, and a third would snatch the hoe from my hand, and say, 'that is not as it should be' ; and so they would worry me until I would give up working and go out of the garden ; so that, what with this thing and that, I was minded to stay there no more, and so I am come hither.   The steward asked me before I left to send him any one whom on my return I might find fit for the work, and I promised ; but God bless his loins, I shall be at no pains to find out and send him any one."

As Nuto thus ran on, Masetto was seized by such a desire to be with these nuns that he quite pined, as he gathered from what Nuto said that his desire might be gratified.   And as that could not be, if he said nothing to Nuto, he remarked :—"Ah ! 'twas well done of thee to come hither.   A man to live with women ! he might as well live with so many devils : six times out of seven they know not themselves what they want."   There the conversation ended ; but Masetto began to cast about how he should proceed to get permission to live with them.   He knew that he was quite competent for the services of which Nuto spoke, and had therefore no fear of failing on that score ; but he doubted he should not be received, because he was too young and well-favoured.   So, after much pondering, he fell into the following train of thought :—The place is a long way off, and no one there knows me ; if I make believe that I am dumb, doubtless I shall be admitted.   Whereupon he made his mind up, laid a hatchet across his shoulder, and saying not a word to any of his destination, set forth, intending to present himself at the convent

in the character of a destitute man.   Arrived there, he had no
sooner entered than he chanced to encounter the steward in the
courtyard, and making signs to him as dumb folk do, he let him
know that of his charity he craved something to eat, and that, if
need were, he would split firewood.   The steward promptly gave
him to eat, and then set before him some logs which Nuto had not
been able to split, all which Masetto, who was very strong, split
in a very short time.   The steward, having occasion to go to the
wood, took him with him, and there set him at work on the lopping;
which done he placed the ass in front of him, and by signs made him
understand that he was to take the loppings back to the convent.
This he did so well that the steward kept him for some days to do
one or two odd jobs.   Whereby it so befell that one day the abbess
saw him, and asked the steward who he was.   " Madam," replied
the steward, " 'tis a poor deaf mute that came here a day or two
ago craving alms, so I have treated him kindly, and have let him
make himself useful in many ways.   If he knew how to do the work
of the kitchen-garden and would stay with us, I doubt not we should
be well served; for we have need of him, and he is strong, and would
be able for whatever he might turn his hand to; besides which you
would have no cause to be apprehensive lest he should be cracking
his jokes with your young women."   " As I trust in God," said the
abbess, " thou sayst sooth; find out if he can do the garden work,
and if he can, do all thou canst to keep him with us; give him a
pair of shoes, an old hood, and speak him well, make much of him,
and let him be well fed."   All which the steward promised to do.

Masetto, meanwhile, was close at hand, making as if he were
sweeping the courtyard, and heard all that passed between the abbess
and the steward, whereat he gleefully communed with himself on
this wise :—Put me once within there, and you will see that I will
do the work of the kitchen-garden as it never was done before.   So
the steward set him to work in the kitchen-garden, and finding that
he knew his business excellently well, made signs to him to know
whether he would stay, and he made answer by signs that he was
ready to do whatever the steward wished.   The steward then signified
that he was engaged, told him to take charge of the kitchen-garden,
and shewed him what he had to do there.   Then, having other
matters to attend to, he went away, and left him there.   Now, as

Masetto worked there day by day, the nuns began to tease him, and make him their butt (as it commonly happens that folk serve the dumb) and used bad language to him, the worst they could think of, supposing that he could not understand them: all which passed scarce heeded by the abbess, who perhaps deemed him as destitute of virility as of speech. Now it so befell that after a hard day's work he was taking a little rest, when two young nuns, who were walking in the garden, approached the spot where he lay, and stopped to look at him, while he pretended to be asleep. And so the bolder of the two said to the other :—" If I thought thou wouldst keep the secret, I would tell thee what I have sometimes meditated, and which thou perhaps mightest also find agreeable." The other replied :— " Speak thy mind freely and be sure that I will never tell a soul." Whereupon the bold one began :—" I know not if thou hast ever considered how close we are kept here, and that within these pre- cincts dare never enter any man, unless it be the old steward or this mute : and I have often heard from ladies that have come hither, that all the other sweets that the world has to offer signify not a jot in comparison of the pleasure that a woman has in connexion with a man. Whereof I have more than once been minded to make experiment with this mute, no other man being available. Nor, indeed, could one find any man in the whole world so meet therefor; seeing that he could not blab if he would; thou seest that he is but a dull clownish lad, whose size has increased out of all proportion to his sense; wherefore I would fain hear what thou hast to say to it." " Alas !" said the other, " what is 't thou sayst ? Knowest thou not that we have vowed our virginity to God ?" " Oh," rejoined the first, " think but how many vows are made to Him all day long, and never a one performed : and so, for our vow, let Him find another or others to perform it." " But," said her com- panion, " suppose that we conceived, how then ?" " Nay but," protested the first, " thou goest about to imagine evil before it befalls thee : time enough to think of that when it comes to pass; there will be a thousand ways to prevent its ever being known, so only we do not publish it ourselves." Thus reassured, the other was now the more eager of the two to test the quality of the male human animal. " Well then," she said, " how shall we go about it ?" and was answered :—" Thou seest 'tis past none ; I make no doubt but

all the sisters are asleep, except ourselves; search we through the
kitchen-garden, to see if there be any there, and if there be none,
we have but to take him by the hand and lead him hither to the
hut where he takes shelter from the rain; and then one shall
mount guard while the other has him with her inside. He is such
a simpleton that he will do just whatever we bid him." No word
of this conversation escaped Masetto, who, being disposed to obey,
hoped for nothing so much as that one of them should take him
by the hand. They, meanwhile, looked carefully all about them,
and satisfied themselves that they were secure from observation:
then she that had broached the subject came close up to Masetto,
and shook him; whereupon he started to his feet. So she took
him by the hand with a blandishing air, to which he replied with
some clownish grins. And then she led him into the hut, where
he needed no pressing to do what she desired of him. Which done,
she changed places with the other, as loyal comradeship required;
and Masetto, still keeping up the pretence of simplicity, did their
pleasure. Wherefore before they left, each must needs make another
assay of the mute's powers of riding; and afterwards, talking the
matter over many times, they agreed that it was in truth not less
but even more delightful than they had been given to understand;
and so, as they found convenient opportunity, they continued to go
and disport themselves with the mute.

Now it so chanced that one of their gossips, looking out of the
window of her cell, saw what they did, and imparted it to two
others. The three held counsel together whether they should not
denounce the offenders to the abbess, but soon changed their mind,
and came to an understanding with them, whereby they became
partners in Masetto. And in course of time by divers chances the
remaining three nuns also entered the partnership. Last of all the
abbess, still witting nought of these doings, happened one very hot
day, as she walked by herself through the garden, to find Masetto,
who now rode so much by night that he could stand very little
fatigue by day, stretched at full length asleep under the shade of
an almond-tree, his person quite exposed in front by reason that the
wind had disarranged his clothes. Which the lady observing, and
knowing that she was alone, fell a prey to the same appetite to
which her nuns had yielded: she aroused Masetto, and took him

with her to her chamber, where, for some days, though the nuns
loudly complained that the gardener no longer came to work in the
kitchen-garden, she kept him, tasting and re-tasting the sweetness
of that indulgence which she was wont to be the first to censure
in others.   And when at last she had sent him back from her
chamber to his room, she must needs send for him again and again,
and made such exorbitant demands upon him, that Masetto, not being
able to satisfy so many women, bethought him that his part of mute,
should he persist in it, might entail disastrous consequences.   So one
night, when he was with the abbess, he cut the tongue-string, and
thus broke silence :—" Madam, I have understood that a cock may
very well serve ten hens, but that ten men are sorely tasked to satisfy
a single woman ; and here am I expected to serve nine, a burden
quite beyond my power to bear ; nay, by what I have already undergone I am now so reduced that my strength is quite spent ; wherefore either bid me Godspeed, or find some means to make matters
tolerable."   Wonder-struck to hear the supposed mute thus speak, the
lady exclaimed :—" What means this ?   I took thee to be dumb."
" And in sooth, Madam, so was I," said Masetto, " not indeed from
my birth, but through an illness which took from me the power
of speech, which only this very night have I recovered ; and so I
praise God with all my heart."   The lady believed him ; and asked
him what he meant by saying that he had nine to serve.   Masetto
told her how things stood ; whereby she perceived that of all her
nuns there was not any but was much wiser than she ; and lest,
if Masetto were sent away, he should give the convent a bad name,
she discreetly determined to arrange matters with the nuns in such
sort that he might remain there.   So, the steward having died
within the last few days, she assembled all the nuns ; and their and
her own past errors being fully avowed, they by common consent,
and with Masetto's concurrence, resolved that the neighbours should
be given to understand that by their prayers and the merits of their
patron saint, Masetto, long mute, had recovered the power of speech ;
after which they made him steward, and so ordered matters among
themselves that he was able to endure the burden of their service.   In
the course of which, though he procreated not a few little monastics,
yet 'twas all managed so discreetly that no breath of scandal stirred,
until after the abbess's death, by which time Masetto was advanced

in years and minded to return home with the wealth that he had
gotten; which he was suffered to do as soon as he made his desire
known.   And so Masetto, who had left Lamporecchio with a
hatchet on his shoulder, returned thither in his old age rich and
a father, having by the wisdom with which he employed his youth,
spared himself the pains and expense of rearing children, and
averring that such was the measure that Christ meted out to the
man that set horns on his cap.

NOVEL II.

A groom lies with the wife of King Agilulf, who learns the fact, keeps his own counsel, finds out the groom and shears him. The shorn shears all his fellows, and so comes safe out of the scrape.

FILOSTRATO's story, which the ladies had received now with blushes now with laughter, being ended, the queen bade Pampinea follow suit. Which behest Pampinea smilingly obeyed, and thus began :—

Some there are whose indiscretion is such that they must needs evince that they are fully cognizant of that which it were best they should not know, and censuring the covert misdeeds of others, augment beyond measure the disgrace which they would fain diminish. The truth whereof, fair ladies, I mean to shew you in the contrary case, wherein appears the astuteness of one that held, perhaps, an even lower place than would have been Masetto's in the esteem of a doughty king.

Agilulf, King of the Lombards, who like his predecessors made the city of Pavia in Lombardy the seat of his government, took to wife Theodelinde, the widow of Authari, likewise King of the Lombards, a lady very fair, wise and virtuous, but who was unfortunate in her lover. For while the Lombards prospered in peace under the wise and firm rule of King Agilulf, it so befell that one of the Queen's grooms, a man born to very low estate, but in native worth far above his mean office, and moreover not a whit less tall and goodly of person than the King, became inordinately enamoured of her. And as, for all his base condition, ne had sense enough to recognize that his love was in the last

184

degree presumptuous, he disclosed it to none, nay, he did not even venture to tell her the tale by the mute eloquence of his eyes. And albeit he lived without hope that he should ever be able to win her favour, yet he inwardly gloried that he had fixed his affections in so high a place; and being all aflame with passion, he shewed himself zealous beyond any of his comrades to do whatever he thought was likely to please the Queen. Whereby it came about, that, when the Queen had to take horse, she would mount the palfrey that he groomed rather than any other; and when she did so, he deemed himself most highly favoured, and never quitted her stirrup, esteeming himself happy if he might but touch her clothes. But as 'tis frequently observed that love waxes as hope wanes, so was it with this poor groom, insomuch that the burden of this great hidden passion, alleviated by no hope, was most grievous to bear, and from time to time, not being able to shake it off, he purposed to die. And meditating on the mode, he was minded that it should be of a kind to make it manifest that he died for the love which he had borne and bore to the Queen, and also to afford him an opportunity of trying his fortune whether his desire might in whole or in part be gratified. He had no thought of speaking to the Queen, nor yet of declaring his love to her by letter, for he knew that 'twould be vain either to speak or to write; but he resolved to try to devise some means whereby he might lie with the Queen; which end might in no other way be compassed than by contriving to get access to her in her bedroom; which could only be by passing himself off as the King, who, as he knew, did not always lie with her. Wherefore, that he might observe the carriage and dress of the King as he passed to her room, he contrived to conceal himself for several nights in a great hall of the King's palace which separated the King's room from that of the Queen: and on one of these nights he saw the King issue from his room, wrapped in a great mantle, with a lighted torch in one hand and a wand in the other, and cross the hall, and, saying nothing, tap the door of the Queen's room with the wand once or twice; whereupon the door was at once opened and the torch taken from his hand. Having observed the King thus go and return, and being bent on doing likewise, he found means to come by a mantle like that which he had seen the King wear, and also a torch and a wand: he then took a warm bath, and having thoroughly cleansed himself, that the smell of the foul straw might not offend the lady, or discover to her the deceit, he in this guise concealed himself as he was wont in the great hall. He waited only until all were asleep, and then, deeming the time come to accomplish his purpose, or by his presumption clear a way to the death which he coveted, he struck a light with the flint and steel which he had brought with him; and having kindled his torch and wrapped himself close in his mantle, he went to the door of the Queen's room, and tapped on it twice with his wand. The door was opened by a very drowsy chambermaid, who took the torch and put it out of sight; whereupon without a word he passed within the curtain, laid aside the mantle, and got into the bed where the Queen lay asleep. Then, taking her in his arms and straining her to him with ardour, making as if he were moody, because he knew that, when the King was in such a frame, he would never hear aught, in such wise, without word said either on his part or on hers, he had more than once carnal cognizance of the Queen. Loath indeed was he to leave her, but, fearing lest by too long tarrying his achieved delight might be converted into woe, he rose, resumed the mantle and the light, and leaving the room without a word, returned with all speed to his bed. He was hardly there when the King got up and entered the Queen's room; whereat she wondered not a little; but, reassured by the gladsome greeting which he gave her as he got into bed, she said :—" My lord, what a surprise is this to-night ! 'Twas but now you left me after an unwonted measure of enjoyment, and do you now return so soon ? consider what you do." From these words the King at once inferred that the Queen had been deceived by some one that had counterfeited his person and carriage; but, at the same time, bethinking himself that, as neither the Queen nor any other had detected the cheat, 'twas best to leave her in ignorance, he wisely kept silence. Which many a fool would not have done, but would have said :—" Nay, 'twas not I that was here. Who was it that was here ? How came it to pass? Who came hither ?" Whereby in the sequel he might have caused the lady needless chagrin, and given her occasion to desire another such experience as she had had; and so have brought disgrace upon himself by uttering that, from which,

unuttered, no shame could have resulted.   Wherefore, betraying
little, either by his mien or by his words, of the disquietude which
he felt, the King replied:—"Madam, seem I such to you that you
cannot suppose that I should have been with you once, and returned
to you immediately afterwards?"   "Nay, not so, my lord," returned
the lady, " but none the less I pray you to look to your health."
Then said the King:—" And I am minded to take your advice;
wherefore, without giving you further trouble I will leave you."
So, angered and incensed beyond measure by the trick which, he
saw, had been played upon him, he resumed his mantle and quitted
the room with the intention of privily detecting the offender,
deeming that he must belong to the palace, and that, whoever he
might be, he could not have quitted it.   So, taking with him a
small lantern which shewed only a glimmer of light, he went into
the dormitory which was over the palace-stables and was of great
length, insomuch that well-nigh all the men-servants slept there
in divers beds, and arguing that, by whomsoever that of which the
Queen spoke was done, his heart and pulse could not after such
a strain as yet have ceased to throb, he began cautiously with one
of the head-grooms, and so went from bed to bed feeling at the
heart of each man to see if it was thumping.   All were asleep,
save only he that had been with the Queen, who, seeing the King
come, and guessing what he sought to discover, began to be mightily
afraid, insomuch that to the agitation which his late exertion had
communicated to his heart, terror now added one yet more violent;
nor did he doubt that, should the King perceive it, he would kill
him.   Divers alternatives of action thronged his mind; but at last,
observing that the King was unarmed, he resolved to make as if
he were asleep, and wait to see what the King would do.   So,
having tried many and found none that he deemed the culprit, the
King came at last to the culprit himself, and marking the thumping
of his heart, said to himself:—This is he.   But being minded to afford
no clue to his ulterior purpose, he did no more than with a pair of
scissors which he had brought with him shear away on one side
of the man's head a portion of his locks, which, as was then the
fashion, he wore very long, that by this token he might recognize
him on the morrow; and having so done, he departed and returned
to his room.   The groom, who was fully sensible of what the King

had done, and being a shrewd fellow understood very well to what
end he was so marked, got up without a moment's delay; and,
having found a pair of scissors—for, as it chanced, there were several
pairs there belonging to the stables for use in grooming the horses—
he went quietly through the dormitory and in like manner sheared
the locks of each of the sleepers just above the ear; which done
without disturbing any, he went back to bed.

On the morrow, as soon as the King was risen, and before the
gates of the palace were opened, he summoned all his men-servants to
his presence, and, as they stood bareheaded before him, scanned them
closely to see whether the one whom he had sheared was there ; and
observing with surprise that the more part of them were all sheared
in the same manner, said to himself :—Of a surety this fellow, whom
I go about to detect, evinces, for all his base condition, a high degree
of sense.   Then, recognising that he could not compass his end
without causing a bruit, and not being minded to brave so great a
dishonour in order to be avenged upon so petty an offender, he was
content by a single word of admonition to shew him that his offence
had not escaped notice.   Wherefore turning to them all, he said :—
" He that did it, let him do it no more, and get you hence in God's
peace." Another would have put them to the strappado, the question,
the torture, and thereby have brought to light that which one should
rather be sedulous to cloak ; and having so brought it to light, would,
however complete the retribution which he exacted, have not
lessened but vastly augmented his disgrace, and sullied the fair fame
of his lady.   Those who heard the King's parting admonition
wondered, and made much question with one another, what the
King might have meant to convey by it ; but 'twas understood by
none but him to whom it referred : who was discreet enough never to
reveal the secret as long as the King lived, or again to stake his life
on such a venture.

NOVEL III.

Under cloak of confession and a most spotless conscience, a lady, enamoured of a young man, induces a booby friar unwittingly to provide a means to the entire gratification of her passion.

WHEN Pampinea had done, and several of the company had commended the hardihood and wariness of the groom, as also the wisdom of the King, the queen, turning to Filomena, bade her follow suit : wherefore with manner debonair Filomena thus began :—

The story which I shall tell you is of a trick which was actually played by a fair lady upon a booby religious, and which every layman should find the more diverting that these religious, being, for the most part, great blockheads and men of odd manners and habits, do nevertheless credit themselves with more ability and knowledge in all kinds than fall to the lot of the rest of the world ; whereas, in truth, they are far inferior, and so, not being able, like others, to provide their own sustenance, are prompted by sheer baseness to fly thither for refuge where they may find provender, like pigs. Which story, sweet my ladies, I shall tell you, not merely that thereby I may continue the sequence in obedience to the queen's behest, but also to the end that I may let you see that even the religious, in whom we in our boundless credulity repose exorbitant faith, may be, and sometimes are, made—not to say by men—even by some of us women the sport of their sly wit.

In our city, where wiles do more abound than either love or faith, there dwelt, not many years ago, a gentlewoman richly endowed (none more so) by nature with physical charms, as also with gracious manners, high spirit and fine discernment. Her name

I know, but will not disclose it, nor yet that of any other who figures in this story, because there yet live those who might take offence thereat, though after all it might well be passed off with a laugh.   High-born and married to an artificer of woollen fabrics, she could not rid her mind of the disdain with which, by reason of his occupation, she regarded her husband ; for no man, however wealthy, so he were of low condition, seemed to her worthy to have a gentle-woman to wife ; and seeing that for all his wealth he was fit for nothing better than to devise a blend, set up a warp, or higgle about yarn with a spinster, she determined to dispense with his embraces, save so far as she might find it impossible to refuse them ; and to find her satisfaction elsewhere with one that seemed to her more meet to afford it than her artificer of woollens.   In this frame of mind she became enamoured of a man well worthy of her love and not yet past middle age, insomuch that, if she saw him not in the day, she must needs pass an unquiet night.   The gallant, meanwhile, remained fancy-free, for he knew nought of the lady's case ; and she, being apprehensive of possible perils to ensue, was far too circumspect to make it known to him either by writing or by word of mouth of any of her female friends.   Then she learned that he had much to do with a religious, a simple, clownish fellow, but nevertheless, as being a man of most holy life, reputed by almost everybody a most worthy friar, and decided that she could not find a better inter-mediary between herself and her lover than this same friar.   So, having matured her plan, she hied her at a convenient time to the convent where the friar abode, and sent for him, saying, that, if he so pleased, she would be confessed by him.   The friar, who saw at a glance that she was a gentlewoman, gladly heard her confession ; which done, she said :—" My father, I have yet a matter to confide to you, in which I must crave your aid and counsel.   Who my kinsfolk and husband are, I wot you know, for I have myself told you.   My husband loves me more dearly than his life, and being very wealthy, he can well and does forthwith afford me whatever I desire.   Wherefore, as he loves me, even so I love him more dearly than myself; nor was there ever yet wicked woman that deserved the fire so richly as should I, were I guilty—I speak not of acts, but of so much as a single thought of crossing his will or tarnishing his honour.   Now a man there is—his name, indeed, I know not, but he seems to me to be a gentleman, and, if I mistake not, he is much with you—a fine man and tall, his garb dun and very decent, who, the bent of my mind being, belike, quite unknown to him, would seem to have laid siege to me, insomuch that I cannot shew myself at door or casement, or quit the house, but forthwith he presents himself before me; indeed I find it passing strange that he is not here now; whereat I am sorely troubled, because, when men so act, unmerited reproach will often thereby be cast upon honest women. At times I have been minded to inform my brothers of the matter; but then I have bethought me that men sometimes frame messages in such a way as to evoke untoward answers, whence follow high words; and so they proceed to rash acts: wherefore, to obviate trouble and scandal, I have kept silence, and by preference have made you my confidant, both because you are the gentleman's friend, and because it befits your office to censure such behaviour not only in friends but in strangers. And so I beseech you for the love of our only Lord God to make him sensible of his fault, and pray him to offend no more in such sort. Other ladies there are in plenty, who may, perchance, be disposed to welcome such advances, and be flattered to attract his fond and assiduous regard, which to me, who am in no wise inclined to encourage it, is but a most grievous molestation."

Having thus spoken, the lady bowed her head as if she were ready to weep. The holy friar was at no loss to apprehend who it was of whom she spoke; he commended her virtuous frame, firmly believing that what she said was true, and promised to take such action that she should not again suffer the like annoyance; nor, knowing that she was very wealthy, did he omit to extol works of charity and almsgiving, at the same time opening to her his own needs. "I make my suit to you," said she, "for the love of God; and if your friend should deny what I have told you, tell him roundly that 'twas from me you had it, and that I made complaint to you thereof." So, her confession ended and penance imposed, bethinking her of the hints which the friar had dropped touching almsgiving, she slipped into his hand as many coins as it would hold, praying him to say masses for the souls of her dead. She then rose and went home.

Not long afterwards the gallant paid one of his wonted visits to the holy friar. They conversed for a while of divers topics, and

then the friar took him aside, and very courteously reproved him for
so haunting and pursuing the lady with his gaze, as from what
she had given him to understand, he supposed was his wont.   The
gallant, who had never regarded her with any attention, and very
rarely passed her house, was amazed, and was about to clear himself,
when the friar closed his mouth, saying :—"Now away with this
pretence of amazement, and waste not words in denial, for 'twill not
avail thee.   I have it not from the neighbours ; she herself, bitterly
complaining of thy conduct, told it me.   I say not how ill this
levity beseems thee ; but of her I tell thee so much as this, that, if
I ever knew woman averse to such idle philandering, she is so ;
and therefore for thy honour's sake, and that she be no more vexed,
I pray thee refrain therefrom, and let her be in peace."   The gallant,
having rather more insight than the holy friar, was not slow to
penetrate the lady's finesse ; he therefore made as if he were rather
shame-stricken, promised to go no further with the matter, and hied
him straight from the friar to the lady's house, where she was always
posted at a little casement to see if he were passing by.   As she saw
him come, she shewed him so gay and gracious a mien that he could
no longer harbour any doubt that he had put the true construction
upon what he had heard from the friar ; and thenceforth, to his own
satisfaction and the immense delight and solace of the lady, he
omitted not daily to pass that way, being careful to make it appear
as if he came upon other business.   'Twas thus not long before the
lady understood that she met with no less favour in his eyes than he
in hers ; and being desirous to add fuel to his flame, and to assure him
of the love she bore him, as soon as time and occasion served, she
returned to the holy friar, and having sat herself down at his feet in
the church, fell a weeping.   The friar asked her in a soothing tone
what her new trouble might be.   Whereto the lady answered :—
"My father, 'tis still that accursed friend of thine, of whom I made
complaint to you some days ago, and who would now seem to have
been born for my most grievous torment, and to cause me to do that
by reason whereof I shall never be glad again, nor venture to place
myself at your feet."   "How ?" said the friar ; "has he not for-
borne to annoy thee ?"   "Not he, indeed," said the lady ; "on the
contrary, 'tis my belief that, since I complained to you of him, he
has, as if in despite, being offended, belike, that I did so, passed my

house seven times for once that he did so before. Nay, would to God he were content to pass and fix me with his eyes; but he is waxed so bold and unabashed that only yesterday he sent a woman to me at home with his compliments and cajoleries, and, as if I had not purses and girdles enough, he sent me a purse and a girdle; whereat I was, as I still am, so wroth, that, had not conscience first, and then regard for you, weighed with me, I had flown into a frenzy of rage. However, I restrained myself, and resolved neither to do nor to say aught without first letting you know it. Nor only so; but, lest the woman who brought the purse and girdle, and to whom I at first returned them, shortly bidding her begone and take them back to the sender, should keep them and tell him that I had accepted them, as I believe they sometimes do, I recalled her and had them back, albeit 'twas in no friendly spirit that I received them from her hand; and I have brought them to you, that you may return them to him and tell him that I stand in no need of such gifts from him, because, thanks be to God and my husband, I have purses and girdles enough to smother him in. And if after this he leave me not alone, I pray you as my father to hold me excused if, come what may, I tell it to my husband and brothers; for much liefer had I that he suffer indignity, if so it must be, than that my fair fame should be sullied on his account: that holds good, friar." Weeping bitterly as she thus ended, she drew from under her robe a purse of very fine and ornate workmanship and a dainty and costly little girdle, and threw them into the lap of the friar, who, fully believing what she said, manifested the utmost indignation as he took them, and said :—
" Daughter, that by these advances thou shouldst be moved to anger, I deem neither strange nor censurable; but I am instant with thee to follow my advice in the matter. I chid him some days ago, and ill has he kept the promise that he made me; for which cause and this last feat of his I will surely make his ears so tingle that he will give thee no more trouble; wherefore, for God's sake, let not thyself be so overcome by wrath as to tell it to any of thy kinsfolk; which might bring upon him a retribution greater than he deserves. Nor fear lest thereby thy fair fame should suffer; for I shall ever be thy most sure witness before God and men that thou art innocent."
The lady made a shew of being somewhat comforted: then, after a pause—for well she knew the greed of him and his likes—she said :—

"Of late, Sir, by night, the spirits of divers of my kinsfolk have appeared to me in my sleep, and methinks they are in most grievous torment; alms, alms, they crave, nought else, especially my mother, who seems to be in so woful and abject a plight that 'tis pitiful to see. Methinks 'tis a most grievous torment to her to see the tribulation which this enemy of God has brought upon me. I would therefore have you say for their souls the forty masses of St. Gregory and some of your prayers, that God may deliver them from this purging fire." So saying she slipped a florin into the hand of the holy friar, who took it gleefully, and having with edifying words and many examples fortified her in her devotion, gave her his benediction, and suffered her to depart.

The lady gone, the friar, who had still no idea of the trick that had been played upon him, sent for his friend; who was no sooner come than he gathered from the friar's troubled air that he had news of the lady, and waited to hear what he would say. The friar repeated what he had said before, and then broke out into violent and heated objurgation on the score of the lady's latest imputation. The gallant, who did not as yet apprehend the friar's drift, gave but a very faint denial to the charge of sending the purse and girdle, in order that he might not discredit the lady with the friar, if, perchance, she had given him the purse and girdle. Whereupon the friar exclaimed with great heat :—"How canst thou deny it, thou wicked man? Why, here they are; she brought them to me in tears with her own hand. Look at them, and say if thou knowest them not." The gallant now feigned to be much ashamed, and said :—"Why, yes, indeed, I do know them; I confess that I did wrong; and I swear to you that, now I know her character, you shall never hear word more of this matter." Many words followed; and then the blockheadly friar gave the purse and girdle to his friend, after which he read him a long lecture, besought him to meddle no more with such matters, and on his promising obedience dismissed him.

Elated beyond measure by the assurance which he now had of the lady's love, and the beautiful present, the gallant, on leaving the friar, hied him straight to a spot whence he stealthily gave the lady to see that he had both her gifts: whereat the lady was well content, the more so as her intrigue seemed ever to prosper more and more. She waited now only for her husband's departure from home to

crown her enterprise with success.   Nor was it long before occasion
required that her husband should go to Genoa.   The very morning
that he took horse and rode away she hied her to the holy friar, and
after many a lamentation she said to him betwixt her sobs :—"My
father, now at last I tell you out and out that I can bear my suffering
no longer.   I promised you some days ago to do nought in this
matter without first letting you know it ; I am now come to crave
release from that promise ; and that you may believe that my
lamentations and complaints are not groundless, I will tell you how
this friend of yours, who should rather be called a devil let loose
from hell, treated me only this very morning, a little before matins.
As ill-luck would have it, he learned, I know not how, that yesterday
morning my husband went to Genoa, and so this morning at the
said hour he came into my garden, and got up by a tree to the
window of my bedroom, which looks out over the garden, and had
already opened the casement, and was about to enter the room, when
I suddenly awoke, and got up and uttered a cry, and should have
continued to cry out, had not he, who was still outside, implored my
mercy for God's sake and yours, telling me who he was.   So, for
love of you I was silent, and naked as I was born, ran and shut the
window in his face, and he—bad luck to him—made off, I suppose,
for I saw him no more.   Consider now if such behaviour be seemly
and tolerable : I for my part am minded to put up with no more of
it ; indeed I have endured too much already for love of you."

Wroth beyond measure was the friar, as he heard her thus speak,
nor knew he what to say, except that he several times asked her if
she were quite certain that it was no other than he.   "Holy name
of God !" replied the lady, "as if I did not yet know him from
another !   He it was, I tell you ; and do you give no credence to his
denial."   "Daughter," said then the friar, "there is here nought
else to say but that this is a monstrous presumption and a most
heinous offence ; and thou didst well to send him away as thou didst.
But seeing that God has preserved thee from shame, I would implore
thee that, as thou hast twice followed my advice, thou do so likewise
on this occasion, and making no complaint to any of thy kinsfolk,
leave it to me to try if I can control this devil that has slipt his chain,
whom I supposed to be a saint; and if I succeed in weaning him from
this insensate folly, well and good ; and if I fail, thenceforth I give

thee leave, with my blessing, to do whatsoever may commend itself to thy own judgment." "Lo now," answered the lady, "once again I will not vex or disobey you; but be sure that you so order matters that he refrain from further annoyance, as I give you my word that never will I have recourse to you again touching this matter." Then, without another word, and with a troubled air, she took leave of him. Scarcely was she out of the church when the gallant came up. The friar called him, took him aside, and gave him the affront in such sort as 'twas never before given to any man, reviling him as a disloyal and perjured traitor. The gallant, who by his two previous lessons had been taught how to value the friar's censures, listened attentively, and sought to draw him out by ambiguous answers. "Wherefore this wrath, Sir?" he began. "Have I crucified Christ?" "Ay, mark the fellow's effrontery!" retorted the friar: "list to what he says! He talks, forsooth, as if 'twere a year or so since, and his villanies and lewdnesses were clean gone from his memory for lapse of time. Between matins and now hast thou forgotten this morning's outrage? Where wast thou this morning shortly before daybreak?" "Where was I?" rejoined the gallant; "that know not I. 'Tis indeed betimes that the news has reached you." "True indeed it is," said the friar, "that the news has reached me: I suppose that, because the husband was not there, thou never doubtedst that thou wouldst forthwith be received by the lady with open arms. Ah! the gay gallant! the honourable gentleman! he is now turned prowler by night, and breaks into gardens, and climbs trees! Dost thou think by sheer importunity to vanquish the virtue of this lady, that thou escaladest her windows at night by the trees? She dislikes thee of all things in the world, and yet thou must still persist. Well indeed hast thou laid my admonitions to heart, to say nothing of the many proofs which she has given thee of her disdain! But I have yet a word for thee: hitherto, not that she bears thee any love, but that she has yielded to my urgent prayers, she has kept silence as to thy misdeeds: she will do so no more: I have given her leave to act as she may think fit, if thou givest her any further annoyance. And what wilt thou do if she informs her brothers?" The gallant, now fully apprised of what it imported him to know, was profuse in promises, whereby as best he might he reassured the friar, and so left him. The very next night, as soon as the matin hour was come, he entered the garden, climbed up the tree, found the window open, entered the chamber, and in a trice was in the embrace of his fair lady. Anxiously had she expected him, and blithely did she now greet him, saying :—" All thanks to master friar that he so well taught thee the way hither." Then, with many a jest and laugh at the simplicity of the asinine friar, and many a flout at distaff-fuls and combs and cards, they solaced themselves with one another to their no small delight. Nor did they omit so to arrange matters that they were well able to dispense with master friar, and yet pass many another night together with no less satisfaction: to which goal I pray that I, and all other Christian souls that are so minded, may be speedily guided of God in His holy mercy.

NOVEL IV.

Dom Felice instructs Fra Puccio how to attain blessedness by doing a penance. Fra Puccio does the penance, and meanwhile Dom Felice has a good time with Fra Puccio's wife.

WHEN Filomena, having concluded her story, was silent, and Dioneo had added a few honeyed phrases in praise of the lady's wit and Filomena's closing prayer, the queen glanced with a smile to Pamfilo, and said :—"Now, Pamfilo, give us some pleasant trifle to speed our delight." "That gladly will I," returned forthwith Pamfilo, and then :—"Madam," he began, "not a few there are that, while they use their best endeavours to get themselves places in Paradise, do, by inadvertence, send others thither: as did, not long ago, betide a fair neighbour of ours, as you shall hear.

Hard by San Pancrazio there used to live, as I have heard tell, a worthy man and wealthy, Puccio di Rinieri by name, who in later life, under an overpowering sense of religion, became a tertiary of the order of St. Francis, and was thus known as Fra Puccio. In which spiritual life he was the better able to persevere that his household consisted but of a wife and a maid, and having no need to occupy himself with any craft, he spent no small part of his time at church ; where, being a simple soul and slow of wit, he said his paternosters, heard sermons, assisted at the mass, never missed lauds (*i. e.* when chanted by the seculars), fasted and mortified his flesh ; nay —so 'twas whispered—he was of the Flagellants. His wife, Monna Isabetta by name, a woman of from twenty-eight to thirty summers, still young for her age, lusty, comely and plump as a casolan[1] apple,

---

[1] Perhaps from Casoli, near Naples.

had not unfrequently, by reason of her husband's devoutness, if not also of his age, more than she cared for, of abstinence ; and when she was sleepy, or, maybe, riggish, he would repeat to her the life of Christ, and the sermons of Fra Nastagio, or the lament of the Magdalen, or the like. Now, while such was the tenor of her life, there returned from Paris a young monk, by name Dom Felice, of the convent of San Pancrazio, a well-favoured man and keen-witted, and profoundly learned, with whom Fra Puccio became very intimate ; and as there was no question which he could put to him but Dom Felice could answer it, and moreover he made great shew of holiness, for well he knew Fra Puccio's bent, Fra Puccio took to bringing him home and entertaining him at breakfast and supper, as occasion served; and for love of her husband the lady also grew familiar with Dom Felice, and was zealous to do him honour. So the monk, being a constant visitor at Fra Puccio's house, and seeing the lady so lusty and plump, surmised that of which she must have most lack, and made up his mind to afford, if he could, at once relief to Fra Puccio and content-ment to the lady. So cautiously, now and again, he cast an admiring glance in her direction with such effect that he kindled in her the same desire with which he burned, and marking his success, took the first opportunity to declare his passion to her. He found her fully disposed to gratify it ; but how this might be, he was at a loss to discover, for she would not trust herself with him in any place what-ever except her own house, and there it could not be, because Fra Puccio never travelled ; whereby the monk was greatly dejected. Long he pondered the matter, and at length thought of an expedient, whereby he might be with the lady in her own house without incurring suspicion, notwithstanding that Fra Puccio was there. So, being with Fra Puccio one day, he said to him :—" Reasons many have I to know, Fra Puccio, that all thy desire is to become a saint ; but it seems to me that thou farest by a circuitous route, whereas there is one very direct, which the Pope and the greater prelates that are about him know and use, but will have it remain a secret, because otherwise the clergy, who for the most part live by alms, and could not then expect alms or aught else from the laity, would be speedily ruined. However, as thou art my friend, and hast shewn me much honour, I would teach thee that way, if I were assured that thou wouldst follow it without letting another soul in the world hear of it." Fra Puccio was now all agog to hear more of the matter, and began most earnestly entreating Dom Felice to teach him the way, swearing that without Dom Felice's leave none should ever hear of it from him, and averring that, if he found it practicable, he would certainly follow it. "I am satisfied with thy promises," said the monk, "and I will shew thee the way. Know then that the holy doctors hold that whoso would achieve blessedness must do the penance of which I shall tell thee ; but see thou take me judiciously. I do not say that after the penance thou wilt not be a sinner, as thou art ; but the effect will be that the sins which thou hast committed up to the very hour of the penance will all be purged away and thereby remitted to thee, and the sins which thou shalt commit thereafter will not be written against thee to thy damnation, but will be quit by holy water, like venial sins. First of all then the penitent must with great exactitude confess his sins when he comes to begin the penance. Then follows a period of fasting and very strict abstinence which must last for forty days, during which time he is to touch no woman whomsoever, not even his wife. Moreover, thou must have in thy house some place whence thou mayst see the sky by night, whither thou must resort at compline ; and there thou must have a beam, very broad, and placed in such a way, that, standing, thou canst rest thy nether part upon it, and so, not raising thy feet from the ground, thou must extend thy arms, so as to make a sort of crucifix, and if thou wouldst have pegs to rest them on thou mayst ; and on this manner, thy gaze fixed on the sky, and never moving a jot, thou must stand until matins. And wert thou lettered, it were proper for thee to say meanwhile certain prayers that I would give thee ; but as thou art not so, thou must say three hundred pater-nosters and as many avemarias in honour of the Trinity ; and thus contemplating the sky, be ever mindful that God was the creator of the heaven and the earth, and being set even as Christ was upon the cross, meditate on His passion. Then, when the matin-bell sounds, thou mayst, if thou please, go to bed—but see that thou undress not —and sleep ; but in the morning thou must go to church, and hear at least three masses, and say fifty paternosters and as many avemarias ; after which thou mayst with a pure heart do aught that thou hast to do, and breakfast ; but at vespers thou must be again at church, and say there certain prayers, which I shall give thee in writing and which are indispensable, and after compline thou must repeat thy former exercise. Do this, and I, who have done it before thee, have good hope that even before thou shalt have reached the end of the penance, thou wilt, if thou shalt do it in a devout spirit, have already a marvellous foretaste of the eternal blessedness." "This," said Fra Puccio, " is neither a very severe nor a very long penance, and can be very easily managed : wherefore in God's name I will begin on Sunday." And so he took his leave of Dom Felice, and went home, and, by Dom Felice's permission, informed his wife of every particular of his intended penance.

The lady understood very well what the monk meant by enjoining him not to stir from his post until matins ; and deeming it an excellent device, she said that she was well content that he should do this or aught else that he thought good for his soul ; and to the end that his penance might be blest of God, she would herself fast with him, though she would go no further. So they did as they had agreed : when Sunday came Fra Puccio began his penance, and master monk, by understanding with the lady, came most evenings, at the hour when he was secure from discovery, to sup with her, always bringing with him abundance both of meat and of drink, and after slept with her till the matin hour, when he got up and left her, and Fra Puccio went to bed. The place which Fra Puccio had chosen for his penance was close to the room in which the lady slept, and only separated from it by the thinnest of partitions ; so that, the monk and the lady disporting themselves with one another without stint or restraint, Fra Puccio thought he felt the floor of the house shake a little, and pausing at his hundredth paternoster, but without leaving his post, called out to the lady to know what she was about. The lady, who dearly loved a jest, and was just then riding the horse of St. Benedict or St. John Gualbert, answered :—"I'faith, husband, I am as restless as may be." " Restless," said Fra Puccio, " how so ? What means this restlessness ? " Whereto with a hearty laugh, for which she doubtless had good occasion, the bonny lady replied :—"What means it ? How should you ask such a question ? Why, I have heard you say a thousand times :—' Who fasting goes to bed, uneasy lies his head.' " Fra Puccio, supposing that her wakefulness and restlessness abed was due to want of food, said in good faith :—" Wife, I told thee I would have thee not fast ; but as thou hast chosen to fast, think not of it, but think how thou mayst compose thyself to sleep ; thou tossest about the bed in such sort that the shaking is felt here." "That need cause thee no alarm," rejoined the lady. "I know what I am about ; I will manage as well as I can, and do thou likewise." So Fra Puccio said no more to her, but resumed his paternosters ; and thenceforth every night, while Fra Puccio's penance lasted, the lady and master monk, having had a bed made up for them in another part of the house, did there wanton it most gamesomely, the monk departing and the lady going back to her bed at one and the same time, being shortly before Fra Puccio's return from his nightly vigil. The friar thus persisting in his penance while the lady took her fill of pleasure with the monk, she would from time to time say jestingly to him :—"Thou layest a penance upon Fra Puccio whereby we are rewarded with Paradise." So well indeed did she relish the dainties with which the monk regaled her, the more so by contrast with the abstemious life to which her husband had long accustomed her, that, when Fra Puccio's penance was done, she found means to enjoy them elsewhere, and ordered her indulgence with such discretion as to ensure its long continuance. Whereby (that my story may end as it began) it came to pass that Fra Puccio, hoping by his penance to win a place for himself in Paradise, did in fact translate thither the monk who had shewn him the way, and the wife who lived with him in great dearth of that of which the monk in his charity gave her superabundant largess.

NOVEL V.

Zima gives a palfrey to Messer Francesco Vergellesi, who in return suffers him to speak with his wife. She keeping silence, he answers in her stead, and the sequel is in accordance with his answer.

WHEN Pamfilo had brought the story of Fra Puccio to a close amid the laughter of the ladies, the queen debonairly bade Elisa follow suit; and she, whose manner had in it a slight touch of severity, which betokened not despite, but was habitual to her, thus began:—

Many there are that, being very knowing, think that others are quite the reverse; and so, many a time, thinking to beguile others, are themselves beguiled; wherefore I deem it the height of folly for any one wantonly to challenge another to a contest of wit. But, as, perchance, all may not be of the same opinion, I am minded, without deviating from the prescribed order, to acquaint you with that which thereby befell a certain knight of Pistoia. Know then that at Pistoia there lived a knight, Messer Francesco, by name, of the Vergellesi family, a man of much wealth and good parts, being both wise and clever, but withal niggardly beyond measure. Which Messer Francesco, having to go to Milan in the capacity of podestà, had provided himself with all that was meet for the honourable support of such a dignity, save only a palfrey handsome enough for him; and not being able to come by any such, he felt himself at a loss. Now there was then in Pistoia a young man, Ricciardo by name, of low origin but great wealth, who went always so trim and fine and foppish of person, that folk had bestowed upon him the name of Zima,[1] by which he was generally known. Zima had long and to no purpose burned and yearned for love of Messer Francesco's very fair and no less virtuous wife. His passion was matter of common notoriety; and so it befell that some one told Messer Francesco that he had but to ask Zima, who was the possessor of one of the handsomest palfreys in Tuscany, which on that account he greatly prized, and he would not hesitate to give him the horse for the love which he bore his wife. So our niggardly knight sent for Zima, and offered to buy the horse of him, hoping thereby to get him from Zima as a gift. Zima heard the knight gladly, and thus made answer:—"Sell you my horse, Sir, I would not, though you gave me all that you have in the world; but I shall be happy to give him to you, when you will, on this condition, that, before he pass into your hands, I may by your leave and in your presence say a few words to your wife so privately that I may be heard by her alone." Thinking at once to gratify his cupidity and to outwit Zima, the knight answered that he was content that it should be even as Zima wished. Then, leaving him in the hall of the palace, he went to his lady's chamber, and told her the easy terms on which he might acquire the palfrey, bidding her give Zima his audience, but on no account to vouchsafe him a word of reply. This the lady found by no means to her mind, but, as she must needs obey her husband's commands, she promised compliance, and followed him into the hall to hear what Zima might have to say. Zima then renewed his contract with the knight in due form; whereupon, the lady being seated in a part of the hall where she was quite by herself, he sate down by her side, and thus began: —"Noble lady, I have too much respect for your understanding to doubt that you have long been well aware of the extremity of passion whereto I have been brought by your beauty, which certainly exceeds that of any other lady that I have ever seen, to say nothing of your exquisite manners and incomparable virtues, which might well serve to captivate every soaring spirit that is in the world; wherefore there need no words of mine to assure you that I love

---

[1] From the Low Latin aczima, explained by Du Cange as "tonture de draps," the process of dressing cloth so as to give it an even nap. Zima is thus equivalent to "nitidus." Cf. Vocab. degli Accademici della Crusca, "Azzimare."

you with a love greater and more ardent than any that man vet bore to woman, and so without doubt I shall do, as long as my woful life shall hold this frame together; nay, longer yet, for, if love there be in the next world as in this, I shall love you evermore. And so you may make your mind secure that there is nothing that is yours, be it precious or be it common, which you may count as in such and so sure a sort your own as me, for all that I am and have. And that thereof you may not lack evidence of infallible cogency, I tell you, that I should deem myself more highly favoured, if I might at your command do somewhat to pleasure you, than if at my command the whole world were forthwith to yield me obedience. And as 'tis even in such sort that I am yours, 'tis not unworthily that I make bold to offer my petitions to Your Highness, as being to me the sole, exclusive source of all peace, of all bliss, of all health. Wherefore, as your most lowly vassal, I pray you, dear my bliss, my soul's one hope, wherein she nourishes herself in love's devouring flame, that in your great benignity you deign so far to mitigate the harshness which in the past you have shewn towards me, yours though I am, that, consoled by your compassion, I may say, that, as 'twas by your beauty that I was smitten with love, so 'tis to your pity that I owe my life, which, if in your haughtiness you lend not ear unto my prayers, will assuredly fail, so that I shall die, and, it may be, 'twill be said that you slew me. 'Twould not redound to your honour that I died for love of you; but let that pass; I cannot but think, however, that you would sometimes feel a touch of remorse, and would grieve that 'twas your doing, and that now and again, relenting, you would say to yourself :—'Ah! how wrong it was of me that I had not pity on my Zima;' by which too late repentance you would but enhance your grief. Wherefore, that this come not to pass, repent you while it is in your power to give me ease, and shew pity on me before I die, seeing that with you it rests to make me either the gladdest or the saddest man that lives. My trust is in your generosity, that 'twill not brook that a love so great and of such a sort as mine should receive death for guerdon, and that by a gladsome and gracious answer you will repair my shattered spirits, which are all a-tremble in your presence for very fear." When he had done, he heaved several very deep sighs, and a few tears started from his eyes, while he awaited the lady's answer.

Long time he had wooed her with his eyes, had tilted in her honour, had greeted her rising with music; and against these and all like modes of attack she had been proof; but the heartfelt words of her most ardent lover were not without their effect, and she now began to understand what she had never till then understood, to wit, what love really means. So, albeit she obeyed her lord's behest, and kept silence, yet she could not but betray by a slight sigh that which, if she might have given Zima his answer, she would readily have avowed. After waiting a while, Zima found it strange that no answer was forthcoming; and he then began to perceive the trick which the knight had played him. However, he kept his eyes fixed on the lady, and observing that her eyes glowed now and again, as they met his, and noting the partially suppressed sighs which escaped her, he gathered a little hope, which gave him courage to try a novel plan of attack. So, while the lady listened, he began to make answer for her to himself on this wise:—"Zima mine, true indeed it is that long since I discerned that thou didst love me with a love exceeding great and whole-hearted, whereof I have now yet ampler assurance by thine own words, and well content I am therewith, as indeed I ought to be. And however harsh and cruel I may have seemed to thee, I would by no means have thee believe, that I have been such at heart as I have seemed in aspect; rather, be assured that I have ever loved thee and held thee dear above all other men; the mien which I have worn was but prescribed by fear of another and solicitude for my fair fame. But a time will soon come when I shall be able to give thee plain proof of my love, and to accord the love which thou hast borne and dost bear me its due guerdon. Wherefore be comforted and of good hope; for, Messer Francesco is to go in a few days' time to Milan as podestà, as thou well knowest, seeing that for love of me thou hast given him thy fine palfrey; and I vow to thee upon my faith, upon the true love which I bear thee, that without fail, within a few days thereafter thou shalt be with me, and we will give our love complete and gladsome consummation. And that I may have no more occasion to speak to thee of this matter, be it understood between us that henceforth when thou shalt observe two towels disposed at the window of my room which overlooks the garden, thou shalt come to me after nightfall of that same day by the garden door (and look

well to it that thou be not seen), and thou shalt find me waiting
for thee, and we will have our fill of mutual cheer and solace all
night long."

Having thus answered for the lady, Zima resumed his own
person and thus replied to the lady:—"Dearest madam, your boon
response so overpowers my every faculty that scarce can I frame
words to render you due thanks; and, were I able to utter all I feel,
time, however long, would fail me fully to thank you as I would
fain and as I ought: wherefore I must even leave it to your sage
judgment to divine that which I yearn in vain to put in words.
Let this one word suffice, that as you bid me, so I shall not fail
to do; and then, having, perchance, firmer assurance of the great
boon which you have granted me, I will do my best endeavour to
thank you in terms the amplest that I may command. For the
present there is no more to say; and so, dearest my lady, I commend you to God; and may He grant you your heart's content of
joy and bliss." To all which the lady returned never a word:
wherefore Zima rose and turned to rejoin the knight, who, seeing
him on his feet, came towards him, and said with a laugh:—"How
sayst thou? Have I faithfully kept my promise to thee?" "Not so,
Sir," replied Zima; "for by thy word I was to have spoken with thy
wife, and by thy deed I have spoken to a statue of marble." Which
remark was much relished by the knight, who, well as he had thought
of his wife, thought now even better of her, and said:—"So thy
palfrey, that was, is now mine out and out." "'Tis even so, Sir,"
replied Zima; "but had I thought to have gotten such fruit as I
have from this favour of yours, I would not have craved it, but
would have let you have the palfrey as a free gift: and would to
God I had done so, for, as it is, you have bought the palfrey and
I have not sold him." This drew a laugh from the knight, who
within a few days thereafter mounted the palfrey which he had
gotten, and took the road for Milan, there to enter on his podestate.
The lady, now mistress of herself, bethought her of Zima's words,
and the love which he bore her, and for which he had parted with
his palfrey; and observing that he frequently passed her house, said
to herself:—"What am I about? Why throw I my youth away?
My husband is gone to Milan, and will not return for six months,
and when can he ever restore them to me? When I am old!

And besides, shall I ever find another such lover as Zima? I am quite by myself. There is none to fear. I know not why I take not my good time while I may: I shall not always have the like opportunity as at present: no one will ever know; and if it should get known, 'tis better to do and repent than to forbear and repent." Of which meditations the issue was that one day she set two towels in the window overlooking the garden, according to Zima's word; and Zima having marked them with much exultation, stole at nightfall alone to the door of the lady's garden, and finding it open, crossed to another door that led into the house, where he found the lady awaiting him. On sight of him she rose to meet him, and gave him the heartiest of welcomes. A hundred thousand times he embraced and kissed her, as he followed her upstairs: then without delay they hied them to bed, and knew love's furthest bourne. And so far was the first time from being in this case the last, that, while the knight was at Milan, and indeed after his return, there were seasons not a few at which Zima resorted thither to the immense delight of both parties.

NOVEL VI.

Ricciarao Minutolo loves the wife of Filippello Fighinolfi, and knowing her to be jealous, makes her believe that his own wife is to meet Filippello at a bagnio on the ensuing day; whereby she is induced to go thither, where, thinking to have been with her husband, she discovers that she has tarried with Ricciardo.

WHEN Elisa had quite done, the queen, after some commendation of Zima's sagacity, bade Fiammetta follow with a story. Whereto Fiammetta, all smiles, responded:—"Madam, with all my heart;" and thus began:—

Richly though our city abounds, as in all things else, so also in instances to suit every topic, yet I am minded to journey some distance thence, and, like Elisa, to tell you something of what goes on in other parts of the world: wherefore pass we to Naples, where you shall hear how one of these sanctified that shew themselves so shy of love, was by the subtlety of her lover brought to taste of the fruit before she had known the flowers of love; whereby at one and the same time you may derive from the past counsel of prudence for the future, and present delectation.

In the very ancient city of Naples, which for loveliness has not its superior or perhaps its equal in Italy, there once lived a young man, renowned alike for noble blood and the splendour of his vast wealth, his name Ricciardo Minutolo. He was mated with a very fair and loving wife; but nevertheless he became enamoured of a lady who in the general opinion vastly surpassed in beauty every other lady in Naples. Catella—such was the lady's name—was married to a young man, likewise of gentle blood, Filippello Fighinolfi by name, whom she, most virtuous of ladies, loved and held dear above all else in the world.   Being thus enamoured of Catella, Ricciardo Minutolo left none of those means untried whereby a lady's favour and love are wont to be gained, but for all that he made no way towards the attainment of his heart's desire: whereby he fell into a sort of despair, and witless and powerless to loose himself from his love, found life scarce tolerable, and yet knew not how to die.   While in this frame he languished, it befell one day that some ladies that were of kin to him counselled him earnestly to be quit of such a love, whereby he could but fret himself to no purpose, seeing that Catella cared for nought in the world save Filippello, and lived in such a state of jealousy on his account that never a bird flew but she feared lest it should snatch him from her.   So soon as Ricciardo heard of Catella's jealousy, he forthwith began to ponder how he might make it subserve his end.   He feigned to have given up his love for Catella as hopeless, and to have transferred it to another lady, in whose honour he accordingly began to tilt and joust and do all that he had been wont to do in honour of Catella.   Nor was it long before well-nigh all the Neapolitans, including Catella herself, began to think that he had forgotten Catella, and was to the last degree enamoured of the other lady.   In this course he persisted, until the opinion was so firmly rooted in the minds of all that even Catella laid aside a certain reserve which she had used towards him while she deemed him her lover, and, coming and going, greeted him in friendly, neighbourly fashion, like the rest.   Now it so befell that during the hot season, when, according to the custom of the Neapolitans, many companies of ladies and gentlemen went down to the sea-coast to recreate themselves and breakfast and sup, Ricciardo, knowing that Catella was gone thither with her company, went likewise with his, but, making as if he were not minded to stay there, he received several invitations from the ladies of Catella's company before he accepted any.   When the ladies received him, they all with one accord, including Catella, began to rally him on his new love, and he furnished them with more matter for talk by feigning a most ardent passion.   At length most of the ladies being gone off, one hither, another thither, as they do in such places, leaving Catella and a few others with Ricciardo, he tossed at Catella a light allusion to a certain love of her husband Filippello, which threw her at once into such a fit of jealousy, that she inly burned with a vehement desire to know what Ricciardo meant. For a while she kept her own counsel; then, brooking no more suspense, she adjured Ricciardo, by the love he bore the lady whom most he loved, to expound to her what he had said touching Filippello. He answered thus:—"You have adjured me by her to whom I dare not deny aught that you may ask of me; my riddle therefore I will presently read you, provided you promise me that neither to him nor to any one else will you impart aught of what I shall relate to you, until you shall have ocular evidence of its truth; which, so you desire it, I will teach you how you may obtain." The lady accepted his terms, which rather confirmed her belief in his veracity, and swore that she would not tell a soul. They then drew a little apart, that they might not be overheard by the rest, and Ricciardo thus began:— "Madam, did I love you, as I once did, I should not dare to tell you aught that I thought might cause you pain; but, now that that love is past, I shall have the less hesitation in telling you the truth. Whether Filippello ever resented the love which I bore you, or deemed that it was returned by you, I know not: whether it were so or no, he certainly never shewed any such feeling to me; but so it is that now, having waited, perhaps, until, as he supposes, I am less likely to be on my guard, he shews a disposition to serve me as I doubt he suspects that I served him; that is to say, he would fain have his pleasure of my wife, whom for some time past he has, as I discover, plied with messages through most secret channels. She has told me all, and has answered him according to my instructions: but only this morning, just before I came hither, I found a woman in close parley with her in the house, whose true character and purpose I forthwith divined; so I called my wife, and asked what the woman wanted. Whereto she answered:—' 'Tis this persecution by Filippello which thou hast brought upon me by the encouraging answers that thou wouldst have me give him: he now tells me that he is most earnestly desirous to know my intentions, and that, should I be so minded, he would contrive that I should have secret access to a bagnio in this city, and he is most urgent and instant that I should consent. And hadst thou not, wherefore I know not, bidden me keep the affair afoot, I would have dismissed him in such a sort that my movements would have been exempt from his prying observation for ever.' Upon this I saw that the affair was going too far; I determined to have no more of it, and to let you know it, that you may understand how he requites your whole-hearted faith, which brought me of late to the verge of death. And that you may not suppose that these are but empty words and idle tales, but may be able, should you so desire, to verify them by sight and touch, I caused my wife to tell the woman who still waited her answer, that she would be at the bagnio to-morrow about none, during the siesta: with which answer the woman went away well content. Now you do not, I suppose, imagine that I would send her thither; but if I were in your place, he should find me there instead of her whom he thinks to find there; and when I had been some little time with him, I would give him to understand with whom he had been, and he should have of me such honour as he deserved. Whereby, I doubt not, he would be put to such shame as would at one and the same time avenge both the wrong which he has done to you and that which he plots against me."

Catella, as is the wont of the jealous, hearkened to Ricciardo's words without so much as giving a thought to the speaker or his wiles, inclined at once to credit his story, and began to twist certain antecedent matters into accord with it ; then, suddenly kindling with wrath, she answered, that to the bagnio she would certainly go ; 'twould cause her no great inconvenience, and if he should come, she would so shame him that he should never again set eyes on woman but his ears would tingle. Satisfied by what he heard, that his stratagem was well conceived, and success sure, Ricciardo added much in corroboration of his story, and having thus confirmed her belief in it, besought her to keep it always close, whereto she pledged her faith.

Next morning Ricciardo hied him to the good woman that kept the bagnio to which he had directed Catella, told her the enterprise which he had in hand, and prayed her to aid him therein so far as she might be able. The good woman, who was much beholden to him, assured him that she would gladly do so, and concerted with him all that was to be said and done. She had in the bagnio a room which was very dark, being without any window to admit the light. This room, by Ricciardo's direction, she set in order, and made up a

bed there as well as she could, into which bed Ricciardo got, as soon
as he had breakfasted, and there awaited Catella's coming.

Now Catella, still giving more credence to Ricciardo's story than
it merited, had gone home in the evening in a most resentful mood,
and Filippello, returning home the same evening with a mind greatly
preoccupied, was scarce as familiar with her as he was wont to be.
Which she marking, grew yet more suspicious than before, and said
to herself :—" Doubtless he is thinking of the lady of whom he expects
to take his pleasure to-morrow, as most assuredly he shall not ; " and
so, musing and meditating what she should say to him after their
rencounter at the bagnio, she spent the best part of the night. But
—to shorten my story—upon the stroke of none Catella, taking with
her a single attendant, but otherwise adhering to her original intention,
hied her to the bagnio which Ricciardo had indicated ; and finding
the good woman there, asked her whether Filippello had been there
that day. Primed by Ricciardo, the good woman asked her, whether
she were the lady that was to come to speak with him; to which she
answered in the affirmative. "Go to him, then," said the good
woman. And so Catella, in quest of that which she would gladly
not have found, was shewn to the chamber where Ricciardo was,
and having entered without uncovering her head, closed the door
behind her. Overjoyed to see her, Ricciardo sprang out of bed, took
her in his arms, and said caressingly : —" Welcome, my soul."
Catella, dissembling, for she was minded at first to counterfeit another
woman, returned his embrace, kissed him, and lavished endearments
upon him ; saying, the while, not a word, lest her speech should
betray her. The darkness of the room, which was profound, was
equally welcome to both ; nor were they there long enough for their
eyes to recover power. Ricciardo helped Catella on to the bed,
where, with no word said on either side in a voice that might be
recognized, they lay a long while, much more to the solace and
satisfaction of the one than of the other party. Then, Catella,
deeming it high time to vent her harboured resentment, burst forth
in a blaze of wrath on this wise :—" Alas ! how wretched is the lot
of women, how misplaced of not a few the love they bear their
husbands ! Ah, woe is me ! for eight years have I loved thee more
dearly than my life ; and now I find that thou, base miscreant that
thou art, dost nought but burn and languish for love of another

woman ! Here thou hast been—with whom, thinkest thou ? Even
with her whom thou hast too long deluded with thy false blandishments, making pretence to love her while thou art enamoured of
another. 'Tis I, Catella, not the wife of Ricciardo, false traitor
that thou art ; list if thou knowest my voice ; 'tis I indeed ! Ah !
would we were but in the light !—it seems to me a thousand years
till then—that I might shame thee as thou deservest, vile, pestilent
dog that thou art ! Alas ! woe is me ! such love as I have borne so
many years—to whom ? To this faithless dog, that, thinking to have a
strange woman in his embrace, has in the brief while that I have
been with him here lavished upon me more caresses and endearments
than during all the forepast time that I have been his ! A lively
spark indeed art thou to-day, renegade dog, that shewest thyself
so limp and enervate and impotent at home ! But, God be praised,
thou hast tilled thine own plot, and not another's, as thou didst believe.
No wonder that last night thou heldest aloof from me ; thou wast
thinking of scattering thy seed elsewhere, and wast minded to shew
thyself a lusty knight when thou shouldst join battle. But praise be
to God and my sagacity, the water has nevertheless taken its proper
course. Where is thy answer, culprit ? Hast thou nought to say ?
Have my words struck thee dumb ? God's faith ! I know not why I
forbear to pluck thine eyes out with my fingers ! Thou thoughtest
to perpetrate this treason with no small secrecy ; but, by God, one is
as knowing as another ; thy plot has failed ; I had better hounds on
thy trail than thou didst think for." Ricciardo, inly delighted by her
words, made no answer, but embraced and kissed her more than
ever, and overwhelmed her with his endearments. So she continued
her reproaches, saying :—" Ay, thou thinkest to cajole me with thy
feigned caresses, wearisome dog that thou art, and so to pacify and
mollify me ; but thou art mistaken. I shall never be mollified, until
I have covered thee with infamy in the presence of all our kinsfolk
and friends and neighbours. Am I not, miscreant, as fair as the wife
of Ricciardo Minutolo ? Am I not as good a lady as she ? Why
dost not answer, vile dog ? Wherein has she the advantage of me ?
Away with thee ! touch me not ; thou hast done feats of arms more
than enough for to-day. Well I know that, now that thou knowest
who I am, thou wilt wreak thy will on me by force : but by God's
grace I will yet disappoint thee. I know not why I forbear to send

for Ricciardo, who loved me more than himself and yet was never able to boast that he had a single glance from me ; nor know I why 'twere wrong to do so. Thou thoughtest to have his wife here, and 'tis no fault of thine that thou hadst her not : so, if I had him, thou couldst not justly blame me."

Enough had now been said : the lady's mortification was extreme ; and, as she ended, Ricciardo bethought him that, if he suffered her, thus deluded, to depart, much evil might ensue. He therefore resolved to make himself known, and disabuse her of her error. So, taking her in his arms, and clipping her so close that she could not get loose, he said :—"Sweet my soul, be not wroth : that which, while artlessly I loved, I might not have, Love has taught me to compass by guile : know that I am thy Ricciardo."

At these words and the voice, which she recognized, Catella started, and would have sprung out of the bed ; which being impossible, she essayed a cry ; but Ricciardo laid a hand upon her mouth, and closed it, saying :—"Madam, that which is done can never be undone, though you should cry out for the rest of your days, and should you in such or any other wise publish this matter to any, two consequences will ensue. In the first place (and this is a point which touches you very nearly) your honour and fair fame will be blasted ; for, however you may say that I lured you hither by guile, I shall deny it, and affirm, on the contrary, that I induced you to come hither by promises of money and gifts, and that 'tis but because you are vexed that what I gave you did not altogether come up to your expectations, that you make such a cry and clamour ; and you know that folk are more prone to believe evil than good, and therefore I am no less likely to be believed than you. The further consequence will be mortal enmity between your husband and me, and the event were as like to be that I killed him as that he killed me : which if I did, you would never more know joy or peace. Wherefore, heart of my body, do not at one and the same time bring dishonour upon yourself and set your husband and me at strife and in jeopardy of our lives. You are not the first, nor will you be the last to be beguiled ; nor have I beguiled you to rob you of aught, but for excess of love that I bear, and shall ever bear, you, being your most lowly vassal. And though it is now a great while that I, and what I have and can and am worth, are yours, yet I am minded that so it shall be henceforth more than ever before. Your discretion in other matters is not unknown to me, and I doubt not 'twill be equally manifest in this."

Ricciardo's admonitions were received by Catella with many a bitter tear; but though she was very wroth and very sad at heart, yet Ricciardo's true words so far commanded the assent of her reason, that she acknowledged that 'twas possible they might be verified by the event. Wherefore she made answer :—" Ricciardo, I know not how God will grant me patience to bear the villainy and knavery which thou hast practised upon me; and though in this place, to which simplicity and excess of jealousy guided my steps, I raise no cry, rest assured that I shall never be happy, until in one way or another I know myself avenged of that which thou hast done to me. Wherefore unhand me, let me go : thou hast had thy desire of me, and hast tormented me to thy heart's content : 'tis time to release me ; let me go, I pray thee." But Ricciardo, seeing that she was still much ruffled in spirit, was resolved not to let her go, until he had made his peace with her. So he addressed himself to soothe her ; and by dint of most dulcet phrases and entreaties and adjurations he did at last prevail with her to give him her pardon ; nay, by joint consent, they tarried there a great while to the exceeding great delight of both. Indeed the lady, finding her lover's kisses smack much better than those of her husband, converted her asperity into sweetness, and from that day forth cherished a most tender love for Ricciardo ; whereof, using all circumspection, they many a time had solace. God grant us solace of ours.

NOVEL VII.

Tedaldo, being in disfavour with his lady, departs from Florence.   He returns thither after a while in the guise of a pilgrim, has speech of his lady, and makes her sensible of her fault.   Her husband, convicted of slaying him, he delivers from peril of death, reconciles him with his brothers, and thereafter discreetly enjoys his lady.

So ceased Fiammetta ; and, when all had bestowed on her their meed of praise, the queen—to lose no time—forthwith bade Emilia resume the narration.   So thus Emilia began :—

I am minded to return to our city, whence my two last predecessors saw fit to depart, and to shew you how one of our citizens recovered the lady he had lost.   Know then that there was in Florence a young noble, his name Tedaldo Elisei, who being beyond measure enamoured of a lady hight Monna Ermellina, wife of one Aldobrandino Palermini, and by reason of his admirable qualities richly deserving to have his desire, found Fortune nevertheless adverse, as she is wont to be to the prosperous.   Inasmuch as, for some reason or another, the lady, having shewn herself gracious towards Tedaldo for a while, completely altered her mien, and not only shewed him no further favour, but would not so much as receive a message from him or suffer him to see her face ; whereby he fell a prey to a grievous and distressful melancholy ; but so well had he concealed his love that the cause of his melancholy was surmised by none.   He tried hard in divers ways to recover the love which he deemed himself to have lost for no fault of his, and finding all his efforts unavailing, he resolved to bid the world adieu, that he might not afford her who was the cause of his distress the satisfaction of seeing him languish. So he got together as much money as he might, and secretly, no word said to friend or kinsman except only a familiar gossip, who knew all, he took his departure for Ancona. Arrived there, he assumed the name of Filippo Santodeccio, and having forgathered with a rich merchant, entered his service. The merchant took him with him to Cyprus aboard one of his ships, and was so well pleased with his bearing and behaviour that he not only gave him a handsome salary but made him in a sort his companion, and entrusted him with the management of no small part of his affairs : wherein he proved himself so apt and assiduous, that in the course of a few years he was himself established in credit and wealth and great repute as a merchant. Seven years thus passed, during which, albeit his thoughts frequently reverted to his cruel mistress, and sorely love smote him, and much he yearned to see her again, yet such was his firmness that he came off conqueror, until one day in Cyprus it so befell that there was sung in his hearing a song that he had himself composed, and of which the theme was the mutual love that was between his lady and him, and the delight that he had of her ; which as he heard, he found it incredible that she should have forgotten him, and burned with such a desire to see her once more, that, being able to hold out no longer, he made up his mind to return to Florence. So, having set all his affairs in order, he betook him, attended only by a single servant, to Ancona ; whence he sent all his effects, as they arrived, forward to Florence, consigning them to a friend of his Ancontan partner, and followed with his servant in the disguise of a pilgrim returned from the Holy Sepulchre. Arrived at Florence, he put up at a little hostelry kept by two brothers hard by his lady's house, whither he forthwith hied him, hoping that, perchance, he might have sight of her from the street ; but, finding all barred and bolted, doors, windows and all else, he doubted much, she must be dead, or have removed thence. So, with a very heavy heart, he returned to the house of the two brothers, and to his great surprise found his own four brothers standing in front of it, all in black. He knew that he was so changed from his former semblance, both in dress and in person, that he might not readily be recognized, and he had therefore no hesitation in going up to a shoemaker and asking him

why these men were all dressed in black. The shoemaker answered:—
"'Tis because 'tis not fifteen days since a brother of theirs, Tedaldo
by name, that had been long abroad, was slain ; and I understand
that they have proved in court that one Aldobrandino Palermini,
who is under arrest, did the deed, because Tedaldo, who loved his
wife, was come back to Florence incognito to forgather with her."
Tedaldo found it passing strange that there should be any one so
like him as to be mistaken for him, and deplored Aldobrandino's evil
plight. He had learned, however, that the lady was alive and well.
So, as 'twas now night, he hied him, much perplexed in mind, into
the inn, and supped with his servant. The bedroom assigned him
was almost at the top of the house, and the bed was none of the
best. Thoughts many and disquieting haunted his mind, and his
supper had been but light. Whereby it befell that midnight came and
went, and Tedaldo was still awake. As thus he watched, he heard
shortly after midnight, a noise as of persons descending from the roof
into the house, and then through the chinks of the door of his room
he caught the flicker of an ascending light. Wherefore he stole
softly to the door, and peeping through a chink to make out what
was afoot, he saw a very fine young woman bearing a light, and three
men making towards her, being evidently those that had descended
from the roof. The men exchanged friendly greetings with the
young woman, and then one said to her :—" Now, God be praised,
we may make our minds easy, for we are well assured that judgment
for the death of Tedaldo Elisei is gotten by his brothers against
Aldobrandino Palermini, and he has confessed, and the sentence is
already drawn up; but still it behoves us to hold our peace; for,
should it ever get abroad that we were guilty, we shall stand in the
like jeopardy as Aldobrandino." So saying, they took leave of the
woman, who seemed much cheered, and went to bed. What he
had heard set Tedaldo musing on the number and variety of the
errors to which men are liable : as, first, how his brothers had
mourned and interred a stranger in his stead, and then charged an
innocent man upon false suspicion, and by false witness brought him
into imminent peril of death : from which he passed to ponder the
blind severity of laws and magistrates, who from misguided zeal to
elicit the truth not unfrequently become ruthless, and, adjudging that
which is false, forfeit the title which they claim of ministers of

God and justice, and do but execute the mandates of iniquity and the Evil One. And so he came at last to consider the possibility of saving Aldobrandino, and formed a plan for the purpose. Accordingly, on the morrow, when he was risen, he left his servant at the inn, and hied him alone, at what he deemed a convenient time, to his lady's house, where, finding, by chance, the door open, he entered, and saw his lady sitting, all tears and lamentations, in a little parlour on the ground-floor. Whereat he all but wept for sympathy; and drawing near her, he said :—"Madam, be not troubled in spirit: your peace is nigh you." Whereupon the lady raised her head, and said between her sobs :—"Good man, what dost thou, a pilgrim, if I mistake not, from distant parts, know either of my peace or of my affliction?" "Madam," returned the pilgrim, "I am of Constantinople, and am but now come hither, at God's behest, that I may give you laughter for tears, and deliver your husband from death." "But," said the lady, "if thou art of Constantinople, and but now arrived, how is 't that thou knowest either who my husband is, or who I am?" Whereupon the pilgrim gave her the whole narrative, from the very beginning, of Aldobrandino's sufferings; he also told her, who she was, how long she had been married, and much besides that was known to him of her affairs : whereat the lady was lost in wonder, and, taking him to be a prophet, threw herself on her knees at his feet, and besought him for God's sake, if he were come to save Aldobrandino, to lose no time, for the matter brooked no delay. Thus adjured, the pilgrim assumed an air of great sanctity, as he said :— "Arise, Madam, weep not, but hearken diligently to what I shall say to you, and look to it that you impart it to none. I have it by revelation of God that the tribulation wherein you stand is come upon you in requital of a sin which you did once commit, of which God is minded that this suffering be a partial purgation, and that you make reparation in full, if you would not find yourself in a far more grievous plight." "Sir," replied the lady, "many sins have I committed, nor know I how among them all to single out that whereof, more than another, God requires reparation at my hands : wherefore, if you know it, tell it me, and what by way of reparation I may do, that will I do." "Madam," returned the pilgrim, "well wot I what it is, nor shall I question you thereof for my better instruction, but that the rehearsal may give you increase of remorse

therefor. But pass we now to fact. Tell me, mind you ever to
have had a lover?" Whereat the lady heaved a deep sigh; then,
marvelling not a little, for she had thought 'twas known to none,
albeit on the day when the man was slain, who was afterwards buried
as Tedaldo, there had been some buzz about it, occasioned by some
indiscreet words dropped by Tedaldo's gossip and confidant, she made
answer:—" I see that there is nought that men keep secret but God
reveals it to you; wherefore I shall not endeavour to hide my secrets
from you. True it is that in my youth I was beyond measure
enamoured of the unfortunate young man whose death is imputed to
my husband; whom I mourned with grief unfeigned, for, albeit I
shewed myself harsh and cruel towards him before his departure, yet
neither thereby, nor by his long absence, nor yet by his calamitous
death was my heart estranged from him." Then said the pilgrim:—
"'Twas not the unfortunate young man now dead that you did love,
but Tedaldo Elisei. But let that pass; now tell me: wherefore lost
he your good graces? Did he ever offend you?" "Nay verily,"
answered the lady, "he never offended me at all. My harshness was
prompted by an accursed friar, to whom I once confessed, and who,
when I told him of the love I bore Tedaldo, and my intimacy with
him, made my ears so tingle and sing that I still shudder to think of
it, warning me that, if I gave it not up, I should fall into the jaws of
the Devil in the abyss of hell, and be cast into the avenging fire.
Whereby I was so terrified that I quite made my mind up to discon-
tinue my intimacy with him, and, to trench the matter, I would
thenceforth have none of his letters or messages; and so, I suppose,
he went away in despair, though I doubt not, had he persevered a
while longer, I should not have seen him wasting away like snow in
sunshine without relenting of my harsh resolve; for in sooth there
was nothing in the world I would so gladly have done." Then said
the pilgrim:—" Madam, 'tis this sin, and this only, that has brought
upon you your present tribulation. I know positively that Tedaldo
did never put force upon you: 'twas of your own free will, and for
that he pleased you, that you became enamoured of him: your
constant visitor, your intimate friend he became, because you yourself
would have it so; and in the course of your intimacy you shewed
him such favour by word and deed that, if he loved you first, you
multiplied his love full a thousandfold. And if so it was, and well

yourself from him? You should have considered the whole matter
before the die was cast, and not have entered upon it, if you deemed
you might have cause to repent you of it as a sin. As soon as he
became yours, you became his. Had he not been yours, you might
have acted as you had thought fit, at your own unfettered discretion;
but, as you were his, 'twas robbery, 'twas conduct most disgraceful,
to sever yourself from him against his will. Now you must know
that I am a friar; and therefore all the ways of friars are familiar to
me; nor does it misbecome me, as it might another, to speak for
your behoof somewhat freely of them; as I am minded to do that
you may have better understanding of them in the future than you
would seem to have had in the past. Time was when the friars were
most holy and worthy men, but those who to-day take the name and
claim the reputation of friars have nought of the friar save only the
habit: nay, they have not even that: for, whereas their founders
ordained that their habits should be strait, of a sorry sort, and of
coarse stuff, apt symbols of a soul that in arraying the body in so mean
a garb did despite to all things temporal, our modern friars will have
them full, and double, and resplendent, and of the finest stuff, and of
a fashion goodly and pontifical, wherein without shame they flaunt it
like peacocks in the church, in the piazza, even as do the laity in their
robes. And as the fisherman casts his net into the stream with
intent to take many fish at one throw: so 'tis the main solicitude and
study, art and craft of these friars to embrace and entangle within
the ample folds of their vast swelling skirts beguines, widows and
other foolish women, ay, and men likewise in great number. Wherefore, to speak with more exactitude, the friars of to-day have nought
of the habit of the friar save only the colour thereof. And, whereas
the friars of old time sought to win men to their salvation, those of
to-day seek to win their women and their wealth; wherefore they
have made it and make it their sole concern by declamation and
imagery to strike terror into the souls of fools, and to make believe
that sins are purged by alms and masses; to the end that they, base
wretches that have fled to friarage not to ensue holiness but to escape
hardship, may receive from this man bread, from that man wine, and
from the other man a donation for masses for the souls of his dead.
True indeed it is that sins are purged by almsgiving and prayer; but,
did they who give the alms know, did they but understand to whom

or throw them to so many pigs.　And, knowing that the fewer be they that share great riches, the greater their ease, 'tis the study of each how best by declamation and intimidation to oust others from that whereof he would fain be the sole owner.　They censure lust in men, that, they turning therefrom, the sole use of their women may remain to the censors : they condemn usury and unlawful gains, that, being entrusted with the restitution thereof, they may be able to enlarge their habits, and to purchase bishoprics and other great preferments with the very money which they have made believe must bring its possessor to perdition.　And when they are taxed with these and many other discreditable practices, they deem that there is no censure, however grave, of which they may not be quit by their glib formula :—' Follow our precepts, not our practice : ' as if 'twere possible that the sheep should be of a more austere and rigid virtue than the shepherds.　And how many of these, whom they put off with this formula, understand it not in the way in which they enunciate it, not a few of them know.　The friars of to-day would have you follow their precepts, that is to say, they would have you fill their purses with coin, confide to them your secrets, practise continence, be long-suffering, forgive those that trespass against you, keep yourselves from evil speaking ; all which things are good, seemly, holy.　But to what end ?　To the end that they may be able to do that which, if the laity do it, they will not be able to do.　Who knows not that idleness cannot subsist without money ?　Spend thy money on thy pleasures, and the friar will not be able to live in sloth in his order.　Go after women, and there will be no place for the friar.　Be not long-suffering, pardon not the wrong-doer, and the friar will not dare to cross thy threshold to corrupt thy family.　But wherefore pursue I the topic through every detail ?　They accuse themselves as often as they so excuse themselves in the hearing of all that have under-standing.　Why seclude they not themselves, if they misdoubt their power to lead continent and holy lives ?　Or if they must needs not live as recluses, why follow they not that other holy text of the Gospel :—Christ began to do and to teach ?[1]　Let

---

[1] As pointed out by Mr. Payne, these words are not from any of the Gospels, but from the first verse of the Acts of the Apostles.　Boccaccio doubtless used " Evangelio " in a large sense for the whole of the New Testament.

them practise first, and school us with their precepts afterwards. A thousand such have I seen in my day, admirers, lovers, philanderers, not of ladies of the world alone, but of nuns ; ay, and they too such as made the most noise in the pulpits. Is it such as they that we are to follow ? He that does so, pleases himself ; but God knows if he do wisely. But assume that herein we must allow that your censor, the friar, spoke truth, to wit, that none may break the marriage-vow without very grave sin. What then ? to rob a man, to slay him, to make of him an exile and a wanderer on the face of the earth, are not these yet greater sins ? None will deny that so they are. A woman that indulges herself in the intimate use with a man commits but a sin of nature ; but if she rob him, or slay him, or drive him out into exile, her sin proceeds from depravity of spirit. That you did rob Tedaldo, I have already shewn you, in that, having of your own free will become his, you reft you from him. I now go further and say that, so far as in you lay, you slew him, seeing that, shewing yourself ever more and more cruel, you did your utmost to drive him to take his own life ; and in the law's intent he that is the cause that wrong is done is as culpable as he that does it. Nor is it deniable that you were the cause that for seven years he has been an exile and a wanderer upon the face of the earth. Wherefore upon each of the said three articles you are found guilty of a greater crime than you committed by your intimacy with him. But consider we the matter more closely : perchance Tedaldo merited such treatment : nay, but assuredly 'twas not so. You have yourself so confessed : besides which I know that he loves you more dearly than himself. He would laud, he would extol, he would magnify you above all other ladies so as never was heard the like, wheresoever 'twas seemly for him to speak of you, and it might be done without exciting suspicion. All his bliss, all his honour, all his liberty he avowed was entirely in your disposal. Was he not of noble birth ? And for beauty might he not compare with the rest of his townsfolk ? Did he not excel in all the exercises and accomplishments proper to youth ? Was he not beloved, held dear, well seen of all men ? You will not deny it. How then could you at the behest of a paltry friar, silly, brutish and envious, bring yourself to deal with him in any harsh sort ? I cannot estimate the error of those ladies who look askance on men and hold them cheap ; whereas, bethinking them of what they are themselves, and what and how great is the nobility with which God has endowed man above all the other animals, they ought rather to glory in the love which men give them, and hold them most dear, and with all zeal study to please them, that so their love may never fail. In what sort you did so, instigated by the chatter of a friar, some broth-guzzling, pastry-gorging knave without a doubt, you know; and peradventure his purpose was but to instal himself in the place whence he sought to oust another. This then is the sin which the Divine justice, which, ever operative, suffers no perturbation of its even balance, or arrest of judgment, has decreed not to leave unpunished: wherefore, as without due cause you devised how you might despoil Tedaldo of yourself, so without due cause your husband has been placed and is in jeopardy of his life on Tedaldo's account, and to your sore affliction. Wherefrom if you would be delivered, there is that which you must promise, ay, and (much more) which you must perform: to wit, that, should it ever betide that Tedaldo return hither from his long exile, you will restore to him your favour, your love, your tender regard, your intimacy, and reinstate him in the position which he held before you foolishly hearkened to the half-witted friar."

Thus ended the pilgrim; and the lady, who had followed him with the closest attention, deeming all that he advanced very sound, and doubting not that her tribulation was, as he said, in requital of her sin, spoke thus:—"Friend of God, well I wot that the matters which you discourse are true, and, thanks to your delineation, I now in great measure know what manner of men are the friars, whom I have hitherto regarded as all alike holy; nor doubt I that great was my fault in the course which I pursued towards Tedaldo; and gladly, were it in my power, would I make reparation in the manner which you have indicated. But how is this feasible? Tedaldo can never return to us. He is dead. Wherefore I know not why I must needs give you a promise which cannot be performed." "Madam," returned the pilgrim, "'tis revealed to me by God that Tedaldo is by no means dead, but alive and well and happy, so only he enjoyed your favour." "Nay, but," said the lady, "speak advisedly; I saw his body done to death by more than one knife-wound; I folded it in these arms, and drenched the dead face with many a tear; whereby, perchance, I gave occasion for the bruit that has been made to my disadvantage." "Say what you may, Madam," rejoined the pilgrim, "I assure you that Tedaldo lives, and if you will but give the promise, then, for its fulfilment, I have good hope that you will soon see him." Whereupon: "I give the promise," said the lady, "and right gladly will I make it good; nor is there aught that might happen that would yield me such delight as to see my husband free and scatheless, and Tedaldo alive." Tedaldo now deemed it wise to make himself known, and establish the lady in a more sure hope of her husband's safety. Wherefore he said:— "Madam, to set your mind at ease in regard of your husband, I must first impart to you a secret, which be mindful to disclose to none so long as you live." Then—for such was the confidence which the lady reposed in the pilgrim's apparent sanctity that they were by themselves in a place remote from observation—Tedaldo drew forth a ring which he had guarded with the most jealous care, since it had been given him by the lady on the last night when they were together, and said, as he shewed it to her:—"Madam, know you this?" The lady recognized it forthwith, and answered:—"I do, Sir; I gave it long ago to Tedaldo." Then the pilgrim, rising and throwing off his sclavine[1] and hat, said with the Florentine accent:—"And know you me?" The lady recognizing forthwith the form and semblance of Tedaldo, was struck dumb with wonder and fear as of a corpse that is seen to go about as if alive, and was much rather disposed to turn and flee from Tedaldo returned from the tomb than to come forward and welcome Tedaldo arrived from Cyprus. But when Tedaldo said to her:—"Fear not, Madam, your Tedaldo am I, alive and well, nor was I ever dead, whatever you and my brothers may think," the lady, partly awed, partly reassured by his voice, regarded him with rather more attention, and inly affirming that 'twas in very truth Tedaldo, threw herself upon his neck, and wept, and kissed him, saying:—"Sweet my Tedaldo, welcome home." "Madam," replied Tedaldo after he had kissed and embraced her, "time serves not now for greetings more intimate. 'Tis for me to be up and doing, that Aldobrandino may be restored to you safe and sound; touching which matter you will, I trust, before to-morrow at even hear tidings that will gladden your heart;

---

[1] *Schiavina*, Low Lat. *sclavina*, the long coarse frock worn, among others, by palmers.

indeed I expect to have good news to-night, and, if so, will come and tell it you, when I shall be less straitened than I am at present." He then resumed his sclavine and hat, and having kissed the lady again, and bade her be of good cheer, took his leave, and hied him to the prison, where Aldobrandino lay more occupied with apprehension of imminent death than hope of deliverance to come. As ministrant of consolation, he gained ready admittance of the warders, and, seating himself by Aldobrandino's side, he said :—"Aldobrandino, in me thou seest a friend sent thee by God, who is touched with pity of thee by reason of thy innocence ; wherefore, if in reverent submission to Him thou wilt grant me a slight favour that I shall ask of thee, without fail, before to-morrow at even, thou shalt, in lieu of the doom of death that thou awaitest, hear thy acquittal pronounced." " Worthy man," replied Aldobrandino, " I know thee not, nor mind I ever to have seen thee ; wherefore, as thou shewest thyself solicitous for my safety, my friend indeed thou must needs be, even as thou sayst. And in sooth the crime, for which they say I ought to be doomed to death, I never committed, though others enough I have committed, which perchance have brought me to this extremity. However, if so be that God has now pity on me, this I tell thee in reverent submission to Him, that, whereas 'tis but a little thing that thou cravest of me, there is nought, however great, but I would not only promise but gladly do it ; wherefore, even ask what thou wilt, and, if so be that I escape, I will without fail keep my word to the letter." " Nay," returned the pilgrim, "I ask but this of thee, that thou pardon Tedaldo's four brothers, that in the belief that thou wast guilty of their brother's death they brought thee to this strait, and, so they ask thy forgiveness, account them as thy brothers and friends." " How sweet," replied Aldobrandino, " is the savour, how ardent the desire, of vengeance, none knows but he that is wronged ; but yet, so God may take thought for my deliverance, I will gladly pardon, nay, I do now pardon them, and if I go hence alive and free, I will thenceforth have them in such regard as shall content thee." Satisfied with this answer, the pilgrim, without further parley, heartily exhorted Aldobrandino to be of good cheer ; assuring him that, before the next day was done, he should be certified beyond all manner of doubt of his deliverance ; and so he left him.

On quitting the prison the pilgrim hied him forthwith to the signory, and being closeted with a knight that was in charge, thus spoke :—" My lord, 'tis the duty of all, and most especially of those who hold your place, zealously to bestir themselves that the truth be brought to light, in order as well that those bear not the penalty who have not committed the crime, as that the guilty be punished. And that this may come to pass to your honour and the undoing of the delinquent, I am come hither to you. You wot that you have dealt rigorously with Aldobrandino Palermini, and have found, as you think, that 'twas he that slew Tedaldo Elisei, and you are about to condemn him ; wherein you are most certainly in error, as I doubt not before midnight to prove to you, delivering the murderers into your hands." The worthy knight, who was not without pity for Aldobrandino, readily gave ear to the pilgrim's words. He conversed at large with him, and availing himself of his guidance, made an easy capture of the two brothers that kept the inn and their servant in their first sleep. He was about to put them the torture, to elicit the true state of the case, when, their courage failing, they confessed without the least reserve, severally at first, and then jointly, that 'twas they that had slain Tedaldo Elisei, not knowing who he was. Asked for why, they answered that 'twas because he had sorely harassed the wife of one of them, and would have constrained her to do his pleasure, while they were out of doors. Whereof the pilgrim was no sooner apprised, than by leave of the knight he withdrew, and hied him privily to the house of Madonna Ermellina, whom (the rest of the household being gone to bed) he found awaiting him alone, and equally anxious for good news of her husband and a complete reconciliation with her Tedaldo. On entering, he blithely exclaimed :—" Rejoice, dearest my lady, for thou mayst rest assured that to-morrow thou shalt have thy Aldobrandino back here safe and sound ; " and to confirm her faith in his words, he told her all that he had done. Greater joy was never woman's than hers of two such glad surprises ; to wit, to have Tedaldo with her alive again, whom she had wailed for verily dead, and to know Aldobrandino, whom she had thought in no long time to wail for dead, now out of jeopardy. Wherefore, when she had affectionately embraced and kissed her Tedaldo, they hied them to bed together, and with hearty goodwill made gracious and gladsome consummation of their peace by interchange of sweet solace.

With the approach of day Tedaldo rose, and having first apprised the lady of his purpose and enjoined her, as before, to keep it most secret, resumed his pilgrim's habit, and sallied forth of her house, to be ready, as occasion should serve, to act in Aldobrandino's interest. As soon as 'twas day, the signory, deeming themselves amply conversant with the affair, set Aldobrandino at large; and a few days later they caused the malefactors to be beheaded in the place where they had done the murder.

Great was Aldobrandino's joy to find himself free, nor less great was that of his lady and all his friends and kinsfolk; and as 'twas through the pilgrim that it had come about, they brought him to their house, there to reside as long as he cared to tarry in the city; nor could they do him honour and cheer enough, and most of all the lady, who knew her man. But after a while, seeing that his brothers were not only become a common laughing-stock by reason of Aldobrandino's acquittal, but had armed themselves for very fear, he felt that their reconciliation with him brooked no delay, and accordingly craved of him performance of his promise. Aldobrandino replied handsomely that it should be had at once. The pilgrim then bade him arrange for the following day a grand banquet, at which he and his kinsfolk and their ladies were to entertain the four brothers and their ladies, adding that he would himself go forthwith as Aldobrandino's envoy, and bid them welcome to his peace and banquet. All which being approved by Aldobrandino, the pilgrim hied him with all speed to the four brothers, whom by ample, apt and unanswerable argument he readily induced to reinstate themselves in Aldobrandino's friendship by suing for his forgiveness: which done, he bade them and their ladies to breakfast with Aldobrandino on the morrow, and they, being assured of his good faith, were consenting to come. So, on the morrow, at the breakfast hour, Tedaldo's four brothers, still wearing their black, came with certain of their friends to Aldobrandino's house, where he awaited them; and, in presence of the company that had been bidden to meet them, laid down their arms, and made surrender to Aldobrandino, asking his pardon of that which they had done against him. Aldobrandino received them compassionately, wept, kissed each on the mouth, and let few words suffice to remit each offence. After them came their sisters and their wives, all habited sadly, and were graciously received by Madonna Ermellina and the other ladies. The guests, men and women alike, found all things ordered at the banquet with magnificence, nor aught unmeet for commendation save the restraint which the yet recent grief, betokened by the sombre garb of Tedaldo's kinsfolk, laid upon speech (wherein some had found matter to except against the banquet and the pilgrim for devising it, as he well knew), but, as he had premeditated, in due time, he stood up, the others being occupied with their dessert, and spoke thus :—" Nothing is wanting to complete the gaiety of this banquet except the presence of Tedaldo ; whom, as you have been long time with him and have not known him, I will point out to you." So, having divested himself of his sclavine and whatever else in his garb denoted the pilgrim, he remained habited in a tunic of green taffeta, in which guise, so great was the wonder with which all regarded him that, though they recognized him, 'twas long before any dared to believe that 'twas actually Tedaldo. Marking their surprise, Tedaldo told them not a little about themselves, their family connexions, their recent history, and his own adventures. Whereat his brothers and the rest of the men, all weeping for joy, hasted to embrace him, followed by the women, as well those that were not, as those that were, of kin to him, save only Madonna Ermellina. Which Aldobrandino observing, said :—" What is this, Ermellina ? How comes it that, unlike the other ladies, thou alone dost Tedaldo no cheer ?" " Cheer," replied the lady in the hearing of all, " would I gladly do him such as no other woman has done or could do, seeing that I am more beholden to him than any other woman, in that to him I owe it that I have thee with me again ; 'tis but the words spoken to my disadvantage, while we mourned him that we deemed Tedaldo, that give me pause." " Now out upon thee," said Aldo-brandino, " thinkest thou that I heed the yelping of these curs ? His zeal for my deliverance has abundantly disproved it, besides which I never believed it. Quick, get thee up, and go and embrace him." The lady, who desired nothing better, was in this not slow to obey her husband ; she rose forthwith, and embraced Tedaldo as the other ladies had done, and did him gladsome cheer. Tedaldo's brothers and all the company, men and women alike, heartily approved Aldo-brandino's handsomeness; and so whatever of despite the rumour had engendered in the minds of any was done away. And, now that all had done him cheer, Tedaldo with his own hands rent his brothers' suits of black upon their backs, as also the sad-hued garments which his sisters and sisters-in-law wore, and bade bring other apparel. Which when they had donned, there was no lack of singing, dancing and other sorts of merry-making; whereby the banquet, for all its subdued beginning, had a sonorous close. Then, just as they were, in the blithest of spirits, they hied them all to Tedaldo's house, where in the evening they supped; and in this manner they held festival for several days.

'Twas some time before the Florentines ceased to look on Tedaldo as a portent, as if he were risen from the dead; and a shadow of doubt whether he were really Tedaldo or no continued to lurk in the minds of not a few, including even his brothers: they had no assured belief; and in that frame had perchance long continued, but for a casual occurrence that shewed them who the murdered man was. It so befell that one day some men-at-arms from Lunigiana passed by their house, and seeing Tedaldo accosted him, saying:—" Good-morrow to thee, Faziuolo." To whom Tedaldo, in the presence of his brothers, answered:—" You take me for another." Whereat they were abashed, and asked his pardon, saying:—" Sooth to tell, you are liker than we ever knew any man like to another to a comrade of ours, Faziuolo da Pontremoli by name, who came hither a fortnight ago, or perhaps a little more, since when we have not been able to learn what became of him. Most true it is that your dress surprised us, because he, like ourselves, was a soldier." Whereupon Tedaldo's eldest brother came forward, and asked how their comrade had been accoutred. They told him, and 'twas found to have been exactly as they said: by which and other evidence 'twas established that 'twas Faziuolo that had been murdered, and not Tedaldo; of whom thenceforth no suspicion lurked in the minds of his brothers or any one else.

So, then, Tedaldo returned home very rich, and remained constant in his love; nor did the lady again treat him harshly; but, using discretion, they long had mutual solace of their love. God grant us solace of ours.

NOVEL VIII.

*Ferondo, having taken a certain powder, is interred for
dead ; is disinterred by the abbot, who enjoys his wife ;
is put in prison and taught to believe that he is in
purgatory ; is then resuscitated, and rears as his own
a boy begotten by the abbot upon his wife.*

ENDED Emilia's long story, which to none was the less pleasing
for its length, but was deemed of all the ladies brief in regard of the
number and variety of the events therein recounted, a gesture of
the queen sufficed to convey her behest to Lauretta, and cause her
thus to begin :—" Dearest ladies, I have it in mind to tell you a true
story, which wears far more of the aspect of a lie than of that which
it really was : 'tis brought to my recollection by that which we
have heard of one being bewailed and buried in lieu of another. My
story then is of one that, living, was buried for dead, and after believed
with many others that he came out of the tomb not as one that had
not died but as one risen from the dead ; whereby he was venerated
as a saint who ought rather to have been condemned as a criminal."
    Know then that there was and still is in Tuscany an abbey,
situate, as we see not a few, in a somewhat solitary spot, wherein the
office of abbot was held by a monk, who in all other matters ordered
his life with great sanctity, save only in the commerce with women,
and therein knew so well how to cloak his indulgence, that scarce any
there were that so much as suspected—not to say detected it—so
holy and just was he reputed in all matters. Now the abbot consorted much with a very wealthy contadino, Ferondo by name, a
man coarse and gross beyond measure, whose friendship the abbot
only cared for because of the opportunities which it afforded of

deriving amusement from his simplicity; and during their intercourse the abbot discovered that Ferondo had a most beautiful wife; of whom he became so hotly enamoured that he could think of nought else either by day or by night.   But learning that, however simple and inept in all other matters, Ferondo shewed excellent good sense in cherishing and watching over this wife of his, he almost despaired. However, being very astute, he prevailed so far with Ferondo, that he would sometimes bring his wife with him to take a little recreation in the abbey-garden, where he discoursed to them with all lowliness of the blessedness of life eternal, and the most pious works of many men and women of times past, insomuch that the lady conceived a desire to confess to him, and craved and had Ferondo's leave therefor. So, to the abbot's boundless delight, the lady came and seated herself at his feet to make her confession, whereto she prefixed the following exordium :—"If God, Sir, had given me a husband, or had not permitted me to have one, perchance 'twould be easy for me, under your guidance, to enter the way, of which you have spoken, that leads to life eternal.   But, considering what manner of man Ferondo is, and his stupidity, I may call myself a widow, while yet I am married in that, so long as he lives, I may have no other husband; and he, fool that he is, is without the least cause so inordinately jealous of me that 'tis not possible but that my life with him be one of perpetual tribulation and woe.   Wherefore, before I address myself to make further confession, I in all humility beseech you to be pleased to give me some counsel of this matter, for here or nowhere is to be found the source of the amelioration of my life, and if it be not found, neither confession nor any other good work will be of any avail." The abbot was overjoyed to hear her thus speak, deeming that Fortune had opened a way to the fulfilment of his heart's desire. Wherefore he said :—"My daughter, I doubt not that 'tis a great affliction to a lady, fair and delicate as you are, to have a fool for a husband, and still more so that he should be jealous : and as your husband is both the one and the other, I readily credit what you say of your tribulation.   But, to come to the point, I see no resource or remedy in this case, save this only, that Ferondo be cured of his jealousy.   The medicine that shall cure him I know very well how to devise, but it behoves you to keep secret what I am about to tell you."   "Doubt not of it, my father," said the lady; "for I had

rather suffer death than tell any aught that you forbade me to tell.
But the medicine, how is it to be devised?" "If we would have
him cured," replied the abbot, "it can only be by his going to purgatory." "And how may that be?" returned the lady; "can he go
thither while he yet lives?" "He must die," answered the abbot;
"and so he will go thither; and when he has suffered pain enough to
be cured of his jealousy, we have certain prayers with which we will
supplicate God to restore him to life, and He will do so." "Then,"
said the lady; "am I to remain a widow?" "Yes," replied the
abbot, "for a certain time, during which you must be very careful
not to let yourself be married to another, because 'twould offend God,
and when Ferondo was restored to life, you would have to go back to
him, and he would be more jealous than ever." "Be it so then,"
said the lady; "if he be but cured of his jealousy, and so I be not
doomed to pass the rest of my days in prison, I shall be content: do
as you think best." "And so will I," said the abbot; "but what
reward shall I have for such a service?" "My father," said the
lady, "what you please; so only it be in my power. But what may
the like of me do that may be acceptable to a man such as you?'
"Madam," replied the abbot, "'tis in your power to do no less for
me than I am about to do for you: as that which I am minded to do
will ensure your comfort and consolation, so there is that which you
may do which will be the deliverance and salvation of my life." "If
so it be," said the lady, "I shall not be found wanting." "In that
case," said the abbot, "you will give me your love, and gratify my
passion for you, with which I am all afire and wasting away."
Whereto the lady, all consternation, replied:—"Alas! my father, what
is this you crave? I took you for a holy man; now does it beseem
holy men to make such overtures to ladies that come to them for
counsel?" "Marvel not, fair my soul," returned the abbot; "here-
by is my holiness in no wise diminished, for holiness resides in the
soul, and this which I ask of you is but a sin of the flesh. But, however it may be, such is the might of your bewitching beauty, that
love constrains me thus to act. And, let me tell you, good cause
have you to vaunt you of your beauty more than other women, in
that it delights the saints, who are used to contemplate celestial
beauties; whereto I may add that, albeit I am an abbot, yet I am a
man even as others, and, as you see, not yet old. Nor need this

matter seem formidable to you, but rather to be anticipated with pleasure, for, while Ferondo is in purgatory, I shall be your nightly companion, and will give you such solace as he should have given you ; nor will it ever be discovered by any, for all think of me even as you did a while ago, or even more so.　Reject not the grace that God accords you ; for 'tis in your power to have, and, if you are wise and follow my advice, you shall have that which women not a few desire in vain to have.　And moreover I have jewels fair and rare, which I am minded shall be yours and none other's.　Wherefore, sweet my hope, deny me not due guerdon of the service which I gladly render you."

The lady, her eyes still downcast, knew not how to deny him, and yet scrupled to gratify him : wherefore the abbot, seeing that she had hearkened and hesitated to answer, deemed that she was already half won, and following up what he had said with much more to the like effect, did not rest until he had persuaded her that she would do well to comply : and so with some confusion she told him that she was ready to obey his every behest ; but it might not be until Ferondo was in purgatory.　The abbot, well content, replied :—"And we will send him thither forthwith : do but arrange that he come hither to stay with me to-morrow or the day after."　Which said, he slipped a most beautiful ring on her finger, and dismissed her. Pleased with the gift, and expecting more to come, the lady rejoined her attendants, with whom she forthwith fell a talking marvellous things of the abbot's sanctity, and so went home with them.

Some few days after, Ferondo being come to the abbey, the abbot no sooner saw him than he resolved to send him to purgatory.　So he selected from among his drugs a powder of marvellous virtue, which he had gotten in the Levant from a great prince, who averred that 'twas wont to be used by the Old Man of the Mountain, when he would send any one to or bring him from his paradise, and that, without doing the recipient any harm, 'twould induce in him, according to the quantity of the dose, a sleep of such duration and quality that, while the efficacy of the powder lasted, none would deem him to be alive.[1]　Whereof he took enough to cause a three days' sleep, and

---

[1] By the Old Man of the Mountain is meant the head of the confraternity of hashish-eaters (Assassins), whose chief stronghold was at Alamut in Persia (1090–1256).　Cf. Marco Polo, ed. Yule, I. cap. xxiii.

gave it to Ferondo in his cell in a beaker that had still some wine in it, so that he drank it unwittingly : after which he took Ferondo to the cloister, and there with some of his monks fell to making merry with him and his ineptitudes.   In no long time, however, the powder so wrought, that Ferondo was seized in the head with a fit of somnolence so sudden and violent that he slept as he stood, and sleeping fell to the ground.   The abbot put on an agitated air, caused him to be untrussed, sent for cold water, and had it sprinkled on his face, and applied such other remedies as if he would fain call back life and sense banished by vapours of the stomach, or some other intrusive force ; but, as, for all that he and his monks did, Ferondo did not revive, they, after feeling his pulse and finding there no sign of life, one and all pronounced him certainly dead.   Wherefore they sent word to his wife and kinsfolk, who came forthwith, and mourned a while ; after which Ferondo in his clothes was by the abbot's order laid in a tomb.   The lady went home, saying that nothing should ever part her from a little son that she had borne Ferondo ; and so she occupied herself with the care of her son and Ferondo's estate.   At night the abbot rose noiselessly, and with the help of a Bolognese monk, in whom he reposed much trust, and who was that very day arrived from Bologna, got Ferondo out of the tomb, and bore him to a vault, which admitted no light, having been made to serve as a prison for delinquent monks ; and having stripped him of his clothes, and habited him as a monk, they laid him on a truss of straw, and left him there until he should revive.   Expecting which event, and instructed by the abbot how he was then to act, the Bolognese monk (none else knowing aught of what was afoot) kept watch by the tomb.

The day after, the abbot with some of his monks paid a pastoral visit to the lady's house, where he found her in mourning weeds and sad at heart ; and, after administering a little consolation, he gently asked her to redeem her promise.   Free as she now felt herself, and hampered neither by Ferondo nor by any other, the lady, who had noticed another beautiful ring on the abbot's finger, promised immediate compliance, and arranged with the abbot that he should visit her the very next night.   So, at nightfall, the abbot donned Ferondo's clothes, and, attended by his monk, paid his visit, and lay with her until matins to his immense delight and solace, and so returned to the abbey ; and many visits he paid her on the same errand; whereby some that met him, coming or going that way, supposed that 'twas Ferondo perambulating those parts by way of penance ; and fables not a few passed from mouth to mouth of the foolish rustics, and sometimes reached the ears of the lady, who was at no loss to account for them.

As for Ferondo, when he revived, 'twas only to find himself he knew not where, while the Bolognese monk entered the tomb, gibbering horribly, and armed with a rod, wherewith, having laid hold of Ferondo, he gave him a severe thrashing. Blubbering and bellowing for pain, Ferondo could only ejaculate :—"Where am I ? " "In purgatory," replied the monk. "How ? " returned Ferondo, "am I dead then ? " and the monk assuring him that 'twas even so, he fell a bewailing his own and his lady's and his son's fate, after the most ridiculous fashion in the world. The monk brought him somewhat to eat and drink. Of which when Ferondo caught sight, "Oh ! " said he, "dead folk eat then, do they ? " "They do," replied the monk ; "and this, which I bring thee, is what the lady that was thy wife sent this morning to the church by way of alms for masses for thy soul ; and God is minded that it be assigned to thee." "Now God grant her a happy year," said Ferondo ; "dearly I loved her while I yet lived, and would hold her all night long in my arms, and cease not to kiss her, ay, and would do yet more to her, when I was so minded." Whereupon he fell to eating and drinking with great avidity, and finding the wine not much to his taste, he said :—"Now God do her a mischief ! Why gave she not the priest of the wine that is in the cask by the wall ? " When he had done eating, the monk laid hold of him again, and gave him another sound thrashing with the rod. Ferondo bellowed mightily, and then cried out :—"Alas ! why servest thou me so ? " "God," answered the monk, "has decreed that thou be so served twice a day." "For why ? " said Ferondo. "Because," returned the monk, "thou wast jealous, notwithstanding thou hadst to wife a woman that has not her peer in thy countryside." "Alas," said Ferondo, "she was indeed all that thou sayst, ay, and the sweetest creature too,—no comfit so honeyed—but I knew not that God took it amiss that a man should be jealous, or I had not been so." "Of that," replied the monk, "thou shouldst have bethought thee while thou wast there, and have amended thy ways; and should it fall to thy lot ever to return thither, be sure that thou so lay to heart the lesson that I now give thee, that thou be no more jealous." "Oh!" said Ferondo; "dead folk sometimes return to earth, do they?" "They do," replied the monk; "if God so will." "Oh!" said Ferondo; "if I ever return, I will be the best husband in the world; never will I beat her or scold her, save for the wine that she has sent me this morning, and also for sending me never a candle, so that I have had perforce to eat in the dark." "Nay," said the monk, "she sent them, but they were burned at the masses." "Oh!" said Ferondo, "I doubt not you say true; and, of a surety, if I ever return, I will let her do just as she likes. But tell me, who art thou that entreatest me thus?" "Late of Sardinia I," answered the monk, "dead too; and, for that I gave my lord much countenance in his jealousy, doomed by God for my proper penance to entreat thee thus with food and drink and thrashings, until such time as He may ordain otherwise touching thee and me." "And are we two the only folk here?" inquired Ferondo. "Nay, there are thousands beside," answered the monk; "but thou canst neither see nor hear them, nor they thee." "And how far," said Ferondo, "may we be from our country?" "Oh! ho!" returned the monk, "why, 'tis some miles clean out of shit-range." "I'faith," said Ferondo, "that is far indeed: methinks we must be out of the world."

In such a course, alternately beaten, fed and amused with idle tales, was Ferondo kept for ten months, while the abbot, to his great felicity, paid many a visit to the fair lady, and had the jolliest time in the world with her. But, as misfortunes will happen, the lady conceived, which fact, as soon as she was aware of it, she imparted to the abbot; whereupon both agreed that Ferondo must without delay be brought back from purgatory to earth and her, and be given to understand that she was with child of him. So the very next night the abbot went to the prison, and in a disguised voice pronounced Ferondo's name, and said to him :—"Ferondo, be of good cheer, for God is minded that thou return to earth; and on thy return thou shalt have a son by thy lady, and thou shalt call him Benedetto; because 'tis in answer to the prayers of thy holy abbot and thy lady, and for love of St. Benedict, that God accords thee this grace." Whereat Ferondo was overjoyed, and said :—"It likes me well.

God give a good year to Master Lord God, and the abbot, and St. Benedict, and my cheese-powdered, honey-sweet wife." Then, in the wine that he sent him, the abbot administered enough of the powder to cause him to sleep for four hours ; and so, with the aid of the monk, having first habited him in his proper clothes, he privily conveyed him back to the tomb in which he had been buried. On the morrow at daybreak Ferondo revived, and perceiving through a chink in the tomb a glimmer of light, to which he had been a stranger for full ten months, he knew that he was alive, and began to bellow :—"Let me out, let me out : " then, setting his head to the lid of the tomb, he heaved amain ; whereby the lid, being insecure, started ; and he was already thrusting it aside, when the monks, matins being now ended, ran to the spot and recognized Ferondo's voice, and saw him issue from the tomb ; by which unwonted event they were all so affrighted that they took to flight, and hied them to the abbot : who, rising as if from prayer, said :—"Sons, be not afraid ; take the cross and the holy water, and follow me, and let us see what sign of His might God will vouchsafe us." And so he led the way to the tomb ; beside which they found Ferondo standing, deathly pale by reason of his long estrangement from the light. On sight of the abbot he ran and threw himself at his feet, saying :—"My father, it has been revealed to me that 'tis to your prayers and those of St. Benedict and my lady that I owe my release from purgatorial pain, and restoration to life ; wherefore 'tis my prayer that God give you a good year and good calends, to-day and all days." "Laud we the power of God!" said the abbot. "Go then, son, as God has restored thee to earth, comfort thy wife, who, since thou didst depart this life, has been ever in tears, and mayst thou live henceforth in the love and service of God." "Sir," answered Ferondo, " 'tis well said ; and, for the doing, trust me that, as soon as I find her, I shall kiss her, such is the love I bear her." So saying, he went his way ; and the abbot, left alone with his monks, made as if he marvelled greatly at the affair, and caused devoutly chant the Miserere. So Ferondo returned to his hamlet, where all that saw him fleeing, as folk are wont to flee from spectacles of horror, he called them back, asseverating that he was risen from the tomb. His wife at first was no less timorous : but, as folk began to take heart of grace, perceiving that he was alive, they plied him with many questions, all which he answered as one that had returned with ripe experience, and gave them tidings of the souls of their kinsfolk, and told of his own invention the prettiest fables of the purgatorial state, and in full folkmoot recounted the revelation vouchsafed him by the mouth of Ragnolo Braghiello [1] before his resuscitation.

Thus was Ferondo reinstated in his property and reunited to his wife, who, being pregnant, as he thought, by himself, chanced by the time of her delivery to countenance the vulgar error that the woman must bear the infant in the womb for exactly nine months, and gave birth to a male child, who was named Benedetto Ferondi. Ferondo's return from purgatory, and the report he brought thence, immeasurably enhanced the fame of the abbot's holiness.   So Ferondo, cured of his jealousy by the thrashings which he had gotten for it, verified the abbot's prediction, and never offended the lady again in that sort.   Wherefore she lived with him, as before, in all outward seemliness ; albeit she failed not, as occasion served, to forgather with the holy abbot, who had so well and sedulously served her in her especial need.

[1] Derisively for Agnolo Gabriello (the *h* having merely the effect of preserving the hardness of the *g* before *i*), *i. e.* Angel Gabriel.

NOVEL IX.

Gillette of Narbonne cures the King of France of a fistula, craves for spouse Bertrand de Roussillon, who marries her against his will, and hies him in despite to Florence, where, as he courts a young woman, Gillette lies with him in her stead, and has two sons by him; for which cause he afterwards takes her into favour and entreats her as his wife.

LAURETTA's story being ended, and the queen being minded not to break her engagement with Dioneo, 'twas now her turn to speak. Wherefore without awaiting the call of her subjects, thus with mien most gracious she began :—Now that we have heard Lauretta's story, who shall tell any to compare with it for beauty ? Lucky indeed was it that she was not the first ; for few that followed would have pleased ; and so, I misdoubt me, 'twill fare ill with those that remain to complete the day's narration. However, for what it may be worth, I will tell you a story which seems to me germane to our theme.

Know, then, that in the realm of France there was a gentleman, Isnard, Comte de Roussillon, by name, who, being in ill-health, kept ever in attendance on him a physician, one Master Gerard of Narbonne. The said Count had an only son named Bertrand, a very fine and winsome little lad; with whom were brought up other children of his own age, among them the said physician's little daughter Gillette; who with a love boundless and ardent out of all keeping with her tender years became enamoured of this Bertrand. And so, when the Count died, and his son, being left a ward of the King, must needs go to Paris, the girl remained beside herself with grief, and, her father dying soon after, would gladly have gone to Paris to see Bertrand, might she but have found a fair excuse; but no decent pretext could she come by, being left a great and sole heiress and very closely guarded. So being come of marriageable age, still cherishing Bertrand's memory, she rejected not a few suitors, to whom her kinsfolk would fain have married her, without assigning any reason.

Now her passion waxing ever more ardent for Bertrand, as she learned that he was grown a most goodly gallant, tidings reached her that the King of France, in consequence of a tumour which he had had in the breast, and which had been ill tended, was now troubled with a fistula, which occasioned him extreme distress and suffering; nor had he as yet come by a physician that was able, though many had essayed, to cure him, but had rather grown worse under their hands; wherefore in despair he was minded no more to have recourse to any for counsel or aid. Whereat the damsel was overjoyed, deeming not only that she might find therein lawful occasion to go to Paris, but, that, if the disease was what she took it to be, it might well betide that she should be wedded to Bertrand. So—for not a little knowledge had she gotten from her father—she prepared a powder from certain herbs serviceable in the treatment of the supposed disease, and straightway took horse, and hied her to Paris. Arrived there she made it her first concern to have sight of Bertrand; and then, having obtained access to the King, she besought him of his grace to shew her his disease. The King knew not how to refuse so young, fair and winsome a damsel, and let her see the place. Whereupon, no longer doubting that she should cure him, she said:—"Sire, so please you, I hope in God to cure you of this malady within eight days without causing you the least distress or discomfort." The King inly scoffed at her words, saying to himself:—"How should a damsel have come by a knowledge and skill that the greatest physicians in the world do not possess?" He therefore graciously acknowledged her good intention, and answered that he had resolved no more to follow advice of physician. "Sire," said the damsel, "you disdain my art, because I am young and a woman; but I bid you bear in mind that I rely not on my own skill, but on the help of God, and the skill of Master Gerard of Narbonne, my father, and a famous physician in his day."

Whereupon the King said to himself:—"Perchance she is sent me by
God; why put I not her skill to the proof, seeing that she says that
she can cure me in a short time, and cause me no distress?" And
being minded to make the experiment, he said:—"Damsel, and if,
having caused me to cancel my resolve, you should fail to cure me,
what are you content should ensue?" "Sire," answered the damsel,
"set a guard upon me; and if within eight days I cure you not, have
me burned; but if I cure you, what shall be my guerdon?" "You
seem," said the King, "to be yet unmarried; if you shall effect the
cure, we will marry you well and in high place." "Sire," returned
the damsel, "well content indeed am I that you should marry me,
so it be to such a husband as I shall ask of you, save that I may not
ask any of your sons or any other member of the royal house."
Whereto the King forthwith consented, and the damsel, thereupon
applying her treatment, restored him to health before the period
assigned. Wherefore, as soon as the King knew that he was cured:—
"Damsel," said he, "well have you won your husband." She
answered:—"In that case, Sire, I have won Bertrand de Roussillon,
of whom, while yet a child, I was enamoured, and whom I have
ever since most ardently loved." To give her Bertrand seemed to
the King no small matter; but, having pledged his word, he would
not break it: so he sent for Bertrand, and said to him:—"Bertrand,
you are now come to man's estate, and fully equipped to enter on it;
'tis therefore our will that you go back and assume the governance
of your county, and that you take with you a damsel, whom we have
given you to wife." "And who is the damsel, Sire?" said Bertrand.
"She it is," answered the King, "that has restored us to health by
her physic." Now Bertrand, knowing Gillette, and that her lineage
was not such as matched his nobility, albeit, seeing her, he had found
her very fair, was overcome with disdain, and answered:—"So, Sire,
you would fain give me a she-doctor to wife. Now God forbid that
I should ever marry any such woman." "Then," said the King,
"you would have us fail of the faith which we pledged to the damsel,
who asked you in marriage by way of guerdon for our restoration to
health." "Sire," said Bertrand, "you may take from me all that
I possess, and give me as your man to whomsoever you may be
minded; but rest assured that I shall never be satisfied with such a
match." "Nay, but you will," replied the King; "for the damsel

is fair and discreet, and loves you well; wherefore we anticipate that you will live far more happily with her than with a dame of much higher lineage." Bertrand was silent; and the King made great preparations for the celebration of the nuptials. The appointed day came, and Bertrand, albeit reluctantly, nevertheless complied, and in the presence of the King was wedded to the damsel, who loved him more dearly than herself. Which done, Bertrand, who had already taken his resolution, said that he was minded to go down to his county, there to consummate the marriage; and so, having craved and had leave of absence of the King, he took horse, but instead of returning to his county he hied him to Tuscany; where, finding the Florentines at war with the Sienese, he determined to take service with the Florentines, and being made heartily and honourably welcome, was appointed to the command of part of their forces, at a liberal stipend, and so remained in their service for a long while. Distressed by this turn of fortune, and hoping by her wise management to bring Bertrand back to his county, the bride hied her to Roussillon, where she was received by all the tenants as their liege lady. She found that, during the long absence of the lord, everything had fallen into decay and disorder; which, being a capable woman, she rectified with great and sedulous care, to the great joy of the tenants, who held her in great esteem and love, and severely censured the Count, that he was not satisfied with her. When the lady had duly ordered all things in the county, she despatched two knights to the Count with the intelligence, praying him, that, if 'twas on her account that he came not home, he would so inform her; in which case she would gratify him by departing. To whom with all harshness he replied :—" She may even please herself in the matter. For my part I will go home and live with her, when she has this ring on her finger and a son gotten of me upon her arm." The ring was one which he greatly prized, and never removed from his finger, by reason of a virtue which he had been given to understand that it possessed. The knights appreciated the harshness of a condition which contained two articles, both of which were all but impossible; and, seeing that by no words of theirs could they alter his resolve, they returned to the lady, and delivered his message. Sorely distressed, the lady after long pondering determined to try how and where the two conditions might be satisfied, that so her husband might be hers again. Having formed her plan, she assembled certain of the more considerable and notable men of the county, to whom she gave a consecutive and most touching narrative of all that she had done for love of the Count, with the result; concluding by saying that she was not minded to tarry there to the Count's perpetual exile, but to pass the rest of her days in pilgrimages and pious works for the good of her soul: wherefore she prayed them to undertake the defence and governance of the county, and to inform the Count that she had made entire and absolute cession of it to him, and was gone away with the intention of never more returning to Roussillon. As she spoke, tears not a few coursed down the cheeks of the honest men, and again and again they besought her to change her mind, and stay. All in vain, however; she commended them to God, and, accompanied only by one of her male cousins and a chambermaid (all three habited as pilgrims and amply provided with money and precious jewels), she took the road, nor tarried until she was arrived at Florence. There she lodged in a little inn kept by a good woman that was a widow, bearing herself lowly as a poor pilgrim, and eagerly expectant of news of her lord.

Now it so befell that the very next day she saw Bertrand pass in front of the inn on horseback at the head of his company; and though she knew him very well, nevertheless she asked the good woman of the inn who he was. The hostess replied:—"'Tis a foreign gentleman—Count Bertrand they call him—a very pleasant gentleman, and courteous, and much beloved in this city; and he is in the last degree enamoured of one of our neighbours here, who is a gentlewoman, but in poor circumstances. A very virtuous damsel she is too, and, being as yet unmarried by reason of her poverty, she lives with her mother, who is an excellent and most discreet lady, but for whom, perchance, she would before now have yielded and gratified the Count's desire." No word of this was lost on the lady; she pondered and meditated every detail with the closest attention, and having laid it all to heart, took her resolution: she ascertained the names and abode of the lady and her daughter that the Count loved, and hied her one day privily, wearing her pilgrim's weeds, to their house, where she found the lady and her daughter in very evident poverty, and after greeting them, told the lady that, if it were agreeable to her, she would speak with her. The gentlewoman

rose and signified her willingness to listen to what she had to say ;
so they went into a room by themselves and sate down, and then
the Countess began thus :—" Madam, methinks you are, as I am,
under Fortune's frown ; but perchance you have it in your power,
if you are so minded, to afford solace to both of us." The lady
answered that, so she might honourably find it, solace indeed was
what she craved most of all things in the world. Whereupon the
Countess continued :—" I must first be assured of your faith, wherein
if I confide and am deceived, the interests of both of us will suffer."
" Have no fear," said the gentlewoman, "speak your whole mind
without reserve, for you will find that there is no deceit in me."
So the Countess told who she was, and the whole course of her love
affair, from its commencement to that hour, on such wise that the
gentlewoman, believing her story the more readily that she had
already heard it in part from others, was touched with compassion
for her. The narrative of her woes complete, the Countess added :—
" Now that you have heard my misfortunes, you know the two
conditions that I must fulfil, if I would come by my husband ; nor
know I any other person than you, that may enable me to fulfil
them ; but so you may, if this which I hear is true, to wit, that
my husband is in the last degree enamoured of your daughter."
" Madam," replied the gentlewoman, " I know not if the Count
loves my daughter, but true it is that he makes great shew of loving
her ; but how may this enable me to do aught for you in the matter
that you have at heart ?" " The how, madam," returned the
Countess, " I will shortly explain to you ; but you shall first hear
what I intend shall ensue, if you serve me. Your daughter, I see, is
fair and of marriageable age, and, by what I have learned and may
well understand, 'tis because you have not the wherewith to marry
her that you keep her at home. Now, in recompense of the service
that you shall do me, I mean to provide her forthwith from my own
moneys with such a dowry as you yourself shall deem adequate for
her marriage." The lady was too needy not to be gratified by the
proposal ; but, nevertheless, with the true spirit of the gentlewoman,
she answered :—" Nay but, madam, tell me that which I may do
for you, and if it shall be such as I may honourably do, gladly will I
do it, and then you shall do as you may be minded." Said then the
Countess :—" I require of you, that through some one in whom you

trust you send word to the Count, my husband, that your daughter
is ready to yield herself entirely to his will, so she may be sure that
he loves her even as he professes ; whereof she will never be con-
vinced, until he send her the ring which he wears on his finger, and
which, she understands, he prizes so much : which, being sent, you
shall give to me, and shall then send him word that your daughter
is ready to do his pleasure, and, having brought him hither secretly,
you shall contrive that I lie by his side instead of your daughter.
Perchance, by God's grace I shall conceive, and so, having his ring
on my finger, and a son gotten of him on my arm, shall have him
for my own again, and live with him even as a wife should live with
her husband, and owe it all to you."

The lady felt that 'twas not a little that the Countess craved of her,
for she feared lest it should bring reproach upon her daughter : but
she reflected that to aid the good lady to recover her husband was
an honourable enterprise, and that in undertaking it she would be
subserving a like end ; and so, trusting in the good and virtuous
disposition of the Countess, she not only promised to do as she was
required, but in no long time, proceeding with caution and secrecy,
as she had been bidden, she both had the ring from the Count, loath
though he was to part with it, and cunningly contrived that the
Countess should lie with him in place of her daughter. In which
first commingling, so ardently sought by the Count, it so pleased
God that the lady was gotten, as in due time her delivery made
manifest, with two sons. Nor once only, but many times did the
lady gratify the Countess with the embraces of her husband, using
such secrecy that no word thereof ever got wind, the Count all the
while supposing that he lay, not with his wife, but with her that he
loved, and being wont to give her, as he left her in the morning,
some fair and rare jewel, which she jealously guarded.

When she perceived that she was with child, the Countess, being
minded no more to burden the lady with such service, said to her :—
"Madam, thanks be to God and to you, I now have that which I
desired, and therefore 'tis time that I make you grateful requital, and
take my leave of you." The lady answered that she was glad if the
Countess had gotten aught that gave her joy ; but that 'twas not as
hoping to have guerdon thereof that she had done her part, but
simply because she deemed it meet and her duty so to do. "Well

said, madam," returned the Countess, "and in like manner that which you shall ask of me I shall not give you by way of guerdon, but because I deem it meet and my duty to give it." Whereupon the lady, yielding to necessity, and abashed beyond measure, asked of her a hundred pounds wherewith to marry her daughter. The Countess, marking her embarrassment, and the modesty of her request, gave her five hundred pounds besides jewels fair and rare, worth, perhaps, no less; and having thus much more than contented her, and received her superabundant thanks, she took leave of her and returned to the inn. The lady, to render purposeless further visits or messages on Bertrand's part, withdrew with her daughter to the house of her kinsfolk in the country; nor was it long before Bertrand, on the urgent entreaty of his vassals and intelligence of the departure of his wife, quitted Florence and returned home. Greatly elated by this intelligence, the Countess tarried awhile in Florence, and was there delivered of two sons as like as possible to their father, whom she nurtured with sedulous care. But by and by she saw fit to take the road, and being come, unrecognized by any, to Montpellier, rested there a few days; and being on the alert for news of the Count and where he was, she learned that on All Saints' day he was to hold a great reception of ladies and gentlemen at Roussillon. Whither, retaining her now wonted pilgrim's weeds, she hied her, and finding that the ladies and gentlemen were all gathered in the Count's palace and on the point of going to table, she tarried not to change her dress, but went up into the hall, bearing her little ones in her arms, and threading her way through the throng to the place where she saw the Count stand, she threw herself at his feet, and sobbing, said to him :—"My lord, thy hapless bride am I, who to ensure thy homecoming and abidance in peace have long time been a wanderer, and now demand of thee observance of the condition whereof word was brought me by the two knights whom I sent to thee. Lo in my arms not one son only but twain, gotten of thee, and on my finger thy ring. 'Tis time, then, that I be received of thee as thy wife according to thy word." Whereat the Count was all dumfounded, recognizing the ring and his own lineaments in the children, so like were they to him; but saying to himself neverthe-less :—"How can it have come about?" So the Countess, while the Count and all that were present marvelled exceedingly, told what had happened, and the manner of it, in precise detail. Wherefore the Count, perceiving that she spoke truth, and having regard to her perseverance and address and her two fine boys, and the wishes of all his vassals and the ladies, who with one accord besought him to own and honour her thenceforth as his lawful bride, laid aside his harsh obduracy, and raised the Countess to her feet, and embraced and kissed her, and acknowledged her for his lawful wife, and the children for his own. Then, having caused her to be rearrayed in garments befitting her rank, he, to the boundless delight of as many as were there, and of all other his vassals, gave up that day and some that followed to feasting and merrymaking; and did ever thenceforth honour, love and most tenderly cherish her as his bride and wife.

NOVEL X.

Alibech turns hermit, and is taught by Rustico, a monk, how the Devil is put in hell. She is afterwards conveyed thence, and becomes the wife of Neerbale.

DIONEO, observing that the queen's story, which he had followed with the closest attention, was now ended, and that it only remained for him to speak, waited not to be bidden, but smilingly thus began :—

Gracious ladies, perchance you have not yet heard how the Devil is put in hell; wherefore, without deviating far from the topic of which you have discoursed throughout the day, I will tell you how 'tis done; it may be the lesson will prove inspiring; besides which, you may learn therefrom that, albeit Love prefers the gay palace and the dainty chamber to the rude cabin, yet, for all that, he may at times manifest his might in wilds matted with forests, rugged with alps, and desolate with caverns : whereby it may be understood that all things are subject to his sway. But—to come to my story—I say that in the city of Capsa[1] in Barbary there was once a very rich man, who with other children had a fair and dainty little daughter, Alibech by name. Now Alibech, not being a Christian, and hearing many Christians, that were in the city, speak much in praise of the Christian Faith and the service of God, did one day inquire of one of them after what fashion it were possible to serve God with as few impediments as might be, and was informed that they served God best who most completely renounced the world and its affairs, like those who had fixed their abode in the wilds of the Thebaid desert. Whereupon, actuated by no sober predilection, but

---

[1] Now Gafsa, in Tunis.

by childish impulse, the girl, who was very simple and about fourteen years of age, said never a word more of the matter, but stole away on the morrow, and quite alone set out to walk to the Thebaid desert ; and, by force of resolution, albeit with no small suffering, she after some days reached those wilds ; where, espying a cabin a great way off, she hied her thither, and found a holy man by the door, who, marvelling to see her there, asked her what she came there to seek. She answered that, guided by the spirit of God, she was come thither, seeking, if haply she might serve Him, and also find some one that might teach her how He ought to be served. Marking her youth and great beauty, the worthy man, fearing lest, if he suffered her to remain with him, he should be ensnared by the Devil, commended her good intention, set before her a frugal repast of roots of herbs, crab-apples and dates, with a little water to wash them down, and said to her :—" My daughter, there is a holy man not far from here, who is much better able to teach thee that of which thou art in quest than I am ; go to him, therefore ; " and he shewed her the way. But when she was come whither she was directed, she met with the same answer as before, and so, setting forth again, she came at length to the cell of a young hermit, a worthy man and very devout—his name Rustico—whom she interrogated as she had the others. Rustico, being minded to make severe trial of his constancy, did not send her away, as the others had done, but kept her with him in his cell, and when night came, made her a little bed of palm-leaves ; whereon he bade her compose herself to sleep. Hardly had she done so before the solicitations of the flesh joined battle with the powers of Rustico's spirit, and he, finding himself left in the lurch by the latter, endured not many assaults before he beat a retreat, and surrendered at discretion : wherefore he bade adieu to holy meditation and prayer and discipline, and fell a musing on the youth and beauty of his companion, and also how he might so order his conversation with her, that without seeming to her to be a libertine he might yet compass that which he craved of her. So, probing her by certain questions, he discovered that she was as yet entirely without cognizance of man, and as simple as she seemed : wherefore he excogitated a plan for bringing her to pleasure him under colour of serving God. He began by giving her a long lecture on the great enmity that subsists between God and the Devil ; after which he gave her to understand that, God having condemned the Devil to hell, to put him there was of all services the most acceptable to God. The girl asking him how it might be done, Rustico answered :—" Thou shalt know it in a trice ; thou hast but to do that which thou seest me do." Then, having divested himself of his scanty clothing, he threw himself stark naked on his knees, as if he would pray ; whereby he caused the girl, who followed his example, to confront him in the same posture. Whereupon Rustico, seeing her so fair, felt an accession of desire, and therewith came an insurgence of the flesh, which Alibech marking with surprise, said :—" Rustico, what is this, which I see thee have, that so protrudes, and which I have not?" " Oh ! my daughter," said Rustico, " 'tis the Devil of whom I have told thee : and, seest thou? he is now tormenting me most grievously, insomuch that I am scarce able to hold out." Then :—" Praise be to God," said the girl, " I see that I am in better case than thou, for no such Devil have I." " Sooth sayst thou," returned Rustico ; " but instead of him thou hast somewhat else that I have not." " Oh !" said Alibech, " what may that be ?" " Hell," answered Rustico : " and I tell thee, that 'tis my belief that God has sent thee hither for the salvation of my soul ; seeing that, if this Devil shall continue to plague me thus, then, so thou wilt have compassion on me and permit me to put him in hell, thou wilt both afford me exceeding great solace, and render to God an exceeding great and most acceptable service, if, as thou sayst, thou art come into these parts for such a purpose." In good faith the girl made answer :— " As I have hell to match your Devil, be it, my father, as and when you will." Whereupon :—" Bless thee, my daughter," said Rustico, " go we then, and put him there, that he leave me henceforth in peace." Which said, he took the girl to one of the beds and taught her the posture in which she must lie in order to incarcerate this spirit accursed of God. The girl, having never before put any devil in hell, felt on this first occasion a twinge of pain : wherefore she said to Rustico :—" Of a surety, my father, he must be a wicked fellow, this devil, and in very truth a foe to God ; for there is sorrow even in hell—not to speak of other places—when he is put there." " Daughter," said Rustico, " 'twill not be always so." And for better assurance thereof they put him there six times before they quitted the bed ; whereby they so thoroughly abased his pride that

he was fain to be quiet.   However, the proud fit returning upon him
from time to time, and the girl addressing herself always obediently
to its reduction, it so befell that she began to find the game agreeable,
and would say to Rustico :—" Now see I plainly that 'twas true,
what the worthy men said at Capsa, of the service of God being so
delightful: indeed I cannot remember that in aught that ever I did
I had so much pleasure, so much solace, as in putting the Devil in
hell ; for which cause I deem it insensate folly on the part of any
one to have a care to aught else than the service of God."   Wherefore many a time she would come to Rustico, and say to him :—
" My father, 'twas to serve God that I came hither, and not to pass
my days in idleness : go we then, and put the Devil in hell."   And
while they did so, she would now and again say :—" I know not,
Rustico, why the Devil should escape from hell ; were he but as
ready to stay there as hell is to receive and retain him, he would
never come out of it."   So, the girl thus frequently inviting and
exhorting Rustico to the service of God, there came at length a time
when she had so thoroughly lightened his doublet that he shivered
when another would have sweated ; wherefore he began to instruct
her that the Devil was not to be corrected and put in hell, save
when his head was exalted with pride ; adding, "and we by God's
grace have brought him to so sober a mind that he prays God he
may be left in peace ; " by which means he for a time kept the girl
quiet.   But when she saw that Rustico had no more occasion for
her to put the Devil in hell, she said to him one day :—" Rustico, if
thy Devil is chastened and gives thee no more trouble, my hell, on
the other hand, gives me no peace ; wherefore, as I with my hell
have holpen thee to abase the pride of thy Devil, so thou wouldst do
well to lend me the aid of thy Devil to allay the fervent heat of my
hell."   Rustico, whose diet was roots of herbs and water, was scarce
able to respond to her demands : he told her that 'twould require
not a few devils to allay the heat of hell ; but that he would do what
might be in his power ; and so now and again he satisfied her ; but
so seldom that 'twas as if he had tossed a bean into the jaws of a lion.
Whereat the girl, being fain of more of the service of God than
she had, did somewhat repine.   However, the case standing thus
(deficiency of power against superfluity of desire) between Rustico's
Devil and Alibech's hell, it chanced that a fire broke out in Capsa,

whereby the house of Alibech's father was burned, and he and all his sons and the rest of his household perished ; so that Alibech was left sole heiress of all his estate. And a young gallant, Neerbale by name, who by reckless munificence had wasted all his substance, having discovered that she was alive, addressed himself to the pursuit of her, and, having found her in time to prevent the confiscation of her father's estate as an escheat for failure of heirs, took her, much to Rustico's relief and against her own will, back to Capsa, and made her his wife, and shared with her her vast patrimony. But before he had lain with her, she was questioned by the ladies of the manner in which she had served God in the desert ; whereto she answered, that she had been wont to serve Him by putting the Devil in hell, and that Neerbale had committed a great sin, when he took her out of such service. The ladies being curious to know how the Devil was put in hell, the girl satisfied them, partly by words, partly by signs. Whereat they laughed exorbitantly (and still laugh) and said to her :—" Be not down-hearted, daughter ; 'tis done here too ; Neerbale will know well how to serve God with you in that way." And so the story passing from mouth to mouth throughout the city, it came at last to be a common proverb, that the most acceptable service that can be rendered to God is to put the Devil in hell ; which proverb, having travelled hither across the sea, is still current. Wherefore, young ladies, you that have need of the grace of God, see to it that you learn how to put the Devil in hell, because 'tis mightily pleasing to God, and of great solace to both the parties, and much good may thereby be engendered and ensue.

A thousand times or more had Dioneo's story brought the laugh to the lips of the honourable ladies, so quaint and curiously entertaining found they the fashion of it. And now at its close the queen, seeing the term of her sovereignty come, took the laurel wreath from her head, and with mien most debonair, set it on the brow of Filostrato, saying :—" We shall soon see whether the wolf will know better how to guide the sheep than the sheep have yet succeeded in guiding the wolves." Whereat Filostrato said with a laugh :—" Had I been hearkened to, the wolves would have taught the sheep to put the Devil in hell even as Rustico taught Alibech. Wherefore call us not wolves, seeing that you have not shewn yourselves sheep : however, as best I may be able, I will govern the kingdom committed to my charge." Whereupon Neifile took him up: "Hark ye, Filostrato," she said, "while you thought to teach us, you might have learnt a lesson from us, as did Masetto da Lamporecchio from the nuns, and have recovered your speech when the bones had learned to whistle without a master."[1] Filostrato, perceiving that there was a scythe for each of his arrows, gave up jesting, and addressed himself to the governance of his kingdom. He called the seneschal, and held him strictly to account in every particular; he then judiciously ordered all matters as he deemed would be best and most to the satisfaction of the company, while his sovereignty should last; and having so done, he turned to the ladies, and said:—"Loving ladies, as my ill luck would have it, since I have had wit to tell good from evil, the charms of one or other of you have kept me ever a slave to Love: and for all I shewed myself humble and obedient and conformable, so far as I knew how, to all his ways, my fate has been still the same, to be discarded for another, and go ever from bad to worse; and so, I suppose, 'twill be with me to the hour of my death. Wherefore I am minded that to-morrow our discourse be of no other topic than that which is most germane to my condition, to wit, of those whose loves had a disastrous close: because mine, I expect, will in the long run be most disastrous; nor for other cause was the name, by which you address me, given me by one that well knew its signification." Which said, he arose, and dismissed them all until supper-time.

So fair and delightsome was the garden that none saw fit to quit it, and seek diversion elsewhere. Rather—for the sun now shone with a tempered radiance that caused no discomfort—some of the ladies gave chase to the kids and conies and other creatures that haunted it, and, scampering to and fro among them as they sate, had caused them a hundred times, or so, some slight embarrassment. Dioneo and Fiammetta fell a singing of Messer Guglielmo and the lady of Vergiù.[2] Filomena and Pamfilo sat them down to a game of chess; and, as thus they pursued each their several

---

[1] *I. e.* when you were so emaciated that your bones made music like a skeleton in the wind.

[2] Evidently some version of the tragical *conte* " de la Chastelaine de Vergi, qui mori por laialment amer son ami." See " Fabliaux et Contes," ed. Barbazan, iv. 296: and cf. Bandello, Pt. iv. Nov. v, and Heptameron, Journée vii. Nouvelle lxx.

diversions, time sped so swiftly that the supper-hour stole upon them almost unawares : whereupon they ranged the tables round the beautiful fountain, and supped with all glad and festal cheer.

When the tables were removed, Filostrato, being minded to follow in the footsteps of his fair predecessors in sway, bade Lauretta lead a dance and sing a song. She answered :—" My lord, songs of others know I none, nor does my memory furnish me with any of mine own that seems meet for so gay a company ; but, if you will be content with what I have, gladly will I give you thereof." " Nought of thine," returned the king, " could be other than goodly and delectable. Wherefore give us even what thou hast." So encouraged, Lauretta, with dulcet voice, but manner somewhat languishing, raised the ensuing strain, to which the other ladies responded :—

> What dame disconsolate
>   May so lament as I,
>   That vainly sigh, to Love still dedicate?
>
> He that the heaven and every orb doth move
>   Formed me for His delight
>   Fair, debonair and gracious, apt for love ;
>   That here on earth each soaring spirit might
>   Have foretaste how, above,
>   That beauty shews that standeth in His sight.
>   Ah ! but dull wit and slight,
>   For that it judgeth ill,
>   Liketh me not, nay, doth me vilely rate.
>
> There was who loved me, and my maiden grace
>   Did fondly clip and strain,
>   As in his arms, so in his soul's embrace,
>   And from mine eyes Love's fire did drink amain,
>   And time that glides apace
>   In nought but courting me to spend was fain ;
>   Whom courteous I did deign
>   Ev'n as my peer to entreat ;
>   But am of him bereft ! Ah ! dolorous fate !
>
> Came to me next a gallant swol'n with pride
>   Brave, in his own conceit,

And no less noble eke. Whom woe betide
That he me took, and holds in all unmeet
Suspicion, jealous-eyed !
And I, who wot that me the world should greet
As the predestined sweet
Of many men, well-nigh
Despair, to be to one thus subjugate.

Ah ! woe is me ! cursed be the luckless day,
When, a new gown to wear,
I said the fatal ay ; for blithe and gay
In that plain gown I lived, no whit less fair ;
While in this rich array
A sad and far less honoured life I bear !
Would I had died, or e'er
Sounded those notes of joy
(Ah ! dolorous cheer !) my woe to celebrate !

So list my supplication, lover dear,
Of whom such joyance I,
As ne'er another, had. Thou that in clear
Light of the Maker's presence art, deny
Not pity to thy fere,
Who thee may ne'er forget ; but let one sigh
Breathe tidings that on high
Thou burnest still for me ;
And sue of God that He me there translate.

So ended Lauretta her song, to which all hearkened attentively,
though not all interpreted it alike. Some were inclined to give it a
moral after the Milanese fashion, to wit, that a good porker was
better than a pretty quean. Others construed it in a higher, better
and truer sense, which 'tis not to the present purpose to unfold.
Some more songs followed by command of the king, who caused
torches not a few to be lighted and ranged about the flowery mead ;
and so the night was prolonged until the last star that had risen had
begun to set. Then, bethinking him that 'twas time for slumber,
the king bade all good-night, and dismissed them to their several
chambers.

Endeth here the third day of the Decameron, beginneth the fourth, in which, under the rule of Filostrato, discourse is had of those whose loves had a disastrous close.

DEAREST ladies, as well from what I heard in converse with the wise, as from matters that not seldom fell within my own observation and reading, I formed the opinion that the vehement and scorching blast of envy was apt to vent itself only upon lofty towers or the highest tree-tops : but therein I find that I misjudged ; for, whereas I ever sought and studied how best to elude the buffetings of that furious hurricane, and to that end kept a course not merely on the plain, but, by preference, in the depth of the valley ; as should be abundantly clear to whoso looks at these little stories, written as they are not only in the vulgar Florentine, and in prose, and without dedicatory flourish, but also in as homely and simple a style as may be ; nevertheless all this has not stood me in such stead but that I have been shrewdly shaken, nay, all but uprooted by the blast, and altogether lacerated by the bite of this same envy. Whereby I may very well understand that 'tis true, what the sages aver, that only misery is exempt from envy in the present life. Know then, discreet my ladies, that some there are, who, reading these little stories, have alleged that I am too fond of you, and that 'tis not a seemly thing that I should take so much pleasure in ministering to your gratification and solace ; and some have found more fault with me for praising you as I do. Others, affecting to deliver a more considered judgment, have said that it ill befits my time of life to ensue such matters, to wit, the discoursing of women, or endeavouring to pleasure them. And not a few, feigning a mighty tender regard to my fame, aver that I should do more wisely to keep

ever with the Muses on Parnassus, than to forgather with you in such
vain dalliance.   Those again there are, who, evincing less wisdom
than despite, have told me that I should shew sounder sense if I
bethought me how to get my daily bread, than, going after these idle
toys, to nourish myself upon the wind; while certain others, in
disparagement of my work, strive might and main to make it appear
that the matters which I relate fell out otherwise than as I set them
forth.   Such then, noble ladies, are the blasts, such the sharp and
cruel fangs, by which, while I champion your cause, I am assailed,
harassed and well-nigh pierced through and through.   Which
censures I hear and mark, God knows, with equal mind : and,
though to you belongs all my defence, yet I mean not to be niggard
of my own powers, but rather, without dealing out to them the
castigation they deserve, to give them such slight answer as may
secure my ears some respite of their clamour ; and that without
delay ; seeing that, if already, though I have not completed the
third part of my work, they are not a few and very presumptuous, I
deem it possible, that before I have reached the end, should they
receive no check, they may have grown so numerous, that 'twould
scarce tax their powers to sink me; and that your forces, great though
they be, would not suffice to withstand them.   However I am
minded to answer none of them, until I have related in my behoof,
not indeed an entire story, for I would not seem to foist my stories in
among those of so honourable a company as that with which I have
made you acquainted, but a part of one, that its very incompleteness
may shew that it is not one of them : wherefore, addressing my
assailants, I say :—That in our city there was in old time a citizen
named Filippo Balducci, a man of quite low origin, but of good
substance and well versed and expert in matters belonging to his
condition, who had a wife that he most dearly loved, as did she him,
so that their life passed in peace and concord, nor there was aught
they studied so much as how to please each other perfectly.   Now it
came to pass, as it does to every one, that the good lady departed this
life, leaving Filippo nought of hers but an only son, that she had had
by him, and who was then about two years old.   His wife's death left
Filippo as disconsolate as ever was any man for the loss of a loved
one : and sorely missing the companionship that was most dear to
him, he resolved to have done with the world, and devote himself

and his little son to the service of God. Wherefore, having dedicated all his goods to charitable uses, he forthwith betook him to the summit of Monte Asinaio, where he installed himself with his son in a little cell, and living on alms, passed his days in fasting and prayer, being careful above all things to say nothing to the boy of any temporal matters, nor to let him see aught of the kind, lest they should distract his mind from his religious exercises, but discoursing with him continually of the glory of the life eternal and of God and the saints, and teaching him nought else but holy orisons : in which way of life he kept him not a few years, never suffering him to quit the cell or see aught but himself. From time to time the worthy man would go Florence, where divers of the faithful would afford him relief according to his needs, and so he would return to his cell. And thus it fell out that one day Filippo, now an aged man, being asked by the boy, who was about eighteen years old, whither he went, told him. Whereupon :—" Father," said the boy, " you are now old, and scarce able to support fatigue ; why take you me not with you for once to Florence, and give me to know devout friends of God and you, so that I, who am young and fitter for such exertion than you, may thereafter go to Florence for our supplies at your pleasure, and you remain here ? "

The worthy man, bethinking him that his son was now grown up, and so habituated to the service of God as hardly to be seduced by the things of the world, said to himself :—" He says well." And so, as he must needs go to Florence, he took the boy with him. Where, seeing the palaces, the houses, the churches, and all matters else with which the city abounds, and of which he had no more recollection than if he had never seen them, the boy found all passing strange, and questioned his father of not a few of them, what they were and how they were named ; his curiosity being no sooner satisfied in one particular than he plied his father with a further question. And so it befell that, while son and father were thus occupied in asking and answering questions, they encountered a bevy of damsels, fair and richly arrayed, being on their return from a wedding ; whom the young man no sooner saw, than he asked his father what they might be. " My son," answered the father, " fix thy gaze on the ground, regard them not at all, for naughty things are they." " Oh ! " said the son, " and what is their name ? " The father, fearing to awaken some mischievous craving of concupiscence in the young man, would not denote them truly, to wit, as women, but said :—" They are called goslings." Whereupon, wonderful to tell! the lad who had never before set eyes on any woman, thought no more of the palaces, the oxen, the horses, the asses, the money, or aught else that he had seen, but exclaimed :— " Prithee, father, let me have one of those goslings." " Alas, my son," replied the father, " speak not of them ; they are naughty things." " Oh ! " questioned the son ; " but are naughty things made like that ? " " Ay," returned the father. Whereupon the son :—" I know not," he said, " what you say, nor why they should be naughty things : for my part I have as yet seen nought that seemed to me so fair and delectable. They are fairer than the painted angels that you have so often shewn me. Oh ! if you love me, do but let us take one of these goslings up there, and I will see that she have whereon to bill." " Nay," said the father, " that will not I. Thou knowest not whereon they bill ; " and straightway, being ware that nature was more potent than his art, he repented him that he had brought the boy to Florence.

But enough of this story : 'tis time for me to cut it short, and return to those, for whose instruction 'tis told. They say then, some of these my censors, that I am too fond of you, young ladies, and am at too great pains to pleasure you. Now that I am fond of you, and am at pains to pleasure you, I do most frankly and fully confess ; and I ask them whether, considering only all that it means to have had, and to have continually, before one's eyes your debonair demeanour, your bewitching beauty and exquisite grace, and there-withal your modest womanliness, not to speak of having known the amorous kisses, the caressing embraces, the voluptuous comminglings, whereof our intercourse with you, ladies most sweet, not seldom is productive, they do verily marvel that I am fond of you, seeing that one who was nurtured, reared, and brought up on a savage and solitary mountain, within the narrow circuit of a cell, without other companion than his father, had no sooner seen you than 'twas you alone that he desired, that he demanded, that he sought with ardour ? Will they tear, will they lacerate me with their censures, if I, whose body Heaven fashioned all apt for love, whose soul from very boyhood was dedicate to you, am not insensible to the power of the light of your eyes, to the sweetness of your honeyed words, to the flame that is kindled by your gentle sighs, but am fond of you and sedulous to pleasure you ; you, again I bid them remember, in whom a hermit, a rude, witless lad, liker to an animal than to a human being, found more to delight him than in aught else that he saw ? Of a truth whoso taxes me thus must be one that, feeling, knowing nought of the pleasure and power of natural affection, loves you not, nor craves your love ; and such an one I hold in light esteem. And as for those that go about to find ground of exception in my age, they do but shew that they ill understand that the leek, albeit its head is white, has a green tail. But jesting apart, thus I answer them, that never to the end of my life shall I deem it shameful to me to pleasure those to whom Guido Cavalcanti and Dante Alighieri in their old age, and Messer Cino da Pistoia in extreme old age, accounted it an honour and found it a delight to minister gratification. And but that 'twere a deviation from the use and wont of discourse, I would call history to my aid, and shew it to abound with stories of noble men of old time, who in their ripest age studied above all things else to pleasure the ladies; whereof if they be ignorant, go they and get them to school. To keep with the Muses on Parnassus is counsel I approve ; but tarry with them always we cannot, nor they with us, nor is a man blameworthy, if, when he happen to part from them, he find his delight in those that resemble them. The Muses are ladies, and albeit ladies are not the peers of the Muses, yet they have their outward semblance ; for which cause, if for no other, 'tis reasonable that I should be fond of them. Besides which, ladies have been to me the occasion of composing some thousand verses, but of never a verse that I made were the Muses the occasion. Howbeit 'twas with their aid, 'twas under their influence that I composed those thousand verses, and perchance they have sometimes visited me to encourage me in my present task, humble indeed though it be, doing honour and paying, as it were, tribute, to the likeness which the ladies have to them ; wherefore, while I weave these stories, I stray not so far from Mount Parnassus and the Muses as not a few perchance suppose. But what shall we say to those, in whom my hunger excites such commiseration that they bid me get me bread ? Verily I know not, save this :—Suppose that in my need I were to beg bread of them, what would be their

answer? I doubt not they would say :—"Go seek it among the
fables." And in sooth the poets have found more bread among their
fables than many rich men among their treasures. And many that
have gone after fables have crowned their days with splendour, while,
on the other hand, not a few, in the endeavour to get them more
bread than they needed, have perished miserably. But why waste
more words on them? Let them send me packing, when I ask
bread of them; not that, thank God, I have yet need of it, and
should I ever come to be in need of it, I know, like the Apostle,
how to abound and to be in want, and so am minded to be beholden
to none but myself. As for those who say that these matters fell out
otherwise than as I relate them, I should account it no small favour,
if they would produce the originals, and should what I write not
accord with them, I would acknowledge the justice of their censure,
and study to amend my ways; but, until better evidence is forthcoming than their words, I shall adhere to my own opinion without
seeking to deprive them of theirs, and give them tit for tat. And
being minded that for this while this answer suffice, I say that with
God and you, in whom I trust, most gentle ladies, to aid and protect
me, and patience for my stay, I shall go forward with my work,
turning my back on this tempest, however it may rage; for I see
not that I can fare worse than the fine dust, which the blast of the
whirlwind either leaves where it lies, or bears aloft, not seldom over
the heads of men, over the crowns of kings, of emperors, and sometimes suffers to settle on the roofs of lofty palaces, and the summits
of the tallest towers, whence if it fall, it cannot sink lower than the
level from which it was raised. And if I ever devoted myself and
all my powers to minister in any wise to your gratification, I am
now minded more than ever so to do, because I know that there is
nought that any can justly say in regard thereof, but that I, and
others who love you, follow the promptings of nature, whose laws
whoso would withstand, has need of powers pre-eminent, and, even
so, will oft-times labour not merely in vain but to his own most
grievous disadvantage. Such powers I own that I neither have, nor,
to such end, desire to have; and had I them, I would rather leave
them to another than use them myself. Wherefore let my detractors
hold their peace, and if they cannot get heat, why, let them shiver
their life away; and, while they remain addicted to their delights,

or rather corrupt tastes, let them leave me to follow my own bent during the brief life that is accorded us. But this has been a long digression, fair ladies, and 'tis time to retrace our steps to the point where we deviated, and continue in the course on which we started.

The sun had chased every star from the sky, and lifted the dank murk of night from the earth, when, Filostrato being risen, and having roused all his company, they hied them to the fair garden, and there fell to disporting themselves : the time for breakfast being come, they took it where they had supped on the preceding evening, and after they had slept they rose, when the sun was in his zenith, and seated themselves in their wonted manner by the beautiful fountain ; where Fiammetta, being bidden by Filostrato to lead off the story-telling, awaited no second command, but debonairly thus began.

NOVEL I.

Tancred, Prince of Salerno, slays his daughter's lover, and sends her his heart in a golden cup: she pours upon it a poisonous distillation, which she drinks and dies.

A DIREFUL theme has our king allotted us for to-day's discourse; seeing that, whereas we are here met for our common delectation, needs must we now tell of others' tears, whereby, whether telling or hearing, we cannot but be moved to pity. Perchance 'twas to temper in some degree the gaiety of the past days that he so ordained, but, whatever may have been his intent, his will must be to me immutable law; wherefore I will narrate to you a matter that befell piteously, nay woefully, and so as you may well weep thereat.

Tancred, Prince of Salerno, a lord most humane and kind of heart, but that in his old age he imbrued his hands in the blood of a lover, had in the whole course of his life but one daughter; and had he not had her, he had been more fortunate.

Never was daughter more tenderly beloved of father than she of the Prince, who, for that cause not knowing how to part with her, kept her unmarried for many a year after she had come of marriageable age: then at last he gave her to a son of the Duke of Capua, with whom she had lived but a short while, when he died and she returned to her father. Most lovely was she of form and feature (never woman more so), and young and light of heart, and more knowing, perchance, than beseemed a woman. Dwelling thus with her loving father, as a great lady, in no small luxury, nor failing to see that the Prince, for the great love he bore her, was at no pains to provide her with another husband, and deeming it unseemly on her part to ask one of him, she cast about how she might come by a gallant to be her secret lover. And seeing at her father's court not a few men, both gentle and simple, that resorted thither, as we know men use to frequent courts, and closely scanning their mien and manners, she preferred before all others the Prince's page, Guiscardo by name, a man of very humble origin, but pre-eminent for native worth and noble bearing; of whom, seeing him frequently, she became hotly enamoured, hourly extolling his qualities more and more highly. The young man, who for all his youth by no means lacked shrewdness, read her heart, and gave her his own on such wise that his love for her engrossed his mind to the exclusion of almost everything else. While thus they burned in secret for one another, the lady, desiring of all things a meeting with Guiscardo, but being shy of making any her confidant, hit upon a novel expedient to concert the affair with him. She wrote him a letter containing her commands for the ensuing day, and thrust it into a cane in the space between two of the knots, which cane she gave to Guiscardo, saying :—" Thou canst let thy servant have it for a bellows to blow thy fire up to night." Guiscardo took it, and feeling sure that 'twas not unadvisedly that she made him such a present, accompanied with such words, hied him straight home, where, carefully examining the cane, he observed that it was cleft, and, opening it, found the letter ; which he had no sooner read, and learned what he was to do, than, pleased as ne'er another, he fell to devising how to set all in order that he might not fail to meet the lady on the following day, after the manner she had prescribed.

Now hard by the Prince's palace was a grotto, hewn in days of old in the solid rock, and now long disused, so that an artificial orifice, by which it received a little light, was all but choked with brambles and plants that grew about and overspread it. From one of the ground-floor rooms of the palace, which room was part of the lady's suite, a secret stair led to the grotto, though the entrance was barred by a very strong door. This stair, having been from time immemorial disused, had passed out of mind so completely that there was scarce any that remembered that it was there : but Love, whose eyes nothing, however secret, may escape, had brought it to the mind of the enamoured lady. For many a day, using all secrecy, that none should discover her, she had wrought with her tools, until she had succeeded in opening the door; which done, she had gone down into the grotto alone, and having observed the orifice, had by her letter apprised Guiscardo of its apparent height above the floor of the grotto, and bidden him contrive some means of descending thereby. Eager to carry the affair through, Guiscardo lost no time in rigging up a ladder of ropes, whereby he might ascend and descend; and having put on a suit of leather to protect him from the brambles, he hied him the following night (keeping the affair close from all) to the orifice, made the ladder fast by one of its ends to a massive trunk that was rooted in the mouth of the orifice, climbed down the ladder, and awaited the lady. On the morrow, making as if she would fain sleep, the lady dismissed her damsels, and locked herself into her room: she then opened the door of the grotto, hied her down, and met Guiscardo, to their marvellous mutual satisfaction. The lovers then repaired to her room, where in exceeding great joyance they spent no small part of the day. Nor were they neglectful of the precautions needful to prevent discovery of their amour; but in due time Guiscardo returned to the grotto; whereupon the lady locked the door and rejoined her damsels. At nightfall Guiscardo reascended his ladder, and, issuing forth of the orifice, hied him home; nor, knowing now the way, did he fail to revisit the grotto many a time thereafter.

But Fortune, noting with envious eye a happiness of such degree and duration, gave to events a dolorous turn, whereby the joy of the two lovers was converted into bitter lamentation. 'Twas Tancred's custom to come from time to time quite alone to his daughter's room, and tarry talking with her a while. Whereby it so befell that he came down there one day after breakfast, while Ghismonda—such was the lady's name—was in her garden with her damsels; so that none saw or heard him enter; nor would he call his daughter, for he was minded that she should not forgo her pleasure. But, finding the windows closed and the bed-curtains drawn down, he seated himself on a divan that stood at one of the corners of the bed, rested his head on the bed, drew the curtain over him, and thus, hidden as if of set purpose, fell asleep. As he slept Ghismonda, who, as it happened, had caused Guiscardo to come that day, left her damsels in the garden, softly entered the room, and having locked herself in, unwitting that there was another in the room, opened the door to Guiscardo,

who was in waiting.   Straightway they got them to bed, as was
their wont; and, while they there solaced and disported them
together, it so befell that Tancred awoke, and heard and saw what
they did: whereat he was troubled beyond measure, and at first was
minded to upbraid them; but on second thoughts he deemed it best
to hold his peace, and avoid discovery, if so he might with greater
stealth and less dishonour carry out the design which was already in
his mind.   The two lovers continued long together, as they were
wont, all unwitting of Tancred; but at length they saw fit to get
out of bed, when Guiscardo went back to the grotto, and the lady
hied her forth of the room.   Whereupon Tancred, old though he
was, got out at one of the windows, clambered down into the garden,
and, seen by none, returned sorely troubled to his room.   By his
command two men took Guiscardo early that same night, as he
issued forth of the orifice accoutred in his suit of leather, and brought
him privily to Tancred; who, as he saw him, all but wept, and
said:—"Guiscardo, my kindness to thee is ill requited by the outrage
and dishonour which thou hast done me in the person of my daughter,
as to-day I have seen with my own eyes."   To whom Guiscardo
could answer nought but:—"Love is more potent than either you
or I."   Tancred then gave order to keep him privily under watch
and ward in a room within the palace; and so 'twas done.   Next
day, while Ghismonda wotted nought of these matters, Tancred,
after pondering divers novel expedients, hied him after breakfast,
according to his wont, to his daughter's room, where, having called
her to him and locked himself in with her, he began, not without
tears, to speak on this wise:—"Ghismonda, conceiving that I knew
thy virtue and honour, never, though it had been reported to me,
would I have credited, had I not seen with my own eyes, that thou
wouldst so much as in idea, not to say fact, have ever yielded thyself
to any man but thy husband: wherefore, for the brief residue of life
that my age has in store for me, the memory of thy fall will ever be
grievous to me.   And would to God, as thou must needs demean
thyself to such dishonour, thou hadst taken a man that matched thy
nobility; but of all the men that frequent my court, thou must needs
choose Guiscardo, a young man of the lowest condition, a fellow
whom we brought up in charity from his tender years; for whose
sake thou hast plunged me into the abyss of mental tribulation,

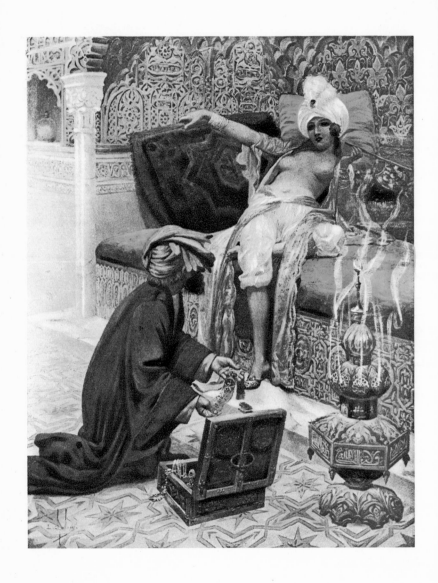

insomuch that I know not what course to take in regard of thee. As to Guiscardo, whom I caused to be arrested last night as he issued from the orifice, and keep in durance, my course is already taken, but how I am to deal with thee, God knows, I know not. I am distraught between the love which I have ever borne thee, love such as no father ever bare to daughter, and the most just indignation evoked in me by thy signal folly; my love prompts me to pardon thee, my indignation bids me harden my heart against thee, though I do violence to my nature. But before I decide upon my course, I would fain hear what thou hast to say to this." So saying, he bent his head, and wept as bitterly as any child that had been soundly thrashed.

Her father's words, and the tidings they conveyed that not only was her secret passion discovered, but Guiscardo taken, caused Ghismonda immeasurable grief, which she was again and again on the point of evincing, as most women do, by cries and tears; but her high spirit triumphed over this weakness; by a prodigious effort she composed her countenance, and taking it for granted that her Guiscardo was no more, she inly devoted herself to death rather than a single prayer for herself should escape her lips. Wherefore, not as a woman stricken with grief or chidden for a fault, but unconcerned and unabashed, with tearless eyes, and frank and utterly dauntless mien, thus answered she her father:—"Tancred, your accusation I shall not deny, neither will I cry you mercy, for nought should I gain by denial, nor aught would I gain by supplication: nay more; there is nought I will do to conciliate thy humanity and love; my only care is to confess the truth, to defend my honour by words of sound reason, and then by deeds most resolute to give effect to the promptings of my high soul. True it is that I have loved and love Guiscardo, and during the brief while I have yet to live shall love him, nor after death, so there be then love, shall I cease to love him; but that I love him, is not imputable to my womanly frailty so much as to the little zeal thou shewedst for my bestowal in marriage, and to Guiscardo's own worth. It should not have escaped thee, Tancred, creature of flesh and blood as thou art, that thy daughter was also a creature of flesh and blood, and not of stone or iron; it was, and is, thy duty to bear in mind (old though thou art) the nature and the might of the laws to which youth is subject; and, though thou hast spent part of thy best years in martial exercises, thou shouldst nevertheless have not been ignorant how potent is the influence even upon the aged—to say nothing of the young—of ease and luxury.   And not only am I, as being thy daughter, a creature of flesh and blood, but my life is not so far spent but that I am still young, and thus doubly fraught with fleshly appetite, the vehemence whereof is marvellously enhanced by reason that, having been married, I have known the pleasure that ensues upon the satisfaction of such desire.   Which forces being powerless to withstand, I did but act as was natural in a young woman, when I gave way to them, and yielded myself to love.   Nor in sooth did I fail to the utmost of my power so to order the indulgence of my natural propensity that my sin should bring shame neither upon thee nor upon me.   To which end Love in his pity, and Fortune in a friendly mood, found and discovered to me a secret way, whereby, none witting, I attained my desire : this, from whomsoever thou hast learned it, howsoever thou comest to know it, I deny not.   'Twas not at random, as many women do, that I loved Guiscardo ; but by deliberate choice I pre- ferred him before all other men, and of determinate forethought I lured him to my love, whereof, through his and my discretion and constancy, I have long had joyance.   Wherein 'twould seem that thou, following rather the opinion of the vulgar than the dictates of truth, find cause to chide me more severely than in my sinful love, for, as if thou wouldst not have been vexed, had my choice fallen on a nobleman, thou complainest that I have forgathered with a man of low condition ; and dost not see that therein thou censurest not my fault but that of Fortune, which not seldom raises the unworthy to high place and leaves the worthiest in low estate.   But leave we this : consider a little the principles of things : thou seest that in regard of our flesh we are all moulded of the same substance, and that all souls are endowed by one and the same Creator with equal faculties, equal powers, equal virtues.   'Twas merit that made the first distinction between us, born as we were, nay, as we are, all equal, and those whose merits were and were approved in act the greatest were called noble, and the rest were not so denoted.   Which law, albeit overlaid by the contrary usage of after times, is not yet abrogated, nor so impaired but that it is still traceable in nature and good manners ; for which cause whoso with merit acts, does plainly shew himself a gentleman; and if any denote him otherwise, the default is his own and not his whom he so denotes. Pass in review all thy nobles, weigh their merits, their manners and bearing, and then compare Guiscardo's qualities with theirs: if thou wilt judge without prejudice, thou wilt pronounce him noble in the highest degree, and thy nobles one and all churls. As to Guiscardo's merits and worth I did but trust the verdict which thou thyself didst utter in words, and which mine own eyes confirmed. Of whom had he such commendation as of thee for all those excellences whereby a good man and true merits commendation? And in sooth thou didst him but justice; for, unless mine eyes have played me false, there was nought for which thou didst commend him but I had seen him practise it, and that more admirably than words of thine might express; and had I been at all deceived in this matter, 'twould have been by thee. Wilt thou say then that I have forgathered with a man of low condition? If so, thou wilt not say true. Didst thou say with a poor man, the impeachment might be allowed, to thy shame, that thou so ill hast known how to requite a good man and true that is thy servant; but poverty, though it take away all else, deprives no man of gentilesse. Many kings, many great princes, were once poor, and many a ditcher or herdsman has been and is very wealthy. As for thy last perpended doubt, to wit, how thou shouldst deal with me, banish it utterly from thy thoughts. If in thy extreme old age thou art minded to manifest a harshness unwonted in thy youth, wreak thy harshness on me, resolved as I am to cry thee no mercy, prime cause as I am that this sin, if sin it be, has been committed; for of this I warrant thee, that as thou mayst have done or shalt do to Guiscardo, if to me thou do not the like, I with my own hands will do it. Now get thee gone to shed thy tears with the women, and when thy melting mood is over, ruthlessly destroy Guiscardo and me, if such thou deem our merited doom, by one and the same blow."

The loftiness of his daughter's spirit was not unknown to the Prince; but still he did not credit her with a resolve quite as firmly fixed as her words implied, to carry their purport into effect. So, parting from her without the least intention of using harshness towards her in her own person, he determined to quench the heat of her love by wreaking his vengeance on her lover, and bade the two men that had charge of Guiscardo to strangle him noiselessly that

same night, take the heart out of the body, and send it to him.   The
men did his bidding: and on the morrow the Prince had a large and
beautiful cup of gold brought to him, and having put Guiscardo's
heart therein, sent it by the hand of one of his most trusted servants
to his daughter, charging the servant to say, as he gave it to her :—
"Thy father sends thee this to give thee joy of that which thou
lovest best, even as thou hast given him joy of that which he loved
best."

Now when her father had left her, Ghismonda, wavering not
a jot in her stern resolve, had sent for poisonous herbs and roots, and
therefrom had distilled a water, to have it ready for use, if that which
she apprehended should come to pass.   And when the servant
appeared with the Prince's present and message, she took the cup
unblenchingly, and having lifted the lid, and seen the heart, and
apprehended the meaning of the words, and that the heart was
beyond a doubt Guiscardo's, she raised her head, and looking straight
at the servant, said :—"Sepulture less honourable than of gold had
ill befitted heart such as this : herein has my father done wisely."
Which said, she raised it to her lips, and kissed it, saying :—"In all
things and at all times, even to this last hour of my life, have I
found my father most tender in his love, but now more so than
ever before ; wherefore I now render him the last thanks which will
ever be due from me to him for this goodly present."   So she spoke,
and straining the cup to her, bowed her head over it, and gazing at
the heart, said :—"Ah ! sojourn most sweet of all my joys, accursed
be he by whose ruthless act I see thee with the bodily eye : 'twas
enough that to the mind's eye thou wert hourly present.   Thou
hast run thy course ; thou hast closed the span that Fortune allotted
thee ; thou hast reached the goal of all ; thou hast left behind thee
the woes and weariness of the world ; and thy enemy has himself
granted thee sepulture accordant with thy deserts.   No circumstance
was wanting to duly celebrate thy obsequies, save the tears of her
whom, while thou livedst, thou didst so dearly love ; which that
thou shouldst not lack, my remorseless father was prompted of God
to send thee to me, and, albeit my resolve was fixed to die with eyes
unmoistened and front all unperturbed by fear, yet will I accord
thee my tears ; which done, my care shall be forthwith by thy
means to join my soul to that most precious soul which thou didst

once enshrine.　And is there other company than hers, in which with more of joy and peace I might fare to the abodes unknown ? She is yet here within, I doubt not, contemplating the abodes of her and my delights, and—for sure I am that she loves me—awaiting my soul that loves her before all else."

Having thus spoken, she bowed herself low over the cup; and, while no womanish cry escaped her, 'twas as if a fountain of water were unloosed within her head, so wondrous a flood of tears gushed from her eyes, while times without number she kissed the dead heart.　Her damsels that stood around her knew not whose the heart might be or what her words might mean, but melting in sympathy, they all wept, and compassionately, as vainly, enquired the cause of her lamentation, and in many other ways sought to comfort her to the best of their understanding and power.　When she had wept her fill, she raised her head, and dried her eyes.　Then :—"O heart," said she, "much cherished heart, discharged is my every duty towards thee ; nought now remains for me to do but to come and unite my soul with thine."　So saying, she sent for the vase that held the water which the day before she had distilled, and emptied it into the cup where lay the heart bathed in her tears ; then, nowise afraid, she set her mouth to the cup, and drained it dry, and so with the cup in her hand she got her upon her bed, and having there disposed her person in guise as seemly as she might, laid her dead lover's heart upon her own, and silently awaited death.　Meanwhile the damsels, seeing and hearing what passed, but knowing not what the water was that she had drunk, had sent word of each particular to Tancred ; who, apprehensive of that which came to pass, came down with all haste to his daughter's room, where he arrived just as she got her upon her bed, and, now too late, addressed himself to comfort her with soft words, and seeing in what plight she was, burst into a flood of bitter tears.　To whom the lady :—" Reserve thy tears, Tancred, till Fortune send thee hap less longed for than this : waste them not on me who care not for them.　Whoever yet saw any but thee bewail the consummation of his desire ?　But, if of the love thou once didst bear me any spark still lives in thee, be it thy parting grace to me, that, as thou brookedst not that I should live with Guiscardo in privity and seclusion, so wherever thou mayst have caused Guiscardo's body to be cast, mine may be united with it in the common view of all." The Prince replied not for excess of grief; and the lady, feeling that her end was come, strained the dead heart to her bosom, saying :—" Fare ye well ; I take my leave of you ; " and with eyelids drooped and every sense evanished departed this life of woe. Such was the lamentable end of the loves of Guiscardo and Ghismonda ; whom Tancred, tardily repentant of his harshness, mourned not a little, as did also all the folk of Salerno, and had honourably interred side by side in the same tomb.

NOVEL II.

Fra Alberto gives a lady to understand that she is beloved of the Angel Gabriel, in whose shape he lies with her sundry times; afterward, for fear of her kinsmen, he flings himself forth of her house, and finds shelter in the house of a poor man, who on the morrow leads him in the guise of a wild man into the piazza, where, being recognized, he is apprehended by his brethren and imprisoned.

MORE than once had Fiammetta's story brought tears to the eyes of her fair companions; but now that it was ended the king said with an austere air :—"I should esteem my life but a paltry price to pay for half the delight that Ghismonda had with Guiscardo : whereat no lady of you all should marvel, seeing that each hour that I live I die a thousand deaths; nor is there so much as a particle of compensating joy allotted me. But a truce to my own concerns : I ordain that Pampinea do next ensue our direful argument, wherewith the tenor of my life in part accords, and if she follow in Fiammetta's footsteps, I doubt not I shall presently feel some drops of dew distill upon my fire." Pampinea received the king's command in a spirit more accordant with what from her own bent she divined to be the wishes of her fair gossips than with the king's words; wherefore, being minded rather to afford them some diversion, than, save as in duty bound, to satisfy the king, she made choice of a story which, without deviating from the prescribed theme, should move a laugh, and thus began :—

'Tis a proverb current among the vulgar, that :—" Whoso, being wicked, is righteous reputed, May sin as he will, and 'twill ne'er be imputed." Which proverb furnishes me with abundant matter of discourse, germane to our theme, besides occasion to exhibit the quality and degree of the hypocrisy of the religious, who flaunt it in ample flowing robes, and, with faces made pallid by art, with voices low and gentle to beg alms, most loud and haughty to reprove in others their own sins, would make believe that their way of salvation lies in taking from us and ours in giving to them; nay, more, as if they had not like us Paradise to win, but were already its lords and masters, assign therein to each that dies a place more or less exalted according to the amount of the money that he has bequeathed to them; which if they believe, 'tis by dint of self-delusion, and to the effect of deluding all that put faith in their words. Of whose guile were it lawful for me to make as full exposure as were fitting, not a few simple folk should soon be enlightened as to what they cloak within the folds of their voluminous habits. But would to God all might have the like reward of their lies as a certain friar minor, no novice, but one that was reputed among their greatest[1] at Venice; whose story, rather than aught else, I am minded to tell you, if so I may, perchance, by laughter and jollity relieve in some degree your souls that are heavy laden with pity for the death of Ghismonda.

Know then, noble ladies, that there was in Imola a man of evil and corrupt life, Berto della Massa by name, whose pestilent practices came at length to be so well known to the good folk of Imola that 'twas all one whether he lied or spoke the truth, for there was not a soul in Imola that believed a word he said: wherefore, seeing that his tricks would pass no longer there, he removed, as in despair, to Venice, that common sink of all abominations, thinking there to find other means than he had found elsewhere to the prosecution of his nefarious designs. And, as if conscience-stricken for his past misdeeds, he assumed an air of the deepest humility, turned the best Catholic of them all, and went and made himself a friar minor, taking the name of Fra Alberto da Imola. With his habit he put on a shew of austerity, highly commending penitence and abstinence, and eating or drinking no sort of meat or wine but such as was to his taste.

1 *de' maggior cassesi.* No such word as *cassesi* is known to the lexicographers or commentators; and no plausible emendation has yet been suggested.

And scarce a soul was there that wist that the thief, the pimp, the cheat, the assassin, had not been suddenly converted into a great preacher without continuing in the practice of the said iniquities, whensoever the same was privily possible. And withal, having got himself made priest, as often as he celebrated at the altar, he would weep over the passion of our Lord, so there were folk in plenty to see, for tears cost him little enough, when he had a mind to shed them. In short, what with his sermons and his tears, he duped the folk of Venice to such a tune that scarce a will was there made but he was its executor and depositary; nay, not a few made him trustee of their moneys, and most, or well-nigh most, men and women alike, their confessor and counsellor: in short, he had put off the wolf and put on the shepherd, and the fame of his holiness was such in those parts that St. Francis himself had never the like at Assisi.

Now it so befell that among the ladies that came to confess to this holy friar was one Monna Lisetta of Ca' Quirino, the young, silly, empty-headed wife of a great merchant, who was gone with the galleys to Flanders. Like a Venetian—for unstable are they all—though she placed herself at his feet, she told him but a part of her sins, and when Fra Alberto asked her whether she had a lover, she replied with black looks:—" How now, master friar? have you not eyes in your head? See you no difference between my charms and those of other women? Lovers in plenty might I have, so I would: but charms such as mine must not be cheapened: 'tis not every man that might presume to love me. How many ladies have you seen whose beauty is comparable to mine? I should adorn Paradise itself." Whereto she added so much more in praise of her beauty that the friar could scarce hear her with patience. Howbeit, discerning at a glance that she was none too well furnished with sense, he deemed the soil meet for his plough, and fell forthwith inordinately in love with her, though he deferred his blandishments to a more convenient season, and by way of supporting his character for holiness began instead to chide her, telling her (among other novelties) that this was vainglory: whereto the lady retorted that he was a blockhead, and could not distinguish one degree of beauty from another. Wherefore Fra Alberto, lest he should occasion her too much chagrin, cut short the confession, and suffered her to depart with the other ladies. Some days after, accompanied by a single trusty friend, he hied him to Monna Lisetta's house, and having withdrawn with her alone into a saloon, where they were safe from observation, he fell on his knees at her feet, and said :—"Madam, for the love of God I crave your pardon of that which I said to you on Sunday, when you spoke to me of your beauty, for so grievously was I chastised there-for that very night, that 'tis but to-day that I have been able to quit my bed." "And by whom," quoth my Lady Battledore, "were you so chastised ?" "I will tell you," returned Fra Alberto. "That night I was, as is ever my wont, at my orisons, when sud-denly a great light shone in my cell, and before I could turn me to see what it was, I saw standing over me a right goodly youth with a stout cudgel in his hand, who seized me by the habit and threw me at his feet and belaboured me till I was bruised from head to foot. And when I asked him why he used me thus, he answered : —''Tis because thou didst to-day presume to speak slightingly of the celestial charms of Monna Lisetta, whom I love next to God Himself.' Whereupon I asked :—'And who are you ?' And he made answer that he was the Angel Gabriel. Then said I :—'O my lord, I pray you pardon me.' Whereto he answered :—'I pardon thee on condition that thou go to her, with what speed thou mayst, and obtain her pardon, which if she accord thee not, I shall come back hither and give thee belabourings enough with my cudgel to make thee a sad man for the rest of thy days.' What more he said, I dare not tell you, unless you first pardon me." Whereat our flimsy pumpion-pated Lady Lackbrain was overjoyed, taking all the friar's words for gospel. So after a while she said :—"And did I not tell you, Fra Alberto, that my charms were celestial ? But, so help me God, I am moved to pity of you, and forthwith I pardon you, lest worse should befall you, so only you tell me what more the Angel said." "So will I gladly, Madam," returned Fra Alberto, "now that I have your pardon ; this only I bid you bear in mind, that you have a care that never a soul in the world hear from you a single word of what I shall say to you, if you would not spoil your good fortune, wherein there is not to-day in the whole world a lady that may compare with you. Know then that the Angel Gabriel bade me tell you that you stand so high in his favour that again and again he would have come to pass the night with you, but that he doubted he should affright you. So now he sends you word through

me that he would fain come one night, and stay a while with you;
and seeing that, being an angel, if he should visit you in his angelic
shape, he might not be touched by you, he would, to pleasure you,
present himself in human shape; and so he bids you send him word,
when you would have him come, and in whose shape, and he will
come; for which cause you may deem yourself more blessed than
any other lady that lives." My Lady Vanity then said that she
was highly flattered to be beloved of the Angel Gabriel; whom she
herself loved so well that she had never grudged four soldi to burn
a candle before his picture, wherever she saw it, and that he was
welcome to visit her as often as he liked, and would always find her
alone in her room; on the understanding, however, that he should
not desert her for the Virgin Mary, whom she had heard he did
mightily affect, and indeed 'twould so appear, for, wherever she saw
him, he was always on his knees at her feet: for the rest he might
even come in what shape he pleased, so that it was not such as to
terrify her.   Then said Fra Alberto:—"Madam, 'tis wisely spoken;
and I will arrange it all with him just as you say.   But 'tis in your
power to do me a great favour, which will cost you nothing; and
this favour is that you be consenting that he visit you in my
shape.   Now hear wherein you will confer this favour: thus will it
be: he will disembody my soul, and set it in Paradise, entering himself into my body; and, as long as he shall be with you, my soul will
be in Paradise."   Whereto my Lady Slenderwit:—"So be it," she
said; "I am well pleased that you have this solace to salve the bruises
that he gives you on my account."   "Good," said Fra Alberto;
"then you will see to it that to-night he find, when he comes, your
outer door unlatched, that he may have ingress; for, coming, as he
will, in human shape, he will not be able to enter save by the door."
"It shall be done," replied the lady.   Whereupon Fra Alberto took
his leave, and the lady remained in such a state of exaltation that her
nether end knew not her chemise, and it seemed to her a thousand
years until the Angel Gabriel should come to visit her.   Fra
Alberto, bethinking him that 'twas not as an angel, but as a cavalier
that he must acquit himself that night, fell to fortifying himself with
comfits and other dainties, that he might not lose his saddle for
slight cause.   Then, leave of absence gotten, he betook him at nightfall, with a single companion, to the house of a woman that was his

friend, which house had served on former occasions as his base when
he went a chasing the fillies ; and having there disguised himself,
he hied him, when he deemed 'twas time, to the house of the lady,
where, donning the gewgaws he had brought with him, he transformed himself into an angel, and going up, entered the lady's
chamber.   No sooner saw she this dazzling apparition than she fell
on her knees before the Angel, who gave her his blessing, raised her
to her feet, and motioned her to go to bed.   She, nothing loath,
obeyed forthwith, and the Angel lay down beside his devotee.   Now
Fra Alberto was a stout, handsome fellow, whose legs bore themselves
right bravely ; and being bedded with Monna Lisetta, who was lusty
and delicate, he covered her after another fashion than her husband
had been wont, and took many a flight that night without wings, so
that she heartily cried him content ; and not a little therewithal did
he tell her of the glory celestial.   Then towards daybreak, all being
ready for his return, he hied him forth, and repaired, caparisoned as
he was, to his friend, whom, lest he should be affrighted, sleeping
alone, the good woman of the house had solaced with her company.
The lady, so soon as she had breakfasted, betook her to Fra Alberto,
and reported the Angel Gabriel's visit, and what he had told her of
the glory of the life eternal, describing his appearance, not without
some added marvels of her own invention.   Whereto Fra Alberto
replied :—"Madam, I know not how you fared with him ; but this
I know, that last night he came to me, and for that I had done his
errand with you, he suddenly transported my soul among such a
multitude of flowers and roses as was never seen here below, and my
soul—what became of my body I know not—tarried in one of the
most delightful places that ever was from that hour until matins."
"As for your body," said the lady, "do I not tell you whose it was ?
It lay all night long with the Angel Gabriel in my arms ; and if you
believe me not, you have but to look under your left pap, where I
gave the Angel a mighty kiss, of which the mark will last for some
days."   "Why then," said Fra Alberto, "I will even do to-day
what 'tis long since I did, to wit, undress, that I may see if you say
sooth."   So they fooled it a long while, and then the lady went
home, where Fra Alberto afterwards paid her many a visit without
any let.   However, one day it so befell that while Monna Lisetta
was with one of her gossips canvassing beauties, she, being minded

to exalt her own charms above all others, and having, as we know, none too much wit in her pumpion-pate, observed :—" Did you but know by whom my charms are prized, then, for sure, you would have nought to say of the rest." Her gossip, all agog to hear, for well she knew her foible, answered :—" Madam, it may be as you say, but still, while one knows not who he may be, one cannot alter one's mind so rapidly." Whereupon my Lady Featherbrain :—" Gossip," said she, " 'tis not for common talk, but he that I wot of is the Angel Gabriel, who loves me more dearly than himself, for that I am, so he tells me, the fairest lady in all the world, ay, and in the Maremma to boot." [1] Whereat her gossip would fain have laughed, but held herself in, being minded to hear more from her. Wherefore she said :—" God's faith, Madam, if 'tis the Angel Gabriel, and he tells you so, why, so of course it must needs be ; but I wist not the angels meddled with such matters." " There you erred, gossip," said the lady : " zounds, he does it better than my husband, and he tells me they do it above there too, but, as he rates my charms above any that are in heaven, he is enamoured of me, and not seldom visits me : so now dost see ? " So away went the gossip so agog to tell the story, that it seemed to her a thousand years till she was where it might be done ; and being met for recreation with a great company of ladies, she narrated it all in detail : whereby it passed to the ladies' husbands, and to other ladies, and from them to yet other ladies, so that in less than two days all Venice was full of it. But among others, whose ears it reached, were Monna Lisetta's brothers-in-law, who, keeping their own counsel, resolved to find this angel and make out whether he knew how to fly ; to which end they kept watch for some nights. Whereof no hint, as it happened, reached Fra Alberto's ears ; and so, one night when he was come to enjoy the lady once more, he was scarce undressed when her brothers-in-law, who had seen him come, were at the door of the room and already opening it, when Fra Alberto, hearing the noise and apprehending the danger, started up, and having no other resource, threw open a window that looked on to the Grand Canal, and plunged into the water. The depth was great, and he was an expert swimmer ; so that he took no hurt, but, having reached the other bank, found a

---

[1] With this ineptitude cf. the friar's " flowers and roses " on the preceding page.

house open, and forthwith entered it, praying the good man that was within, for God's sake to save his life, and trumping up a story to account for his being there at so late an hour, and stripped to the skin. The good man took pity on him, and having occasion to go out, he put him in his own bed, bidding him stay there until his return ; and so, having locked him in, he went about his business.

Now when the lady's brothers-in-law entered the room, and found that the Angel Gabriel had taken flight, leaving his wings behind him, being baulked of their prey, they roundly rated the lady, and then, leaving her disconsolate, betook themselves home with the Angel's spoils. Whereby it befell, that, when 'twas broad day, the good man, being on the Rialto, heard tell how the Angel Gabriel had come to pass the night with Monna Lisetta, and, being surprised by her brothers-in-law, had taken fright, and thrown himself into the Canal, and none knew what was become of him. The good man guessed in a trice that the said Angel was no other than the man he had at home, whom on his return he recognized, and, after much chaffering, brought him to promise him fifty ducats that he might not be given up to the lady's brothers-in-law. The bargain struck, Fra Alberto signified a desire to be going. Whereupon :—" There is no way," said the good man, " but one, if you are minded to take it. To-day we hold a revel, wherein folk lead others about in various disguises ; as, one man will present a bear, another a wild man, and so forth ; and then in the piazza of San Marco there is a hunt, which done, the revel is ended ; and then away they hie them, whither they will, each with the man he has led about. If you are willing to be led by me in one or another of these disguises, before it can get wind that you are here, I can bring you whither you would go ; otherwise I see not how you are to quit this place without being known ; and the lady's brothers-in-law, reckoning that you must be lurking somewhere in this quarter, have set guards all about to take you." Loath indeed was Fra Alberto to go in such a guise, but such was his fear of the lady's relations that he consented, and told the good man whither he desired to be taken, and that he was content to leave the choice of the disguise to him. The good man then smeared him all over with honey, and covered him with down, set a chain on his neck and a vizard on his face, gave him a stout cudgel to carry in one hand, and two huge dogs, which he had brought from the shambles, to lead with

the other, and sent a man to the Rialto to announce that whoso would
see the Angel Gabriel should hie him to the piazza of San Marco ; in
all which he acted as a leal Venetian.   And so, after a while, he led
him forth, and then, making him go before, held him by the chain
behind, and through a great throng that clamoured :—" What manner
of thing is this ? what manner of thing is this ?" he brought him
to the piazza, where, what with those that followed them, and those
that had come from the Rialto on hearing the announcement, there
were folk without end.   Arrived at the piazza, he fastened his wild
man to a column in a high and exposed place, making as if he were
minded to wait till the hunt should begin ; whereby the flies and
gadflies, attracted by the honey with which he was smeared, caused
him most grievous distress.   However, the good man waited only
until the piazza was thronged, and then, making as if he would
unchain his wild man, he tore the vizard from Fra Alberto's face,
saying :—"Gentlemen, as the boar comes not to the hunt, and the hunt
does not take place, that it be not for nothing that you are come hither,
I am minded to give you a view of the Angel Gabriel, who comes
down from heaven to earth by night to solace the ladies of Venice."
The vizard was no sooner withdrawn than all recognized Fra Alberto,
and greeted him with hootings, rating him in language as offensive
and opprobrious as ever rogue was abused withal, and pelting him in
the face with every sort of filth that came to hand : in which plight
they kept him an exceeding great while, until by chance the bruit
thereof reached his brethren, of whom some six thereupon put themselves in motion, and, arrived at the piazza, clapped a habit on his
back, and unchained him, and amid an immense uproar led him off
to their convent, where, after languishing a while in prison, 'tis believed
that he died.

So this man, by reason that, being reputed righteous, he did evil,
and 'twas not imputed to him, presumed to counterfeit the Angel
Gabriel, and, being transformed into a wild man, was in the end put
to shame, as he deserved, and vainly bewailed his misdeeds.   God
grant that so it may betide all his likes.

NOVEL III.

Three young men love three sisters, and flee with them to Crete. The eldest of the sisters slays her lover for jealousy. The second saves the life of the first by yielding herself to the Duke of Crete. Her lover slays her, and makes off with the first: the third sister and her lover are charged with the murder, are arrested and confess the crime. They escape death by bribing the guards, flee destitute to Rhodes, and there in destitution die.

PAMPINEA's story ended, Filostrato mused a while, and then said to her :—"A little good matter there was that pleased me at the close of your story, but, before 'twas reached, there was far too much to laugh at, which I could have wished had not been there." Then, turning to Lauretta, he said :—"Madam, give us something better to follow, if so it may be." Lauretta replied with a laugh :—"Harsh beyond measure are you to the lovers, to desire that their end be always evil ; but, as in duty bound, I will tell a story of three, who all alike came to a bad end, having had little joyance of their loves ; " and so saying, she began.

Well may ye wot, young ladies, for 'tis abundantly manifest, that there is no vice but most grievous disaster may ensue thereon to him that practises it, and not seldom to others ; and of all the vices that which hurries us into peril with loosest rein is, methinks, anger ; which is nought but a rash and hasty impulse, prompted by a feeling of pain, which banishes reason, shrouds the eyes of the mind in thick darkness, and sets the soul ablaze with a fierce frenzy. Which, though it not seldom befall men, and one rather than another, has nevertheless been observed to be fraught in women with more disastrous consequences, inasmuch as in them the flame is both more readily kindled, and burns more brightly, and with less impediment to its vehemence. Wherein is no cause to marvel, for, if we consider it, we shall see that 'tis of the nature of fire to lay hold more readily of things light and delicate than of matters of firmer and more solid substance ; and sure it is that we (without offence to the men be it spoken) are more delicate than they, and much more mobile. Wherefore, seeing how prone we are thereto by nature, and considering also our gentleness and tenderness, how soothing and consolatory they are to the men with whom we consort, and that thus this madness of wrath is fraught with grievous annoy and peril ; therefore, that with stouter heart we may defend ourselves against it, I purpose by my story to shew you, how the loves of three young men, and as many ladies, as I said before, were by the anger of one of the ladies changed from a happy to a most woeful complexion.

Marseilles, as you know, is situate on the coast of Provence, a city ancient and most famous, and in old time the seat of many more rich men and great merchants than are to be seen there to-day, among whom was one Narnald Cluada by name, a man of the lowest origin, but a merchant of unsullied probity and integrity, and boundless wealth in lands and goods and money, who had by his lady several children, three of them being daughters, older, each of them, than the other children, who were sons. Two of the daughters, who were twins, were, when my story begins, fifteen years old, and the third was but a year younger, so that in order to their marriage their kinsfolk awaited nothing but the return of Narnald from Spain, whither he was gone with his merchandise. One of the twins was called Ninette, the other Madeleine ; the third daughter's name was Bertelle. A young man, Restagnon by name, who, though poor, was of gentle blood, was in the last degree enamoured of Ninette, and she of him ; and so discreetly had they managed the affair, that, never another soul in the world witting aught of it, they had had joyance of their love, and that for a good while, when it so befell that two young friends of theirs, the one Foulques, the other Hugues by name, whom their fathers, recently dead, had left very wealthy, fell in love, the one with Madeleine, the other with Bertelle.

Whereof Restagnon being apprised by Ninette bethought him that in their love he might find a means to the relief of his necessities. He accordingly consorted freely and familiarly with them, accompanying, now one, now the other, and sometimes both of them, when they went to visit their ladies and his; and when he judged that he had made his footing as friendly and familiar as need was, he bade them one day to his house, and said :—"Comrades most dear, our friendship, perchance, may not have left you without assurance of the great love I bear you, and that for you I would do even as much as for myself: wherefore, loving you thus much, I purpose to impart to you that which is in my mind, that in regard thereof, you and I together may then resolve in such sort as to you shall seem the best. You, if I may trust your words, as also what I seem to have gathered from your demeanour by day and by night, burn with an exceeding great love for the two ladies whom you affect, as I for their sister. For the assuagement whereof, I have good hope that, if you will unite with me, I shall find means most sweet and delightsome; to wit, on this wise. You possess, as I do not, great wealth : now if you are willing to make of your wealth a common stock with me as third partner therein, and to choose some part of the world where we may live in careless ease upon our substance, without any manner of doubt I trust so to prevail that the three sisters with great part of their father's substance shall come to live with us, wherever we shall see fit to go; whereby, each with his own lady, we shall live as three brethren, the happiest men in the world. 'Tis now for you to determine whether you will embrace this proffered solace, or let it slip from you." The two young men, whose love was beyond all measure fervent, spared themselves the trouble of deliberation : 'twas enough that they heard that they were to have their ladies : wherefore they answered, that, so this should ensue, they were ready to do as he proposed. Having thus their answer, Restagnon a few days later was closeted with Ninette, to whom 'twas a matter of no small difficulty for him to get access. Nor had he been long with her before he adverted to what had passed between him and the young men, and sought to commend the project to her for reasons not a few. Little need, however, had he to urge her : for to live their life openly together was the very thing she desired, far more than he : wherefore she frankly answered that she would have it so, that her sisters would do, more especially in this matter, just as she wished, and that he should lose no time in making all the needful arrangements. So Restagnon returned to the two young men, who were most urgent that it should be done even as he said, and told them that on the part of the ladies the matter was concluded. And so, having fixed upon Crete for their destination, and sold some estates that they had, giving out that they were minded to go a trading with the proceeds, they converted all else that they possessed into money, and bought a brigantine, which with all secrecy they handsomely equipped, anxiously expecting the time of their departure, while Ninette on her part, knowing well how her sisters were affected, did so by sweet converse foment their desire that, till it should be accomplished, they accounted their life as nought. The night of their embarcation being come, the three sisters opened a great chest that belonged to their father, and took out therefrom a vast quantity of money and jewels, with which they all three issued forth of the house in dead silence, as they had been charged, and found their three lovers awaiting them; who, having forthwith brought them aboard the brigantine, bade the rowers give way, and, tarrying nowhere, arrived the next evening at Genoa, where the new lovers had for the first time joyance and solace of their love.

Having taken what they needed of refreshment, they resumed their course, touching at this port and that, and in less than eight days, speeding without impediment, were come to Crete. There they bought them domains both beautiful and broad, whereon, hard by Candia they built them mansions most goodly and delightsome, wherein they lived as barons, keeping a crowd of retainers, with dogs, hawks and horses, and speeding the time with their ladies in feasting and revelling and merrymaking, none so light-hearted as they. Such being the tenor of their life, it so befell that (as 'tis matter of daily experience that, however delightsome a thing may be, superabundance thereof will breed disgust) Restagnon, much as he had loved Ninette, being now able to have his joyance of her without stint or restraint, began to weary of her, and by consequence to abate somewhat of his love for her. And being mightily pleased with a fair gentlewoman of the country, whom he met at a merry-making, he set his whole heart upon her, and began to shew himself marvellously courteous and gallant towards her; which Ninette per-

ceiving grew so jealous that he might not go a step but she knew of
't, and resented it to his torment and her own with high words. But
as, while superfluity engenders disgust, appetite is but whetted when
fruit is forbidden, so Ninette's wrath added fuel to the flame of
Restagnon's new love. And whichever was the event, whether in
course of time Restagnon had the lady's favour or had it not, Ninette,
whoever may have brought her the tidings, firmly believed that he
had it; whereby from the depths of distress she passed into a tower-
ing passion, and thus was transported into such a frenzy of rage that
all the love she bore to Restagnon was converted into bitter hatred,
and, blinded by her wrath, she made up her mind to avenge by
Restagnon's death the dishonour which she deemed that he had done
her. So she had recourse to an old Greek woman, that was very
skilful in compounding poisons, whom by promises and gifts she
induced to distill a deadly water, which, keeping her own counsel,
she herself gave Restagnon to drink one evening, when he was
somewhat heated and quite off his guard : whereby—such was the
efficacy of the water—she despatched Restagnon before matins. On
learning his death Foulques and Hugues and their ladies, who knew
not that he had been poisoned, united their bitter with Ninette's
feigned lamentations, and gave him honourable sepulture. But so it
befell that, not many days after, the old woman, that had compounded
the poison for Ninette, was taken for another crime; and, being put
to the torture, confessed the compounding of the poison among other
of her misdeeds, and fully declared what had thereby come to pass.
Wherefore the Duke of Crete, breathing no word of his intent, came
privily by night, and set a guard around Foulques' palace, where
Ninette then was, and quietly, and quite unopposed, took and carried
her off; and without putting her to the torture, learned from her in
a trice all that he sought to know touching the death of Restagnon.
Foulques and Hugues had learned privily of the Duke, and their
ladies of them, for what cause Ninette was taken; and, being mightily
distressed thereby, bestirred themselves with all zeal to save Ninette
from the fire, to which they apprehended she would be condemned,
as having indeed richly deserved it; but all their endeavours seemed
to avail nothing, for the Duke was unwaveringly resolved that justice
should be done. Madeleine, Foulques' fair wife, who had long been
courted by the Duke, but had never deigned to shew him the least

ravour, thinking that by yielding herself to his will she might redeem her sister from the fire, despatched a trusty envoy to him with the intimation that she was entirely at his disposal upon the twofold condition, that in the first place her sister should be restored to her free and scatheless, and, in the second place, the affair should be kept secret. Albeit gratified by this overture, the Duke was long in doubt whether he should accept it; in the end, however, he made up his mind to do so, and signified his approval to the envoy. Then with the lady's consent he put Foulques and Hugues under arrest for a night, as if he were minded to examine them of the affair, and meanwhile quartered himself privily with Madeleine. Ninette, who, he had made believe, had been set in a sack, and was to be sunk in the sea that same night, he took with him, and presented her to her sister in requital of the night's joyance, which, as he parted from her on the morrow, he prayed her might not be the last, as it was the first, fruit of their love, at the same time enjoining her to send the guilty lady away that she might not bring reproach upon him, nor he be compelled to deal rigorously with her again. Released the same morning, and told that Ninette had been cast into the sea, Foulques and Hugues, fully believing that so it was, came home, thinking how they should console their ladies for the death of their sister; but, though Madeleine was at great pains to conceal Ninette, Foulques nevertheless, to his no small amazement, discovered that she was there; which at once excited his suspicion, for he knew that the Duke had been enamoured of Madeleine; and he asked how it was that Ninette was there. Madeleine made up a long story by way of explanation, to which his sagacity gave little credit, and in the end after long parley he constrained her to tell the truth. Where-upon, overcome with grief, and transported with rage, he drew his sword, and, deaf to her appeals for mercy, slew her. Then, fearing the vengeful justice of the Duke, he left the dead body in the room, and hied him to Ninette, and with a counterfeit gladsome mien said to her:—"Go we without delay whither thy sister has appointed that I escort thee, that thou fall not again into the hands of the Duke." Ninette believed him, and being fain to go for very fear, she forewent further leave-taking of her sister, more particularly as it was now night, and set out with Foulques, who took with him such little money as he could lay his hands upon; and so they made their way to the coast, where they got aboard a bark, but none ever knew where their voyage ended.

Madeleine's dead body being discovered next day, certain evil-disposed folk, that bore a grudge to Hugues, forthwith apprised the Duke of the fact ; which brought the Duke—for much he loved Madeleine—in hot haste to the house, where he arrested Hugues and his lady, who as yet knew nothing of the departure of Foulques and Ninette, and extorted from them a confession that they and Foulques were jointly answerable for Madeleine's death. For which cause being justly apprehensive of death, they with great address corrupted the guards that had charge of them, giving them a sum of money which they kept concealed in their house against occasions of need ; and together with the guards fled with all speed, leaving all that they possessed behind them, and took ship by night for Rhodes, where, being arrived, they lived in great poverty and misery no long time. Such then was the issue, to which Restagnon, by his foolish love, and Ninette by her wrath brought themselves and others.

NOVEL IV.

Gerbino, in breach of the plighted faith of his grandfather, King Guglielmo, attacks a ship of the King of Tunis to rescue thence his daughter. She being slain by those aboard the ship, he slays them, and afterwards he is beheaded.

LAURETTA, her story ended, kept silence; and the king brooded as in deep thought, while one or another of the company deplored the sad fate of this or the other of the lovers, or censured Ninette's wrath, or made some other comment. At length, however, the king roused himself, and raising his head, made sign to Elisa that 'twas now for her to speak. So, modestly, Elisa thus began :—Gracious ladies, not a few there are that believe that Love looses no shafts save when he is kindled by the eyes, contemning their opinion that hold that passion may be engendered by words; whose error will be abundantly manifest in a story which I purpose to tell you; wherein you may see how mere rumour not only wrought mutual love in those that had never seen one another, but also brought both to a miserable death.

Guglielmo, the Second,[1] as the Sicilians compute, King of Sicily, had two children, a son named Ruggieri, and a daughter named Gostanza. Ruggieri died before his father, and left a son named Gerbino; who, being carefully trained by his grandfather, grew up a most goodly gallant, and of great renown in court and camp, and that not only within the borders of Sicily, but in divers other parts

---

[1] First, according to the now accepted reckoning. He reigned from 1154 to 1166.

of the world, among them Barbary, then tributary to the King of Sicily. And among others, to whose ears was wafted the bruit of Gerbino's magnificent prowess and courtesy, was a daughter of the King of Tunis, who, by averment of all that had seen her, was a creature as fair and debonair, and of as great and noble a spirit as Nature ever formed. To hear tell of brave men was her delight, and what she heard, now from one, now from another, of the brave deeds of Gerbino she treasured in her mind so sedulously, and pondered them with such pleasure, rehearsing them to herself in imagination, that she became hotly enamoured of him, and there was none of whom she talked, or heard others talk, so gladly. Nor, on the other hand, had the fame of her incomparable beauty and other excellences failed to travel, as to other lands, so also to Sicily, where, falling on Gerbino's ears, it gave him no small delight, to such effect that he burned for the lady no less vehemently than she for him. Wherefore, until such time as he might, upon some worthy occasion, have his grandfather's leave to go to Tunis, yearning beyond measure to see her, he charged every friend of his, that went thither, to give her to know, as best he might, his great and secret love for her, and to bring him tidings of her. Which office one of the said friends discharged with no small address; for, having obtained access to her, after the manner of merchants, by bringing jewels for her to look at, he fully apprised her of Gerbino's passion, and placed him, and all that he possessed, entirely at her disposal. The lady received both messenger and message with gladsome mien, made answer that she loved with equal ardour, and in token thereof sent Gerbino one of her most precious jewels. Gerbino received the jewel with extreme delight, and sent her many a letter and many a most precious gift by the hand of the same messenger; and 'twas well understood between them that, should Fortune accord him opportunity, he should see and know her.

On this footing the affair remained somewhat longer than was expedient; and so, while Gerbino and the lady burned with mutual love, it befell that the King of Tunis gave her in marriage to the King of Granada; [1] whereat she was wroth beyond measure, for that

---

[1] An anachronism; the Moorish kingdom of Granada not having been founded until 1238.

she was not only going into a country remote from her lover, but, as she deemed, was severed from him altogether; and so this might not come to pass, gladly, could she but have seen how, would she have left her father and fled to Gerbino. In like manner, Gerbino, on learning of the marriage, was vexed beyond measure, and was oft-times minded, could he but find means to win to her husband by sea, to wrest her from him by force. Some rumour of Gerbino's love, and of his intent, reached the King of Tunis, who, knowing his prowess and power, took alarm, and as the time drew nigh for conveying the lady to Granada, sent word of his purpose to King Guglielmo, and craved his assurance that it might be carried into effect without let or hindrance on the part of Gerbino, or any one else. The old King had heard nothing of Gerbino's love affair, and never dreaming that 'twas on such account that the assurance was craved, granted it without demur, and in pledge thereof sent the King of Tunis his glove. Which received, the King made ready a great and goodly ship in the port of Carthage, and equipped her with all things meet for those that were to man her, and with all appointments apt and seemly for the reception of his daughter, and awaited only fair weather to send her therein to Granada. All which the young lady seeing and marking, sent one of her servants privily to Palermo, bidding him greet the illustrious Gerbino on her part, and tell him that a few days would see her on her way to Granada ; wherefore 'twould now appear whether, or no, he were really as doughty a man as he was reputed, and loved her as much as he had so often protested. The servant did not fail to deliver her message exactly, and returned to Tunis, leaving Gerbino, who knew that his grandfather, King Guglielmo, had given the King of Tunis the desired assurance, at a loss how to act. But prompted by love, and goaded by the lady's words and loath to seem a craven, he hied him to Messina ; and having there armed two light galleys, and manned them with good men and true, he put to sea, and stood for Sardinia, deeming that the lady's ship must pass that way. Nor was he far out in his reckoning ; for he had not been there many days, when the ship, sped by a light breeze, hove in sight not far from the place where he lay in wait for her. Where-upon Gerbino said to his comrades :—" Gentlemen, if you be as good men and true as I deem you, there is none of you but must have felt, if

he feel not now, the might of love; for without love I deem no
mortal capable of true worth or aught that is good; and if you are
or have been in love, 'twill be easy for you to understand that which
I desire. I love, and 'tis because I love that I have laid this travail
upon you; and that which I love is in the ship that you see before
you, which is fraught not only with my beloved, but with immense
treasures, which, if you are good men and true, we, so we but play
the man in fight, may with little trouble make our own; nor for
my share of the spoils of the victory demand I aught but a lady,
whose love it is that prompts me to take arms : all else I freely cede
to you from this very hour. Forward, then; attack we this ship;
success should be ours, for God favours our enterprise, nor lends her
wind to evade us." Fewer words might have sufficed the illustrious
Gerbino; for the rapacious Messinese that were with him were
already bent heart and soul upon that to which by his harangue he
sought to animate them. So, when he had done, they raised a
mighty shout, so that 'twas as if trumpets did blare, and caught up
their arms, and smiting the water with their oars, overhauled the
ship. The advancing galleys were observed while they were yet a
great way off by the ship's crew, who, not being able to avoid the
combat, put themselves in a posture of defence. Arrived at close
quarters, the illustrious Gerbino bade send the ship's masters aboard
the galleys, unless they were minded to do battle. Certified of the
challenge, and who they were that made it, the Saracens answered
that 'twas in breach of the faith plighted to them by their assailants'
king that they were thus attacked, and in token thereof displayed
King Guglielmo's glove, averring in set terms that there should be
no surrender either of themselves or of aught that was aboard the
ship without battle. Gerbino, who had observed the lady standing
on the ship's poop, and seen that she was far more beautiful than he
had imagined, burned with a yet fiercer flame than before, and to
the display of the glove made answer, that, as he had no falcons there
just then, the glove booted him not; wherefore, so they were not
minded to surrender the lady, let them prepare to receive battle.
Whereupon, without further delay, the battle began on both sides
with a furious discharge of arrows and stones; on which wise it was
long protracted to their common loss; until at last Gerbino, seeing
that he gained little advantage, took a light bark which they had

brought from Sardinia, and having fired her, bore down with her, and both the galleys, upon the ship. Whereupon the Saracens, seeing that they must perforce surrender the ship or die, caused the King's daughter, who lay beneath the deck weeping, to come up on deck, and led her to the prow, and shouting to Gerbino, while the lady shrieked alternately "mercy" and "succour," opened her veins before his eyes, and cast her into the sea, saying :—" Take her; we give her to thee on such wise as we can, and as thy faith has merited." Maddened to witness this deed of barbarism, Gerbino, as if courting death, recked no more of the arrows and the stones, but drew alongside the ship, and, despite the resistance of her crew, boarded her ; and as a famished lion ravens amongst a herd of oxen, and tearing and rending, now one, now another, gluts his wrath before he appeases his hunger, so Gerbino, sword in hand, hacking and hewing on all sides among the Saracens, did ruthlessly slaughter not a few of them; till, as the burning ship began to blaze more fiercely, he bade the seamen take thereout all that they might by way of guerdon, which done, he quitted her, having gained but a rueful victory over his adversaries. His next care was to recover from the sea the body of the fair lady, whom long and with many a tear he mourned : and so he returned to Sicily, and gave the body honourable sepulture in Ustica, an islet that faces, as it were, Trapani, and went home the saddest man alive.

When these tidings reached the King of Tunis, he sent to King Guglielmo ambassadors, habited in black, who made complaint of the breach of faith and recited the manner of its occurrence. Which caused King Guglielmo no small chagrin ; and seeing not how he might refuse the justice they demanded, he had Gerbino arrested, and he himself, none of his barons being able by any entreaty to turn him from his purpose, sentenced him to forfeit his aead, and had it severed from his body in his presence, preferring to suffer the loss of his only grandson than to gain the reputation of a faithless king. And so, miserably, within the compass of a few brief days, died the two lovers by woeful deaths, as I have told you, and without having known any joyance of their love.

NOVEL V.

*Lisabetta's brothers slay her lover : he appears to her in
a dream, and shews her where he is buried : she
privily disinters the head, and sets it in a pot of
basil, whereon she daily weeps a great while. The
pot being taken from her by her brothers, she dies
not long after.*

ELISA's story ended, the king bestowed a few words of praise
upon it, and then laid the burden of discourse upon Filomena, who,
full of compassion for the woes of Gerbino and his lady, heaved a
piteous sigh, and thus began:—My story, gracious ladies, will not
be of folk of so high a rank as those of whom Elisa has told us, but
perchance 'twill not be less touching. 'Tis brought to my mind by
the recent mention of Messina, where the matter befell.

Know then that there were at Messina three young men, that
were brothers and merchants, who were left very rich on the death
of their father, who was of San Gimignano ; and they had a sister,
Lisabetta by name, a girl fair enough, and no less debonair, but
whom, for some reason or another, they had not as yet bestowed in
marriage. The three brothers had also in their shop a young Pisan,
Lorenzo by name, who managed all their affairs, and who was so
goodly of person and gallant, that Lisabetta bestowed many a glance
upon him, and began to regard him with extraordinary favour ;
which Lorenzo marking from time to time, gave up all his other
amours, and in like manner began to affect her, and so, their loves
being equal, 'twas not long before they took heart of grace, and did
that which each most desired. Wherein continuing to their no
small mutual solace and delight, they neglected to order it with due

secrecy, whereby one night as Lisabetta was going to Lorenzo's room, she, all unwitting, was observed by the eldest of the brothers, who, albeit much distressed by what he had learnt, yet, being a young man of discretion, was swayed by considerations more seemly, and, allowing no word to escape him, spent the night in turning the affair over in his mind in divers ways. On the morrow he told his brothers that which, touching Lisabetta and Lorenzo, he had observed in the night, which, that no shame might thence ensue either to them or to their sister, they after long consultation determined to pass over in silence, making as if they had seen or heard nought thereof, until such time as they in a safe and convenient manner might banish this disgrace from their sight before it could go further. Adhering to which purpose, they jested and laughed with Lorenzo as they had been wont; and after a while pretending that they were all three going forth of the city on pleasure, they took Lorenzo with them ; and being come to a remote and very lonely spot, seeing that 'twas apt for their design, they took Lorenzo, who was completely off his guard, and slew him, and buried him on such wise that none was ware of it. On their return to Messina they gave out that they had sent him away on business ; which was readily believed, because 'twas what they had been frequently used to do. But as Lorenzo did not return, and Lisabetta questioned the brothers about him with great frequency and urgency, being sorely grieved by his long absence, it so befell that one day, when she was very pressing in her enquiries, one of the brothers said :—" What means this ? What hast thou to do with Lorenzo, that thou shouldst ask about him so often ? Ask us no more, or we will give thee such answer as thou deservest." So the girl, sick at heart and sorrowful, fearing she knew not what, asked no questions ; but many a time at night she called piteously to him, and besought him to come to her, and bewailed his long tarrying with many a tear, and ever yearning for his return, languished in total dejection.

But so it was that one night, when, after long weeping that her Lorenzo came not back, she had at last fallen asleep, Lorenzo appeared to her in a dream, wan and in utter disarray, his clothes torn to shreds and sodden ; and thus, as she thought, he spoke :— " Lisabetta, thou dost nought but call me, and vex thyself for my long tarrying, and bitterly upbraid me with thy tears ; wherefore be

it known to thee that return to thee I may not, because the last day
that thou didst see me thy brothers slew me." After which, he
described the place where they had buried him, told her to call and
expect him no more, and vanished. The girl then awoke, and
doubting not that the vision was true, wept bitterly. And when
morning came, and she was risen, not daring to say aught to her
brothers, she resolved to go to the place indicated in the vision, and
see if what she had dreamed were even as it had appeared to her.
So, having leave to go a little way out of the city for recreation in
company with a maid that had at one time lived with them and
knew all that she did, she hied her thither with all speed ; and having
removed the dry leaves that were strewn about the place, she began
to dig where the earth seemed least hard. Nor had she dug long,
before she found the body of her hapless lover, whereon as yet
there was no trace of corruption or decay ; and thus she saw without
any manner of doubt that her vision was true. And so, saddest of
women, knowing that she might not bewail him there, she would
gladly, if she could, have carried away the body and given it more
honourable sepulture elsewhere ; but as she might not so do, she
took a knife, and, as best she could, severed the head from the trunk,
and wrapped it in a napkin and laid it in the lap of her maid ; and
having covered the rest of the corpse with earth, she left the spot,
having been seen by none, and went home. There she shut herself
up in her room with the head, and kissed it a thousand times in every
part, and wept long and bitterly over it, till she had bathed it in her
tears. She then wrapped it in a piece of fine cloth, and set it in a
large and beautiful pot of the sort in which marjoram or basil is
planted, and covered it with earth, and therein planted some roots
of the goodliest basil of Salerno, and drenched them only with her
tears, or water perfumed with roses or orange-blossoms. And 'twas
her wont ever to sit beside this pot, and, all her soul one yearning, to
pore upon it, as that which enshrined her Lorenzo, and when long
time she had so done, she would bend over it, and weep a great
while, until the basil was quite bathed in her tears.

Fostered with such constant, unremitting care, and nourished by
the richness given to the soil by the decaying head that lay therein,
the basil burgeoned out in exceeding great beauty and fragrance.
And, the girl persevering ever in this way of life, the neighbours from

time to time took note of it, and when her brothers marvelled to see her beauty ruined, and her eyes as it were evanished from her head, they told them of it, saying :—"We have observed that such is her daily wont." Whereupon the brothers, marking her behaviour, chid her therefore once or twice, and as she heeded them not, caused the pot to be taken privily from her. Which, so soon as she missed it, she demanded with the utmost instance and insistence, and, as they gave it not back to her, ceased not to wail and weep, insomuch that she fell sick ; nor in her sickness craved she aught but the pot of basil. Whereat the young men, marvelling mightily, resolved to see what the pot might contain ; and having removed the earth they espied the cloth, and therein the head, which was not yet so decayed, but that by the curled locks they knew it for Lorenzo's head. Passing strange they found it, and fearing lest it should be bruited abroad, they buried the head, and, with as little said as might be, took order for their privy departure from Messina, and hied them thence to Naples. The girl ceased not to weep and crave her pot, and, so weeping, died. Such was the end of her disastrous love ; but not a few in course of time coming to know the truth of the affair, there was one that made the song that is still sung : to wit :—

> A thief he was, I swear,
> A sorry Christian he,
> That took my basil of Salerno fair, etc.[1]

---

[1] This Sicilian folk-song, of which Boccaccio quotes only the first two lines, is given in extenso from MS. Laurent. 38, plut. 42, by Fanfani in his edition of the *Decameron* (Florence, 1857). The following is a free rendering—

> A thief he was, I swear,
> A sorry Christian he,
> That took my basil of Salerno fair,
> That flourished mightily.
> Planted by mine own hands with loving care
> What time they revelled free :
> To spoil another's goods is churlish spite.
>
> To spoil another's goods is churlish spite,
> Ay, and most heinous sin.

A basil had I (alas! luckless wight!),
The fairest plant: within
Its shade I slept: 'twas grown to such a height
But some folk for chagrin
'Reft me thereof, ay, and before my door.

'Reft me thereof, ay, and before my door.
Ah! dolorous day and drear!
Ah! woe is me! Would God I were no more!
My purchase was so dear!
Ah! why that day did I to watch give o'er?
For him my cherished fere
With marjoram I bordered it about.

With marjoram I bordered it about
In May-time fresh and fair,
And watered it thrice ere each week was out,
And marked it grow full yare:
But now 'tis stolen. Ah! too well 'tis known![1]

But now 'tis stolen. Ah! too well 'tis known!
That no more may I hide:
But had to me a while before been shewn
What then should me betide,
At night before my door I had laid me down
To watch my plant beside.
Yet God Almighty sure me succour might.

Ay, God Almighty sure me succour might,
So were it but His will,
'Gainst him that me hath done so foul despite,
That in dire torment still
I languish, since the thief reft from my sight
My plant that did me thrill,
And to my inmost soul such comfort lent!

And to my inmost soul such comfort lent!
So fresh its fragrance blew,
That when, what time the sun uprose, I went
My watering to do,
I'd hear the people all in wonderment
Say, whence this perfume new?
And I for love of it of grief shall die.

[1] This stanza is defective in the original.

And I for love of it of grief shall die,
　　Of my fair plant for dole.
Would one but shew me how I might it buy!
　　Ah! how 'twould me console!
Ounces [1] an hundred of fine gold have I:
　　Him would I give the whole,
Ay, and a kiss to boot, so he were fain.

[1] The "oncia" was a Sicilian gold coin worth rather more than a zecchino.

NOVEL VI.

Andreuola loves Gabriotto : she tells him a dream that she has had; he tells her a dream of his own, and dies suddenly in her arms. While she and her maid are carrying his corpse to his house, they are taken by the Signory. She tells how the matter stands, is threatened with violence by the Podestà, but will not brook it. Her father hears how she is bested; and, her innocence being established, causes her to be set at large; but she, being minded to tarry no longer in the world, becomes a nun.

GLAD indeed were the ladies to have heard Filomena's story, for that, often though they had heard the song sung, they had never yet, for all their enquiries, been able to learn the occasion upon which it was made. When 'twas ended, Pamfilo received the king's command to follow suit, and thus spoke :—By the dream told in the foregoing story I am prompted to relate one in which two dreams are told, dreams of that which was to come, as Lisabetta's was of that which had been, and which were both fulfilled almost as soon as they were told by those that had dreamed them. Wherefore, loving ladies, you must know that 'tis the common experience of mankind to have divers visions during sleep; and albeit the sleeper, while he sleeps, deems all alike most true, but, being awake, judges some of them to be true, others to be probable, and others again to be quite devoid of truth, yet not a few are found to have come to pass. For which cause many are as sure of every dream as of aught that they see in their waking hours, and so, as their dreams engender in them fear or hope, are sorrowful or joyous. And on the other hand there are those that credit no dream, until they see themselves fallen into the very peril whereof they were forewarned. Of whom I approve neither sort, for in sooth neither are all dreams true, nor all alike false. That they are not all true, there is none of us but may many a time have proved ; and that they are not all alike false has already been shewn in Filomena's story, and shall also, as I said before, be shewn in mine. Wherefore I deem that in a virtuous course of life and conduct there is no need to fear aught by reason of any dream that is contrary thereto, or on that account to give up any just design ; and as for crooked and sinister enterprises, however dreams may seem to favour them, and flatter the hopes of the dreamer with auspicious omens, none should trust them : rather should all give full credence to such as run counter thereto. But come we to the story.

In the city of Brescia there lived of yore a gentleman named Messer Negro da Ponte Carraro, who with other children had a very fair daughter, Andreuola by name, who, being unmarried, chanced to fall in love with a neighbour, one Gabriotto, a man of low degree, but goodly of person and debonair, and endowed with all admirable qualities ; and aided and abetted by the housemaid, the girl not only brought it to pass that Gabriotto knew that he was beloved of her, but that many a time to their mutual delight he came to see her in a fair garden belonging to her father. And that nought but death might avail to sever them from this their gladsome love, they became privily man and wife ; and, while thus they continued their clandestine intercourse, it happened that one night, while the girl slept, she saw herself in a dream in her garden with Gabriotto, who to the exceeding great delight of both held her in his arms ; and while thus they lay, she saw issue from his body somewhat dark and frightful, the shape whereof she might not discern ; which, as she thought, laid hold of Gabriotto, and in her despite with prodigious force reft him from her embrace, and bore him with it underground, so that both were lost to her sight for evermore : whereby stricken with sore and inexpressible grief, she awoke ; and albeit she was overjoyed to find that 'twas not as she had dreamed, yet a haunting dread of what she had seen in her vision entered her soul. Wherefore, Gabriotto being minded to visit her on the ensuing night, she did her best endeavour to dissuade him from coming ; but seeing that he was bent upon it, lest he should suspect somewhat, she received him in her garden, where, having culled roses many, white and red—for 'twas summer—she sat herself down with him at the base of a most fair and lucent fountain. There long and joyously they dallied, and then Gabriotto asked her wherefore she had that day forbade his coming. Whereupon the lady told him her dream of the night before, and the doubt and fear which it had engendered in her mind. Whereat Gabriotto laughed, and said that 'twas the height of folly to put any faith in dreams, for that they were occasioned by too much or too little food, and were daily seen to be, one and all, things of nought, adding :—" Were I minded to give heed to dreams, I should not be here now, for I, too, had a dream last night, which was on this wise :—Methought I was in a fair and pleasant wood, and there, a hunting, caught a she-goat as beautiful and loveable as any that ever was seen, and, as it seemed to me, whiter than snow, which in a little while grew so tame and friendly that she never stirred from my side. All the same so jealous was I lest she should leave me, that, meseemed, I had set a collar of gold around her neck, and held her by a golden chain. And presently meseemed that, while the she-goat lay at rest with her head in my lap, there came forth, I knew not whence, a greyhound bitch, black as coal, famished, and most fearsome to look upon ; which made straight for me, and for, meseemed, I offered no resistance, set her muzzle to my breast on the left side and gnawed through to the heart, which, meseemed, she tore out to carry away with her. Whereupon ensued so sore a pain that it brake my sleep, and as I awoke I laid my hand to my side to feel if aught were amiss there ; but finding nothing I laughed at myself that I had searched. But what signifies it all ? Visions of the like sort, ay, and far more appalling, have I had in plenty, and nought whatever, great or small, has come of any of them. So let it pass, and think we how we may speed the time merrily."

What she heard immensely enhanced the already great dread which her own dream had inspired in the girl; but, not to vex Gabriotto, she dissembled her terror as best she might. But, though she made great cheer, embracing and kissing him, and receiving his embraces and kisses, yet she felt a doubt, she knew not why, and many a time, more than her wont, she would gaze upon his face, and ever and anon her glance would stray through the garden to see if any black creature were coming from any quarter. While thus they passed the time, of a sudden Gabriotto heaved a great sigh, and embracing her, said :—" Alas ! my soul, thy succour ! for I die." And so saying, he fell down upon the grassy mead. Where-upon the girl drew him to her, and laid him on her lap, and all but wept, and said :—" O sweet my lord, what is't that ails thee ? " But Gabriotto was silent, and gasping sore for breath, and bathed in sweat, in no long time departed this life.

How grievous was the distress of the girl, who loved him more than herself, you, my ladies, may well imagine. With many a tear she mourned him, and many times she vainly called him by his name ; but when, having felt his body all over, and found it cold in every part, she could no longer doubt that he was dead, knowing not what to say or do, she went, tearful and woebegone, to call the maid, to whom she had confided her love, and shewed her the woeful calamity that had befallen her. Piteously a while they wept together over the dead face of Gabriotto, and then the girl said to the maid :—" Now that God has reft him from me, I have no mind to linger in this life ; but before I slay myself, I would we might find apt means to preserve my honour, and the secret of our love, and to bury the body from which the sweet soul has fled." " My daughter," said the maid, "speak not of slaying thyself, for so wouldst thou lose in the other world, also, him that thou hast lost here ; seeing that thou wouldst go to hell, whither, sure I am, his soul is not gone, for a good youth he was ; far better were it to put on a cheerful courage, and bethink thee to succour his soul with thy prayers or pious works, if perchance he have need thereof by reason of any sin that he may have committed. We can bury him readily enough in this garden, nor will any one ever know ; for none knows that he ever came hither ; and if thou wilt not have it so, we can bear him forth of the garden, and leave him there ; and on the morrow he will be found, and carried home, and buried by his kinsfolk." The girl, heavy-laden though she was with anguish, and still weeping, yet gave ear to the counsels of her maid, and rejecting the former alternative, made answer to the latter on

this wise :—" Now God forbid that a youth so dear, whom I have
so loved and made my husband, should with my consent be buried
like a dog, or left out there in the street.　He has had my tears, and
so far as I may avail, he shall have the tears of his kinsfolk, and
already wot I what we must do."　And forthwith she sent the maid
for a piece of silken cloth, which she had in one of her boxes; and
when the maid returned with it, they spread it on the ground, and
laid Gabriotto's body thereon, resting the head upon a pillow.　She
then closed the eyes and mouth, shedding the while many a tear,
wove for him a wreath of roses, and strewed upon him all the roses
that he and she had gathered; which done, she said to the maid :—
" 'Tis but a short way hence to the door of his house ; so thither we
will bear him, thou and I, thus as we have dight him, and will lay
him at the door.　Day will soon dawn, and they will take him up ;
and, though 'twill be no consolation to them, I, in whose arms he
died, shall be glad of it."　So saying, she burst once more into a
torrent of tears, and fell with her face upon the face of the dead, and
so long time she wept.　Then, yielding at last to the urgency of her
maid, for day was drawing nigh, she arose, drew from her finger the
ring with which she had been wedded to Gabriotto, and set it on
his finger, saying with tears :—" Dear my lord, if thy soul be witness
of my tears, or if, when the spirit is fled, aught of intelligence or
sense still lurk in the body, graciously receive the last gift of her
whom in life thou didst so dearly love."　Which said, she swooned,
and fell upon the corpse ; but, coming after a while to herself, she
arose ; and then she and her maid took the cloth whereon the body
lay, and so bearing it, quitted the garden, and bent their steps towards
the dead man's house.　As thus they went, it chanced that certain
of the Podestà's guard, that for some reason or another were abroad
at that hour, met them, and arrested them with the corpse. Andreuola, to whom death was more welcome than life, no sooner knew
them for the officers of the Signory than she frankly said :—"I know
you, who you are, and that flight would avail me nothing : I am
ready to come with you before the Signory, and to tell all there is to
tell; but let none of you presume to touch me, so long as I obey
you, or to take away aught that is on this body, if he would not that
I accuse him."　And so, none venturing to lay hand upon either her
person or the corpse, she entered the palace.

So soon as the Podestà was apprised of the affair, he arose, had
her brought into his room, and there made himself conversant with
the circumstances : and certain physicians being charged to inquire
whether the good man had met his death by poison or otherwise, all
with one accord averred that 'twas not by poison, but that he was
choked by the bursting of an imposthume near the heart. Which
when the Podestà heard, perceiving that the girl's guilt could but
be slight, he sought to make a pretence of giving what it was not
lawful for him to sell her, and told her that he would set her at
liberty, so she were consenting to pleasure him ; but finding that he
did but waste his words he cast aside all decency, and would have
used force. Whereupon Andreuola, kindling with scorn, waxed
exceeding brave, and defended herself with a virile energy, and with
high and contumelious words drove him from her.

When 'twas broad day, the affair reached the ears of Messer
Negro, who, half dead with grief, hied him with not a few of his
friends to the palace ; where, having heard all that the Podestà had
to say, he required him peremptorily to give him back his daughter.
The Podestà, being minded rather to be his own accuser, than that
he should be accused by the girl of the violence that he had meditated
towards her, began by praising her and her constancy, and in proof
thereof went on to tell what he had done ; he ended by saying, that,
marking her admirable firmness, he had fallen mightily in love with
her, and so, notwithstanding she had been wedded to a man of low
degree, he would, if 'twere agreeable to her and to her father, Messer
Negro, gladly make her his wife. While they thus spoke, Andreuola
made her appearance, and, weeping, threw herself at her father's feet,
saying :—" My father, I wot I need not tell you the story of my
presumption, and the calamity that has befallen me, for sure I am
that you have heard it and know it ; wherefore, with all possible
humility I crave your pardon of my fault, to wit, that without your
knowledge I took for my husband him that pleased me best. And
this I crave, not that my life may be spared, but that I may die as
your daughter and not as your enemy ; " and so, weeping, she fell at
his feet. Messer Negro, now an old man, and naturally kindly and
affectionate, heard her not without tears, and weeping raised her
tenderly to her feet, saying :—" Daughter mine, I had much liefer
had it that thou hadst had a husband that I deemed a match for thee ;

and in that thou hadst taken one that pleased thee I too had been pleased ; but thy concealing thy choice from me is grievous to me by reason of thy distrust of me, and yet more so, seeing that thou hast lost him before I have known him.   But as 'tis even so, to his remains be paid the honour which, while he lived for thy content-ment, I had gladly done him as my son-in-law."   Then, turning to his sons and kinsmen, he bade them order Gabriotto's obsequies with all pomp and honourable circumstance.

Meanwhile the young man's kinsmen and kinswomen, having heard the news, had flocked thither, bringing with them almost all the rest of the folk, men and women alike, that were in the city.   And so his body, resting on Andreuola's cloth, and covered with her roses, was laid out in the middle of the courtyard, and there was mourned not by her and his kinsfolk alone, but publicly by well-nigh all the women of the city, and not a few men ; and shouldered by some of the noblest of the citizens, as it had been the remains of no plebeian but of a noble, was borne from the public courtyard to the tomb with exceeding great pomp.

Some days afterwards, as the Podestà continued to urge his suit, Messer Negro would have discussed the matter with his daughter ; but, as she would hear none of it, and he was minded in this matter to defer to her wishes, she and her maid entered a religious house of great repute for sanctity, where in just esteem they lived long time thereafter.

NOVEL VII.

*Simona loves Pasquino; they are together in a garden;
Pasquino rubs a leaf of sage against his teeth, and
dies; Simona is arrested, and, with intent to shew
the judge how Pasquino died, rubs one of the leaves of
the same plant against her teeth, and likewise dies.*

WHEN Pamfilo had done with his story, the king, betraying no
compassion for Andreuola, glancing at Emilia, signified to her his
desire that she should now continue the sequence of narration.
Emilia made no demur, and thus began :—

Dear gossips, Pamfilo's story puts me upon telling you another in
no wise like thereto, save in this, that as Andreuola lost her lover in
a garden, so also did she of whom I am to speak, and, being arrested
like Andreuola, did also deliver herself from the court, albeit 'twas
not by any vigour or firmness of mind, but by a sudden death.   And,
as 'twas said among us a while ago, albeit Love affects the mansions
of the noble, he does not, therefore, disdain the dominion of the
dwellings of the poor, nay, does there at times give proof of his might
no less signal than when he makes him feared of the wealthiest as a
most potent lord.   Which, though not fully, will in some degree
appear in my story, wherewith I am minded to return to our city,
from which to-day's discourse, roving from matter to matter, and
one part of the world to another, has carried us so far.

Know then that no great while ago there dwelt in Florence a
maid most fair, and, for her rank, debonair—she was but a poor
man's daughter—whose name was Simona; and though she must
needs win with her own hands the bread she ate, and maintain
herself by spinning wool ; yet was she not, therefore, of so poor a

spirit, but that she dared to give harbourage in her mind to Love, who for some time had sought to gain entrance there by means of the gracious deeds and words of a young man of her own order that went about distributing wool to spin for his master, a wool-monger. Love being thus, with the pleasant image of her beloved Pasquino, admitted into her soul, mightily did she yearn, albeit she hazarded no advance, and heaved a thousand sighs fiercer than fire with every skein of yarn that she wound upon her spindle, while she called to mind who he was that had given her that wool to spin. Pasquino on his part became, meanwhile, very anxious that his master's wool should be well spun, and most particularly about that which Simona span, as if, indeed, it and it alone was to furnish forth the whole of the cloth. And so, what with the anxiety which the one evinced, and the gratification that it afforded to the other, it befell that, the one waxing unusually bold, and the other casting off not a little of her wonted shyness and reserve, they came to an understanding for their mutual solace ; which proved so delightful to both, that neither waited to be bidden by the other, but 'twas rather which should be the first to make the overture.

While thus they sped their days in an even tenor of delight, and ever grew more ardently enamoured of one another, Pasquino chanced to say to Simona that he wished of all things she would contrive how she might betake her to a garden, whither he would bring her, that there they might be more at their ease, and in greater security. Simona said that she was agreeable ; and, having given her father to understand that she was minded to go to San Gallo for the pardoning, she hied her with one of her gossips, Lagina by name, to the garden of which Pasquino had told her. Here she found Pasquino awaiting her with a friend, one Puccino, otherwise Stramba ; and Stramba and Lagina falling at once to love-making, Pasquino and Simona left a part of the garden to them, and withdrew to another part for their own solace.

Now there was in their part of the garden a very fine and lovely sage-bush, at foot of which they sat them down and made merry together a great while, and talked much of a junketing they meant to have in the garden quite at their ease. By and by Pasquino, turning to the great sage-bush, plucked therefrom a leaf, and fell to rubbing his teeth and gums therewith, saying that sage was an excellent detergent of aught that remained upon them after a meal. Having done so, he returned to the topic of the junketing of which he had spoken before. But he had not pursued it far before his countenance entirely changed, and forthwith he lost sight and speech, and shortly after died. Whereupon Simona fell a weeping and shrieking and calling Stramba and Lagina ; who, notwithstanding they came up with all speed, found Pasquino not only dead but already swollen from head to foot, and covered with black spots both on the face and on the body ; whereupon Stramba broke forth with :—" Ah ! wicked woman ! thou hast poisoned him ; " and made such a din that 'twas heard by not a few that dwelt hard by the garden ; who also hasted to the spot, and seeing Pasquino dead and swollen, and hearing Stramba bewail himself and accuse Simona of having maliciously poisoned him, while she, all but beside herself for grief to be thus suddenly bereft of her lover, knew not how to defend herself, did all with one accord surmise that 'twas even as Stramba said. Wherefore they laid hands on her, and brought her, still weeping bitterly, to the palace of the Podestà : where at the instant suit of Stramba, backed by Atticciato and Malagevole, two other newly-arrived friends of Pasquino, a judge forthwith addressed himself to question her of the matter ; and being unable to discover that she had used any wicked practice, or was guilty, he resolved to take her with him and go see the corpse, and the place, and the manner of the death, as she had recounted it to him ; for by her words he could not well understand it. So, taking care that there should be no disturbance, he had her brought to the place where Pasquino's corpse lay swollen like a tun, whither he himself presently came, and marvelling as he examined the corpse, asked her how the death had come about. Whereupon, standing by the sage-bush, she told him all that had happened, and that he might perfectly apprehend the occasion of the death, she did as Pasquino had done, plucked one of the leaves from the bush, and rubbed her teeth with it. Whereupon Stramba and Atticciato, and the rest of the friends and comrades of Pasquino, making in the presence of the judge open mock of what she did, as an idle and vain thing, and being more than ever instant to affirm her guilt, and to demand the fire as the sole condign penalty, the poor creature, that, between grief for her lost lover and dread of the doom demanded by Stramba, stood mute and helpless, was stricken no less suddenly, and in the same manner, and for the same cause (to wit, that she had rubbed her teeth with the sage leaf) as Pasquino, to the no small amazement of all that were present.

Oh! happy souls for whom one and the same day was the term of ardent love and earthly life! Happier still, if to the same bourn ye fared! Ay, and even yet more happy, if love there be in the other world, and there, even as here, ye love! But happiest above all Simona, so far as we, whom she has left behind, may judge, in that Fortune brooked not that the witness of Stramba, Atticciato and Malagevole, carders, perchance, or yet viler fellows, should bear down her innocence, but found a more seemly issue, and, appointing her a like lot with her lover, gave her at once to clear herself from their foul accusation, and to follow whither the soul, that she so loved, of her Pasquino had preceded her!

The judge, and all else that witnessed the event, remained long time in a sort of stupefaction, knowing not what to say of it; but at length recovering his wits, the judge said:—"'Twould seem that this sage is poisonous, which the sage is not used to be. Let it be cut down to the roots and burned, lest another suffer by it in like sort." Which the gardener proceeding to do in the judge's presence, no sooner had he brought the great bush down, than the cause of the deaths of the two lovers plainly appeared: for underneath it was a toad of prodigious dimensions, from whose venomous breath, as they conjectured, the whole of the bush had contracted a poisonous quality. Around which toad, none venturing to approach it, they set a stout ring-fence of faggots, and burned it together with the sage. So ended Master Judge's inquest on the death of hapless Pasquino, who with his Simona, swollen as they were, were buried by Stramba, Atticciato, Guccio Imbratta, and Malagevole in the church of San Paolo, of which, as it so happened, they were parishioners.

NOVEL VIII.

Girolamo loves Salvestra : yielding to his mother's prayers he goes to Paris ; he returns to find Salvestra married ; he enters her house by stealth, lays himself by her side, and dies ; he is borne to the church, where Salvestra lays herself by his side, and dies.

WHEN Emilia's story was done, Neifile at a word from the king thus began :—Some there are, noble ladies, who, methinks, deem themselves to be wiser than the rest of the world, and are in fact less so ; and by consequence presume to measure their wit against not only the counsels of men but the nature of things ; which presumption has from time to time been the occasion of most grievous mishaps ; but nought of good was ever seen to betide thereof. And as there is nought in nature that brooks to be schooled or thwarted so ill as love, the quality of which is such that it is more likely to die out of its own accord than to be done away of set purpose, I am minded to tell you a story of a lady, who, while she sought to be more wise than became her, and than she was, and indeed than the nature of the matter, wherein she studied to shew her wisdom, allowed, thinking to unseat Love from the heart that he had occupied, and wherein perchance the stars had established him, did in the end banish at one and the same time Love and life from the frame of her son.

Know, then, that, as 'tis related by them of old time, there was once in our city a very great and wealthy merchant, Leonardo Sighieri by name, who had by his lady a son named Girolamo, after whose birth he departed this life, leaving his affairs in meet and due order ; and well and faithfully were they afterwards administered in the interest of the boy by his mother and guardians. As he grew up, consorting more frequently with the neighbours' children than any others of the quarter, he made friends with a girl of his own age that was the daughter of a tailor ; and in course of time this friendship ripened into a love so great and vehement, that Girolamo was ever ill at ease when he saw her not ; nor was her love for him a whit less strong than his for her. Which his mother perceiving would not seldom chide him therefor and chastise him. And as Girolamo could not give it up, she confided her distress to his guardians, speaking—for by reason of her boy's great wealth she thought to make, as it were, an orange-tree out of a bramble—on this wise :—" This boy of ours, who is now scarce fourteen years old, is so in love with a daughter of one of our neighbours, a tailor— Salvestra is the girl's name—that, if we part them not, he will, per- adventure, none else witting, take her to wife some day, and I shall never be happy again ; or, if he see her married to another, he will pine away ; to prevent which, methinks, you would do well to send him away to distant parts on the affairs of the shop ; for so, being out of sight she will come at length to be out of mind, and then we can give him some well-born girl to wife." Whereto the guardians answered, that 'twas well said, and that it should be so done to the best of their power: so they called the boy into the shop, and one of them began talking to him very affectionately on this wise :— " My son, thou art now almost grown up ; 'twere well thou shouldst now begin to learn something for thyself of thy own affairs : where- fore we should be very well pleased if thou wert to go stay at Paris a while, where thou wilt see how we trade with not a little of thy wealth, besides which thou wilt there become a much better, finer, and more complete gentleman than thou couldst here, and when thou hast seen the lords and barons and seigneurs that are there in plenty, and hast acquired their manners, thou canst return hither." The boy listened attentively, and then answered shortly that he would have none of it, for he supposed he might remain at Florence as well as another. Whereupon the worthy men plied him with fresh argument, but were unable to elicit other answer from him, and told his mother so. Whereat she was mightily incensed, and gave him a great scolding, not for his refusing to go to Paris, but for his love ; which done, she plied him with soft, wheedling words, and endearing expressions and gentle entreaties that he would be pleased to do as his guardians would have him; whereby at length she prevailed so far, that he consented to go to Paris for a year and no more; and so 'twas arranged. To Paris accordingly our ardent lover went, and there under one pretext or another was kept for two years. He returned more in love than ever, to find his Salvestra married to a good youth that was a tent-maker; whereat his mortification knew no bounds. But, seeing that what must be must be, he sought to compose his mind; and, having got to know where she lived, he took to crossing her path, according to the wont of young men in love, thinking that she could no more have forgotten him than he her. 'Twas otherwise, however; she remembered him no more than if she had never seen him; or, if she had any recollection of him, she dissembled it: whereof the young man was very soon ware, to his extreme sorrow. Nevertheless he did all that he could to recall himself to her mind; but, as thereby he seemed to be nothing advantaged, he made up his mind, though he should die for it, to speak to her himself. So, being instructed as to her house by a neighbour, he entered it privily one evening when she and her husband were gone to spend the earlier hours with some neighbours, and hid himself in her room behind some tent-cloths that were stretched there, and waited till they were come back, and gone to bed, and he knew the husband to be asleep. Whereupon he got him to the place where he had seen Salvestra lie down, and said as he gently laid his hand upon her bosom:—"O my soul, art thou yet asleep?" The girl was awake, and was on the point of uttering a cry, when he forestalled her, saying:—"Hush! for God's sake. I am thy Girolamo." Whereupon she, trembling in every limb:—"Nay, but for God's sake, Girolamo, begone: 'tis past, the time of our childhood, when our love was excusable. Thou seest I am married; wherefore 'tis no longer seemly that I should care for any other man than my husband, and so by the one God, I pray thee, begone; for, if my husband were to know that thou art here, the least evil that could ensue would be that I should never more be able to live with him in peace or comfort, whereas, having his love, I now pass my days with him in tranquil happiness." Which speech caused the young man grievous distress; but 'twas in vain that he reminded her of the past, and of his love that distance had not impaired, and therewith mingled many a prayer and the mightiest protestations.

Wherefore, yearning for death, he besought her at last that she would suffer him to lie a while beside her till he got some heat, for he was chilled through and through, waiting for her, and promised her that he would say never a word to her, nor touch her, and that as soon as he was a little warmed he would go away. On which terms Salvestra, being not without pity for him, granted his request. So the young man lay down beside her, and touched her not ; but, gathering up into one thought the love he had so long borne her, the harshness with which she now requited it, and his ruined hopes, resolved to live no longer, and in a convulsion, without a word, and with fists clenched, expired by her side.

After a while the girl, marvelling at his continence, and fearing lest her husband should awake, broke silence, saying :—" Nay, but, Girolamo, why goest thou not ? " But, receiving no answer, she supposed that he slept. Wherefore, reaching forth her hand to arouse him, she touched him and found him to her great surprise cold as ice ; and touching him again and again somewhat rudely, and still finding that he did not stir, she knew that he was dead. Her grief was boundless, and 'twas long before she could bethink her how to act. But at last she resolved to sound her husband's mind as to what should be done in such a case without disclosing that 'twas his own. So she awakened him, and told him how he was then bested, as if it were the affair of another, and then asked him, if such a thing happened to her, what course he would take. The good man answered that he should deem it best to take the dead man privily home, and there leave him, bearing no grudge against the lady, who seemed to have done no wrong. "And even so," said his wife, " it is for us to do ; " and taking his hand, she laid it on the corpse. Whereat he started up in consternation, and struck a light, and without further parley with his wife, clapped the dead man's clothes upon him, and forthwith (confident in his own innocence) raised him on his shoulders, and bore him to the door of his house, where he set him down and left him.

Day came, and the dead man being found before his own door, there was a great stir made, particularly by his mother ; the body was examined with all care from head to foot, and, no wound or trace of violence being found on it, the physicians were on the whole of opinion that, as the fact was, the man had died of grief. So the corpse was borne to a church, and thither came the sorrowing mother and other ladies, her kinswomen and neighbours, and began to wail and mourn over it without restraint after our Florentine fashion. And when the wailing had reached its height, the good man, in whose house the death had occurred, said to Salvestra :—" Go wrap a mantle about thy head, and hie thee to the church, whither Girolamo has been taken, and go about among the women and list what they say of this matter, and I will do the like among the men, that we may hear if aught be said to our disadvantage." The girl assented, for with tardy tenderness she now yearned to look on him dead, whom living she would not solace with a single kiss, and so to the church she went. Ah ! how marvellous to whoso ponders it, is the might of Love, and how unsearchable his ways ! That heart, which, while Fortune smiled on Girolamo, had remained sealed to him, opened to him now that he was fordone, and, kindling anew with all its old flame, melted with such compassion that no sooner saw she his dead face, as there she stood wrapped in her mantle, than, edging her way forward through the crowd of women, she stayed not till she was beside the corpse ; and there, uttering a piercing shriek, she threw herself upon the dead youth, and as her face met his, and before she might drench it with her tears, grief that had reft life from him had even so reft it from her.

The women strove to comfort her, and bade her raise herself a little, for as yet they knew her not ; then, as she did not arise, they would have helped her, but found her stiff and stark, and so, raising her up, they in one and the same moment saw her to be Salvestra and dead. Whereat all the women that were there, overborne by a redoubled pity, broke forth in wailing new and louder far than before. From the church the bruit spread itself among the men, and reached the ears of Salvestra's husband, who, deaf to all that offered comfort or consolation, wept a long while ; after which he told to not a few that were there what had passed in the night between the youth and his wife ; and so 'twas known of all how they came to die, to the common sorrow of all. So they took the dead girl, and arrayed her as they are wont to array the dead, and laid her on the same bed beside the youth, and long time they mourned her : then were they both buried in the same tomb, and thus those, whom love had not been able to wed in life, were wedded by death in indissoluble union.

NOVEL IX.

Sieur Guillaume de Roussillon slays his wife's paramour, Sieur Guillaume de Cabestaing, and gives her his heart to eat. She, coming to wit thereof, throws herself from a high window to the ground, and dies, and is buried with her lover.

NEIFILE's story, which had not failed to move her gossips to no little pity, being ended, none now remained to speak but the king and Dioneo, whose privilege the king was minded not to infringe: wherefore he thus began :—I propose, compassionate my ladies, to tell you a story, which, seeing that you so commiserate ill-starred loves, may claim no less a share of your pity than the last, inasmuch as they were greater folk of whom I shall speak, and that which befell them was more direful.

You are to know, then, that, as the Provençals relate, there were once in Provence two noble knights, each having castles and vassals under him, the one yclept Sieur Guillaume de Roussillon, and the other Sieur Guillaume de Cabestaing ; [1] and being both most doughty warriors, they were as brothers, and went ever together, and bearing the same device, to tournament or joust, or other passage of arms. And, albeit each dwelt in his own castle, and the castles were ten good miles apart, it nevertheless came to pass that, Sieur Guillaume de Roussillon having a most lovely lady, and amorous withal, to wife, Sieur Guillaume de Cabestaing, for all they were such friends and comrades, became inordinately enamoured of the lady, who, by this, that, and the other sign that he gave, dis-

---

[1] Boccaccio writes Guardastagno, but the troubadour, Cabestaing, or Cabestany, is the hero of the story.

covered his passion, and knowing him for a most complete knight,
was flattered, and returned it, insomuch that she yearned and burned
for him above all else in the world, and waited only till he should
make his suit to her, as before long he did ; and so they met from
time to time, and great was their love. Which intercourse they
ordered with so little discretion that 'twas discovered by the husband,
who was very wroth, insomuch that the great love which he bore to
Cabestaing was changed into mortal enmity ; and, dissembling it
better than the lovers their love, he made his mind up to kill Cabestaing. Now it came to pass that, while Roussillon was in this
frame, a great tourney was proclaimed in France, whereof Roussillon
forthwith sent word to Cabestaing, and bade him to his castle, so he
were minded to come, that there they might discuss whether (or no)
to go to the tourney, and how. Cabestaing was overjoyed, and
made answer that he would come to sup with him next day without
fail. Which message being delivered, Roussillon wist that the
time was come to slay Cabestaing. So next day he armed himself,
and, attended by a few servants, took horse, and about a mile from
his castle lay in ambush in a wood through which Cabestaing must
needs pass. He waited some time, and then he saw Cabestaing
approach unarmed with two servants behind, also unarmed, for he
was without thought of peril on Roussillon's part. So Cabestaing
came on to the place of Roussillon's choice, and then, fell and vengeful, Roussillon leapt forth lance in hand, and fell upon him, exclaim-
ing :—"Thou art a dead man ! " and the words were no sooner
spoken than the lance was through Cabestaing's breast. Powerless
either to defend himself or even utter a cry, Cabestaing fell to the
ground, and soon expired. His servants waited not to see who had
done the deed, but turned their horses' heads and fled with all speed
to their lord's castle. Roussillon dismounted, opened Cabestaing's
breast with a knife, and took out the heart with his own hands,
wrapped it up in a banderole, and gave it to one of his servants to
carry : he then bade none make bold to breathe a word of the affair,
mounted his horse and rode back—'twas now night—to his castle.
The lady, who had been told that Cabestaing was to come to supper
that evening, and was all impatience till he should come, was greatly
surprised to see her husband arrive without him. Wherefore :—
" How is this, my lord ? " said she. " Why tarries Cabestaing ? "

"Madam," answered her husband, "I have tidings from him that he cannot be here until to-morrow:" whereat the lady was somewhat disconcerted.

Having dismounted, Roussillon called the cook, and said to him:—"Here is a boar's heart; take it, and make thereof the daintiest and most delicious dish thou canst, and when I am set at table serve it in a silver porringer." So the cook took the heart, and expended all his skill and pains upon it, mincing it and mixing with it plenty of good seasoning, and made thereof an excellent ragout; and in due time Sieur Guillaume and his lady sat them down to table. The meat was served, but Sieur Guillaume, his mind engrossed with his crime, ate but little. The cook set the ragout before him, but he, feigning that he cared to eat no more that evening, had it passed on to the lady, and highly commended it. The lady, nothing loath, took some of it, and found it so good that she ended by eating the whole. Whereupon:—"Madam," quoth the knight, "how liked you this dish?" "In good faith, my lord," replied the lady, "not a little." "So help me, God," returned the knight, "I dare be sworn you did; 'tis no wonder that you should enjoy that dead, which living you enjoyed more than aught else in the world." For a while the lady was silent; then:—"How say you?" said she; "what is this you have caused me to eat?" "That which you have eaten," replied the knight, "was in good sooth the heart of Sieur Guillaume de Cabestaing, whom you, disloyal woman that you are, did so much love: for assurance whereof I tell you that but a short while before I came back, I plucked it from his breast with my own hands." It boots not to ask if the lady was sorrow-stricken to receive such tidings of her best beloved. But after a while she said:—"'Twas the deed of a disloyal and recreant knight; for if I, unconstrained by him, made him lord of my love, and thereby did you wrong, 'twas I, not he, should have borne the penalty. But God forbid that fare of such high excellence as the heart of a knight so true and courteous as Sieur Guillaume de Cabestaing be followed by aught else." So saying she started to her feet, and stepping back to a window that was behind her, without a moment's hesitation let herself drop backwards therefrom. The window was at a great height from the ground, so that the lady was not only killed by the fall, but almost reduced to atoms. Stunned and conscience-stricken by the spectacle, and fearing the vengeance of the country folk, and the Count of Provence, Sieur Guillaume had his horses saddled and rode away. On the morrow the whole countryside knew how the affair had come about ; wherefore folk from both of the castles took the two bodies, and bore them with grief and lamentation exceeding great to the church in the lady's castle, and laid them in the same tomb, and caused verses to be inscribed thereon signifying who they were that were there interred, and the manner and occasion of their death.

NOVEL X.

The wife of a leech, deeming her lover, who has taken an opiate, to be dead, puts him in a chest, which, with him therein, two usurers carry off to their house. He comes to himself, and is taken for a thief; but, the lady's maid giving the Signory to understand that she had put him in the chest which the usurers stole, he escapes the gallows, and the usurers are mulcted in moneys for the theft of the chest.

Now that the king had told his tale, it only remained for Dioneo to do his part, which he witting, and being thereto bidden by the king, thus began :—Sore have I—to say nought of you, my ladies— been of eyne and heart to hear the woeful histories of ill-starred love, insomuch that I have desired of all things that they might have an end. Wherefore, now that, thank God, ended they are, unless indeed I were minded, which God forbid, to add to such pernicious stuff a supplement of the like evil quality, no such dolorous theme do I purpose to ensue, but to make a fresh start with somewhat of a better and more cheerful sort, which perchance may serve to suggest to-morrow's argument.

You are to know, then, fairest my damsels, that 'tis not long since there dwelt at Salerno a leech most eminent in surgery, his name, Master Mazzeo della Montagna, who in his extreme old age took to wife a fair damsel of the same city, whom he kept in nobler and richer array of dresses and jewels, and all other finery that the sex affects, than any other lady in Salerno. Howbeit, she was none too warm most of her time, being ill covered abed by the doctor ;

who gave her to understand—even as Messer Ricciardo di Chinzica, of whom we spoke a while since, taught his lady the feasts—that for once that a man lay with a woman he needed I know not how many days to recover, and the like nonsense : whereby she lived as ill content as might be ; and, lacking neither sense nor spirit, she determined to economize at home, and taking to the street, to live at others' expense. So, having passed in review divers young men, she at last found one that was to her mind, on whom she set all her heart and hopes of happiness. Which the gallant perceiving was mightily flattered, and in like manner gave her all his love. Ruggieri da Jeroli—such was the gallant's name—was of noble birth, but of life and conversation so evil and reprehensible that kinsman or friend he had none left that wished him well, or cared to see him ; and all Salerno knew him for a common thief and rogue of the vilest character. Whereof the lady took little heed, having a mind to him for another reason ; and so with the help of her maid she arranged a meeting with him. But after they had solaced themselves a while, the lady began to censure his past life, and to implore him for love of her to depart from such evil ways ; and to afford him the means thereto, she from time to time furnished him with money. While thus with all discretion they continued their intercourse, it chanced that a man halt of one of his legs was placed under the leech's care. The leech saw what was amiss with him, and told his kinsfolk, that, unless a gangrened bone that he had in his leg were taken out, he must die, or have the whole leg amputated ; that if the bone were removed he might recover ; but that otherwise he would not answer for his life : whereupon the relatives assented that the bone should be removed, and left the patient in the hands of the leech ; who, deeming that by reason of the pain 'twas not possible for him to endure the treatment without an opiate, caused to be distilled in the morning a certain water of his own concoction, whereby the patient, drinking it, might be ensured sleep during such time as he deemed the operation, which he meant to perform about vespers, would occupy. In the meantime he had the water brought into his house, and set it in the window of his room, telling no one what it was. But when the vesper hour was come, and the leech was about to visit his patient, a messenger arrived from some very great friends of his at Amalfi, bearing tidings of a great riot there had been there, in which not a few had been wounded, and bidding him on no account omit to hie him thither forthwith. Wherefore the leech put off the treatment of the leg to the morrow, and took boat to Amalfi; and the lady, knowing that he would not return home that night, did as she was wont in such a case, to wit, brought Ruggieri in privily, and locked him in her chamber until certain other folk that were in the house were gone to sleep. Ruggieri, then, being thus in the chamber, awaiting the lady, and having—whether it were that he had had a fatiguing day, or eaten something salt, or, perchance, that 'twas his habit of body—a mighty thirst, glancing at the window, caught sight of the bottle containing the water which the leech had prepared for the patient, and taking it to be drinking water, set it to his lips and drank it all, and in no long time fell into a deep sleep.

So soon as she was able the lady hied her to the room, and there finding Ruggieri asleep, touched him and softly told him to get up: to no purpose, however; he neither answered nor stirred a limb. Wherefore the lady, rather losing patience, applied somewhat more force, and gave him a push, saying:—"Get up, sleepy-head; if thou hadst a mind to sleep, thou shouldst have gone home, and not have come hither." Thus pushed Ruggieri fell down from a box on which he lay, and, falling, shewed no more sign of animation than if he had been a corpse. The lady, now somewhat alarmed, essayed to lift him, and shook him roughly, and took him by the nose, and pulled him by the beard; again to no purpose: he had tethered his ass to a stout pin. So the lady began to fear he must be dead: however, she went on to pinch him shrewdly, and singe him with the flame of a candle; but when these methods also failed she, being, for all she was a leech's wife, no leech herself, believed for sure that he was dead; and as there was nought in the world that she loved so much, it boots not to ask if she was sore distressed; wherefore silently, for she dared not lament aloud, she began to weep over him and bewail such a misadventure. But, after a while, fearing lest her loss should not be without a sequel of shame, she bethought her that she must contrive without delay to get the body out of the house; and standing in need of another's advice, she quietly summoned her maid, shewed her the mishap that had befallen her, and craved her counsel. Whereat the maid marvelled not a little; and she too fell to pulling Ruggieri this way and that, and pinching him, and, as she found no sign of life in him, concurred with her mistress that he was verily dead, and advised her to remove him from the house. " And where," said the lady, "shall we put him, that to-morrow, when he is discovered, it be not suspected that 'twas hence he was carried ?" " Madam," answered the maid, " late last evening I marked in front of our neighbour the carpenter's shop a chest, not too large, which, if he have not put it back in the house, will come in very handy for our purpose, for we will put him inside, and give him two or three cuts with a knife, and so leave him. When he is found, I know not why it should be thought that 'twas from this house rather than from any other that he was put there ; nay, as he was an evil-liver, 'twill more likely be supposed, that, as he hied him on some evil errand, some enemy slew him, and then put him in the chest." The lady said there was nought in the world she might so ill brook as that Ruggieri should receive any wound ; but with that exception she approved her maid's proposal, and sent her to see if the chest were still where she had seen it. The maid, returning, reported that there it was, and, being young and strong, got Ruggieri, with the lady's help, upon her shoulders ; and so the lady, going before to espy if any folk came that way, and the maid following, they came to the chest, and having laid Ruggieri therein, closed it and left him there.

Now a few days before, two young men, that were usurers, had taken up their quarters in a house a little further on : they had seen the chest during the day, and being short of furniture, and having a mind to make great gain with little expenditure, they had resolved that, if it were still there at night, they would take it home with them. So at midnight forth they hied them, and finding the chest, were at no pains to examine it closely, but forthwith, though it seemed somewhat heavy, bore it off to their house, and set it down beside a room in which their women slept ; and without being at pains to adjust it too securely they left it there for the time, and went to bed.

Towards matins Ruggieri, having had a long sleep and digested the draught and exhausted its efficacy, awoke, but albeit his slumber was broken, and his senses had recovered their powers, yet his brain remained in a sort of torpor which kept him bemused for some days ;

and when he opened his eyes and saw nothing, and stretched his hands hither and thither and found himself in the chest, it was with difficulty that he collected his thoughts. " How is this ? " he said to himself. "Where am I ? Do I sleep or wake ? I remember coming this evening to my lady's chamber ; and now it seems I am in a chest. What means it ? Can the leech have returned, or somewhat else have happened that caused the lady, while I slept, to hide me here ? That was it, I suppose. Without a doubt it must have been so." And having come to this conclusion, he composed himself to listen, if haply he might hear something, and being somewhat ill at ease in the chest, which was none too large, and the side on which he lay paining him, he must needs turn over to the other, and did so with such adroitness that, bringing his loins smartly against one of the sides of the chest, which was set on an uneven floor, he caused it to tilt and then fall ; and such was the noise that it made as it fell that the women that slept there awoke, albeit for fear they kept silence. Ruggieri was not a little disconcerted by the fall, but, finding that thereby the chest was come open, he judged that, happen what might, he would be better out of it than in it ; and not knowing where he was, and being otherwise at his wits' end, he began to grope about the house, if haply he might find a stair or door whereby he might take himself off. Hearing him thus groping his way, the alarmed women gave tongue with :—" Who is there ? " Ruggieri, not knowing the voice, made no answer : wherefore the women fell to calling the two young men, who, having had a long day, were fast asleep, and heard nought of what went on. Which served to increase the fright of the women, who rose and got them to divers windows, and raised the cry :—" Take thief, take thief ! " At which summons there came running from divers quarters not a few of the neighbours, who got into the house by the roof or otherwise as each best might : likewise the young men, aroused by the din, got up ; and, Ruggieri being now all but beside himself for sheer amazement, and knowing not whither to turn him to escape them, they took him and delivered him to the officers of the Governor of the city, who, hearing the uproar, had hasted to the spot. And so he was brought before the Governor, who, knowing him to be held of all a most arrant evil-doer, put him forthwith to the torture, and, upon his confessing that he had entered the house of the usurers with intent to rob, was minded to make short work of it, and have him hanged by the neck.

In the morning 'twas bruited throughout all Salerno that Ruggieri had been taken a thieving in the house of the usurers. Whereat the lady and her maid were all amazement and bewilderment, insomuch that they were within an ace of persuading themselves that what they had done the night before they had not done, but had only dreamed it; besides which, the peril in which Ruggieri stood caused the lady such anxiety as brought her to the verge of madness. Shortly after half tierce the leech, being returned from Amalfi, and minded now to treat his patient, called for his water, and finding the bottle empty made a great commotion, protesting that nought in his house could be let alone. The lady, having other cause of annoy, lost temper, and said:—"What would you say, Master, of an important matter, when you raise such a din because a bottle of water has been upset? Is there never another to be found in the world?" "Madam," replied the leech, "thou takest this to have been mere water: 'twas no such thing, but an artificial water of a soporiferous virtue;" and he told her for what purpose he had made it. Which the lady no sooner heard, than, guessing that Ruggieri had drunk it, and so had seemed to them to be dead, she said:—"Master, we knew it not; wherefore make you another." And so the leech, seeing that there was no help for it, had another made. Not long after, the maid, who by the lady's command had gone to find out what folk said of Ruggieri, returned, saying:— "Madam, of Ruggieri they say nought but evil, nor, by what I have been able to discover, has he friend or kinsman that has or will come to his aid; and 'tis held for certain that to-morrow the Stadic [1] will have him hanged. Besides which, I have that to tell you which will surprise you; for, methinks, I have found out how he came into the usurers' house. List, then, how it was: you know the carpenter in front of whose shop stood the chest we put Ruggieri into: he had to-day the most violent altercation in the world with one to whom it would seem the chest belongs, by whom he was required to make good the value of the chest, to which he made answer that he had not sold it, but that it had been stolen from him in the night. 'Not

---

[1] The Neapolitan term for the chief of police.

so,' said the other ; ' thou soldst it to the two young usurers, as they themselves told me last night, when I saw it in their house at the time Ruggieri was taken.' 'They lie,' replied the carpenter. ' I never sold it them, but they must have stolen it from me last night ; go we to them.' So with one accord off they went to the usurers' house, and I came back here. And so, you see, I make out that 'twas on such wise that Ruggieri was brought where he was found ; but how he came to life again, I am at a loss to conjecture." The lady now understood exactly how things were, and accordingly told the maid what she had learned from the leech, and besought her to aid her to get Ruggieri off, for so she might, if she would, and at the same time preserve her honour. "Madam," said the maid, "do but shew me how ; and glad shall I be to do just as you wish." Where-upon the lady, to whom necessity taught invention, formed her plan on the spur of the moment, and expounded it in detail to the maid ; who (as the first step) hied her to the leech, and, weeping, thus addressed him :—"Sir, it behoves me to ask your pardon of a great wrong that I have done you." "And what may that be ?" inquired the leech. "Sir," said the maid, who ceased not to weep, "you know what manner of man is Ruggieri da Jeroli. Now he took a fancy to me, and partly for fear, partly for love, I this year agreed to be his mistress ; and knowing yestereve that you were from home, he coaxed me into bringing him into your house to sleep with me in my room. Now he was athirst, and I, having no mind to be seen by your lady, who was in the hall, and knowing not whither I might sooner betake me for wine or water, bethought me that I had seen a bottle of water in your room, and ran and fetched it, and gave it him to drink, and then put the bottle back in the place whence I had taken it ; touching which I find that you have made a great stir in the house. Verily I confess that I did wrong ; but who is there that does not wrong sometimes ? Sorry indeed am I to have so done, but 'tis not for such a cause and that which ensued thereon that Ruggieri should lose his life. Wherefore, I do most earnestly beseech you, pardon me, and suffer me to go help him as best I may be able." Wroth though he was at what he heard, the leech replied in a bantering tone :—" Thy pardon thou hast by thine own deed ; for, whereas thou didst last night think to have with thee a gallant that would thoroughly dust thy pelisse for thee, he was but a sleepy-head ; wherefore get thee gone, and do what thou mayst for the deliverance of thy lover, and for the future look thou bring him not into the house ; else I will pay thee for that turn and this to boot." The maid, deeming that she had come off well in the first brush, hied her with all speed to the prison where Ruggieri lay, and by her cajoleries prevailed upon the warders to let her speak with him ; and having told him how he must answer the Stadic if he would get off, she succeeded in obtaining preaudience of the Stadic ; who, seeing that the baggage was lusty and mettlesome, was minded before he heard her to grapple her with the hook, to which she was by no means averse, knowing that such a preliminary would secure her a better hearing. When she had undergone the operation and was risen :—"Sir," said she, "you have here Ruggieri da Jeroli, apprehended on a charge of theft ; which charge is false." Whereupon she told him the whole story from beginning to end, how she, being Ruggieri's mistress, had brought him into the leech's house and had given him the opiate, not knowing it for such, and taking him to be dead, had put him in the chest ; and then recounting what she had heard pass between the carpenter and the owner of the chest, she shewed him how Ruggieri came into the house of the usurers. Seeing that 'twas easy enough to find out whether the story were true, the Stadic began by questioning the leech as to the water, and found that 'twas as she had said : he then summoned the carpenter, the owner of the chest and the usurers, and after much further parley ascertained that the usurers had stolen the chest during the night, and brought it into their house : finally he sent for Ruggieri, and asked him where he had lodged that night, to which Ruggieri answered that where he had lodged he knew not, but he well remembered going to pass the night with Master Mazzeo's maid, in whose room he had drunk some water by reason of a great thirst that he had ; but what happened to him afterwards, except that, when he awoke, he found himself in a chest in the house of the usurers, he knew not. All which matters the Stadic heard with great interest, and caused the maid and Ruggieri and the carpenter and the usurers to rehearse them several times. In the end, seeing that Ruggieri was innocent, he released him, and mulcted the usurers in fifteen ounces for the theft of the chest. How glad Ruggieri was thus to escape, it boots not to ask ; and glad beyond measure was his lady. And so, many a time did they laugh and make merry together over the affair, she and he and the dear maid that had proposed to give him a taste of the knife ; and remaining constant in their love, they had ever better and better solace thereof. The like whereof befall me, sans the being put in the chest.

Heartsore as the gentle ladies had been made by the preceding stories, this last of Dioneo provoked them to such merriment, more especially the passage about the Stadic and the hook, that they lacked not relief of the piteous mood engendered by the others. But the king observing that the sun was now taking a yellowish tinge, and that the end of his sovereignty was come, in terms most courtly made his excuse to the fair ladies, that he had made so direful a theme as lovers' infelicity the topic of their discourse ; after which, he rose, took the laurel wreath from his head, and, while the ladies watched to see to whom he would give it, set it graciously upon the blond head of Fiammetta, saying :—" Herewith I crown thee, as deeming that thou, better than any other, wilt know how to make to-morrow console our fair companions for the rude trials of to-day." Fiammetta, whose wavy tresses fell in a flood of gold over her white and delicate shoulders, whose softly rounded face was all radiant with the very tints of the white lily blended with the red of the rose, who carried two eyes in her head that matched those of a peregrine falcon, while her tiny sweet mouth shewed a pair of lips that shone as rubies, replied with a smile :—" And gladly take I the wreath, Filostrato, and that thou mayst more truly understand what thou hast done, 'tis my present will and pleasure that each make ready to discourse to-morrow of good fortune befalling lovers after divers direful or disastrous adventures." The theme propounded was approved by all ; whereupon the queen called the seneschal, and having made with him all meet arrangements, rose and gaily dismissed all the company until the supper hour ; wherefore, some straying about the garden, the beauties of which were not such as soon to pall, others bending their steps towards the mills that were grinding without, each, as and where it seemed best, they took meanwhile their several pleasures. The supper hour come, they all gathered, in their wonted order, by the fair fountain, and in the gayest of spirits and well served they supped. Then rising they addressed them, as was their wont, to dance and song, and while

Filomena led the dance :—"Filostrato," said the queen, "being minded to follow in the footsteps of our predecessors, and that, as by their, so by our command a song be sung ; and well witting that thy songs are even as thy stories, to the end that no day but this be vexed with thy misfortunes, we ordain that thou give us one of them, whichever thou mayst prefer." Filostrato answered that he would gladly do so ; and without delay began to sing on this wise :—

> Full well my tears attest,
> > O traitor Love, with what just cause the heart,
> > With which thou once hast broken faith, doth smart.
>
> Love, when thou first didst in my heart enshrine
> > Her for whom still I sigh, alas ! in vain,
> > Nor any hope do know,
> > A damsel so complete thou didst me shew,
> > That light as air I counted every pain,
> > Wherewith behest of thine
> > Condemned my soul to pine.
> > Ah ! but I gravely erred ; the which to know
> > Too late, alas ! doth but enhance my woe.
>
> The cheat I knew not ere she did me leave,
> > She, she, in whom alone my hopes were placed :
> > For 'twas when I did most
> > Flatter myself with hope, and proudly boast
> > Myself her vassal lowliest and most graced,
> > Nor thought Love might bereave,
> > Nor dreamed he e'er might grieve,
> > 'Twas then I found that she another's worth
> > Into her heart had ta'en, and me cast forth.
>
> A plant of pain, alas ! my heart did bear,
> > What time my hapless self cast forth I knew ;
> > And there it doth remain ;
> > And day and hour I curse and curse again,
> > When first that front of love shone on my view
> > That front so queenly fair,
> > And bright beyond compare !
> > Wherefore at once my faith, my hope, my fire
> > My soul doth imprecate, ere she expire.

My lord, thou knowest how comfortless my woe,
  Thou, Love, my lord, whom thus I supplicate
    With many a piteous moan,
    Telling thee how in anguish sore I groan,
  Yearning for death my pain to mitigate.
  Come death, and with one blow
  Cut short my span, and so
    With my curst life me of my frenzy ease;
    For wheresoe'er I go, 'twill sure decrease.

Save death no way of comfort doth remain:
  No anodyne beside for this sore smart.
    The boon, then, Love bestow;
    And presently by death annul my woe,
  And from this abject life release my heart.
  Since from me joy is ta'en,
  And every solace, deign
    My prayer to grant, and let my death the cheer
    Complete, that she now hath of her new fere.

Song, it may be that no one shall thee learn:
  Nor do I care; for none I wot, so well
    As I may chant thee; so,
    This one behest I lay upon thee, go
  Hie thee to Love, and him in secret tell,
  How I my life do spurn,
  My bitter life, and yearn,
    That to a better harbourage he bring
    Me, of all might and grace that own him king.

Full well my tears attest, etc.

Filostrato's mood and its cause were made abundantly manifest by the words of this song; and perchance they had been made still more so by the looks of a lady that was among the dancers, had not the shades of night, which had now overtaken them, concealed the blush that suffused her face. Other songs followed until the hour for slumber arrived: whereupon at the behest of the queen all the ladies sought their several chambers.

END OF VOL. I.